KT-407-436

ACC. No: 05033178

BRYANT & MAY
Strange Tide

www.**transworldbooks**.co.uk

Also by Christopher Fowler,
featuring Bryant & May

FULL DARK HOUSE
THE WATER ROOM
SEVENTY-SEVEN CLOCKS
TEN-SECOND STAIRCASE
WHITE CORRIDOR
THE VICTORIA VANISHES
BRYANT & MAY ON THE LOOSE
BRYANT & MAY OFF THE RAILS
BRYANT & MAY AND THE MEMORY OF BLOOD
BRYANT & MAY AND THE INVISIBLE CODE
BRYANT & MAY: THE BLEEDING HEART
BRYANT & MAY: THE BURNING MAN
BRYANT & MAY: LONDON'S GLORY

PAPERBOY: A MEMOIR
FILM FREAK

For more information on Christopher Fowler and his books,
see his website at www.christopherfowler.co.uk

BRYANT & MAY
Strange Tide

CHRISTOPHER FOWLER

Doubleday

LONDON · TORONTO · SYDNEY · AUCKLAND · JOHANNESBURG

TRANSWORLD PUBLISHERS
61–63 Uxbridge Road, London W5 5SA
www.transworldbooks.co.uk

Transworld is part of the Penguin Random House group of companies
whose addresses can be found at global.penguinrandomhouse.com

First published in Great Britain in 2016 by Doubleday
an imprint of Transworld Publishers

Copyright © Christopher Fowler 2016

Christopher Fowler has asserted his right under the Copyright,
Designs and Patents Act 1988 to be identified as the author of this work.

This book is a work of fiction and, except in the case of historical fact,
any resemblance to actual persons, living or dead, is purely coincidental.

Every effort has been made to obtain the necessary permissions with
reference to copyright material, both illustrative and quoted. We apologize
for any omissions in this respect and will be pleased to make the
appropriate acknowledgements in any future edition.

A CIP catalogue record for this book
is available from the British Library.

ISBN 9780857523426

Typeset in 11/13pt Sabon by Falcon Oast Graphic Art Ltd.
Printed and bound by Clays Ltd, Bungay, Suffolk.

Penguin Random House is committed to a sustainable
future for our business, our readers and our planet. This book
is made from Forest Stewardship Council® certified paper.

1 3 5 7 9 10 8 6 4 2

For Peter Chapman

PART ONE

GOING AWAY

I walk till the stars of London wane
And dawn creeps up the Shadwell Stair.
But when the crowing syrens blare
I with another ghost am lain.

WILFRED OWEN

The Thames is too dark to lack a god.

CARRIE ETTER

I

QUEENS & KINGS

Nothing gave Arthur Bryant greater satisfaction than making his first blotch on a fresh white page. The scratch of the nib as it scarred the paper always sent a tingle through his fingertips.

'I've decided to write up that business of the Clapham Common Casanova,' he announced, turning to the new notebook on his desk and opening it with a theatrical flourish. Uncapping his fountain pen, he made a grand downward stroke.

Nothing came out.

He shook the pen violently. Ink spots flew all over the office. Crippen had been happily sleeping beside his desk and sprinted from the room.

'I thought Raymond didn't want you circulating any more of your dodgy memoirs,' said John May. 'You make our investigations sound like terrible old paperback murder mysteries.' He swiped irritably at his smartphone. 'Why won't this thing sync properly?'

'Nothing modern works properly,' Bryant cheerfully replied. 'Everything is over-complicated. The office teabags are sentient, apparently. They have a Twitter account. It says so on the box. Dan Banbury bought me electronic bathroom scales for my birthday. They told everyone on Facebook how much I weigh. I don't need inanimate objects slagging me off.'

'But you still use them?' asked May.

'No, tragically they fell under the wheels of my car. Your phone is probably working fine, you're just losing the ability to keep up with it. You're deteriorating, like everything else around here.

'Things fall apart; the centre cannot hold;
Mere anarchy is loosed upon the world,
The blood-dimmed tide is loosed, and everywhere
The ceremony of innocence is drowned. – Yeats.

'No amount of colouring your hair and sucking in your gut will change that.' Pleased with himself, he sat back and took a sip from his tea mug.

It is said that the hallmark of a gentleman is that he is only ever rude intentionally. Arthur Bryant was no gentleman. His rudeness came from an inability to cloak his opinions in even the most cursory civility. He believed in good manners at the meal table and bad manners almost everywhere else.

'You're a very unpleasant old man,' May replied, returning to his phone.

'What's the point in consensual opinion?' Bryant asked, exasperated. 'If you only discuss matters of interest with like-minded individuals you never learn anything new. Why would I want a peer group on Twitter? They're just going to agree with me.'

'Nobody ever agrees with you, and besides you're not even supposed to be here. You're—'

'Yes, I know what I am, thank you, but I'm feeling a lot better this morning so can we not talk about it until we absolutely have to?'

'Very well.' May peered across the desks at his partner's open notebook. 'If you're planning to set down those cases in chronological order, the Bride in the Tide should be next.'

Bryant raised the fingers of his right hand. 'Three – no, two things. One, please don't call it by the name a tabloid reporter coined after a five-bottle lunch, and B, it's the only case I won't ever be able to write up in my superbly erudite and illuminating chronicles.'

May gave up with his phone and set it aside. 'Why not?'

'Because,' Bryant pointed out, 'it's one of the only times we nailed the culprit and were given the slip. My public wants to read about the successes, not the failures.' He rose and walked over to the window, to jingle the change in his pockets and survey his kingdom.

'Your public?' asked May. 'You haven't got a public. You were complaining about your phone not ringing the other day. There's nothing wrong with it; you've never given anyone your number. Anyway, the case wasn't an entire failure. Your suspicions turned out to be justified.'

'It still didn't end up with a spell in the pokey for – I forget the name of the malefactor now. It was on the tip of my tongue, began with a B. Boadicea.'

May looked up. 'I'm sorry?'

Bryant was still looking down into the street. The houses on the other side were ochreish and meanly windowed. 'Queen Boadicea. She's over the road, just past the fried-chicken shop. How very odd.'

'Take one of your yellow pills,' said May, allowing his fingers to creep back towards his phone.

Boadicea, the great warrior queen, was sitting on a garden wall opposite, dangling her silver sandals over its edge, her coarse-woven purple robe gathered about her waist, her golden breastplate glinting in the cold morning sunlight. The breeze ruffled the dyed red leveret fur on her bronze helmet. She was contemplatively licking the side of a 99.

'I don't know how you can eat that,' said the Roman centurion next to her. 'It's bloody freezing.'

'I'm the Queen of the Iceni,' said Boadicea. 'I don't feel the cold.'

The centurion pointed to her ice cream. 'Why is it that the flakes in those things never taste as good as the Cadbury's Flakes you buy in the yellow wrappers?'

'I can't comment,' said Boadicea. 'Chocolate hasn't been invented yet.'

'You don't have to stay in character all the time.'

'When I was a kid we spelled it B-O-A-D-I-C-E-A. That was how everybody spelled it. Then all of a sudden it was B-O-U-D-I-C-C-A. Where did that come from?'

'You were a Victorian misprint.'

'I've got my own statue on Westminster Bridge. You'd think they could sort out my name.'

'It's B-U-D-D-U-G in Welsh,' said the centurion, who was Welsh.

'They don't even know where I died! It was either Watling Street, East Anglia or over there, under platform nine.' She pointed to the great arched glass roof of King's Cross Station in the distance.

'You're thinking of Harry Potter,' said the centurion.

'Did you even bother to do any research before you took this part?' Boadicea asked, gnawing the end off her cone.

'It was hardly worth it,' said the centurion. 'I just come on, shout a bit and get a spear shoved through me.' In the gardens behind him, the second assistant director called everyone back to their places. 'Looks like they're going for another take,' he said. 'Are you in this scene?'

'No, I've finished for the day.' She crunched up the last of her wafer and wiped her fingers on a dock leaf. 'I'm going to get out of this clobber. I thought it would be a bit of a novelty doing location work instead of green-screening everything down at Pinewood, but I've spent most of my time staring out at King's Cross, watching plain-clothes coppers going in and out of that building on the corner.' She pointed up at the headquarters of the Peculiar Crimes Unit on Caledonian Road.

'How do you know they're coppers if they're in plain clothes?' the centurion asked.

'They have big feet and matching jackets and they're always carrying takeaways,' said Boadicea. 'What else could they be? I wonder what they do in there all day.'

The centurion shrugged. 'What do you care? You've been dead for nearly two thousand years.'

'You don't understand,' said the warrior queen. 'I'm an *actor*. I observe humanity.'

'You're an extra, love,' said the centurion. 'And what could you possibly learn from watching a bunch of plain-clothes plods?'

Boadicea waved a ringed finger in the direction of Raymond Land's first-floor window in the Peculiar Crimes Unit. 'I've learned that the bloke who sits in that room doesn't do any work,' she said.

Across the road from Boadicea in the offices of the PCU, two rooms along from where Bryant and May sat, Land also stared down into the street, just as he had on the Monday morning before he or anyone else at the PCU had ever heard of the Bride in the Tide murder . . .

Look at it, Land thought, *King's Bloody Cross, the armpit of the northern hemisphere. I looked out of the window earlier this morning thinking there was a rare bird in that tree opposite, but it turned out to be a pigeon with a plastic bag stuck over its head. I know how it feels. What do I have to do to get out of here, apart from die?*

With an exhausted sigh he sat at his desk and examined the 'Lifemates' dating form on his screen once more.

Tick the Adjective that Best Describes Your Personality:
Assertive. Serious. Amusing. Calm. Outgoing. Adventurous.

He ticked 'Outgoing'. Just last week the City of London Police Commissioner had described him in a meeting as 'our outgoing head of analogue services'. He moved on to the next question.

Tick the Adjective that Best Sums Up Your Approach to Life:
Daring. Cautious. Analytical. Impetuous. Outrageous. Risk-Averse.

He hovered over 'Cautious' but finally ticked 'Risk-Averse'.

Tick the Adjective that Friends Are Most Likely to Use When Describing You to Others:
Charming. Witty. Intellectual. Powerful. Courageous. Manly.

After staring at the choice for a full minute he irritably shut the page and turned his attention to more important things: namely, the weekly spreadsheet his detective sergeant had prepared for him.

Peculiar Crimes Unit
The Old Warehouse
231 Caledonian Road
London N1 9RB

STAFF ROSTER MONDAY 18 NOVEMBER

Raymond Land, Unit Chief
Arthur Bryant, Senior Detective
John May, Senior Detective
Janice Longbright, Detective Sergeant
Dan Banbury, Crime Scene Manager
Fraternity DuCaine, Information/Technology

Meera Mangeshkar, Detective Constable
Colin Bimsley, Detective Constable
Giles Kershaw, Forensic Pathologist (off-site)
Crippen, staff cat

Having checked that the date was correct he thought for a moment about what he should dictate, then decided it was better not to think because he would only get himself into a tangle. Instead he clicked the microphone symbol on the screen to make it start recording and emptied his mind into a staff memo, as he did every Monday morning.

PRIVATE & CONFIDENTIAL MEMO
FROM: RAYMOND LAND
TO: ALL PCU STAFF

Well, I never expected our handling of the so-called 'Burning Man' case to earn us a commendation, but I didn't think the Police Commissioner would actually insult us in public. At the Benevolent Society Fundraising Dinner last night he told everyone that the Peculiar Crimes Unit reminded him of a Remington typewriter, 'noisy, slow and cumbersome, but still capable of hammering out results if you punched it hard enough'. The Met officer next to me laughed so hard that trifle came down his nose.

This is all your fault. Do I have to remind you yet again of this unit's remit? We're here to 'prevent crimes capable of causing social panic, violent disorder and general malaise in the public areas of the city, without alarming the populace or alerting it to ongoing operations'. That's a direct quote from the original 'Particular' Crimes Unit handbook of 1947, and it means you don't throw the baby out with the bathwater.

In our most recent investigation you not only threw the baby out with the bathwater, you killed the baby and burned down the bathroom. You upset everyone from the Governor of the Bank of England to the executive board of the Better Business Bureau, while managing to ruin the nation's biggest firework display in the process. The idea is to get the public to trust us. That means not having to duck into doorways when they walk past. Good God, if I'd wanted to be feared and hated I'd have joined the Special Branch.

Why do I feel like I'm dealing with a bunch of bright students who can't resist sticking a traffic cone on a statue of Winston Churchill? Sometimes I sit here trying to imagine ways in which this unit could be more disrespected than it already is. Maybe Mr Bryant could apply for a post as a Selfridge's Santa this Christmas and traumatize hundreds of small children, or you could falsely arrest a national treasure: Dame Judi Dench perhaps, or Paddington Bear.

From now on, none of you makes a move without me approving it first, do you understand? Do nothing. If you're struck by an epiphany, sit on your hands. Pretend you're in the Met. You don't catch them thinking. Take a leaf out of their book; if you come up with a unique way of single-handedly slashing the capital's crime rate, go to Costa Coffee and read *Hello!* magazine until you've forgotten it. You're not here to innovate, you're here to keep a few seats warm in an outmoded government department until it expires.

And just for once, can you not go around arresting high-ranking government officials and public figures? We're supposed to be engaged in police investigations, not class warfare.

There are days when I honestly miss the Metropolitan Police Service. It would be nice to catch an Essex plumber with a car boot full of lead for a change. I'd be very happy to go back to the days of shining an anglepoise in some nonce's face and taking away his fags until he talks, but that's not how we're meant to do it any more. The City of London wants us to 'engage in meaningful dialogue' every time some junked-up razzhead carrying bolt-cutters swears blind he was on his way to the shops at two a.m. and tweets accusations of harassment while you're questioning him. The Met can hire yoga instructors and take young offenders to the opera for all I care. What their officers do is no concern of mine. Not my circus, not my monkeys.

I care about what happens to this unit. I used to dread coming to work in the mornings, but that was before I realized I'd never swing a transfer so now I'm making the best of it, and so should you. After all, you nick all the most interesting cases. Met officers are so busy untangling neighbourhood disputes about bin bags that they never get to find headless bodies in canals. That's why they hate us so much: we have job satisfaction. We're a crack team of highly skilled professionals.

(*Indistinct.*) Don't spill it in the saucer, Janice. Aren't there any custard creams? I thought we had – Look, now I've got tea all over my trousers.

But we're back-room operatives, not social reformers. We don't qualify for Orders of Merit. Even the duty officer at Bloomsbury Police Station gets sent a tray of cupcakes from the neighbours whenever he threatens to duff up a traffic warden, but we have to settle for being treated like piranhas.

'I think he means "pariahs",' said John May, reading the memo aloud to the rest of the staff, an occupation which afforded them weekly amusement.

So can you not go around making matters worse? Take a tip from my ex-wife. Whenever you start to feel passionate about something, eat an orange and do the *Daily Mail* crossword.

A word about the chain of command. All investigations must come to us via the City of London HQ in Love Lane. Cases can only be opened once we've received full clearance from Leslie Faraday, their public liaison officer. I know he's an utter tool but he has his uses, so try buttering him up a bit. Dan, that means not pretending to be Chinese when he rings your direct line. You can't do the accent and it just sounds racist.

STAFF BULLETINS

All right, some housekeeping. Our dustman – sorry, *disposal operative* – has complained that he lost his fingerprints after handling something one of you left by the back door in a Tesco bag. I know I told you to use bags but this one leaked after eating its way through the carpet tiles outside Mr Bryant's office. I saw *Alien*, I know how these things turn out. Acids, combustibles and other toxic materials don't go into the sinks or the bins. And certainly not down the toilet, as Colin discovered last week to his discomfort.

You'll notice we are now down to a staff of nine, but if everyone works a bit harder we can make up for the shortfall caused by Jack Renfield suddenly leaving us. I understand we were planning to hold a little party for him, but he'd already cleared out his desk and left before anyone had a chance to sign his card. Perhaps he had a train to catch. Or he simply didn't like us. Maybe

Janice would care to explain what happened, and why she returned his staff card by attaching it to my desk with a nail-gun.

The two Daves are staying with us for another month because the first floor still has too much electricity. If you want to use the light switch in the upstairs toilet make sure you're wearing rubber gloves.

There's some kind of a tomb in the basement. If anyone knows what an eight-foot box with symbols scratched all over it is doing down there, could they come and tell me? It's probably just an old electrical substation, but until we know for sure I don't want you calling up any of your weird contacts. We can do without druids dancing around it burning herbs and singing in funny voices.

After the banking riots some of you had the nerve to put in expense claims for fire-damaged uniforms. This is a crime unit, not Top Shop. No one expects you to look good. Look at me: I've resigned myself to living in unironed shirts until I get married again.

Dan Banbury tells me we're to be issued with tablets. I told him I thought it was about time as I'd finished my ex-wife's supply of anti-depressants, but it turns out he means electronic notebooks. Why you can't use pads and pencils is beyond me. But then, most things are these days.

I've decided we should take turns choosing films for the PCU's Saturday Night Cinema Club. Meera's choice, *The Assassination of Trotsky*, wasn't exactly a thigh-slapper, so this week's film will be one of my favourites. *Carry On Up the Khyber* will start at eight p.m.; bring your own snacks. No kebabs this time, Colin.

The fumigators will be in during the week as we have an infestation of cockroaches that's even worse than Crippen's infamous flea outbreak. I've been assured it won't smell any worse than Mr Bryant's pipe. Speaking of whom, Mr Bryant isn't feeling very perky at the moment. I've asked him to take some time off and he has agreed to take it easy until he gets – that is – if – er . . .

(Pause.)

I'm sure we all hope he makes a full recovery, although at the moment I don't think he knows whether it's Christmas Day or Marble Arch. Still, all good things come to an end. Let's show him how well we can manage without him until I can find a replacement.

'I'm sure he didn't mean it like that, Arthur,' said May. 'Don't do anything to him that you'll regret.'

In the meantime, just get on with your work, and remember I'm the king around here from now on, so no funny business.

2

WATER & FIRE

Several years before Boadicea sat on a wall in King's Cross, and several oceans away, a more desperate situation was unfolding off the Libyan coast.

Freezing water, icy sky; it was so dark that Ali could not tell one from the other. There was no breath of a breeze. The glassine depths mirrored the universe. He tilted his head to one side, and thought for a moment that the world had turned over. There was no sound but the faint creak of wood and here or there a cough, a rustle, as someone stirred in uneasy sleep. Those awake kept silent, such was their fear of discovery.

Only Ali Bensaud made a sound. He shook his head and whispered, 'It's taking too long. Why won't he run the engine?'

Ismael Rahman shrugged. 'He says his company doesn't give him enough gasoline to make the round trip. He is lying. He's pocketing the money.'

Ali passed his friend the Russian vodka bottle that had been refilled with *bokha*. Ismael took a swig that caught in his throat. He wiped his mouth. 'I keep thinking it was wrong to run away.'

'Half of bravery is running away, brother,' said Ali.

'But my business is in Tripoli. To leave my homeland—'

'What is homeland?' Ali shook his head. 'I have no loyalty to Libya. My parents are Armenian. My name is short for Alishan; that's a traditional Armenian name.'

'You tell me this once a day,' said Ismael. 'But you've lived there all your life—'

'Yes, and now I will live somewhere else. I will make it to England and be more English than the most English man alive.' His grin shone in the dark. 'I will make so much money that we will wash in it. You know why? The English are Britons, and where did they first travel from? Armenia! Libya is your homeland, not mine. What is left for me there?' He shifted closer, lowering his voice. 'The Martyrs Brigade is using missile launchers on its own people. You've seen such things with your own eyes. I have a clever tongue, but how many more times could I get caught by the militiamen and talk my way out of it? My own father threatened to turn me in. You know this to be true.'

'You put all those things online, Ali, you kept a diary for everyone to read,' said Ismael. 'I warned you often enough.'

'Yes, and perhaps I was wrong to do so. What's done is done. Sooner or later they were going to come for me. My luck was all used up, brother. This was the only way. What other option did we have? All will be well now. We're going to a land where people don't even bother to count the things they own. We'll look out for each other, just as we've always done. I will look after you. We will be well, *insha'allah*. Now try to get some rest.'

'How can I sleep?' Ismael moaned. The gunwale was digging into his back. 'We should have been picked up by now. There are NATO boats out there, and American Navy SEALs.'

'They're looking for oil-runners,' Ali reminded him, 'not a bunch of people trying to get to somewhere with a McDonald's. We're not important to them. Let me take your mind off such things. Want me to show you a magic trick? It's a new one.'

But Ismael shook his head. Even Ali's sleight-of-hand games couldn't help him relax tonight.

They could not sleep; their excitement was too great. They sat side by side with their chins on their knees, and an itchy grey blanket that smelled of engine oil wrapped around their shoulders. There was no coastline. There was no horizon at all. No world existed beyond the overcrowded cargo vessel with the silver jellyfish on its hull. The boat had been freshly painted and had looked smart enough when they first saw it from a distance, but it was much smaller than they had been led to believe, and was barely seaworthy. It had no lifeboats, no radar, no crew except the captain and his mate. They had cut the engine to conserve fuel and now they were adrift.

The escape route ran from North Africa to Greece and Italy, but since the start of the crisis the borders were closing up across Europe. The EU's border security force was now planning to line the Greek–Turkish frontier with a reinforced steel fence, and Israel was talking of doing the same with its Egyptian border in the Sinai Desert. Until recently it had been possible to effect an easy entry through Spain's Moroccan enclaves, Melilla and Ceuta, then everyone tried to leave from the empty, unpatrolled coast of Libya. The thirty-hour boat journey into Italian waters was undertaken only by the truly desperate. The migrants were still being rescued by the Italian coastguard, but even as they were scooped from sinking boats twice their number were lining up back on the shore, ready to risk their lives. All bets were off; it was now a matter of praying for protection and getting out of countries like Libya and Syria any way you could.

Ali had an advantage over the others. He had been taught English by a teacher from London and had been his favourite pupil. The teacher had presented him with a pack of cards and the first of many books on magic; they provided cheap amusement for a boy with no money. He'd promised to take Ali to London one day, but had eventually gone home on the advice of the British Foreign Office. He'd left behind a young man with an unquenchable thirst for a culture he had never experienced.

Ali studied the slope of the deck. The little cruiser seemed to be listing. Even though it wasn't running, the engine was leaking gasoline and the smell made them feel sick. Eventually Ismael dozed with his head on Ali's shoulder. Ali stayed awake making plans for them both.

Shortly after daybreak the mate opened the water can and those who could rouse themselves gathered to drink, but he warned them that after noon today he would start charging for containers. Although Ismael had managed to sleep for a while he now felt disoriented and only half-awake. Ali was far too alert to settle. The blue nylon bag at his feet contained all he dared to bring on the journey. Finally he could no longer stay still, and took water around to those who were too tightly wedged into the corners of the boat to move.

The night had been surprisingly cold, but the refugees were kept warm by their mass and number. They remained most tightly packed together at the stern, which offered better shelter, but the vessel was sitting too low in the water. Ali had seen the danger even as they were being transferred from the mother ship that had brought them beyond Libyan waters. He wondered what they were carrying below decks to weigh the boat down so much, but knew it was dangerous to ask.

It was two hundred miles from the coast to Lampedusa, the first Italian territory they would reach. They had each paid a thousand dollars to the *passeurs*, who had promised them that the French-registered boat would have a satellite phone. The plan, as they understood it, was for one of the *passeurs* to call a relative on the rocky island, who in turn would alert the coastguard. *Lampedusa* meant 'rock' and 'oyster' and 'torch', which perfectly summed up their destination: a closed-off cliff with a beacon that led to a new world.

But things had gone wrong; there was no phone on the boat, and the vessel's plank deck was so rotten that Ali found he could leave deep depressions in it just by kicking down with his heel. Nobody seemed to be in charge, least of all the captain, who had been drinking the whole time. There was no food on board. Several of the Eritreans were sick and unable to rouse themselves. Those around them tried to move away from the pools of infected vomit but there was nowhere to go.

Ali had the sense that they were drifting, waiting for someone to find them. Surely there had to be a better plan than this. On his surreptitious inspection tour he had seen one yellow rubber life raft stowed aft. It was the only one, and absurdly small for a vessel this size, better suited for a boating lake than an ocean, but still he thought about stealing it.

'What if the Italian navy refuses to pick us up? Look what happened to the last boat.' Ismael stroked the silver crescent moon he wore on his neck-chain, something he had always done when he was anxious, ever since they were children. 'They know boats like this come over and wait to be rescued. What if—'

'If you're so worried why don't you just jump overboard and swim home?' Ali snapped, worn down by his friend's fears. 'We both chose this. There's no going back and nothing we can do, so there's no point in complaining now.'

Ismael knew that his friend was right. They were closer than brothers, having spent their entire lives together, playing outside Ismael's father's camera shop, going to watch football matches in the stadium that was now used for public executions. Ali had always been the showman, the silvered-tongued charmer, the one with drive and brains and ambition. Ismael had been happy to walk in his shadow. They were family to each other. But there were few loyalties left behind them now, only fear and suspicion, and as the West hardened against them in uncaring ignorance it was time for everyone to help themselves and get out while they could.

'Besides,' said Ali, 'your brother made it, didn't he? You must have the same strength.'

'Zakaria left seven years ago,' said Ismael. 'He promised to send money. There has been no word from him in the last four years. He is dead to me.'

'You can't say that. You share his blood.'

'Then if I'm of his blood why wouldn't he help us? Why didn't he get in touch?'

Ali had no answer for this, and stayed silent. By his reckoning they had now been in the boat for forty-two hours. They had no food left and very little water. There was still no sign of land.

He looked between the supine figures hugging their sacks of meagre belongings. The yellow rubber raft lay just ahead of them, under the bench, unnoticed. The darker-skinned Africans had been forced to pay more for the trip, and were stowed below deck. No one had seen them since they were transferred on board.

Just before dusk the weather suddenly changed. Where the sea had been aquamarine glass it was now opaque and stippled, then black and swelling. The wind rose and cloud cover swept in with the speed of someone unrolling a carpet across the sky. There were no moans of fear from the almost two hundred souls within the boat, only an unnerving silence and stillness as the passengers grimly clamped their jaws and waited for the storm to pass.

No rain came, which Ali knew was good because the clear air kept them visible. As the night descended once more, he raised his head and searched the horizon for the lights of Lampedusa. If they made it there, they could get to Sicily and the mainland beyond. He feared that the few older ones on board would not have the strength to make the journey.

The boat began to creak alarmingly, as if it was trying to pull itself in different directions. The sea looked like a great table that someone was trying to tip over, first this way, then that. As they pitched and rolled to steeper degrees, the refugees started to stir and then scream. A sudden commotion exploded near the bow. The vessel was taking on water. Ali tried to stand and see what was happening, but was thrown to the deck.

'What's going on?' asked Ismael. 'Are we near the shore?'

'I don't think so. They've seen something. Maybe another boat.' He slapped his friend's shoulder. 'Mare Nostrum.'

The Mare Nostrum project had been set up to provide air-sea rescue for refugees, and to halt human trafficking from mother ships in the waters around Sicily.

The Eritreans and Somalis were sitting separately from the Syrians and Libyans, and now an argument broke out. The mate shouted a warning at them.

'They're saying it's a naval vessel,' Ali confirmed. 'Somewhere over there.' They both tried to rise and search for lights but the storm-swell forced them to wait for a view.

'There, to the left,' said Ismael excitedly. But the lights of the vessel were too far past them. The ship hadn't noticed the little craft. In a few moments it would be too late and their chance would have slipped away . . .

Warmth and yellow light suddenly bathed the refugees' faces. The mate had doused a blanket in petrol and set it alight. He was waving it wildly above his head. Burning pieces detached themselves and showered the passengers.

'Is he mad?' cried Ali. The cargo vessel stank of gasoline, which was stored in unstoppered plastic drums near the engine. Some of the men were trying to snatch the burning blanket away from the mate, but only succeeded in spreading the flames.

The explosion sent a ball of fire into the sky and blew out the entire port side of the vessel. Nearly everyone seated on that side was doused with fiery meteors and sent into the water.

The boat had moments left to live before it capsized. Ali and Ismael tried to help the older men and women around them, pulling them to their feet, but a palpable terror was spreading through the passengers. Already the craft was starting to sink. Many more were pitched into the sea on top of one another.

The deck was now sharply angled. Chunks of burning wood were raining down on them. Below Ali, a woman in a flaming blanket stumbled into the water. As the boat shuddered and rolled over, Ali dived in and grabbed at her, pushing her burning clothes beneath the waves to extinguish them, but he was too late; she floundered for a moment, then disappeared beneath him. A single cork sandal returned to the surface.

The craft groaned and whined in its death throes. A great steel panel smacked into the water beside him, shearing its way to the depths. It didn't seem possible that the vessel could have broken up so quickly. There was now a danger of being pulled down with the wreckage.

Ali still had his bag. Looking for Ismael, he saw the yellow life raft flop into the sea. No one was swimming to it; they hadn't realized that it could be inflated by pulling the painter out of the CO_2 canister and yanking it. He tried to see if Ismael was still on the boat, but now the vessel was standing vertically and sliding down at an incredible speed. Moments later all sign of it had gone. Refugees were clinging to pieces of burning wood. Many were quickly lost from sight.

The water was cold but not unbearable. When Ismael and Ali went fishing they often stayed wet until they returned home, and barely felt the bitter chill. For the journey they wore light hooded sweatshirts, cut-off jeans and trainers, but the Somalis wore long brown cloaks that were impossible to remove once they were waterlogged, and the heavy fabric dragged at their limbs, pulling them down even faster.

Ali could not see his friend now. He clung to a barely buoyant cross-plank, paddling this way and that, searching among the few survivors. Ismael was wearing a red Ohio State Buckeyes shirt with yellow lettering. It should have been easy to spot him.

He lost track of time. His limbs grew tired. He knew he

was a stronger swimmer than Ismael. Soon there were fewer heads in the water. Many of the passengers had already been made frail by hunger and thirst, and the sea began to swallow them. They slipped silently beneath the surface like players forfeiting a game. Soon there would be no one left. A vast shoal of silvered jellyfish caused some to scream and flounder. They did not realize that the best way to avoid being stung was to stay still.

As Ali sought his childhood friend, he saw figures flopping listlessly in the dark water like cormorants trapped in oil, and knew that he was looking at the dead. A wax-white face with draggled hair floated past, staring into the stars.

The moon rose higher. No boat came near. He floated close to a cluster of swimmers weakly thrashing and crying to Allah, and suddenly spotted Ismael's sweatshirt.

Leaving the safety of the plank, he swam towards it. As he drew alongside, he realized that Ismael's head was facing down in the water. Turning him over, he saw that his friend had blanched in death. There was a blackened spear of wood protruding from Ismael's neck, blasted into him by the igniting boat.

Ali refused to release his brother. At that moment he wanted to join him; it was all that he deserved for failing to protect him. Even if he only lived for a few more minutes, it felt shameful that he had been spared.

He spotted the crumpled yellow raft in the distance, floating just behind the handful of oblivious survivors. Holding on tightly to Ismael's sweatshirt, Ali towed him towards it. He caught the raft's edge and felt for the canister. He needed to swim away and inflate it some distance from the wreck-site. This was not selfishness on his part but expediency; he knew that the tiny raft could quickly be over-whelmed by those who remained.

The starscape turned. The sea calmed. The moon disap-peared behind clouds, forsaking them. Now that he could no longer hear crying, Ali inflated the little raft and clambered in, dragging Ismael's corpse behind him. The little yellow dinghy finished plumping itself up, but was barely as long as Ali's body. An old man spotted it and tried to swim near. Ali could not deny him the chance of survival and reached out a hand, but the old man had no strength left and suddenly raised his hands above his head, vanishing below the surface of the sea.

Ali took the chain with the silver crescent moon from Ismael's neck and fastened it around his own. He kissed Ismael on the forehead, whispered a prayer and released him to the depths. He watched the spot where his friend sank, but despite all his efforts to stay awake, he lost consciousness.

The lights grew brighter as the patrol ship approached. He opened his eyes and saw something extraordinary: what appeared to be a bright orange plastic fence was floating above the water. Ali realized he was looking at the crew of an Italian naval vessel, lined along the deck railings in dayglo rescue jackets.

Of the 197 refugees on board the Libyan cargo boat, just seventeen were pulled from the ocean alive. Ali Bensaud was thankful that Ismael Rahman had been returned to the sea he loved so much. If he had kept the body of his friend on the raft he would have been forced to leave it in the care of the navy, and they would have refused to tell him what would happen to it, for the simple reason that they could not know.

Nobody knew what would happen to the survivors, let alone the fate of the dead.

3

RAGS & RICHES

'Piston rings,' said Fred Tamworth. 'I might have known.'

'You're going back a long way,' said Joan, his wife. 'That was the old days. I thought there were some biscuits left.'

'What are you talking about?' Fred took his eyes away from the windscreen for a second and watched his wife rooting about on the floor beneath the passenger seat. She always seemed to have her head in something: a handbag, a shopping bag, a kitchen cupboard, a washing machine. Sometimes it seemed as if he didn't see the top half of her body for days. 'Cars still need pistons otherwise there'd be nothing to power the engine. It's all very well having motherboards and heated wing mirrors but you wouldn't get very far without internal combustion. Ginger nuts. There's a packet of them by your right foot.'

The A2 from Dover was still misted with the remains of a thick grey sea-fret, but at least the traffic was light. Fred kept his speed down, partly because the more time they spent on the road, the less they'd have left to spend with Joan's sister in Crawley. In the rear of their Fiat Panda were four crates of decent plonk from the Calais hypermarket that Fred insisted they needed for Christmas in case anyone popped round, not that anyone had ever shown the slightest inclination to do so except Alfie from the office, who had no friends because his only topics of conversation were geography, Christianity and the installation of boilers.

'It has to be the gaskets,' said Fred emphatically. 'This thing's been feeling underpowered ever since we came off the ferry.'

Joan found the ginger nuts, put them in the glove box and patted her hair back in place. 'I think it's time we traded this in for something with a bit more oomph,' she said, possibly considering the same for her husband.

'Don't move my mirror,' warned Fred. There was a lay-by approaching. He flicked on the indicator.

'*Now* what's wrong?'

'I'm just going to take a quick look, all right?' He pulled over and turned off the engine, fumbling for the bonnet catch.

Joan sighed and sat back with her *Mail on Sunday*. That new Bond girl said she was playing the role as an empowered feminist, so why was she being photographed in a thong? An articulated lorry hurtled past, rocking the car. Under the bonnet, Fred swore.

'What's wrong?' Joan called.

'Nothing, I've cut myself, that's all.'

'There are plasters in the first-aid box.' Joan folded away the paper, knowing that he would never bother with them, and wearily clambered from the vehicle. The booze runs were never much fun, and constituted Fred's sole idea of a day out. There was a time when they'd at least have managed a National Trust house, if only to stock up on marmalade. Just once she would like to go somewhere with a bit of culture, Bruges or Amsterdam, but he wouldn't hear of it.

She went around to the rear of the vehicle and released the hatch door, allowing it to rise. She didn't remember putting their tartan travel rug over the wine boxes. Why would he have done that?

As she pulled away the blanket she saw that the wine boxes had disappeared. In their space a young man was folded up, Arabic-looking with wide brown eyes, dressed in a ragged, filthy sweatshirt and torn shorts. Before she could utter a single word he slid out and ran past her, swinging a blue nylon bag on to his shoulder, vaulting the low fence beside the lay-by, leaving a trail through the wet grass, heading for the safety of the woods beyond. Joan stood staring after him in wonder. Moments later the sea-fret had closed about the young man in a disappearing act that was worthy of a master magician.

The gates of Buckingham Palace gleamed in spring sunshine. Pressed against the railings peering in were tourists from every corner of the globe. To the guards posted on the other side, it must have been like looking at a cage full of badly dressed monkeys.

The young man studied the tourists and broke them down into groups. The ones in spotless white trainers were Americans; Ali had seen their coach parked around the corner. They were watchful and harder to fool. The very orderly line of sightseers mostly dressed in black were Japanese. All of them wore high-quality cameras around their necks, so they were no good. The third party looked the most promising because their coach was from County Durham, which he knew was in North Yorkshire. He had memorized all of the counties and their main cities by now, although some of the pronunciation still defeated him.

One couple seemed ideal. They looked well off but weren't rich enough to be suspicious.

Ali had lightened his hair and wore dark Northern European clothes that made him less likely to stand out. Tourists never seemed to understand that blending in meant wearing neutral colours, not loud patterned shirts. He straightened his collar, rubbed his second-hand shoes on the back of his jeans and stood closer to listen.

'Well, it's not working,' the woman next to him was saying as she jabbed away at her phone, trying to take a picture of her husband standing at the railings.

'It can't be that bloody difficult,' he said. 'I've shown you how to do it a hundred times, Margery. Have you opened the right application? It's got a picture of a camera – it couldn't be any plainer.'

Ali stepped in. 'You want me to take a picture with you both in the shot?' he offered in impeccably precise English.

'No thank you,' said the man.

'Yes please,' said the lady at the same time. She happily surrendered her phone and scuttled over to her husband's side.

'Just press the button at the bottom of the screen,' said the husband briskly.

Ali attempted to take several photographs and allowed the couple to notice his frown of frustration. He fiddled with the phone, looking increasingly puzzled. 'I used to have one of these but there's something wrong with the display on this one,' he said.

'I told you,' said the wife, feeling vindicated. 'It's not always me.'

It was important to act before the husband came forward. 'Why don't I take a picture and send it to you?' he offered, holding up a much larger and fancier phone than the one they had. 'This is twelve meg and takes better shots in soft light than cameras with twice the amount of pixels. The quality should be very good.'

A flicker of suspicion crossed the husband's face but disappeared when Ali said, 'That's perfect – say *London*!' and took the shot. 'Just one more to be sure.'

The couple stepped forward to see the photograph, and loved what they saw. Ali had framed the picture professionally. Those years spent hanging around Ismael's father's camera shop were paying off. 'Oh, that's lovely,' said the wife. 'My husband couldn't do that. He hasn't got the eye for it.'

'What's your email address? I'll send it to you right now,' he said cheerfully.

Before her husband could stop her, his wife told him their address. 'That's all one word,' she added unnecessarily.

He tapped it in and pressed SEND. 'There you are,' he said, gallantly waiting until they heard it ping in their inbox.

'Thank you, you're very kind,' said the lady.

'You're welcome, and enjoy the rest of your stay,' he told them both, sauntering away and pretending to take his own photographs. His scanner had transferred their personal, bank and credit card details, their contacts, email addresses and some pretty obvious clues about their passcodes. He could get anything else he needed from their daughter's social network profiles. As soon as he was out of sight he would collate everything and send the information to a third party. Ali would get a small cash cut at the end of the week. Maybe the couple would remain unaware that the information about their lives was changing hands for money, and maybe he'd get a chance to skim a little off for himself; it made no difference as they had no way of tracing him. He managed to cull the details of over fifty tourists a day, so the law of averages put him into profit.

Taking small amounts hurt nobody, and if he got enough of them he would be rich. There were a dozen other ways to get your hands on money using identity theft, but most required going through a hacker who would take the largest cut. What he needed was a bespoke system of his own. If he could just build that, he would be on his way to proving that even a poor refugee with nothing but the rags on his back and fast learning skills could become a rich man in London.

He stayed clear of the ubiquitous CCTV cameras dotted around the tourist areas, knowing that the police had software that could check the crowds for recurring faces. The trick was to think like the security forces and stay one step ahead. He knew exactly what he was doing. London was too rich and confident. Its people could afford to lose a little.

Hell, half of them probably never even noticed anything was missing. If he decided they were deserving, there would be plenty of time to give something back when he was as wealthy as they were.

Ali changed his name whenever he felt it necessary. Eventually he knew he would have to settle on a single permanent identity. He would get enough money together to buy a dead man's passport, and live under that name for the rest of his life. But for now he was young and free, so his personality fluctuated according to his needs. There were so many ways of getting money in this city if you just looked around for opportunities. Nobody here seemed hungry. They were all in such a hurry, and rushing distracted them from what was important. He did not believe in hurting people. He would not take a penny from the desperate or disadvantaged. He would never do what had been done to him and his family in Tripoli. He would always remember Ismael and what their desperate flight had cost him.

Ali was not a bad man, but he could not afford to be an entirely good one either.

4

TIME & TIDE

Suddenly she was no longer frightened.

Not now that it was real and the end was here. She had thought about how she might die so many times before. She had first cut her arms when she was twelve, just to see if she could sense a movement towards something eternal and unknowable. At first it had the desired effect; the pressure on her disappeared as her parents turned upon each other instead. So she did it again, but each time she cut herself the effect lessened until they finally lost patience with her. 'You don't want to kill yourself at all,' her mother said accusingly, 'you're just after attention.'

She wondered what they would say if they could see her now.

She tried to raise herself a little, but her head hurt too much. She felt the wet sand against her knees, her forearms.

Feeling strangely disconnected, she turned to face the night sky and was surprised to find it was cleared of clouds. Diamond stars sparkled down, but the rippling black water cast aside their reflections. Over on the Queen's Walk, the tumorous stump of City Hall was colonnaded by piercing shafts of light and surrounded by glass towers angled as sharply as knives, as if to warn Londoners that they would be cut if they came too close. From this distance the penthouses looked more like part of a penitentiary. She viewed everything with a distant disregard. The night and the river and the strange burning pain in her head had drained away all sensation. Clear thought was impossible. What could she remember?

Lowering her head to the cold stones, she wondered if it would take her a long time to die. The back of her head stung when she rested it. Her left wrist was sore, and the cold wet sand made her skin bristle. Now that this little life was over, she could distance herself from futile human emotions and accept what had happened. *When Death comes to the door,* her father had once told her in his typically fatalistic way, *it's important to have your bags packed and ready. Nobody should be caught unawares at such a time.*

Instead of thinking about what lay beyond, she tried to focus her blurred thoughts. She concentrated on her senses.

Touch: the rough edge of the concrete, the chill grit of the sand, something by her right foot, a stick of driftwood perhaps, some tide-smoothed pebbles.

Sight: the ancient embanked wall with its worn green steps, the dank stanchions of the pier, a few saturnine trees, the glimmering river and the pale mother moon, controlling everything.

Smell: brackish, stale and damp but not unpleasant, like mildew, moss or mud, or dead wet foliage.

Sound: the gentle flopping of the tide, *ker-lep, ker-lep,* rhythmic and calming, the clock of the river ticking away her life.

Taste: the water, brackish but too cold to be completely unpleasant, a touch of brine from the distant sea, a strangely lifeless flavour which was yet alive. Wasn't it always moving?

A sudden flood surged about her head, sending a fresh bolt of fire through it, and now she came fully awake and began to panic. Her hair was caught on something in the sand and she could not turn her face. The next little wave was enough to wash into her mouth and make her choke.

She tried to lift her left wrist but the chain tore a strip of pain around her flesh. The more she struggled the worse everything became. The moon pulled at the night, bringing another little wave just as she was breathing in, and this time she swallowed and retched.

It was the fault of the moon. The sun was male because he was larger and angrier, worshipped by all men. He gave violent life to everything he touched. The moon was female because she was smaller and calmer, and moved in cycles that shifted the oceans of the world, something even the sun could not do. At night she was accompanied by her children, the stars.

She much preferred to die at night, in the reflected light of the Earth's only natural satellite. *The moon is so strong and kind that it won't kill me,* she thought, *I will become a part of the tide, and I'll flow back in, renewed.* She opened her mouth to accept the rising waters, the cold blackness, the flowing eternal dark.

Just past Sugar Quay on the north bank of the Thames there were, until very recently, some overhanging plane trees and, on one corner, a flight of stone steps leading down to the ragged shoreline.

This access to the river is still known as the Queen's Stairs, and stands in front of the Tower of London. Carved into the nearby wall are dates and initials: 'ST D. E. AD 1819', a boundary marker representing St Dunstan-in-the-East. The church had been destroyed in the Blitz, and its overgrown ruins had lain undisturbed for years.

Once the Thames had been slow and wide, and many of the buildings had water gates that gave direct access to the river. Now, the remnants of St Dunstan's were cut off from the river by a thunderous arterial road, and beyond was only a windswept plaza of grey stone, the rear of another corpse-grey office block, a steel-ribbed castle of finance guarded by impassive wardens in headsets. Near the gleaming brushed-chrome embankment railing stood a sign that summed up the city's new attitude, a pictogram of a pedestrian with a diagonal red bar passing through it. Humans were not wanted here, just drones for the hive who would climb over the bodies of their fallen predecessors to continue making money.

The shore of the Thames was inaccessible, sealed off by the glass edifice on one side and a tiny old stone house on the other. A wooden walkway led out to the T-shaped Tower Millennium Pier. The narrow gap beside the house – the only route of access – had been blocked by a two-metre-tall gate of polished black steel.

But if you could still reach the steps, at the bottom you would find something unexpected; along with the green and white stones, pink chunks of pottery, cream clay pipes, weathered groynes, half-buried tyres and decayed chunks of wood there was sand – all that remained of Tower Hill Pleasure Beach, once London's only seaside resort.

In 1934 King George V promised the children of London that they could have 'free access forever' to this specially constructed sandy foreshore, and over the next five years half a million people swam and sunbathed among the vendors and entertainers, hiring threepenny rowing boats to go under Tower Bridge and back. On sunny days you could almost hear the echoes of their laughter.

It was far too early on Monday morning, and a pale grey mist like a sea-fret had yet to dissipate from the shore. John May and Dan Banbury passed through the now-unlocked gate and stood at the top of the stone stairway looking down. A plastic marker topped with a small green pennant indicated the spot they were looking for. The police had been careful not to draw attention to the site. There was a constable on guard somewhere; they couldn't see him but every few minutes his headset crackled.

'I still can't find her,' said May, shielding his eyes. Watery sunlight was starting to spread out through the mist.

'Let's get closer. I've got what I need from here.' Banbury unclipped his camera and folded up the tripod. The steps were slippery with grass-green algae. May steadied himself against the wall as they descended.

'Keep to the stones,' Banbury instructed. 'Give me a six-metre perimeter, come in close behind me and try not to disturb anything. We haven't got long. The tide's on the turn. It's a good job we haven't got your partner with us. He'd be tromping all over the place and showing off his sandcastle-building skills by now.'

The constable who had placed the pennant had reached the spot by stepping on a series of slippery stones in shallow water, but these were already submerged. May was wearing expensive handmade shoes from Church's – his one great luxury in life – and he wasn't at all happy about getting them wet.

From here he could just about make out the body. Clad in dark fabrics, it was small and folded into a foetal position, and looked like nothing more than a bundle of wet rags.

Banbury was nimble for his size and reached her first. 'She was spotted by someone on a river bus,' he said.

'Must have had good eyesight.'

'Camera viewfinder. He was enlarging the shot. Captain called the MPU.'

The Marine Policing Unit took care of forty-seven miles of the river between Hampton Court and Dartford, and had been tackling crime on the Thames for well over two centuries. It had nearly eighty working officers, but few of the city's employees were even aware that the unit existed.

'How come they're not handling this?' May waited for Dan to finish photographing before he got closer to the corpse, then knelt beside it.

'The foreshore here is in dispute,' Dan explained. 'City of London says it's theirs. The MPU doesn't agree but there's not a lot that they can do about it.'

May looked around. 'I remember Arthur telling me he used to make pocket money renting out deckchairs down here.'

'What, in the thirties? Blimey, how old is he?'

'The beach didn't close until 1971, just as the river finally got clean,' said May, checking about for access. The beach felt oddly claustrophobic at the tide level, with the pier, the walkway and the stone wall hemming them into a small shadow-filled rectangle of shore. He looked up at the embankment offices above, but their opaque windows revealed no interior life. 'In theory there's still nothing to stop you from swimming here,' he said, 'but the beach is technically shut. Most people wouldn't dream of doing it, anyway.'

'Yeah, I had a mate who fell in and had to have his stomach pumped. I say "fell in" – he got chucked off the pier in a Hawaiian skirt and a pair of coconuts. Stag do.'

'He's lucky he lived. Once you get out there the riptides are pretty treacherous.' A tug passed them, giving a mournful hoot.

'Besides, hell, look at it,' said Banbury. 'It might have been all right before they built the pier, when it still had a decent view of Tower Bridge, but now it's all boxed in by supports. You wouldn't if you had any sense, would you? OK, it looks like she's in one piece. I want to try and move her.'

Banbury pulled out his pocket recorder and crouched down. 'We've got a female Caucasian aged around twenty-four, brown eyes, black hair, around five foot two, about a hundred and fifteen pounds. Two tattoos on the backs of the legs, a little man—'

'That's Gautama Buddha, the Enlightened One,' said May. 'The other one's Parvati, the Indian goddess of love and devotion.'

'Thank you, Einstein – and a possible TBI to the back of the skull. There's a bruise behind the left ear and the skin's broken.'

'A contusion like that could have caused a haematoma.' May hitched his trousers and leaned forward to examine the wound. He'd seen something like it before, usually on gang members who'd been in confrontations. It looked as if she had been jabbed with a spike, something blunt-sided but sharp at the tip. Teen gangs kept screwdrivers on them, but the bruising and force from this suggested the weapon was bigger.

'Giles is your man for the effects of a knock on the head. What have we here? Her hand's held down by something.' Banbury carefully pulled back a waterlogged cardigan sleeve and turned a pale left wrist with his gloved forefinger, pointing it out to May. A length of thick silver chain had been pulled around it and passed through a rusty iron ring embedded in a rough circle of stone, which was in turn partially buried in the sand.

A chill wind whipped along the foreshore. Dan rocked back on his heels and took more shots. 'Quite a distinctive chain,' he said. 'Hallmarked, with a crescent moon at one end. Did the Met officers even see this? They couldn't have or they'd have gone for it like a rat up a drain. Stands to reason, a nice juicy homicide.'

'Show some respect, Dan.'

'Sorry, John, no disrespect intended.' Banbury took a plastic spatula from his portable kit and began probing beneath the chain. The tide bloomed around the corpse's free arm, momentarily restoring it to life.

Considering the location, it was an oddly lonely spot. 'I'm not sure I can get this off.' Banbury raised the links of the chain with his forefinger.

'There's a trick to it,' said May. 'I used to have one when I was younger. One of the links is on a spring. If you're not familiar with this type of chain you'll never get it off.' He pushed on the links, found the one that opened, removed the chain and handed it to Banbury for bagging. 'It should be traceable,' he said. 'Funny thing to use. Strong, though. I suppose it came readily to hand.'

At moments like this, Banbury was grateful for being with

the PCU. He wouldn't have been allowed to touch the chain under regular City of London jurisdiction. The site would have been swarming with technicians, officers and various surplus jobsworths building timelines and photographic records. CoL had a court history of prosecutors accusing officers, so every stage had to be documented in great detail. Against this was the need to act fast. Banbury could load stats online with the contents of his case, which removed the need for couriers. He had a grey plastic body tray, a laptop and a fold-up forensics tent so it was possible to carry out his report without anyone on the shore spotting any activity, not that they could see much down here. The one thing he hadn't allowed for was the unimpeded wind.

May must have been thinking along the same lines. 'If she was here for a while, why didn't anyone notice her?'

'She'd be pretty invisible from up there,' Banbury answered, studying their surroundings. Above, an office worker stopped at the railings and looked down, but only for a moment, as if realizing that his non-productive time was being wasted.

'I'll try the river-facing offices, see if there was anyone working overnight.'

'Look at her, John, she's dressed in green, grey and brown. She blends in with her surroundings. Nobody comes down to any part of the shore when it's cold; why would they? Besides, they can't even get to this part any more. Look at what we had to go through. Public thoroughfare, my arse. The only other way you can access the old beach is by passing through one of the corporate reception areas and subjecting yourself to a grilling by a headset-chimp.'

'High and low tides must vary a lot at this time of the year,' said May, squinting up. A few rags of mist were still clinging to the pier stanchions. 'They should give you a rough time of death. What was holding her in place?'

'Well, this is weird,' said Banbury, digging the sand away. 'Come a bit closer.' May found himself looking at the stone stump, about a foot in diameter, into which a rusty iron ring was embedded. 'It's the top of an old stanchion, probably used to tie up boats, late 1940s, early 1950s.'

'How can you tell the period?' May asked.

'Post-war concrete.' The CSM held up a fragment of wet cement and rubbed it in his fingers, watching it dissolve. 'The good stuff was in short supply so they bulked it up with pebbles and shale. You don't think she was chained here alive, do you?'

'God, I hope not. I wouldn't want to die by ingesting this stuff.'

'Our noble Mayor says the Thames is clean now.'

'I think it's safe to say that drowning in it would still be a fairly unpleasant experience. What a lonely, miserable death.' May frowned. The ghost of an idea had formed.

Banbury fought the breeze and erected the tent. 'If I get this logged in the next half-hour you can whip her straight over to Giles and he can run tests on her lungs.'

'Punishment.'

'Sorry?'

'Isn't that what it feels like to you?' May pointed at the position of the body. 'Chaining someone to a post in a public place and letting them die? It's almost a tradition in this part of the city. Smithfield is just behind us. Thousands died there. Like putting someone in the stocks.'

'You're talking about centuries ago,' said Banbury. 'Don't start sounding like Mr Bryant.'

'Somebody has to, now that he's not around.' May rose unsteadily to his feet and stretched his tight spine. The November air was damp and cruel to older bones. 'If she was still alive when she was chained up, why didn't she cry out? You'd think somebody might have heard her.'

'Why would they?' Banbury wrestled with a telescopic leg. 'It's deserted around here after midnight, and if you go back a bit there's the noise of all-night traffic on the A3211. Maybe she did scream and there was nobody to hear her.' As if on cue, a shriek of laughter came from somewhere on the walkway – the sound of children was rare in this part of the city.

'A good spot for a murder, if you can reach it.' May studied the few boats that traversed the greenish-brown expanse ahead of him. 'I don't suppose there's any CCTV on the river itself, or the foreshores. But there must be on Lower Thames Street and at the entrances to the underpasses. Know what I'd do if I wanted to kill someone here? Strangle them in the middle of the subway, out of the sight of cameras, lift the body over that steel gate – causing the contusion on the back of the head – then drag them down to the beach.'

'Then you wouldn't make a very good murderer,' said Banbury. 'Why not leave her in the subway? And you're going to toss a dead weight over an eight-foot gate? Why go out of your way to make things complicated?'

May shrugged. 'You're right, we're missing something. After I've got her off to St Pancras, see what you can turn up in the way of video footage. Can you make—' He stopped and turned. 'Wait, that's no good.'

'What?' Banbury rose and followed May's eyeline.

'I was going to say can you make casts, but there shouldn't be anything to make a cast from.' The sand had dried a little while the tide was out, but the high water table and the deep green shadows would ensure that it remained permanently damp, even in the height of summer. The same ancient mix of sand and clay had preserved the most unlikely items all along this part of the Thames, from the phallic silver brothel-brooches of Southwark's whores to a single banana found in 1999, which had been discovered lying whole under the waterlogged beach and dated back to 1560, a full century before the fruit was ever known to be exported to Britain.

Banbury heard nothing more and looked up. 'Sorry, John, not with you.'

May pointed down at a faint wavering line of crescent indentations in the sand, leading from the embankment wall to the concrete stanchion. 'You don't think they could still be the remains of footprints?' He tried to see where they ended.

'Why would there be any prints at all?' asked Banbury, checking his watch. 'It's past noon. The tide's been in and gone out again.'

May headed to the edge and bent down, placing his fingers in the water to feel its pressure against them. 'Maybe there weren't many waves last night. There's no river traffic passing near here. The Tower's restricted and boats can't get in close because the pier's in the way.'

'But there's still the current, John. I would have thought it would wash out most of the markings.'

'The tidal flow must be less pronounced in this stretch. Look at the rise in the shoreline. There's a hump left by the residue of the old Tower Beach.' A row of seagulls regarded May insolently. One of them was pulling at something best left unexamined. 'They didn't take the sand away when they closed it, they just left it where it was, so the water washes around it. Those marks – OK, there are no details left but they're definitely prints from a small shoe size.'

'If they're the remains of hers, where are his?' asked Banbury. 'How did he get her down here? I mean, seriously? It would be impossible. If she was already dead he would have had to drag her right across the forecourt to the offices, get her through the building and out of the back. Either that or over that gate beside the stone house. Come to think of it, if she was alive he'd have had the same problem.' He stood and stretched his back. The cold river air was getting to him as well.

May felt a chill. 'The water at the front, the wall at the back, one set of prints, it doesn't make sense.'

'There's something else about these prints,' said Banbury. 'The heavy indentation is the heel. They're facing towards the waterline, as if she went down there alone.'

May traced the route with his raised hand. 'If she was alive he could have rendered her unconscious on the staircase and carried her out on to the strand.'

'What, you think they had a fight on the embankment and he knocked her out by reaching around to the back of her head with something long and heavy? Without anyone seeing or hearing a thing? Even though it's empty, this section of the river walk is still pretty exposed. There's usually a bit of foot traffic nearby.' Banbury turned and stared back at the green staves supporting the embankment like animal ribs. 'You might be able to see it from the next reach.'

'But not at night.'

'Even so, you'd think *someone* would have noticed them.' He took out a fresh packet of gloves and tore it open. 'The last time I walked down this new stretch was after a mate's birthday. I thought I'd take a look at the commemorative poppies in the Tower of London moat. It must have been around midnight. I don't really remember, I wasn't exactly sober.'

'Why would you have come down this bit?' asked May. 'It doesn't lead anywhere.'

'Oh, I probably needed a wee. It certainly wasn't for the view. Apart from the police launches there were only one or two private vessels moored along the reaches of the river. Maybe she was already on the shore, and he came in by boat and surprised her.'

'God, Dan, I hope there's a simpler explanation than that.' May sighed. 'I wish Arthur was here.' Working without his partner was like having his hands tied behind his back.

Above them, an ambulance had arrived. As its crew disembarked, one of the EMTs came to the railing and called out, 'How do we get down there?'

'You have to go through the office building to your right,' May shouted back. The pair stood beside the tent waiting for the emergency team. They might have been extras on location, waiting for the director to go for a take.

'John, before they get here, can I ask you something?' said Banbury, concerned.

'If it's about—'

'You know who it's about. Is he coming back?'

'I don't see how he can.' May glanced down at the damp sand on his shoes. 'I've been summoned to a meeting with his doctor. I don't suppose he has any good news for me. I think he's going to say that Arthur's reached the end of the line.'

'We won't survive without him, John. The only reason why our strike rate is so high—'

'You think they don't know that?' said May angrily. 'The performance targets come up in every Home Office assessment we've ever had. They stood us in good stead while everything was running smoothly. You know how many officers would be covering a case like this if CoL had to handle it? They save a fortune by using us.'

Banbury didn't like suggesting the idea, but he felt somebody had to say it. 'Don't take this the wrong way, John, but have you thought about finding a replacement for Mr Bryant?'

'There's no one who could take his place,' said May flatly.

'What about promoting Fraternity DuCaine? He's young, he's smart, he's got a lot of energy.'

'He doesn't have enough experience, and he certainly doesn't have Arthur's weird way of looking at things.'

'You're right, but you're never going to find someone who has that. Maybe what's needed now is a fresh approach.'

'It wouldn't be any good. Fraternity's mainly a tech-head. Can we not talk about this right now?'

'It's just that . . . there's a woman I worked with a few months ago,' said Banbury, shifting the last of his equipment. 'She's a forensic specialist with a lot of unusual ideas, clever, geeky, a bit on the autism spectrum. She came to the CoL from Munich and is looking for a change. Her name's Steffi Vesta. Maybe you could trial her.'

'It's out of the question,' said May. 'Can you imagine what it would do to Arthur, knowing he'd been replaced? It would destroy him. This unit is all he has left to live for.'

Dan glanced back at the steps and lowered his voice. 'You

don't have to tell him, John. You always said the case has to come first. This girl was chained to a rock and left to drown. We're going to need more help. What are you going to do, tell Raymond to turn it over to the CoL? It's our case; nobody else will be able to do a better job, even without Mr Bryant.'

'This German woman,' said May. 'What's her special-ization?'

'She's a lab rat but prefers being out on the street. Not a lateral thinker but very determined. Hell, she's so keen to get into an outsource unit that she's prepared to intern with us. What harm could it do?'

'No, maybe later,' said May stubbornly. 'I'll see Arthur's doctor first. I owe it to him to exhaust every possibility.'

The Emergency Medical Team had followed Banbury's path and were standing by, awaiting a briefing session. 'What if Dr Gillespie says there's absolutely no hope?' Banbury insisted.

'Then we'll have to consider taking someone else on board,' May replied. 'But not before. I'm not giving up yet.'

5

CAUTION & TRUST

Ali Bensaud kept on the move and constantly changed the way he looked. This week he was in Victoria, the next in Hampstead. He worked out in the public parks. He knew he was handsome. When he smiled, even the most suspicious people were drawn to him.

He had tried to find Zakaria Rahman in London, without any luck. He missed Ismael, his brother in all but blood. He missed his family. He sent a message to his father to say that he was fine, but heard nothing back. He would send money when he could, even if he heard nothing. This was a different world, where all about you people shed cash unthinkingly. You could almost see it falling from them like goat hairs. In small amounts: pounds for ice creams and soft drinks; ten-pound notes for beers. In large amounts: credit cards for designer clothes and theatre tickets and restaurant bills, cards placed unthinkingly into the hands of total strangers. If they were told that something would cost more they just shrugged and paid. No one ever apologized to them or offered a better service, they just took more money, and more money. The British were trusting and lacking in caution because these amounts meant nothing to them. They didn't seem to know what anything was worth. Would this amount buy a loaf of bread, a packet of cigarettes, a phone? Half of them had no idea. There was water in every tap but they bought it in bottles. There were meals you could make but they paid fortunes to have them cooked. He stood in the station watching people buying railway tickets, being charged different amounts for the same ticket again and again, and hardly anyone complained. He saw a sea of opening wallets.

Londoners were the worst; they were far too worried about time to care about money. There was a sign outside the Armenian barber shop in Victoria that promised to cut hair in five minutes or your money back. If a haircut took a minute more, would the world end? The Queen lived in Victoria. Did Prince Philip go there to get his hair cut? No, because he did not care about time. But everyone else who was rich did. People would hand over their phones because they could not be bothered to learn how to take a photograph. They left food, binned clothes and threw away computers because a new one had come out. Why shouldn't you take from them that which they wouldn't miss?

He listened to them on tube trains and in shops, always talking about the time it took to do this or that. Then there was the thing about houses. Every day, the same conversations about houses, how much they were worth, how near they were to schools and stations, how much they could be sold for. Why would two people choose to live in a building that had ten rooms? An unused room was a sin. Why would they send their parents into care homes when they had room in their houses? He longed for a day when he could take the houses from them too, to make them see that they could be happier with less. To make them rediscover themselves and each other.

There were other city-dwellers, ones who shopped in the cheapest supermarkets and went to sales and ate in junk-food outlets, and watched every last penny. They got fat from sugar and corn starch, and smoked and drank hard. They had a tough time raising kids and in them he recognized something of his own background, so he left them alone to concentrate on the rich ones.

Ali did not have to pay to enter the nightclub in Greek Street. The Syrian on the door had come over in a vegetable truck and eye contact was all it took for the red ropes to be parted. Inside, the music was like a magnified heartbeat. He was making good money now, but had to be careful. He stood at the bar with a beer and looked around because in here he could not hear anyone speaking. He understood much from the way people stood, their hand gestures, the closeness of their faces.

There were three girls grouped together, lambs protecting themselves from wolves. Any two would back up the third. They were of no use to him. There were girls everywhere, some of them beautiful, some dressed like whores. Sullen girls paired with angry, mean-eyed men; clutches of drunk girls quacking like ducks, who had no need of partners tonight. There were hunters looking for prey and invisible people who arrived with prettier, thinner friends. There was hardly anyone alone, except her.

He guessed – rightly, it later turned out – that she had been abandoned, but her pride would not allow her to leave. Instead she had ordered another white wine and stood tapping her cobalt nails on the counter while a José Padilla track brought the Mediterranean into the basement. Padilla had been popular in Libyan beach bars but you couldn't tell that to an Englishman; they thought you lived in mud huts. Besides, he never spoke about his roots. He was a Londoner now. Being a Londoner was, he learned, a state of mind that anyone could attain with a little hard work. You learned to say please and thank you and sorry, always sorry. You said sorry in a thousand different intonations and circumstances. You even apologized for being in the way when you weren't. And you always had to be in a hurry, otherwise you didn't look important.

There was a long list of things you needed to do before becoming a Londoner, starting with learning how to use the system with intelligence and reason. And there were small things to learn, like the trick of catching the right part of the Northern line at King's Cross and knowing how to cross a road diagonally and how to look right through the people you didn't want to see, and having a favourite pub where the barman would, after two or three weeks, send you the faintest nod of greeting as you approached.

By now Ali had been a hotel cleaner, an unregistered tour guide, a café busboy, a barman and a car-park attendant. He was living in a council flat with five others, and made sure that he hardly ever saw them. He paid cash because there were only supposed to be two people renting. The flat was sublet by a Greek electrician who had more than a dozen properties scattered across Camden and Dalston in a scheme he'd arranged without the councils knowing; lots of people ran scams like that.

There were still little things that gave Ali away. He didn't have a bank account or a credit card. He couldn't pronounce 'Greenwich' or find a fast route across Covent Garden. He watched a lot of films and read a lot of books, but they couldn't teach him everything he needed to know. Up until now the only people who had helped him to move up were those who were getting a cut. It was time to find someone who would help him out of loyalty, even love. Which meant that he would have to make himself appealing in a new way.

This was the hardest part of all. He'd had no practice, which was why he picked the girl standing at the end of the bar tapping her hand to the music. It was important not to look too eager or ingratiating. Better barely to care at all.

He talked to her. If she had looked any less interested she would have fallen asleep. That was fine; it was just her style. He was careful not to stand too close. People here had a circle of space around them that you could not enter without permission. He had seen a film about a boy who was a vampire, and learned that you had to be invited inside. It was like that with girls. She was wearing a very short dress of white lace with black leggings underneath, the kind of outfit the girls at home wore when they were babies, and she had very high heels because she was worried about being short. She looked away from him and flicked her hair, catching sight of herself in the bar mirror. When she looked back she stole a glance at his face, then looked straight ahead.

He casually turned to her. 'Hey, how you doing?' That was how it was done, as if you could hardly be bothered to open your mouth. He'd watched others and could copy their movements exactly.

'OK.'

He waited until his own glass was finished before offering. 'I'm going to the bar – you want . . . ?'

She shook her head. 'No.' But this was part of the game. She wanted him to try a little harder.

'Your glass is empty. It's Saturday night. I'm going anyway.' He made to move away.

She shrugged and nodded imperceptibly at her glass. *I'm not bothered but if you're going* . . . The thing about Londoners was, you had to interpret everything. No intention was ever made plain. If someone said, 'Yes, we must do that,' it usually meant, 'Piss off.' Was this a mark of sophistication or merely a sign that they were emotionally backward? He had already learned the hard way that an angry look from a London girl could crack mirrors, blight crops and freeze the Thames solid. There was a point where you became so refined that it made you stupid.

But this one gave a guarded smile when he returned with the drinks, just a slight turning of the lips. Then she looked ahead again and listened to the music, sipping. They were facing the same direction together. He had read about body language, *matching and mirroring.* He had cracked part of the code but still had much to learn. It helped that he didn't drink. Others revealed too much of themselves when they became drunk.

She finally talked, and after that they moved to a spot where she could actually hear his replies.

Her name was Cassie, short for Cassandra. She had a husky voice and said she came from Henley, had been there all her life until now. It was a town outside London that pretended it was in the countryside. The man she'd come with tonight had turned out to be a *total tosser* (he filed the new phrase) and she was better off without him because – and this she said in a single breath – in seven months he'd like bought her a drink one time only because he had this thing about her making more money than him because she worked for like a really high-end Kensington estate agent and was really ambitious and he was in IT and it paid like really badly but he didn't care because he liked the job but he was all like bent *totally* out of shape about it plus he didn't like her smoking?

He understood the gist of what she was saying, even if he had trouble with some of the words she used. Although he had no knowledge of the English class system, he instinctively knew she came from somewhere in the middle of it. He listened to her and tried to copy the way she spoke. *Hen*ley. *Fox*tons. *Un*believable. *Glas*tonbury. Funny how so many words had the accent on the first syllable.

Ali had an exceptional memory, and filed away all the strange phrases he heard on the street. Earlier in the month he had met a young Indian man in a club on Brick Lane who seemed to be speaking an alien language. He quickly learned that *110s* were expensive trainers. *Bait* was stupid. *Rinsed* was something used up. A *ginul* was a con. *Mash* was a gun. At first he exhausted himself trying to remember everything, but then he realized that he didn't need to; many words belonged to different social groups, and he had not yet decided who he wanted to be. Cassie used none of these words but it was still hard to understand her because she never paused for breath, hurling herself at sentences and then lapsing into silence.

She was still angry with the man who had left her. She

wanted to get her own back, and just knowing that she needed something gave him an opening. He was thinking about this when he suddenly realized that she was speaking to him, asking his name. His eyes darted to the bar shelves lined with up-lit bottles behind her head. 'Gordon,' he said without missing a beat. 'Gordon Hendrick.'

'You're kidding, right?'

'No.' He laughed. 'That's my name. My mother was an alcoholic.' They both laughed. He was bright, not in the sense of having had a good education, but clever, quick, feral, fast. Because he remembered everything he could not be tricked by anyone.

He said, 'You have an accent, just a trace, something Russian.' She gave him a long, hard look and said her mother had given her a different name, Natalya, but she had changed it. She had been born in Kazakhstan. How was that possible? She looked so English. Suddenly he realized that he still had a lot to learn. Cassie's parents had brought her to London when she was three years old, so that made her a Londoner. Wasn't everyone from somewhere else?

She told him about her other jobs. She had worked for Allied Breweries but left because everyone drank too much, then went to the FCO, the Foreign & Commonwealth Office, as a translator writing press releases and sitting in on immigration interviews. She had a Mazda car and her own flat. What she didn't have, as of an hour ago, was a boyfriend. She seemed as driven and determined as he was.

It was too good to be true. Ali found himself on his best behaviour. It was suddenly very important that Cassie liked him. He had places to go and worlds to conquer. He needed a partner whose ferocious loyalty would cover his weaknesses and hide them from suspicious eyes. He knew what a *power couple* was and sensed great reserves of strength in her. She was pretty in an obvious, over-made-up way and her strength would probably become unbearable when she was older. Right now, though, she was just what he needed.

He turned and smiled slightly and nodded. She was drinking faster than him. 'Get you another,' he said, and this time he did not have to wait for a reply because he knew he could walk away to the bar and find her there when he got back. Cassie had instinctively lied about her background upon meeting him. That was good. She knew how to protect herself. She was tough. They weren't so different from one another.

While he waited for the barman to pour their drinks, he thought about a possible future for both of them that would be something other than a romantic match. It would be an alliance, and woe betide anyone who was stupid enough to cross them.

6

REMEMBERING & FORGETTING

Dr Gillespie's third-floor office was situated directly behind the eye-damaging LED Coca-Cola sign in Piccadilly Circus, halfway along a dingy sepia-painted hallway filled with threadbare Indian carpets, African masks and earthenware pots of indeterminate origin. It was extraordinary to think that such places still existed in the heart of the city, but for the moment the building's byzantine lease protected its few remaining tenants. London had more offices, clubs, bars and bedrooms hidden in tunnels, cellars, basements and chambers than anywhere else in Europe.

John May stopped before the doctor's door and knocked. An explosion of coughing subsided and a voice gasped, 'Come in.'

The room had no windows and smelled of Vick's VapoRub and liniment oil. Dr Gillespie had a black eye. He was wearing a flesh-coloured neck brace that forced up his chin and squashed his features into a funhouse-mirror version of his old self. He turned awkwardly and indicated the seat opposite his desk. 'Impacted vertebrae,' he said.

'Car accident?' May asked.

'A difference of opinion with the wife about whose turn it

was to bleed the radiators. I dodged a jar of pickled onions and fell over the dog. Your partner.' He searched around for his notes, but couldn't see his desktop.

'Here, let me.' May passed him a fat folder that looked as if it went back at least fifty years.

'I've been doing some research. As I told you before, it's not straightforward Alzheimer's, at least not as I've ever experienced it. Excuse me.' Gillespie extracted an enormous white linen handkerchief from his sleeve and released a snotty blast into it, wincing when the shock travelled to his spine. 'Mr Bryant's bouts of cognitive impairment have distinct phases. I thought at first that his so-called "blank moments" might be due to transient ischaemic episodes triggered by lapses in his brain's blood supply.'

'You mean mini-strokes.'

'In layman's terms. Except that there are anomalies. The disease is not taking its traditional path.' Gillespie winced and gingerly touched his eye. 'For example, he doesn't seem to forget words. His memory is relatively undamaged. There are no indicative genetic markers in his background. He's never had high blood pressure – that's your problem, not his. You're both getting on, you know.'

'I'm three and a half years younger,' said May defensively.

Gillespie ignored him. 'He does lose his place occasionally. He's undergone quite a bit of sensory loss, ears and eyes, but that's natural at his age. Balancing that, he's far more physically and mentally active than most people of similar advanced years. And he never seems to get depressed. Why is that?'

May shrugged. 'Arthur loves his work.'

Gillespie squinted down at his notes. 'I suppose you could say death keeps him alive. Well, there's good news too. His weight is constant, he doesn't have diabetes, he communicates well and says he doesn't suffer mood changes. As far as I can tell, there's no traditional history of Alzheimer's or dementia in his family. He's had a brain scan, but that didn't reveal anything untoward. It's almost impossible to pin down the cause of these episodes. So we'll tackle a biopsy next.'

'He won't be happy about that.'

'There's something else. There are cycles.' Another spasm of hacking produced more pained grimaces. 'Sorry about this, the coughing stops if I take the brace off, but then my head falls on one side. Where was I? Most of his attacks occur at roughly the same times of the day. Now that doesn't make any sense at all. If stress and fatigue were the only factors he'd suffer most after a tough day at work, but he doesn't. And there's the matter of his cognitive perceptions. Is he experiencing behavioural changes? Has he started acting inappropriately, saying whatever's on his mind, being rude, upsetting those around him?'

May gave the medic a long, hard look. 'Dr Gillespie, that's not a disease. Arthur has never been able to say anything polite or even remotely appropriate. He leaves a trail of embarrassment wherever he goes. Are you telling me he's going to get even worse?'

'Well, yes. This illness may manifest itself in some very surprising ways.'

'So you think he'll continue to deteriorate.'

'I can't see any other likelihood. The attacks are growing in severity, and the periods between them are shrinking. I see Alzheimer's following the same growth pattern in many of my older patients, with very little deviation. I've just never seen anything exactly like his before.'

'What can you do to manage the problem?'

Gillespie stuck a pencil under his neck brace and gave himself a good scratch. 'Therein lies the paradox, you see. If I sign him off work and we leave him at home, there'll be nothing to occupy his mind and he'll deteriorate much more quickly. If you keep him working so that his mind and body remain active, you'll help him but you may be placing other people at risk.'

May was stumped. 'Then what do you suggest I do?'

'There's an old book . . .' Gillespie tried to point to the bookcase but had such trouble turning around that he looked like a very old gun turret seeking its target. 'Third shelf, at the end, black leather cover.'

May searched the shelf and found a heavy volume that looked as if it had travelled the world. 'This one?'

'That's it. May be of some help.'

'Is this for Arthur?'

'No, no. *He* gave the book to *me*. Apparently he's been researching his own case.'

May searched the cover but failed to find a title. Inside were a thousand thin pages and columns of dense type. 'What is it, a medical casebook?'

'No, it's a history of the Belgian Congo. Your partner seems to think it contains the explanation for his condition. He was terribly excited. Mind you, after he'd gone I found he'd stolen my lunch, so I'm not too convinced he was *compos mentis* at the time.'

May opened the volume and turned to the title page, unsurprised by what he read. *Diseases and Treatments of Congolese Tribal Elders 1870–1914.*

Typical light reading for Arthur, he thought as he left.

'I need the book,' said Arthur Bryant aloud. 'It must be here somewhere. Where else could I have left it?' Grunting with the effort, he stood on tiptoe but still could not clearly read the spines on the bookcase.

Looking around the living room he saw a small wooden set of stairs on wheels, with a carved pole to hold on to. He didn't recall buying any library steps, but wheeled them over anyway. On the way he passed a garish orange sofa that he did not remember seeing before either. *Perhaps Alma's been spring-cleaning again,* he thought, setting the steps before the bookcase. That was more like it. He could reach the top three shelves now. It had to be here somewhere. Climbing up, he searched the titles, but nothing was right: *Treasure Island,*

Two Years Before the Mast, The Life of Lord Nelson, Hornblower in the West Indies, Master and Commander, The Battle of Trafalgar. What on earth were all these naval volumes doing here? He didn't remember putting them up on display like this. He arranged books alphabetically, not by themes, and certainly didn't mix fact and fiction. Could someone have given him them? Perhaps they contained inscriptions.

Pulling down the first, *The Conquest of Scurvy*, he opened it and examined the contents.

The pages were blank.

He grabbed the next book, *Rigging and Practical Seamanship*, and threw it open.

A sea of bare white pages swam up before him.

And the next. Blank. And the next. And the next.

In a deepening state of panic, he hurled the volumes on to the floor. The words had all vanished. What would he do without them? Where had the words gone? How would he survive? His beloved books!

He tore at the naval library until the entire shelf was cleared, then stumbled down the steps and fell on to the sofa, no longer able to contain the sense of devastation that filled his heart.

'You, what are you doing?' barked a shiny young man in a too-tight suit, threaded eyebrows and a Germanic haircut. What he saw in front of him was something that, like the grace of God, defied rational explanation. It looked as if someone had fired a tramp out of a cannon into his prized centrepiece. 'That's our Royal Devonshire Buffalo-Grain Faux-Leather Autumn Collection,' he cried. 'It's not for sitting on! Where do you think you are?'

He's got a point, thought Bryant, *where on earth am I?*

'What seems to be the problem?' said a middle-aged woman with too much make-up and even stranger hair.

'A tramp, Morwenna,' said the young man, flustered.

Morwenna took charge. She came over and stood before

him with her hands on her dimpled fat knees. 'Do you know where you are?' she asked, kindly enough, but speaking loudly as if to a child.

'Of course I do, you silly woman,' Bryant snapped. 'I'm at number seventeen, Albion House, Harrison Street, Bloomsbury.'

'No,' she said, flourishing her palm at the rest of the view behind her, 'you're in the soft-furnishings department of British Home Stores, Oxford Street.'

He looked around and took stock of the scene. Shoppers were drifting about, hypnotized by swivel chairs, standard lamps and other knick-knackery. He looked down at himself. He was wearing his oldest and most worn-out brown tweed suit. He had one torn sock and there were mud splashes all over his legs. 'I'm most frightfully sorry,' he said, trying to extricate himself from the sofa's powerful gravitational pull and failing. 'I seem to have lost my bearings for a moment.'

'Here,' said the sales lady, a look of empathy crossing her features. 'Give me your hand.' And reaching down she gently pulled him to his feet, patiently waiting until he had found his sea-legs.

'Thank you, Morwenna,' he said, grateful for this small gesture of kindness. 'I'm afraid my confusion about being here is far greater than yours. I'm sorry about all the books.'

'Well, I hope you find what you're looking for,' she said, watching him go before turning to berate her junior employee.

Find what I'm looking for, thought Bryant as he tacked towards the exit. *Fat chance of that. I've lost my mind. How can I ever find that again?*

As he stepped out among the blank-faced shoppers of Oxford Street, there before him at the pavement's edge was a familiar figure. John May, resplendent in his navy Savile Row overcoat, was standing beside a waiting black cab, welcoming him towards its open door.

7

HIDDEN & DROWNED

'What were you doing there, anyway?' asked May as they settled back in the taxi for the short journey to King's Cross.

'I think I meant to buy something for Alma's birthday,' Bryant decided. He always picked up a little gift for her, a china owl for her collection, or bedsocks (prior to his discovery that no woman in the world liked being bought bedsocks). Alma Sorrowbridge had been his landlady for decades, and had moved with him to a flat in Bloomsbury after they had foolishly mislaid their old home. Although it had been agreed that they would now share on equal terms, the devout Antiguan found herself cooking and cleaning for her former tenant, a role she adopted with an air of resignation, feeling it was God's will that she should do so, although why this devotion should extend to peeling his corn plasters off the cooker hood – he tended to treat them like Post-it notes – was beyond her.

'What, and then you confused the shop with your home?'

'I suppose I must have done. I really have no idea how I got there.'

'So how did you remember that it was her birthday?'

Bryant rattled his lips. 'Oh, that's easy. November the

eighteenth, 1686. It's exactly three hundred and thirty years after Charles-François Félix famously operated on King Louis XIV of France's anal fistula. In order not to incur the wrath of the king, he first practised the surgery on several peasants. Understandably, most of them died in agony. It's also the day of the state funeral of the Duke of Wellington in 1852, the end of the Battle of the Somme in 1916, the date of the first appearance of Mickey Mouse in *Steamboat Willie* in 1928 and Alma's birthday.'

'So you can remember all that, but not where you live?'

'Oh, I've always favoured abstruse facts over prosaic ones.' Bryant removed his damp felt hat and gave it a bash on the door handle. 'Of course, it's more useful to remember where your keys are than to recall the details of Charles II's exile in Holland, but that's just the way my mind works. I can't bear those people who only talk about arthritis and ring roads and television and mending gutters, although one does recognize the need for them, if only because they occasionally provide babies who grow up to be more interesting.'

'That's generous of you,' said May, not without sarcasm. 'I have a dilemma.'

'Ah. What to do with me, I imagine.'

'Precisely so.'

'I'm not having a carer.'

'No, but the problem is suddenly pressing.'

'You mean a case has come in.'

'You have an encyclopaedic knowledge of the Thames. I really need your help but I can't risk you wandering off again. Arthur, I'm trying to be delicate about this—'

'Please don't be. Delicacy is the curse of the Englishman.'

'That morning on Waterloo Bridge.'

'Ah.' Bryant's face scrunched into a map of wrinkles as if the thought pained him.

'I thought I'd lost you. I watched you head off into the fog to say your goodbyes to London and honestly thought I'd never see you again. You can be a right sod sometimes.'

Bryant bounced back in his seat. 'I have the theatrical gene. And I *did* go to say goodbye to London. But perhaps London isn't quite finished with me.'

'What do you mean?'

'I mean that there are still a few things I have to do.'

'Dr Gillespie doesn't think you have much time left.'

'What if I stayed at the office and didn't take on any field-work, would that satisfy you?'

'I'd much rather you were in the office, but it's not up to me,' said May, wiping condensation from the window and gazing out into the sodden November world. 'I'm afraid it's Raymond's decision.'

Bryant brushed aside the idea. 'Oh, I can wrap him around my little finger.'

'Not this time, old sock. The PCU's performance is being monitored. Raymond's being watched every step of the way. City of London HQ know about your doctor's report and they don't want you anywhere near the case. They need to see how the unit fares without your help.'

'So they can take away its powers once I'm gone,' scoffed Bryant. 'What if nobody knew I was there?'

'How would that work?'

'Get me picked up and dropped off at the building in the morning, send me home by cab at night. No one from outside would need to know.'

'If they found out, we'd be for the chop.'

'Then they won't find out,' said Bryant, attempting to look innocent. 'I promise. We must stand firm and do what we know to be right. We always knew this day was coming. You have to lie.'

'Wait a minute,' said May, 'what happened to "we"?'

The taxi had stopped a little way before the great bronze statue of Isaac Newton at the British Library. 'The traffic's bad,' said Bryant. 'Before we arrive at the unit why don't you quickly fill me in?'

'All right,' May conceded, realizing he had agreed to do

something illegal without actually saying he would. 'A young woman was found on the Thames foreshore this morning, on the site of the old Tower Hill Beach near the Queen's Stairs. She'd been chained to a stone post by her left wrist some time the night before and left to drown. The tide had come in and gone out, but we have some remains of footprints. Unfortunately they belong to only one person going in one direction, down to the water.'

'Well, that throws up at least a dozen anomalies in itself,' said Bryant, intrigued.

'Name one.'

'You say "chained". Explain in more detail, please.'

'Exactly what I said. Chained by a silver neck-chain with a crescent moon on one end.'

'Hers?'

'I imagine so. Dan's working on the hallmark. Her wrist had been attached to an iron ring in the concrete.'

'Why not both wrists? Why only one? Is Giles examining her?'

'He should be by now.'

'Then let's go over there.'

'Now wait a minute.' May pushed his old partner back into the taxi seat. 'You just said you'd stay hidden in the office.'

'Yes, but the coroner's office is right on the way,' Bryant reasoned. 'We virtually have to drive past the place. In fact we could cut out the infernal traffic that way. We just drop off the cab, look in and walk back to the PCU together afterwards. It's right here. Couldn't we?'

'Don't do the orphaned puppy eyes.'

'*Couldn't* we?'

Against his better judgement May gave in, as he always knew he would.

The canalside around King's Cross in the spring did not adopt an inner-city appearance. Colonies of bluebells and forget-me-nots would come into flower around the elder bushes, thrusting through nettle, mint and rose, honeysuckle and cow parsley, while bursts of buddleia, ceanothus and horse chestnut were overhung by frothy plumes of lilac, *No whit less still and lonely fair than the high cloudlets in the sky,* Arthur Bryant often thought. Unfortunately it was November, and all he could see from the road today were two drunk kids kicking McDonald's boxes into the litter-strewn water and a tramp taking a dump behind a diseased plane tree.

The St Pancras Coroner's Office on Camley Street was a building you might expect to find in one of Grimm's less logical fairy tales, and certainly not in the centre of town. Yet here it still stood, at the edge of a graveyard associated with folklore and myth, beside a church that was purportedly 1,700 years old, a damp-looking red-bricked, crook-chimneyed, moss-covered miracle lost in a gleaming futuropolis of steel and concrete, where the only difference between one tower block and the next was the finish on the window frames.

The detectives headed through the cemetery's ornate black and gold gates, pushed past wet overgrown hedgerows and reached the front door, where Rosa Lysandrou answered their knock. Although the Greek coroner's assistant wore her usual shapeless black smock and Birkenstocks, she was also sporting a pair of pink sparkly bunny ears.

'Now I know I'm one carrot short of a casserole,' said Bryant. 'Rosa, what on earth have you got on your head? Have they increased your HRT?'

'I'm being photographed for a calendar,' she sniffed, holding the door wide.

'You're not posing nude?'

'Certainly not.'

'That's a relief. A calendar, eh? What are you, the last day of December?'

'It's for the Co-operative Women's Guild. It shows that we have a sense of humour.'

'Nothing's that funny. Wouldn't you be happier holding a scythe? Is Giles in?'

Rosa pulled her ears off, offended. 'I don't suppose you have an appointment.'

'Good Lord, I don't need an appointment, I used to employ him.'

'Well, you don't any more.'

'No, but I still outrank him in seniority. If we were in ancient Persia, he would be a wizard but I'd be the Grand Wazir.' Bryant shucked off his overcoat and swept past her, followed by the helplessly apologetic May. 'That's confused her,' he said. 'She'll be telling everyone I've gone potty now.'

Giles Kershaw looked up as the door opened. 'Mr Bryant! I didn't think I'd see you—'

'Rumours of my death have been slightly exaggerated,' said Bryant, looking for somewhere to hang his hat. 'Why are you always so smartly attired? Look at you, with your wavy hair and your high thread-count shirt: you look like a male model.'

'A side effect of the job,' Giles said cheerfully. 'People's insides can get in the most frightful messes; it makes you want to put a tie on. I gather you mentioned our Jane Doe in the Thames, John?'

'Of course he did,' said Bryant irritably. 'He's my partner. You should hear what we say about you behind your back.' May glared at him.

The young pathologist pointed across the room with the metal antenna he had been given by his predecessor, a treasured heirloom he mostly used for pointing out diseased lung tissue. 'She's right here. I'm just finishing up.'

'You're still doing all your own prep-work?' said May. 'I thought you were finally getting an assistant.'

'I think your last little escapade put an end to that,' said Giles. 'Take a look at her, just don't touch.'

The body was covered to the shoulders. Bryant examined the girl's pale features. Her skin was the greenish-grey of a turtle's stomach. 'I used to think there was a dark romance to drowning,' he said, slipping beneath the waves amid billow-ing petticoats.'

'Not if you're chained to a post,' said Giles. 'Drowning is usually fast. This wasn't.'

'It sounds like someone took pleasure in making her suffer,' said Bryant, walking around the cadaver tray. 'Are there any externals?'

'Let me get to that in a minute. Janice has already sent us an ID. Her prints were on record. Lynsey Dalladay, twenty-four. We've notified the next of kin. She was seven weeks pregnant.'

'A rather Victorian reason for murder. Bit unlikely these days.'

'I guess that depends on whom she told. I'm waiting to hear back from her physician.'

'Was she dead before she was attached to the rock?'

'There's no mucus in her air passages, no distension of the lungs, no broken blood vessels. She didn't struggle so I'd have to conclude that she was either rendered unconscious and carried out to the site, then awoke, or that she'd been tranquillized.'

Bryant unwrapped a stick of barley sugar. 'What about her natural state of composure?'

'You mean she let it happen? That would be very unusual. I'm on the toxicology now.'

'Wouldn't the cold water have woken her?' May asked.

'She was face down when the tide came in, wasn't she? There's sand in her left ear.' Giles tapped her on the side of the head with his antenna. 'She wouldn't have been able to breathe. If you're in deep water and fighting for breath you can't think about calling for help. You want to keep your body upright, so your arms go straight out – you make a clawing motion.' He demonstrated. 'That stage only lasts for up to a minute. Then you submerge and hold your breath for as long as possible, up to about ninety seconds. After that you suddenly inhale water, splutter, cough, maybe throw up, inhale more. The water blocks the gas exchange in delicate tissues and triggers your airway to seal shut – that's laryngo-spasm. It burns deep in your chest. After the pain you feel suddenly calm because you're losing consciousness from oxygen deprivation. Your heart stops and your brain dies. It's not entirely unpleasant, by all accounts.'

'Unless the victim is in shallow water,' May countered.

'Right, so in this case it played out a little differently. If you can't move and you're being forced to breathe water, your first reaction is still to hold your breath. You reach a breaking point and involuntarily inhale, but you do it too sharply, taking in a large amount of liquid, which ends up in the stomach. That's what happened here. She didn't vomit much prior to cerebral hypoxia, so I'm thinking she hyperventi-lated, decreased her CO_2 levels, suffered hypoxia, passed out and *then* drew in the water. It was cold and we don't know how long she was trapped there, so there may have been numbness that lessened the pain of laryngospasm, sending her directly into a comatose state. All I can tell you is that she wasn't dead when she was chained to the post, probably just unconscious.'

Gently cradling her head, he slowly rotated it and parted her hair. 'I took a careful look at this. The contusion at the base of her skull is consistent with a blow from some kind of metal spike; it's four-sided. It's possible that whoever did it knocked her out, which would explain why she didn't scream and attract anyone. Of course, that scenario creates other physical problems.'

'Presumably it was dark and misty and there was no one to see what happened,' said Bryant. 'Tower Bridge is lit up like a funfair these days but it's still a little too far away to throw much light on the beach, and the pier blocks it.'

May agreed. 'We searched the foreshore for weapons but didn't come up with anything.'

'Do you have any CCTV footage?' Giles asked.

'Dan's working on that as well,' said May. 'We'll see when we get to the PCU.'

Giles was studying Bryant. 'Are you back at the ranch?' he asked casually. 'I thought—'

'You thought what?' said Bryant, sucking the barley sugar. 'I was told you were taking some time off.'

'Oh for God's sake, can you stop trying to be so tactful?' Bryant clattered the stick around his false teeth. 'My mind is dying, my body is not. Right now I'm all there, but sometimes I'm not here. When I'm all there you'll know because I'll be here, but when I'm not here you won't know because I won't be here. All clear?'

'Yes. No. Not really,' said Giles.

'He means that he'll either be in the office or at home, depending on whether he's suffering another attack,' said May.

'And please don't talk about me as if I'm not here,' Bryant warned. 'Giles, are you going to file a Category Two or Three?'

'I don't know yet, but I imagine it'll have to be a Two,' said Giles.

'But she was chained up. Surely that indicates murder or manslaughter.'

'There's no way of knowing that chaining her there indicates an intention to kill.'

'I can't see what else it would indicate.'

'You'd be surprised what people do for kicks,' Giles replied.

'Realistically, what are we looking at – misadventure or an open verdict?'

'Probably the former. I'll only go with an open verdict as the last resort. I can't file yet anyway, not without a more accurate time of death. Assuming she drowned at around—'

'The tide started coming in at one fifteen a.m.,' Bryant interrupted.

'I didn't tell you that,' said May.

Bryant pulled an old-fashioned printed Thames tide table from his back pocket. 'I always have one on me.'

'Of course you do.' Giles folded away his antenna. 'Then I'll wait for your report, shall I?'

'We're sending the team out to track down witnesses,' said May, 'but don't get your hopes up. I'll call you from the office.' He turned to his partner, who was about to head off without him. 'And you – don't you dare stray out of my line of vision.'

'There are things I need to do so I'll see you back there,' said Bryant, disappearing around the corner.

'No, Arthur, I promised I'd stay by your side. You can't just go off—'

But Bryant had already done so.

8

SECRETS & LIES

Cassie North wore a crimson spangled swimsuit and matching high heels. The outfit wasn't her idea, but audiences had an expectation of tradition. It was now a few months after Ali had first met her in the club, and she was ready to be chopped into pieces.

Ali held the cabinet door open for her. The box was black and silver, as tall as a person. She settled herself inside and he closed the three sections, locking each one with theatrical prestiges. Cassie's face, hands and left foot were visible through openings in the front of the cabinet. Ali stepped back and watched her. Cassie smiled up into the spotlight.

He looked out at the expectant audience, knowing that he could afford to wait for another few seconds before starting. He had them in the palm of his hand. *Piano, drums and trumpet,* he thought, looking down into the orchestra pit. *Not exactly the big time.* The musician handling the drum roll hadn't been sober for a single performance.

The auditorium held four hundred but was less than a quarter full. Saturday matinees always seemed to coincide with mall sales, and the few who were here were not enjoying themselves. At least there was no shuffling or talking

– audiences of this generation had been raised to behave politely in theatres – but they were a very old, very English crowd. After all, who else would be attracted to a show called *The Good Old Times Variety Show*?

He was in the Roebuck Theatre, Sevenoaks, typical of a thousand small venues scattered across the country. A painted ceiling, gold cherubs, red velvet curtains, unused side boxes smelling of damp, a provincial lighting rig with a single follow-spot and a box flood, coughing pensioners and an uninter-ested girl hawking programmes at the rear of the stalls.

Ali picked up the first of the rectangular metal blades and inserted it horizontally in the cabinet's midsection. He added a second, dividing the box into thirds. He pretended to push at the blades, as if they were encountering resistance. Cassie gave a squeal. There were murmurs of interest in the audience.

With a flourish Ali slid the cabinet's midsection apart from the top and bottom, pulling Cassie's torso away from the rest of her. Then he summoned a member of the audience.

He usually picked a pretty young girl. Pensioners took too long to reach the stage and children were liable to start poking around the back, trying to spoil the illusion. Today nobody wanted to come up, so the programme-seller stepped in.

Ali opened a small door on the cabinet's midsection so that the usher could make a point of examining and prodding Cassie's stomach. The drummer missed his cue again because he'd been at the bar in the intermission.

The trick was old and easy to perform. The black stripes down the sides of the casket made it look narrower, and the blades weren't as wide as their handles. The left foot was false, and could be moved from inside. Some assistants could perform the so-called 'Zig-Zag' by actually sticking their feet out, but Cassie didn't have enough flexibility.

The illusion only received a patter of applause. They were used to seeing better on TV. He released Cassie and they took their bows. They had only just started the act together, but he already knew they needed to move on to something bigger. If they stayed on this circuit they would never make real money. By the time they'd paid off the booking agent they hardly had anything left over, and the receipts would never make them rich. They'd only managed to get this far by sabotaging the resident magician's van.

After years of sitting on the sun-warmed stone of the dock, staring at the sea's horizon and waiting for each day to pass, Ali was facing a world of opportunity. It was already becoming hard to remember who he had been. Everything was new, everything was exciting, everything was there for the taking.

A plan was fizzing inside his brain, but he needed to run it past Cassie. She would know whether it was something they could handle; she had a good head for business. As the curtains swished shut behind them and they headed offstage to make way for Olga and her Performing Poodles, he decided to tell her about his idea that night. The decision would eventually, in the fullness of time, bring him into contact with the detectives of the PCU.

Back in the present, DS Janice Longbright turned sideways in the mirror and pinched the roll of flesh at her waist. She usually blamed her weight gain not on portion control but corset failure. Her hair was currently Harlow Blonde, but the roots needed touching up. On the right side of her desk sat some pumpkin seed crackers and a tub of quinoa with edamame beans, prepared for her by Meera's sister. On the left, challenging these, was a sausage sandwich oozing brown sauce, lovingly placed there by Colin Bimsley. Life was full of such choices. She loved the fact that everyone called the condiment 'brown sauce' without knowing what was in it. On the other hand, South American farmers were suffering because of the sudden increased demand for quinoa. So really it was a matter of putting the planet's needs before her own.

No contest: she took a bite from the sausage sandwich and

slumped back at her desk. Longbright had put up with a lot of aggravation during her time in law enforcement, from the bad old days of institutional sexism to cruel personal comments about her racy past in the press. It didn't seem to matter that she was on the front line when it came to protecting the city; someone was always ready to dredge up old stories about her student days, when she had paid for her education by performing in Soho's now-vanished burlesque shows. Her years at the Peculiar Crimes Unit had dealt their fair share of blows, too, starting with the death of her mother and ending, most recently, with the departure of a lover. She had made more sacrifices than she had ever intended, and now, somewhere between lying about her age and proudly telling everyone what it was, found herself alone and facing an uncertain future.

At least she had always been able to take refuge in the company of her fellow officers. She thought of John May as her surrogate father, and the idea that she would have to watch him losing his greatest friend and ally was almost too much to bear. Now they would have to fight for stability in the face of irrevocable change.

Arthur Bryant was sitting in the armchair opposite her, his prehistoric overcoat rucked up about his shrinking form like a mammoth-skin, his white tonsure standing vertically above his ears like frightened fur.

He had shuffled in and asked to talk to her, a permission he had never bothered to seek before. She knew at once that he was going to officially take her into his confidence, not realizing that John May had already spoken to her about the doctor's prognosis.

'The worst part,' said Bryant, typically beginning in the middle of a thought, 'is feeling so powerless. Illness is an insidious trickster, a time-thief that plays spiteful emotional games. I really feel I must apologize.'

'Don't be ridiculous,' she said briskly, knowing that she wouldn't be able to stand it if he became maudlin.

'It's a progression that's hard to calibrate,' he continued, accepting the tea mug she handed him. 'Fascinating, really. In its later stages it will become unforgivably dreary, rather like a dull partner brought to a party by a gregarious guest, a parasite attached to its host. I'll be boring to be around, and I'll be bored by doctors and nurses and waiting about, and all those ghastly prosaic things I've never had to bother with before, and the conversation will be about illness and nothing else. You know I have no patience. If there's anything more spectacularly mind-numbing than having to undergo *tests*, it's people wanting to talk to you about them.'

'Do you want me to come with you to the hospital?' she offered.

Bryant's blue eyes widened. 'Good Lord, no, why would you want to do that? I'll take a paperback. Reading a book is the finest way of attaining inner peace. It seems as though our adult lives are entirely spent fighting to regain ground, first against stasis and then against actual decay, but it's a battle we can never fully win. What was the point of me learning so much if all that knowledge is simply going to be chucked into the soil? *Shall I at least set my lands in order?* – T. S. Eliot.' He suddenly clapped his hands. 'But that isn't why I wanted to talk to you. I'm going to need your help.'

She had half expected something like this. 'Oh yes?' she said warily.

'I struck a deal with poor old Raymondo. I promised I would stay home whenever I felt seedy, and that John would secretly cart me to and from the office. It's only a ten-minute walk but there is a slight risk that I'll wander off into traffic or start pretending I'm Catherine of Aragon or something. But I want to be involved.'

'In what?'

'The case, of course – the girl in the river. John says she was pregnant and thinks it's simply a matter of *cherchez l'homme*, but he's wrong. It rather goes without saying that there are several alternative courses of action you can take if you get a girl pregnant, not one of which is chaining her to a concrete post in the Thames. There's much more to this than meets the eye, and I have a few ideas about where to start looking. However, it will involve a certain amount of subterfuge.'

Longbright was puzzled. 'Why? If John is going to bring you to the PCU whenever you feel up to working, what kind of subterfuge are you thinking of?'

'That's the thing. I can't just sit behind a desk. I'll need to take trips out and get my hands dirty in the great seething metropolis. But I don't want to get John into trouble. He won't if someone else covers for me.'

'By "covers" you mean "lies" and by "someone" you mean me.'

Bryant pursed his lips, thinking. 'That's about the size of it, yes.'

'You already know what I'll say.' Longbright talked to the ceiling. 'Why do I do this? Why me?'

'Because—'

'It was a rhetorical question. I'll do it on one condition: that you wear the transmitter Dan made for you. If you won't turn on your phone's GPS tracker you can at least do that.'

'It's a deal,' said Bryant, rising and flashing a grin made wider by his oversized false teeth.

He knows all of our flaws and works them, she thought irritably as he left. *Not bad for someone who's losing his mind.*

9

FLOW & CURRENT

As the two Daves had now cordoned off the basement and one of the staircases while awaiting instructions about what to do with their coffin-sized discovery, the staff met in the temporary ground-floor common room. It was a little after 3.00 p.m. on Monday when Dan Banbury turned his laptop to the others and began running footage.

'I've sent these files to all of you,' he said, 'just in case you spot anything I've missed. Lynsey Dalladay was found chained up here, between the pier and the shore wall, just after dawn this morning.' He tapped the centre of the visual, which showed an area of sand at the base of the river steps. 'She'd just turned twenty-four. She'd been rendered unconscious with a blow to the back of the head, but the contusion is abraded and therefore ambiguous. Giles found particles of grit in the wound that match the concrete she was chained to. She drowned in a few centimetres of water as the tide came in. There was nothing in the pockets of her jeans, no tube card, no wallet, no mobile phone. She has an old Nokia but it hasn't contacted any of her network provider's transmitters since yesterday afternoon, when she rang her mother but hung up before it answered.'

'What have you got on the pregnancy?' asked May.

'I was getting to that. She attended a walk-in clinic at the Cavendish Health Centre just off Oxford Street on the previous Wednesday and was informed that she was seven weeks pregnant. Before then she was registered at the Royal Free. We're still trying to find her medical files. They've got computer problems.'

He raised a small evidence bag so that they could see it clearly. 'This is the chain that attached her wrist to the iron ring. We're assuming it belonged to her and the killer slipped it from around her neck. Now, at this point the tide – what did you say about that, Mr Bryant?'

Bryant unfolded his trifocals and checked his book of tide tables. 'At this time of the year the tide comes up high and fast. Look at the figures.'

Bimsley read over his shoulder and gave a low whistle. 'Does it normally do that?'

'At London Bridge there's a tidal range of nearly eight metres. The speed of flow increases the further downstream you go, as other tributaries add their water. It's a good way to kill someone.'

'And yet there's no CCTV on the shore?' asked Raymond Land.

'There are several areas of increased sensitivity like the Houses of Parliament, MI5 and the Tower of London, but generally why should there be?' asked Bryant. 'There's been no need to patrol the tideline since the docks were moved out. Before, when thieving was rampant in the Pool of London, it was policed—'

'Pool of London?' Meera repeated. 'Where's that?'

'You were born in the Elephant and Castle and you don't know where the Pool of London is?' Bryant was incredulous. 'It's the part of the Thames that goes from London Bridge to Limehouse. There are two parts, Upper and Lower. It's where ships arrived from the rest of the world to deliver their cargoes for inspection by the customs officials. And it was where most of the smuggling went on. That's why there's a bloody great wall running along one side of East Smithfield and the old Ratcliffe Highway: to stop tea leaves from getting in. You don't know about the Night Plunderers? A representation of the Londoner in his most atavistic form? A thousand-year-old history that starts—'

Land flagged down the conversation with his hands. 'Wait, wait, before you get into all that old history rubbish let's stick to the facts. What about Dalladay's boyfriend?'

'Fraternity's located him,' said Longbright, checking her notes. 'His name's Freddie Cooper. John and I are going over there in a few minutes.'

'If we can get back to the problem of the CCTV,' said Banbury doggedly, knowing how easily the PCU staff could be derailed from any topic, 'there's only one camera that picks up any footage of the foreshore around there and it's hardly ever checked because, well, there's never anything interesting on it. It's jointly shared by the companies that own the embankment terrace. We've got a patchy feed from the night before, but nothing for the hours of darkness. It's programmed to lift time-lapse shots through working hours only, or when the light sensors are tripped. Seems it's there mainly to check up on employees. The owners say it's their land and they can do what they like.'

'So there's nothing covering the actual river at that point?' asked May.

'Private craft aren't allowed out on to that stretch without authorization, and not at all after hours of darkness. If anyone did try it, the River Police would pick them up straight away. Now, you can clearly see this lump here.' He tapped at the monochrome scene with his biro. 'That's Lynsey Dalladay right there in the water. You can understand why nobody on the embankment picked her out. She's almost invisible from the shoreside. The pier was shut for the night and inaccessible. She had to have been placed there while the tide was out. The neap tide had occurred the week before.'

'That's the point when high and low tides are the least

different,' Bryant interrupted. 'It happens twice a month.'

Banbury checked his notes. 'There's an approximate six-hour time difference between high and low tides. She was placed at the farthest exposed point of the shore, which gives us a pretty narrow window of operation, probably around thirty minutes, but I'll have to take expert advice on that. Perhaps Mr Bryant could—'

'I'll do it,' said May hastily. 'What have you got on the footprints?'

'This is where it gets murky,' said Banbury. 'See this single line of indentations here?' Turning back to his laptop screen, he traced the faint markings on the beach with his pen. 'These are definitely the remains of human tracks, but the tide washed away their fine detailing. We tried to match the shoes and the leg stride, but we only have approximates because of the tidal pattern. There are no other prints on the beach either before or after she was placed there.'

'That's impossible,' said Land.

'We went down to the site and saw for ourselves,' said May. 'There were no other indentations. Whoever killed her found a way to get out there without leaving a mark.'

'Maybe he left a single set of tracks going to the shoreline and then swam away.'

'You mean he walked in women's shoes?' asked Land, incredulous. 'This isn't an Agatha Christie. Criminals don't leave annoying little puzzles for you to unravel.'

'What about that woman who drowned in her own house?' asked Bryant. 'Ruth Singh, found with river water in her throat, in a terraced house in Kentish Town which she never left.* A classic example of misinterpreting the signs. I remember everything about that investigation. We nearly drowned.'

Of course, now he remembers everything, thought Land, annoyed. *Earlier today he couldn't remember where he lived.*

---

* See *The Water Room.*

'What if he lowered himself off the pier and swam there with her when the tide was partly in?' asked May.

'Why would anybody do that? Besides, you can't get on to the pier except from the embankment, and that's sealed off. The pier entrance is on the other side of the railings that separate the Tower of London from the surrounding area. Actually, it does look like something out of an Agatha Christie,' Bryant mused. 'Or rather more accurately an R. Austin Freeman novel. *The Man With the Nailed Shoes* entirely hinges on a study of footprints.'

'I'm sorry, can we just pop back from the Land of Make-Believe for a moment?' asked Land, his patience exhausted. 'How did they get down to the beach at all?'

'That's another problem,' May admitted. 'There are only two access routes. One is by a locked gate consisting of tall spiked-iron bars specifically designed to stop anyone from climbing over it. And before you ask, no, the spikes don't match Dalladay's contusion. The other route requires you to pass through the front door of the office building on the far side and out the back, which presents further problems. Either the murderer had to negotiate his way past the security guards, or he was already in the building and let himself out with the victim. If it was the latter, Dalladay would still have had to come inside the building at some point as she wasn't an employee and didn't have a pass on her, and there's always someone on the reception desk. The land is owned by Ceto Holdings, who also occupy the main building.'

'How appropriate,' said Bryant, offering a discontinued tube of Fruit Spangles around. 'Ceto is the goddess of the dangers of the ocean, and of sea monsters.'

Land was becoming visibly frustrated. 'What else are you lot doing to sort out this mess?'

'Meera's checking all vehicles in the area the night before and looking for witnesses,' said Longbright, accepting a Spangle without thinking how old the packet must be. 'Colin and Fraternity are talking to employees in the building. Dan and I are on to Dalladay's home, family, employment and medical records.'

'The river,' said Bryant, apropos of nothing in particular.

'I'm sorry?' Land looked at his most senior detective in puzzlement. 'Is there something you wish to add, Mr Bryant? You're not even supposed to be here.' He didn't have the nerve to march Bryant off the premises.

'We have an impossible murder, not committed on London soil but on the disputed jurisdiction of the Thames.' Bryant opened an A2 drawing pad and drew a wiggly blue line across it. 'When you lean over the railings, what do you see? Swirling currents. They seem to encourage violent death. That's hardly surprising, as the Thames is the main artery that runs through the body of the city and takes away its human refuse. Criminals are drawn to it.'

He emptied the rest of the Spangles packet into his fist. 'John Christie, the Ten Rillington Place murderer, was found on Putney Embankment, here.' He marked each of the sites with one of the boiled sweets. 'The Bulgarian Secret Service murdered George Markov on Waterloo Bridge, here. The gravediggers at St Clement Danes used to throw human remains into the Thames, here. Roberto Calvi, the Vatican banker, was murdered under Blackfriars Bridge, either by the Mafia or the Masons, just here. The poet William Cowper tried to commit suicide by jumping into the Thames but the tide was out. That African boy the Met named "Adam" was dismembered in a ritualistic Muti killing and found at Tower Bridge. The pirate Captain Kidd was hanged at Execution Dock – damn, I shouldn't have eaten all the blackcurrant ones.'

He had run out of sweets.

'Look, this is all incredibly riveting, Mr Bryant, but if we could return from Planet Bonkers for a moment we might want to think about finding the bastard who did this,' said Land tactlessly. He was wondering if Bryant was having another lapse, whereas it seemed to everyone else that the old man was just being his usual self.

'You didn't have to put it like that,' said May afterwards as they dispersed back to their offices.

Land looked miffed. 'I can't just keep making allowances for him,' he complained. 'I'm sorry he's ill but I have a unit to run and targets to hit.'

'Let's be clear about one thing,' said May. 'You don't have a unit without him. If you cut him out, you kill us all off.'

'That's not fair,' Land cried, 'I have everyone's best interests at heart—'

Ignoring his supervisor's entreaties, May grabbed his coat and headed off.

10

ROUGH & SMOOTH

'Bad timing,' Longbright warned as she pulled on her jacket and joined May in the corridor. 'The passenger on the river service who took the photograph of Dalladay just posted the shot online and the press picked it up. They're already running it as breaking news.'

'Bugger,' said May. 'What else do they have?'

'Not much. A body removed by ambulance believed to be that of a young woman, but they've already dubbed her "The Bride in the Tide". There's some grainy stock footage of the Tower Hill site, but luckily the tide's over the stanchion at the moment and they're only getting shots of it from a distance. If someone realizes she was chained up there they won't wait for clearance. They'll find a way of getting down on to the beach.'

'Great, so they can post the usual panic-stricken clickbait,' said May. 'Put the fear up that company, Ceto, will you? Make sure they don't grant anyone access. Has anyone warned Giles Kershaw?'

'I spoke to him as soon as I heard,' said Longbright. 'He knows how to deal with camera crews.'

'OK. Let's see what we get from the boyfriend.' May held

open the door for her. 'I assume someone's done the knock. How much more does he know?'

'They've only told him about the location of Dalladay's body and that she drowned, nothing else. I've got an address for Cooper. I think you'll have to drive.'

To the north of the Thames is a ghost shadow of another waterway, roughly tracing the same curves. The Regent Canal extends from the Paddington arm of the Grand Union Canal for eight miles until it reaches the Limehouse Basin, and passes through some of London's more overlooked neighbourhoods. De Beauvoir Town lies between Shoreditch and Dalston, and had been earmarked for the upper classes, but after the canal's construction the ward filled with warehouses. They still stood between tower blocks and Victorian mansions set back from wide, tree-lined streets, a conservation area few Londoners ever had cause to visit.

'Wait, isn't this where the Mole Man of Hackney lived?' asked May as they searched for door numbers.

'His house was alive with rats,' said Longbright. 'We all thought they were going to tear it down, but I heard they just sold it for over a million.'

A retired engineer known as the Mole Man had dug a series of tunnels and caverns under his house, spreading out in every direction, causing many of the pavements to collapse. It was that kind of area, populated by quiet families and eccentric loners, rarely finding its way into the press unless something extraordinary surfaced.

The grand façade of the detached three-storey Edwardian house was kept dark by tall unkempt hedges and a peeling white plaster portico, a shabby old lady of a property badly in need of kindness.

'This one must be worth a few bob,' said May. 'You'd think he'd do it up.'

The man who answered the front door was at the dissipated end of handsome, mid-forties, dressed in a tightly tailored business suit that looked simultaneously sharp and cheap. His black shoulder-length hair was held with a plastic grip, and a tattoo of a rose could be glimpsed below his shirt cuff. Freddie Cooper looked like a man who was no longer surprised by anything life might throw at him. Pushing the door wide he headed back into the house, expecting them to follow him.

The house was musty and smelled of damp, its rooms filled with a mix of generic furniture inherited from other properties and personal items that belonged somewhere else: valuable church candlesticks, expensive Indian rugs, a nineteenth-century wrought-iron table covered in Catalan tiles, some minor Pre-Raphaelite sketches in gilt frames.

Longbright and May seated themselves in the cavernous living room opposite Cooper, keeping a distant cordiality, a double-act they had finessed over the years until it reached the level of a top-notch production of *Waiting For Godot*.

May instinctively knew it was important to take a tough stance with Dalladay's boyfriend, despite his loss; everything about him suggested shiftiness. He looked like a man used to subterfuge and the withholding of information. As he waited for them his left leg bounced up and down, dispersing agitation.

Longbright was getting the same bad feeling. Certain men never looked entirely clean. On a coffee table pushed into the corner of the huge living room were the carelessly swept-up remains of a heavy night: a mirror, a biro tube, two empty coke wraps, vodka and beer bottles, shot glasses.

'You don't look very distraught,' said May, turning to Longbright. 'Does he seem distraught to you?'

'Not remotely,' said Longbright. 'Quite a party you've had here.'

'You can skip the routine, I still have some important appointments to get to,' said Cooper, looking as if he'd never had an important appointment in his life. 'Is this going to take long?'

'It all depends on you,' said May. 'Lynsey Dalladay, how long have you known her?'

Cooper searched the ceiling for an answer. 'Just under a year.'

'Living together, that right?' asked Longbright, checking her pad.

'Yeah, she moved in about six months ago.'

'Where was she before that?'

'I don't know. Hanging out with the rest of the Botox set, I imagine.'

'Is that all you know?' asked Longbright, looking at her notes again.

'There's not much else to say,' said Cooper.

'Try telling us about her.'

Cooper wiped his nose, looking vaguely bored. 'Posh bird, privately educated; I met her at the bar of the Hoxton Hotel with all her frozen-faced pals looking down their noses at me. She thought a bit of rough would make a nice change.'

You're not that rough, thought Longbright, *not with an original Burne-Jones on the wall.* 'The street accent,' she said. 'Have we got some Received Pronunciation under that? You went to Westminster, didn't you?' She had already done some checking.

'Well, yeah—'

'Which university did you drop out of?'

Cooper shrugged. 'Oxford, Worcester College.'

'So, Frederick, Posh Freddie, what's the history here? You came to town, banged through your trust fund while squatting in one of your old man's Primrose Hill properties, then invested in an up-and-coming area like this, or has the money already run out? You met Dalladay and thought you'd sponge off her for a while?'

'You should watch how you talk to me, I'm not the villain here, I'm a successful businessman,' Cooper warned, a short fuse lit.

'So who is the villain?' Longbright asked.

'I don't know. Dalladay was damaged goods, a real mess.

Women like her can drag you down with them. She said she was trying to "find herself". She found plenty of others on the way. Spent a year bumming around Goa and Kerala, ashrams, tantric sex, lots of drugs. Used her connections to get a few media jobs but always got fired.'

'Why?'

'Because that's what happens when you can't concentrate on anything for more than ten minutes at a time. She went to Thailand, joined a religious group, discovered her inner goddess, came back to London and cleaned up her act, so she told me.'

'And then she met you,' said Longbright, eyeing the table with the badly wiped-up coke-line, the suspicious inlaid wooden box next to it.

'Yeah, I tried to keep her straight.'

'Sure you did.'

May withdrew his smart new PCU-issue tablet and ran down its history. 'You've got two convictions for possession of a controlled drug and intent to supply. So she was a free spirit or, as we call them, a "Person at Risk", and she teamed up with someone who, historically speaking, is a bit of—'

'—an entrepreneur.'

'—a scumbag. Not that it's my job to judge. How was that going to straighten her out?'

'I told you, I'm a businessman,' said Cooper. 'Like a few million others in this city. We were both on the same road back from a bad place. I thought I could help her.'

'So what went wrong?' May asked.

Cooper made an attempt to look hurt. 'Who said anything went wrong?'

'Do you share this place with anyone else?' May nodded at the table. 'Class As, that's up to seven years. You don't care about that?'

'Come on, man.' Cooper waved the idea aside. 'You've got bigger things to think about than a bit of blow. I had a few mates around from the office.'

'So you weren't exactly missing her,' said Longbright.

'What, that's a crime now? She was the one who lost interest in me.'

'How did that show itself?'

'Let me see. That would be when she started disappearing for several days at a time.'

'You mean she was using again.' May had seen Giles's report and knew this not to be the case.

'No, I don't think so. But she must have been seeing someone.'

'You don't know where she went?' May asked. 'It says here she was working at the Cossack Club in Dalston. That doesn't sound very Henley.'

'I have no idea what happened to her, and that's the God's honest truth,' said Cooper, taking pains to look as if he might be telling the truth. 'She stayed away more and more, wouldn't tell me where she was going or where she'd been, and certainly couldn't remember enough to lie properly. Finally she moved out.'

'Or did you throw her out?' asked May.

'No, it was her decision to go.'

'When was this?'

'About two weeks ago. And before you say it, yeah, I knew she was pregnant, but I also knew it wasn't mine.'

'How did you find out?' asked Longbright. 'She called you?'

'No, someone else, I don't remember who. I meet a lot of people, hear a lot of rumours.'

'Something like that, I'd have thought you'd remember. Did somebody pop a postcard through?'

'We've got some shared friends who talk too much, OK?'

'Was she happy about it?'

Cooper all but exploded. 'How the hell would I know? Are you even listening to me? She wasn't saying and she sure as hell wasn't sleeping with me.'

'But you must have had *some* idea of where she was going

and who she was going with,' Longbright persisted. 'Did you never hear a phone ring or see any texts?'

'No, she had this old phone that barely worked, and nobody rings the house phone except my foreman, usually to tell me that something's gone wrong at work, or my mother, who can't figure out how to call my mobile number.'

'Did Dalladay have a laptop?'

'You're joking. I bought her an iPad a few months back. It's still in its box.'

'So a fortnight ago she just announced she was leaving.'

'She didn't announce anything, just packed a bag and walked out.'

'Did you have a fight?'

'You can't have a fight with someone who makes no sense.'

'And she left no forwarding address.'

'She washed her hands of me, man. Like all the little rich girls who clean up their acts. She got *bored*. I bored her. She was bipolar and scary and she was driving me nuts.'

'So you got tired of her too.'

'That's an understatement. She wore me down. After she walked out it was like a weight had lifted. I opened a bottle of champagne.'

'Anything else we need to know before we find out?' Longbright asked, looking around the room.

'There's nothing I can tell you about her that would surprise you.' Cooper shrugged, as if the matter was closed. 'I felt sorry for her, but she was just another high-maintenance princess with an exaggerated sense of entitlement who went ballistic when people stopped paying attention to her.'

'When she took off, you didn't try to find her?'

'I didn't look too hard, if that's what you mean. Can't you track her movements over the last couple of weeks?'

'Tell me about the Cossack Club,' said May.

Cooper raised his hands. 'It's just an after-hours place people go. You're going to look into it and find out some bad stuff, but I swear that has nothing to do with me, or this.'

'What kind of bad stuff?' asked Longbright.

'If you're going to ask me anything else, I want a lawyer.'

'Tell you what, we'll take a swab and a blood sample for now,' said May, rising. 'Just to – you know.'

'And you can show us where you keep your shoes,' said Longbright, also rising.

'What, you think I was involved in her death?' Cooper asked as he chased behind them.

Longbright deadpanned. 'Were you?'

'I'm not the most honest bloke in the world, but if I wanted to deal with a problem I wouldn't take it down to the river and drown it like a cat.'

'No, I imagine not,' said the detective sergeant. 'At the moment we have no reason to assume that you killed her. By the way, did she wear any jewellery?'

'Not much,' said Cooper. 'Some rings, cheap things.'

'Nothing around her neck?'

'Like what?'

'A silver chain with a crescent moon and a lock.'

'No, I never saw anything like that.'

They headed upstairs to the main bedroom, which had a freestanding white marble bath at one end. May opened the antique wardrobe and emptied out Cooper's boots and trainers. He was careful not to touch the outsides, knowing that Banbury would be able to tell if any pair had been specially cleaned. He took some shots of the wardrobe's layout. 'Don't touch anything; we'll send someone along,' he said. 'Where's Dalladay's stuff?'

'She never left anything here.'

'Nothing at all?'

'She always dragged a bag around with her.'

'Where were you on Sunday night around midnight?'

'I was here, at home, alone in front of the telly, like I always am. I start work at six a.m. on Mondays.'

'What's your business?'

'I run a road-haulage company. So I am a suspect?'

'Only if you keep asking me.'

As they left, Longbright stopped May in the gloomy hallway. 'Do you want to bust him?'

'For recreationals? A bit of work-hard-play-hard? No. He knows we could whenever we wanted. He'd have cleared it away if he was dealing. If we turn a blind eye now he may be useful to us in the future.'

'You know what the Met Drugs Directorate would have to say about that.'

'We're PCU; they have no influence over us.'

As they reached the car it was starting to rain finely, glossing the pavements. 'So, what do you reckon?' Longbright asked.

'About Cooper? He thinks he's smooth. He's just another Flash Harry,' said May. 'But I suppose there could be something. Let's dig a little deeper.'

'Dalladay sounds like she was a pain in the arse.'

'She's not able to give an account of herself,' May reminded Longbright. 'Someone robbed her of that right. I want you to go and see where she worked. We need someone who spoke to her in the last couple of weeks. She couldn't just have vanished.'

'Maybe she went back to Henley.'

'Not to her parents.'

'You've spoken to them?'

'I got somebody local to do the knock. You heard Cooper. She left with an overnight bag.' May dug out his keys. 'Can I give you a lift up to Dalston?'

'It's not far, I'll walk,' said Longbright. 'Where are you going?'

May checked his watch. 'We've been gone a while. I have to keep an eye on Arthur. I think each day's going to be a surprise from now on.'

11

RATS & LIONS

'Of course, there are only a handful of real motives for murder,' said Raymond Land, concluding his argument with all the authority of someone who doesn't know what he's talking about. 'It's always sex or money, stands to reason.'

As everyone else was out working on the case, Land found himself answering phones, making weak tea, reorganizing paperwork in such a way that no one would be able to find anything and babysitting his befuddled detective. It was unfortunate that in this case the baby was a faintly unsanitary pipe-smoking senior with oversized false teeth, a whistling hearing aid and a lethal walking stick.

'I must disagree with you there,' said Bryant, who looked forward to disagreeing with anyone, especially his unit chief. 'There are many more motives.' He ticked them off on his fingers. 'Revenge and power and anger and damage control and cruelty, warnings to others, the hiding of evidence – and plain, simple insanity. Meanwhile you've got the Met spending their days chucking quasi-military teams into every postcode with a gang problem when London needs more community workers, not goons inviting themselves into council flats with battering rams. We need to spot the symptoms instead of dishing out cures.'

Beyond the office windows a sudden squall of rain increased its strength, causing the other side of the road mercifully to disappear. Land blinked back at his charge. He found it hard to believe that this was the same man who'd been reported lost in a department store just a few hours earlier. Bryant never ceased to wrongfoot him.

'Do you know what's happened to the murder rate in London, Raymondo? It's dropped by 30 per cent in five years and is still falling.' Bryant poked at his pipe bowl with a meat skewer, disrespectfully emptying its reeking contents on to Land's desk. 'Great Britain now has one of the lowest murder rates in the world. It's lower than Norway's, for heaven's sake. Have you ever met a Norwegian? If they were any gentler they'd be hamsters. Do you know who has the highest murder rate? Honduras. Now before you tell me it's down to hot-blooded Latins, let me point out that it can't be related to temperature because the place with the lowest murder rate in the world is Polynesia. I suppose you can't hide a gun in a grass skirt.'

'Wait, wait,' said Land, feeling as if he was once more stepping into the wobbly funhouse corridor of Bryant's mind. 'You have no way of knowing how each country classifies its cases. In the UK you can't count homicides unless there's a conviction. There's no international standard. Knife crimes are up.'

'True,' Bryant agreed, 'and the number of unexplained deaths has risen sharply in London. By "unexplained", I mean open verdicts, unsolved cases, disappearances, people simply dropping off the grid and ceasing to exist. Now, what does that suggest to you?'

'Poor accounting?' asked Land hopefully.

'No, *mon petit débile*, it suggests that the nature of lawbreaking is changing. London is much more populous and transitory these days, so theoretically the crime rate per capita should have risen. I think it *has* risen, and we're misreading the figures.'

'How would that make a difference?' Land eyed the pipe debris with disgust. 'A person is either there to be counted or not.'

'Not strictly true, if you believe in quantum super-position.'

Land gave him the blankest of looks.

'Schrödinger's Cat? No?' Bryant shrugged. 'Never mind, you were talking about motives, and forgive me but the motives you selected are the same ones that have been trotted out for the past century and a half. Motives for murders that were committed by rats.'

Land was lost. 'What do you mean, rats?'

'Germ-riddled squeakers that flee from the light, hungry and cowardly opportunists from what used to be called the criminal classes. What if crime rates haven't changed but criminals have? We're in a fast-evolving, fluid society that's almost impossible to track, despite the fact that you can't nip out for a Kit-Kat without triggering an electronic Post-it note. There's no nice old PC Plod popping in for a cup of tea and keeping a friendly eye on all at 999, Letsby Avenue any more.' Bryant squinted into his pipe and blew. 'Look up "police station" for this area and you know what the interweb tells you? That there *is* one, only it doesn't seem to exist at the listed address. That's because it got closed down due to lack of use, which just leaves specialist units like us. We tackle crime after the event, we don't keep the peace. Nobody keeps the peace any more. We punish but we don't prevent. The politicians are letting society do that for us.' Bryant saw that Land was still having trouble following him. 'Look, if someone chucks a McDonald's bag on to the pavement in front of you, you don't tell him off for fear of getting a knife in your gut, right? You keep your head down and your eyes averted, and hope that someone else does something. Fear is what's keeping the population in line nowadays.'

Land shot him a look of concern. 'Are you feeling all right?'

'No, of course I'm not. Victims go unnoticed because we no longer know who's preying on them, and they don't report half the things that happen for fear of having their own histories investigated. What kind of a person would tie a pregnant girl to a post and let the tide drown her? Maybe she wanted to have the child and expected this Cooper fellow to support her, so he did her in.'

'I think he'd have tried to talk through the options before dragging her down to the river and planning an impossible crime, don't you?' said Land.

Bryant patted his pockets, looking for tobacco. 'We don't know enough about the girl yet. The father of her child could be a married man with a lot to lose. We need to drive her family and friends mad with questions. And I want Dan to tear Cooper's house apart. I want him pushed through the hoops. I should have gone with them this afternoon. I feel like I'm under house arrest being stuck here with you. No offence.'

'There's plenty for you to do here,' said Land. 'You can give us moral support, and there are your books, and the phones and the internet.' He sounded like a sports teacher consoling a child who'd forgotten his kit for the big match.

'Fine,' said Bryant, unwrapping a packet of HMS Nautilus Rough Cut Rolling Tobacco. 'If you're going to patronize me, I shall retire to my thought-chamber and ponder the problem. But don't expect me to get very much further without being allowed out in the field. You might do me a favour, though. That so-called "public-private area" near Tower Hill Beach. Find out if it bans dogs, will you? And see if there's a bright red coach parked by the Tower called "Golden Dreams".'

Savouring the mystified look on his colleague's face, Bryant returned to his own office and threw himself down into his old green leather armchair, taking in his half of the room, which had been filled with even more furniture while the two Daves were laying new floors.

To his left were the bowed bookcases stuffed with forgotten periodicals, lost treatises, banned tracts, esoteric
catalogues and misleading textbooks. Next to them was a
late-nineteenth-century Vernis Martin *bonheur du jour*
writing desk with slender cabriole legs and ormolu mounts,
its top inlaid with cherrywood marquetry, its value somewhat diminished by the half-litre of 'Peach Bellini' Dulux
matt emulsion Bryant had accidentally tipped over it during
an experiment. The staff had trodden pink paint around the
building for days. There was also an astonishingly ugly sideboard, a veritable Quasimodo of Victorian furniture that
contained several hundred files, souvenirs, mementoes, gee-
gaws and postcards of a distinctly dodgy nature, as well as a
hundred millilitres of nitroglycerine stored in an old bottle of
Dr Japp's Colonic Rejuvenator. There was a ventriloquist's
dummy that had once belonged to Charles Dickens and a
plaster figurine of Dame Nellie Melba minus its right leg. It
was a measure of Bryant's mind that he thought such items
might one day come in useful.

In amongst this old rubbish were far more serious effects,
of course, including a number of documents so sensitive that
they still had the power to destabilize governments. Bryant
was very selective about what he kept, and everything was
stored for a reason. Like Edgar Allen Poe in 'The Purloined
Letter' he believed in hiding the most important items in
plain sight, which was why his black book of contacts lay
open on his desk.

As a lay historian and a self-taught academic there was
very little he did not know about the secret synchronicities
of London, but very occasionally he drew a blank, and then
the black book came into its own, for its pages contained the
addresses of hundreds of men and women who shared his odd
passions. He searched for names now, carefully jotting down
the details of a few eccentrics and social misfits who might
prove useful. Then he sat back for a quiet smoke and a think.

By the time the pipe was finished he had decided that the

key was the river. It gave life to London, but could just as easily take it away. The question that hung in his mind was this: Why keep Dalladay alive until the Thames consumed her? Why not kill her and weight the body, throwing it from a bridge as so many had done before? Why tie only the left hand? And what was to be gained by taking such a risk, by doing something so utterly cruel? What kind of devious mind were they dealing with?

Bryant's bookshelves contained half a dozen esoteric histories of the Thames, but none proved to be of any help. He stuck a hand into his overcoat pocket and pulled out two leaking cheddar and chutney sandwiches, making a mental note to ask Alma to wrap them before leaving them inside the brain-pan of the carved Tibetan skull he kept beside his bed. *What kind of person are we looking for?* he asked himself as he munched. *Does he have a special association with the river? Does she? Or is it simply because that spot is dark and inaccessible and free from cameras? How did the killer get in there anyway?*

So far, they didn't have enough physical evidence to answer his questions. For all of London's much-vaunted crime-prevention technology, it was amazing how often the system failed to record illegal activities. Hard drives froze, motherboards overheated, lights burned out, substations flooded, suspects blurred before camera lenses; for every major advance it seemed there was half a step back.

He needed to go and look at the site, just walk around on the foreshore and get a feel for what had happened. Janice was off paying a visit to the Cossack Club. It was already dark. Tower Hill was less than twenty minutes away. He could slip out via the fire escape and get back before John returned. No one would ever know that he had even been away.

Knotting his favourite green scarf tightly around his neck and chin, Bryant crept off down the stairs and out into the street, keeping close to the wall just in case Raymond Land was looking out of his window. It was still raining, and London in the rain had its own scent. It was the smell of weeds and wet brickwork, and in the new Square Mile it was becoming rarer with each passing day. Glass and steel were odourless.

A short walk from Tower Hill Station took him towards the banks of the Thames. Visitors were still milling about the new entrance to the Tower of London, tickets for which now included access to the Tower and the Crown Jewels, exhibitions and guided tours, historical re-enactments, activity trails and fish and chips. *It's only a matter of time before they add a roller-coaster,* Bryant decided.

He made his way down to the river's edge, where the wind-swept stone concourse that presented itself did indeed display a 'No Dogs' sign. Anyone with a pet in the private apartments opposite would have to walk it farther along the embankment at night, so there was no point in searching among them for witnesses.

The Thames did not possess the romantic outlook of the Danube or the Seine. There was a harshness about it that rankled in the nostrils and blossomed in the brown-green depths like a series of submerged thunderstorms. Bryant knew that if you fell into its central channel during an ebb tide there was little chance of your body ever being recovered. Mothers no longer allowed their children to play on the shoreline. Its reaches had a gloomy, melancholy aura on even the sunniest days. Ancient weathered posts, the gangrenous remains of the wharves that had bristled all along the shore, still rose up like dinosaur bones.

Bryant considered the problem of access. To get her here, Dalladay's attacker must have carried or walked her through some of the most heavily guarded and photographed streets in the city. If he drove in from the east he would have had to pass through the security checkpoints. From the west he would have been under the gaze of numerous CCTV banks, and once at the Thames he had the impossible problem of reaching the actual beach, so why take a risk when less than a mile down the road he would have found any number of secluded tidal spots?

The river edge was a liminal space of dank corrosion, the exposed gut of the city, the source of its nourishment and the eliminator of its wastes. It seeped into the bones and spread malign thoughts. There was nothing kind or graceful about its unreflective surface, nothing but danger in its depths.

He made his way down the side of the unadorned brick house that stood beyond the Tower of London gift shop and tried the spiked steel gate, noting that although the tall bars were new the lock itself was old and rusted solid. It had clearly not been opened in years. Not impossible to climb over though, if you were determined enough. But not carrying a dead weight. He was about to take his leave of the spot when he saw something move on the river.

A wall of fog was approaching. Fascinated, he stopped to watch.

It billowed over the water in great grey-green curls, obliterating the opposite bank within seconds. Filled with a terrible sense of foreboding, Bryant remained frozen. The noise of traffic faded away and the sound of lapping water assailed him. He remembered an ancient saying: 'When the lions drink, London will drown.'

The green bronze lion-heads held rings in their bared teeth and were set all along the Thames embankments as mooring points. It had long been thought that if the river rose above them it would flood the city's great plain and London would be lost. Any passing policeman who couldn't see the lions was to immediately report the fact so that the tube system could be shut down at once. The fog obscured them now.

Glancing down, Bryant saw that his boots were wet with coalescing droplets. The fog was completely enveloping him. He turned around. The view had vanished in every direction. He sniffed the wet air and wrinkled his nose. He could smell fish-guts spilling from the gutters of Billingsgate Market, coal dust, leather and oil, horse dung, bad meat and rotted wood, and above all the river, unclean, unhealthy, dense and dark.

The fog roiled and parted for a moment, revealing a forest of masts, tall chimneys belching black smoke and, in the distance, the sign of the White Lion Wharf. Mountainously overfilled lighters and barges were drawn up on the foreshore before Locket & Judkins, the coal merchants, its discoloured clapboard building poking out beside the ironmonger's, whose sign advertised stove ranges and castings. These were separated by rickety planked wharves and surrounded by a dozen or so small cranes. Nosing through the black waters was a hay barge, a 'stackie', its cargo loaded to the reefed brown sails of its rigging. On the shore red-faced men in surtouts, paletots and brown waistcoats lolled about smoking clay pipes, waiting for the 'calling foremen' to arrive with their hire-books. The purl-men, who were licensed to sell wormwood-infused ale from their casks, rang their handbells and pushed their carts, attracting thirsty ballast-heavers and coal porters.

Out in the deep channel a black-sided wooden battleship was silently gliding downriver, its rigging filled with capering sailors as it set off with its cargo of human suffering, convicts from the Fleet Prison bound for Australia.

Digging at his scarf's constricting coils, Bryant tore them away from his throat and took great gulping gasps of air that reeked of hides and horns, shit and sulphur, coal dust, cinnamon and nutmeg. He turned and saw the great tree of Queenhithe dock, which had survived from the ninth century to the late twentieth, and the great dark dome of St Paul's Cathedral, by far the tallest building in the city. The thin November daylight shaded into dusk and darkness as time itself stretched and shrank.

It was impossible, absurd – this was the pungent, chaotic Thames shoreline of the 1890s, not the bare antiseptic riverside of the twenty-first century. *This is worse than being lost*, he thought, *I'm hallucinating. It's ridiculous, I'm bringing to life a London I never knew. I could only have seen these images in my books.*

He jumped when he felt fingers tapping at his left shoulder.

'Are you all right, sir?' The constable wore a high-waisted blue serge coat with a wooden truncheon fastened at his side. In his right gloved hand he held the strap of a wooden-cased lamp. 'Not the safest spot for a gentleman at this time of night, if I might be so bold. There's no public footpath to the river. Only thieves and swivers come down to the Pool after dark.'

'I'd lost my way—' Bryant turned about, confused, and looked back, hoping to see something familiar.

The constable stroked the tip of his moustache, pondering. 'Perhaps you was headed for the service at All Hallows tonight? I was listening to the choir meself just five minutes ago. This is a foul night to be out and no mistake.'

'Why on earth are you talking like an extra from a BBC costume drama?' Bryant asked irritably. 'I'm half expecting Sherlock Holmes to come wandering around the corner.'

'There's no need to take that tone of voice, sir. I'm a constable of this parish. I does what I likes and I likes what I do.'

'Now, I happen to know that's one of Dick Van Dyke's lines from *Mary Poppins*,' said Bryant firmly. 'You've overstepped the mark there. And what have you done with Tower Bridge?' He pointed to where the bridge should have been and found only black water.

'Either you're a visitor to these parts or you know as well as I do that London Bridge is the last Thames crossing before open sea.'

'But that would make the date earlier than 1894,' said Bryant reasonably. 'Getting lost is one thing, but if I'm going to be hurled back in time by over a century, I may have to think about self-medication.'

The constable had clearly tired of the confused old gentleman and pointed ahead. 'You should be able to get a hansom on Trinity Square, sir. There's a rank there. I'd accompany you but I have to finish my rounds.'

Bryant had an idea. He laid his hand on the constable's arm, pointing to the small brick house, noting that it no longer had a modern steel gate standing beside it but a low wooden fence. 'Before you go, could you tell me who lives there?' he asked.

'Why, only the watchman. That's just the old gate lodge.'

'Is it the only way to reach the shore?'

'It used to be "for free and public use by all" as I believe they say,' said the constable. 'But that was before the pillagers took their toll along this stretch of the river. So now you has to go through old Barney the gatekeeper. There's nothing for a gentleman such as yourself down there, though. The language that floats up to my ears on some nights, it's a mite too salty for those of a refined temperament. At night these reaches belong to the bone-grubbers and pure-finders. They lead a wandering, unsettled sort of life.'

'Pure-finding? What's that?' Bryant asked.

The constable shook his head, sucking at his teeth. 'Oh, a nasty, unclean business that is. They collect dog dung for the tanning yards. For the purifying of skins. They reckon they can always earn seven and six a week along this stretch, on account of there being so many tan-yards in Bermondsey, but to my mind there must be easier ways to get your crust. That's the trouble here, sir. Where the water meets the city it's a sort of no man's land, unscrupled you might say. Always has been, always will be. Well, I must be on my rounds so let me bid you goodnight.'

He gave a cheerful salute and faded into the fog, until just the soft yellow glow of his lantern remained.

And then there was the noise of traffic once more, modern petrol-engine traffic, not the clatter of carthorses and hansoms, and the fog had gone and some Japanese tourists were waving selfie sticks in the direction of the Tower of London, and everything was normal again.

Except that it wasn't. It wasn't normal at all. Everything was wrong.

Bryant had expected a stately deterioration of the senses, gradual but consistent, a gentle dissipation into the nether-world of dementia, and instead there were these frightful lurches: first his periodic inability to recognize people and places, and now a time machine back to a history-book blur of fact and fantasy. He would have to see Dr Gillespie as soon as possible. In the meantime, it was imperative that he returned to the PCU before anyone else noticed he was missing.

Flicking Dan's GPS tracker back on, Bryant headed for the tube station. But when he took one last quick look back over his shoulder, checking that the present was still in place, he felt that he could almost overlay the scene he had just wit-nessed on the world that had replaced it. And the one might just inform the other.

12

SWORDS & SCIMITARS

Cassie had never believed that Ali's name was really Gordon Hendrick, not for a minute, but she went along with it to keep things smooth between them. They fitted together comfortably. As the months passed she came to think of him not as a foreigner but as a Londoner. He never spoke of his old life, just about his new one, and for all his talk about making a fortune he still seemed to believe that there was money to be made in magic. When he held his cards or his magic books in his hands, it was as if he was recalling some happy distant memory and trying to recapture it.

Ali was smart; he picked up any subject he knew nothing about and quickly become proficient in it. He was a sponge, a chameleon, an opportunist, and he had come up with a new name for the act: the Great Hidini, which had been the name of one of Houdini's rivals.

In an old bookshop off the Edgware Road he had found a paperback condensation of Houdini's notebooks, and it became his constant companion. Cassie wouldn't allow him to attempt the more dangerous escapes, like the Chinese Water Torture Cell, the Damsel Sliced by Swords or anything that involved being suspended in a straitjacket, and besides, they didn't have the money to purchase the paraphernalia for the tricks. Joining a professional group was out of the question as it would involve registration forms that Ali was reluctant to fill in, so they kept to variety acts that had elements of Houdini's magic, touring the satellite commuter towns, being paid cash in hand, gradually working their way towards the centre.

Ali quickly realized that Houdini had been a master of marketing as much as magic – he had once paid seven top-hatted men to sit in the street and expose their bald heads simultaneously, revealing the word 'HOUDINI' painted on their pates – but he knew the pair of them had to keep a low profile for now and continue quietly amassing money until he could at least afford to buy a passport with an undetectable provenance. He and Cassie were lovers by convenience, linked more by ambition than romance.

Their next show was at Carpenters' Hall in South London, a shabby concert venue that had been reclaimed as a community theatre. There was no orchestra pit, so shows had to make do with an onstage resident band which usually consisted of a piano and drums.

Their days were long and hard: finding bookings and renting lodgings, travelling and practising, always practising. For now Cassie was happy enough to follow him and tried to avoid asking awkward questions. She was so undemanding and loyal that Ali suspected she was escaping a difficult past of her own.

The Milk Can was the best escape Houdini ever invented. The props were simple to build from salvage but it was a tricky act to pull off. Ali created a metal cylinder out of scrap, and welded it into shape with tools borrowed from a used-car dealer. The trick, he knew, hinged on the audience's fear of drowning, so he made Cassie describe the effects of such a death beforehand in great detail. He was working on his London accent but had trouble with Ts and certain vowel sounds, and still felt self-conscious when addressing audiences.

After inviting a member of the public up onstage to inspect the can and find it escape-proof, Cassie topped it up with a garden hose and produced a pair of handcuffs. With his wrists locked together before him Ali climbed into the cylinder, displacing water everywhere, which only disturbed the audience more.

Cassie seemed barely able to lift the steel cover, although it was actually made of aluminium and easy to handle, and bolted it into place, fastening it with a padlock. The first few times she had drawn a screen around the can before counting down, but now they had dispensed with that in order to heighten the drama of the trick.

Its secret was simple and undetectable. Ali's escape depended on the fact that the top of the can's tapering section was not actually riveted to the lid. Once inside the milk can he could easily separate the two portions at the joint, and as the lid was much lighter than Cassie made it appear, escape was guaranteed. The churn sat on a wooden pallet to prove that there was no trapdoor beneath it (the public were obsessed with trapdoors, he had discovered, even though they were rarely used). When he climbed inside, he made sure that his body displaced enough water to provide a narrow breathing space at the top. They had performed the trick half a dozen times with great success. Then one night it went wrong.

The house was never more than half-full but tonight it was particularly poor; snow had shut several railway stations and caused many of the older audience members to cancel their tickets.

'We could shorten the slot tonight and skip the escape,' Cassie suggested, tugging at the crimson and gold bugle-beaded panels of her assistant's outfit. 'I've been getting a lot of stick from front of house about the water spilling over on to the aisle carpet.'

'No, we go on,' Ali told her, his brown eyes shining with the anticipation of performance. 'We have to give them value for money so they will tell their friends. How will we ever build a reputation otherwise?'

She checked that his bow-tie was straight. 'You do know that we're never going to get rich doing this? We still owe money on the outfits.'

'I know that,' he said. 'I'm working on something new. We'll become famous because I'll make it happen. We're going to get the money and respect we deserve very soon now.'

He moved around her, getting ready to go on, but she placed a hand on his chest. 'I don't understand you. Why are you in such a hurry all the time? London's not going to disappear overnight. Why is it so important for you to make it big?'

He shrugged off her hand. 'You wouldn't understand. You're already on the inside. People like me, we have to work harder to get in.'

Two old ladies dressed in Pearly Queen outfits came off the stage, having just sang 'The Lambeth Walk'. 'They're all yours, love,' said one of them, 'and bleedin' good luck.'

Ali and Cassie dragged the props onstage themselves because the centre couldn't afford stage hands. After the usual card tricks and a mentalism feat performed with a borrowed phone, Ali moved on to producing bottles from empty tubes. The council had banned the use of animals in acts, so dragging a rabbit from a top hat was out of the question.

Finally it was time for the Milk Can escape. Cassie finished filling the churn with tepid water and, amid wolf whistles from the old ladies in the front row, Ali tore open the Velcro strips on his suit to reveal sunbed-tanned musculature. As Cassie handcuffed him she described the dire consequences of the stunt going wrong. Ali climbed up and over the rim of the churn. As he made a display of lowering himself inside, Cassie turned to the audience and asked for silence. Ali began to work on removing the handcuffs even before she had locked the lid of the can in place.

The cuffs came off easily. He could hold his breath for a minute and eighteen seconds, but never needed more than thirty seconds to effect his escape. The rest was just waiting until the last possible moment, feeling the tension ramp up in the audience.

But tonight when he pushed at the lid nothing happened. He had very little leverage inside the cramped can, but it usually lifted with ease. Trying not to panic, he thought back through the preparations. He had heard Cassie making an effort of rolling, then lifting the lid. She had dropped it into place and hammered it down.

That was it. She had hit one side harder than the other and jammed it. He punched at the lid with his fist but nothing happened. Pushing himself up into the air-space at the top of the can, he knew that if he panicked now he would start breathing too quickly and run out of air before he could be rescued. It was better to keep very still, conserving breath and energy. So he sat there with his unlocked wrists before him, imagining what it would be like to drown, as Ismael had drowned in the dark ocean off the coast of Lampedusa. He, Ali, had been spared for a higher purpose. He would face drowning a second time, and he would survive again.

Cassie would quickly realize that something was wrong when she couldn't hear him moving about. Everything would be all right. It *had* to be.

But tonight the music cues were different. The piano and drums started too soon and drowned out the lack of sound from the can. Cassie checked the clock behind her and saw that it was coming up to eighty seconds.

She had faith in him. She was sure he was just playing the audience, who had started to get fidgety and nervous. *Good call, Ali,* she thought, *we'll really get them this time.* She acted out a bit of stage business, pretending that she was really worried, enjoying the feedback she felt coming off the front rows.

But the can hadn't moved. Walking to the back of the

churn she climbed the steps and tried to see if something really had gone wrong. The audience was highly agitated now, sensing trouble.

She tested the lid and found it wedged firmly down, as it always was. What could have happened? The clock had hit ninety seconds, the second-hand deep into the red danger zone. Her fingers fumbled around the edge of the lid. Then she realized; it was pushed further down on one side than the other. The metal had buckled, wedging it shut. She thumped at the edge with her fist but it would not budge a centimetre. There was no one in the wings to help her.

The churn was heavy with the weight of a human body and many litres of water, so she had to slam her back into it. On her third attempt the churn rocked and passed beyond its tipping point, crashing to the stage, where its lid burst off, allowing water to flood the stage and blow the footlights.

Ali was unconscious. She had to drag him out, and surprised herself by remembering how to clear his lungs of water, something she had learned at school. He spluttered back into consciousness, coughing.

Management was very upset about the state of the stage, because water passed through the floorboards and blew the main electrics. They didn't care that one of their performers had very nearly died, and charged him for the damage.

Back in the dressing room Ali was back to his usual ebullient self. 'I should have oiled the lid,' he said. 'Now we've lost the gig. We'll need to find a new revenue stream.'

Cassie held his wrists and made him look into her eyes. 'Listen to me,' she said. 'You're alive. You could have died. Do you understand?'

'I knew you'd figure out what had gone wrong,' Ali said. 'We needed this booking, and the milk can is wrecked. We'll have to start over.'

'No,' she said, 'that's our last time doing this. There are better ways of making money – maybe not easier, just better.'

Cassie was right. It was the last performance in the

short-lived career of the Great Hidini. They fled their debts, and Ali decided to implement a new game which he hoped would prove more lucrative. This time it involved stepping closer to the edge of the law. Every step he took brought him closer to a future meeting with the PCU.

Janice Longbright arrived at the spot where the Cossack Club should have been and found nothing. This was an area, she reminded herself, where a fashionable cocktail bar could be hidden behind the frontage of a derelict newsagent's. At number 273, Dalston High Road there was a Turkish barber shop that shared its premises, in true Sweeney Todd style, with a butcher. A scratched black doorway stood between the two halves.

Then she saw the letters, gold italic diamonds that had lost their adhesive and slipped from their position above the letter box:

CO SACK CLU – Ring bell twice

Classy joint, she thought, ringing and stepping back. The Victorian terrace had been carved into shops, bars, cafés and dingy spaces that defied glancing interpretation, each sublet property flirting inventively with the council rulebook.

The lock buzzed and she pushed inward to a claustrophobic hall of black-painted walls and sticky green carpet. Beyond that, a narrow staircase led down to a nightclub that managed to be both garish and penumbral. Nearly a dozen rooms ran off the lower corridor, which finally opened into a dance floor and bar. On the wall was a pair of crossed scimitars, vaguely Baltic in origin.

The man behind the counter, an ex-army type, now morbidly obese and mottled with the brick-coloured features of a heavy drinker, rested his tattooed forearms on the beer pumps, nodding at her warily. Janice could tell that he sensed the presence of a police officer, even though she was wearing the PCU's non-regulation winter uniform of black sweater and Puffa jacket. To settle the matter she flicked him her badge and asked his name. Joe Easter said he was the bar manager. He also appeared to be reading Virginia Woolf's *To the Lighthouse*, if the dog-eared copy next to the beer pumps was his.

'Lynsey Dalladay. Name ring a bell?' she asked, looking around.

'Hang on,' said Easter. 'Are you new CO14?'

CO14 was Clubs and Vice. The manager had obviously had his collar felt before, and wasn't bothered about letting her know.

'Special unit,' she said. 'Dalladay, twenty-four, dark-haired, petite, very pretty. Come on, it's not rocket science.'

'Why, what's she done?'

'Your turn first.'

'She didn't turn up for her shift, if that's what you mean.'

'When?'

'She was due in Saturday night. I tried her phone but it was switched off.'

'Any contact since?'

'Not a dickey.'

Longbright looked around at the scarlet walls, the blue leather sofas, the absurd paintings of naked Eurasian women in gold plastic frames. The decor was either ironic or a genuine throwback to the clip joints of the late 1990s. The latter, she decided, noting the pink and green neon strip lights behind the bar. Even in her own days as a night-club hostess she had never worked in a place as grim as this. 'First time she's gone missing?' she asked.

'No. She hardly ever turns up when she's supposed to.'

'Then why do you keep her?'

Easter scratched his neck and checked under his fingernail. 'She makes the punters happy.'

'Happy? Are we talking about a cocktail waitress or something more?'

'Look around, love.' He nodded at the table lamp, which consisted of a tasselled shade balancing on a headless nude female torso. 'What do you think?'

'How far does she go?'

'That's up to her, if you're fishing for a licence infringement. I never saw her do anything dodgy.'

'What's a bit of posh doing down here? Do you get many girls like her?'

'You having a laugh? Hardly ever.'

'Then why her? Why here?' she wondered aloud. 'What would bring her to a rathole like this?'

'A bit of *nostalgie de la boue*, I imagine,' said the bar manager, taking Longbright aback somewhat. 'Doing it for kicks. Some girls just get the yearning for it. The punters like that.'

'What sort of punters?'

'Turkish, mostly. Russians who fancy themselves as oligarchs just because they've bought a four-bedroom house at the wrong end of Islington. A few Chinese. The odd high-roller, but mostly meatheads looking for a cheap thrill on the way home. There's plenty of upmarket clubs they could go to before hitting Dalston, but the girls would be more . . . demanding. Lynsey knew which ones she was after, and picked off the best of them. I used to watch her sometimes, studying their form like she was picking racehorses.'

'I guess that didn't make her too popular with the other girls.'

Easter snorted, then had to wipe his nose on his wrist. 'They asked me to get rid of her, but why should I? She brought in bigger spenders.'

'And you need the bigger spenders because . . .' She let the question hang in the air.

He tilted his head on one side and studied her coolly. 'You know as well as I do that we don't have a gambling licence, so there's no gambling going on here, is there?'

'What, no tables behind any of those doors?' Longbright

asked. 'You'd be the only club around here without them.'

'What's she supposed to have done, anyway?'

'Done? She's carked it, pal. Currently lying on a steel tray in the St Pancras Mortuary.'

'Bloody hell.'

'Who did you last see her with? Did she have regulars?'

'Not really. Blokes asked for her but she was moody, rarely saw anyone twice.'

'Because she didn't have to.' The air down here was unpleasantly beery and stale. Longbright was ready to get back out into the rain. 'You kept her on,' she reminded him. 'You must have formed an opinion of her.'

Easter scratched at himself again, thinking. 'Well, it's a type, innit? She'd been here nearly four months, vanished every three or four weeks; I gave it another month or so before she quit for good. Stands to reason, a girl like that.'

'What do you mean?'

Easter cracked his knuckles, or it might have just been his signet rings. 'Come on, you know the type,' he said. 'Lost girls, isn't that what they call them? The smooth life didn't work out so she was trying the rough. She had this idea she could start her life again. Into all that astro-bollocks, karma, crystals, Buddhism. You know, lady-science.' He checked himself. 'No offence, love.'

Longbright smiled darkly. 'Did you ever try it on with her? Force it a bit, offer to look after her?'

'Not me. First, this is my place of work. Second, she was too hyper. Liable to stab you with an ice pick if you looked at her the wrong way.'

'I want a list out of you before I go,' she said. 'Every man she met in here; everyone who called her or asked for her.'

'People don't give their real names—' Easter began.

'You're a private club so you're legally required to keep membership documents with a name, proof of age and a valid contact number. If you can't furnish those from your ID scanner, consider yourself closed down as of this moment.'

She tapped the cover of the paperback. 'That's not her best book, by the way. Try *Orlando*.'

Half an hour later Longbright left with the membership forms in a box under her arm. Even if only a quarter of the names were real, at least she had somewhere to start.

13

NARCOTICS & STIMULANTS

The DS fished the pages from her overburdened desk and handed them over. 'He knew nobody was likely to leave their real names and addresses at a dive like the Cossack Club, so he had them photographed at the counter in the corridor. Joe Easter isn't as dumb as he looks. He was a big deal in a jazz band back in the nineties, a clarinettist. Now he's got arthritis and can't do his collar buttons up, let alone play. His wife probably leaves them undone when he annoys her, just to get her own back. If he was my husband and he upset me I'd put things on the top shelves of cupboards.'

'Remind me never to get on the wrong side of you.' John May turned over the sheets, mostly generic Russian and Turkish names. Attached were small photographs of the punters as they stood at the counter, waiting for entry.

Longbright tapped the notes she had added beneath the photographs. 'He said the shots were for security purposes. The punters use credit cards to clear their tabs. Put their personal details together with their head-shots and I think you'll find the club is probably doing something interesting with the data. They're also running some kind of gambling deal. I saw card tables and chairs stacked in one of the rooms.'

'That's not our concern,' said Bryant, who had been listening at the door. 'If you get sidetracked into chasing down their extracurricular activities instead of following the girl you'll be heading away from the target.'

'The club could be our only way of finding out who got Dalladay pregnant,' said May.

'You mean it wasn't Freddie Cooper?' Longbright was genuinely surprised. 'Damn, I had him pegged as the type.'

May stared at pages of unrecognizable faces, then handed the forms back. 'Not according to Giles,' he said. 'Cooper was telling the truth. He's definitely not the father. The samples came back negative.'

'Then we need to look somewhere else.' Bryant manoeuvred himself above his green leather chair and dropped into it with a sigh.

'We talked to Dalladay's parents,' said May. 'She had—'

'—a bright older brother who worked in the City and died of a heroin overdose,' Bryant interrupted. 'I checked too. Her mother's a former dancer; her father was a professional tennis player who was forced to give up his shot at Wimbledon after a botched hamstring operation. You know what that means, don't you? Mother regretful, father bitter, favoured son lost, daughter obliquely blamed, hand-wringing and incomprehension at her lifestyle choices, the usual complaints: "We gave her everything"; "Where did we go wrong?" Some theatrics, but not enough to cover their selfishness at being denied perfect kids.'

'You're assuming a lot – and being very cynical,' Longbright pointed out. 'They're probably feeling pretty guilty right now.'

'Cynical, *moi*?' Bryant's blue eyes widened so far that he looked like a lemur with conjunctivitis. 'How many times have you heard that story before? The parents don't even realize they're not being original. I'm sure they expressed mystification for your benefit. They know what happened to their daughter, they just choose not to think too hard about it.'

'You can't be sure of that,' said Longbright. 'Maybe it's what they genuinely believe.'

Bryant looked up at the ceiling, listening to the steady drip of water somewhere. 'People choose what they want to believe. I believe that London was once called New Troy,' he said, 'and that it was founded by the giants Gog and Magog. I believe that the London Stone once stood in the centre of the Thames long before the Romans arrived. I believe that every single legend about this city has at its root a grain of truth, so if a pregnant young woman is found chained in the river instead of being dumped on a piece of waste ground, I believe there is premeditation and a logical reason why the site was selected for her death.'

Even May couldn't entirely argue with that. 'But it's not to do with the river, Arthur, it can't be,' he said. 'The club – there were drug busts in the past but no convictions. Why not?'

'That's a question for CO14, not us,' said Longbright. 'Dalston is Darren Link's old territory. He headed up the local vice unit before he moved to the City of London. Do you want to ask him what happened?'

It was never a good idea to lock horns with Darren 'Missing' Link. The superintendent now worked for the City of London's Serious Crime Directorate, and was an old-school copper who came on like a cross between a betrayed Presbyterian and a recently woken bear. He believed he was morally superior to his weak-willed officers, a minatory man who preached a gospel of expiation before proof of guilt and punishment before rehabilitation. In the fluctuating miasma of urban criminality, where officers had powers to determine the fate of offenders before trial in order to alleviate pressure on the courts, it was not fashionable to be so unbending. Hard-to-prove cases could be resolved with a handshake and a warning in order to save everyone time and money, but that was never good enough for Link; he expected to see some Old Testament suffering. He would have closed down all the shady clubs in his district if he could, and if he hadn't shut the Cossack it was because he had found a better way to hurt them.

'You think Link's mob were on the take, is that it?' asked May. 'It would have to have been without his knowledge.'

'I heard his officers in CO14 regularly raided the clubs and brothels around Dalston in the name of combatting trafficking and coercion,' Longbright told him. 'They checked the girls' employment status and National Insurance numbers, and reported them to the immigration authorities. Sometimes in the process money went missing without receipts. Link wouldn't have been too worried about that so long as he kept them all in check.'

'Why would Dalladay work there at all?' asked May. 'She could have got all the money she needed from her folks.'

'Only someone who loves women a lot can misunderstand them as much as you, John,' said Longbright with a wry smile. 'She did it for herself. For pleasure or power, to be in control of something for once in her life. But she had no discernment. Maybe she mixed with the clients and maybe some of them were on Link's squad. She could have got into something she couldn't get out of. We have to dig deeper.'

'You know what Link will say,' warned May.

'You're asking if my team used the club as *clients*?' asked Superintendent Darren Link twenty minutes later. Raymond Land had him on the speaker in Bryant and May's office, and hastily turned down its volume with a wince. 'Do you want a moment to think about this before you go any further?'

Land beckoned the detectives closer. 'The Cossack had several run-ins with vice during the time you were in charge of the squad, so it makes sense to check with you first,' said May reasonably. 'The present owner is currently living in Moscow. We're having trouble tracking him down. The bar manager admits they had a problem with dealers operating out of the club in the past, but insists they're clean now. If they were professionals they'd supply their own.' May knew that the high-end clubs employed suppliers to ensure that nobody died of bad MDMA on their premises. 'Whatever they're up to – and they're definitely up to plenty – could still be going on.'

Link stonewalled them. 'If you have hard evidence you should be talking to the current vice squad, not to me,' he warned.

'I've got three separate raids dating from your watch,' said May. 'All of your cases were closed; none of the charges stuck.'

'I'm not prepared to go through the fine print of investigations that occurred outside your jurisdiction,' said Link with weary disdain in his voice. 'You don't deal with vice. Anything you uncover in that area has to be turned over to the appropriate agency.'

'It may have a direct bearing on the Dalladay death,' said May.

'If it does we'll have to take the case away from you.'

Bryant made an urgent throat-cutting gesture. May took the point. 'We'll get back to you when we have something solid,' he said, killing the line.

Land was annoyed. 'You must have known that would happen. It's not our area of expertise, John. The girl was murdered because someone didn't want to be linked with a hooker, pure and simple.'

'You don't know that,' said May. 'Janice says some of the other girls saw local officers on a professional basis but not Dalladay. Giles says she showed signs of regular cocaine use. She was a wild card who kept bad company. That doesn't make her a hooker.'

'You won't find her killer through a hair sample.' Land knew that cocaine caused hair growth to slow down. 'You've nothing to connect her death to the club, or to any of Link's old team-mates.'

'Then we'll concentrate on Freddie Cooper,' said Bryant, perking up. 'I'll go and talk to him this time.'

'Oh no you don't,' warned Land, 'you're staying right where we can keep an eye on you. Freddie Cooper isn't the father. You're not leaving this room. I can't have you wandering around out there like—'

'Marley's ghost? Coleridge's Ancient Mariner?' Bryant suggested. 'Or someone you've already written off as no longer being capable of the job?'

'Come on, Arthur,' said May gently. 'It's late anyway. I'll take you home.'

It was only a short walk to Bryant's Bloomsbury flat, but the night was bleak and grey with damp, so May drove him back. They sat in the car looking up at the building in Hastings Street. Alma's light was still on; she always waited up for him.

'There's something strange at the heart of this case,' said Bryant, peeping over the top of his moulting green scarf. 'You see a girl who was killed because she was pregnant. I see a victim sacrificed to the city's most ancient deities. I try to look at it your way, the obvious logical way, but I never could and I still can't even now, just when I need everything to be cogent and consistent.'

'But that's your great strength,' said May gently. 'Are you sure you want to get further involved in this?'

'Are you asking me if I'm up to it?' Bryant gave a sigh. 'I can cope with any debilitation if it's simply a matter of finding the strength. What I can't handle is the sheer unpredictability of my senses. They're altering as they depart, and I have no idea what to expect next from them. You know, I always thought of long-term illness as a series of battles with incremental losses, but I swear this is proving to be more like a stimulant. It doesn't make sense. Earlier this evening when I was down by the river I had a kind of waking dream. I saw and heard and *smelled* things that were impossible.'

'What do you mean? What sort of things?'

'It's going to sound ridiculous. I imagined I was back in Victorian times.' Bryant held his hands before him, as if daring the visions to return. 'It was as though my subconscious mind was pointing me in a particular direction. I don't know where the next stop on this strange journey might be.'

'Then make sure you stay close. Alma will keep watch on you when you're in the flat and I'll ferry you to and from the unit. But you can't go out on your own from now on. You know that, don't you? I need a promise from you.'

'I promise I'll try,' said Bryant, and May knew it was the closest he would get to an assurance.

14

INVISIBLE & VISIBLE

Monday had been a long day. Tuesday morning was drained of light and life, the landscape as damp and drab as codfish skin. No computer model of the city's thrusting new tower blocks had ever envisioned them huddled beneath such lugubrious skies, their gleaming carapaces as mottled and clouded as antique mirrors.

In Highgate, Janice Longbright finished applying Smudge-Proof Cherrybloom Foundation ('Alma Cogan's Favourite!' said the jar) and closed the 1950s make-up box she had inherited from her mother. She glanced back at her neatly made bed, feeling a pang of regret for driving away the man who had filled its other side. Her independence had quickly reasserted itself but right now it would have been nice to depend on someone again, just to pick up a few of their habits rather than always falling back on her own. Being in control was different from being a control freak, but she knew that sometimes one state led to the other. *That won't be me,* she thought, defiantly pulling off her black unit sweater and replacing it with a Jezebel Crimson Leopard Bust Dress and leggings.

In Shad Thames, John May stood at the front door of his

manicured minimalist apartment, looking out at the falling rain. Reluctantly, he exchanged his elegant Church's shoes for a pair of hated but practical Adidas trainers. Once the narrow street beyond had been filled with the rumble of coopers' trolleys, the clanking of cranes, the aroma of cardamom, cloves, pepper and tea. Now there were only single professionals with cyberspace jobs who had no time for anything as unproductive as passing conversation. The thirty-somethings took one look at his silver mane and neatly knotted tie and fled back to their phones. No matter how non-judgemental they tried to be in their day jobs, they couldn't countenance the idea of talking to older people in their precious spare time.

Since moving to the flat from St John's Wood he had failed to make a single friend in the building. Residents' meetings had been abandoned after it was discovered that most of the owners existed as offshore addresses lodged in company ledgers. May's world revolved around the unit. It was where he came to life. The question was what would happen when his tenure ended. He had no safety net of family, friends or even savings to rely on. He would simply cease to exist.

You know what Arthur would say, he thought disapprovingly. *This is no time for morbidity, stop being a miserable old ratbag and pull yourself together.* Choosing his favourite red scarf, he stepped out into the half-light and prepared to face the day.

In Bloomsbury, Arthur Bryant folded his Rupert the Bear pyjamas beneath his pillow and removed the sardine and tomato sandwiches Alma had left in his Tibetan skull, sliding them into a paper bag which he then squashed into the pocket of his overcoat. The sight of the falling rain pleased him immensely. It would rinse the pavements and keep the day dark enough for thinking. Who knew what it held? Would there be hours missing? Would he black out and come round in the Whispering Gallery or the London Sewing Machine Museum? Would he find himself serving under Boadicea in her final battle against the Romans, performing before a Jacobean audience as Ferdinand in *The Duchess of Malfi* or agreeing to bomb the *Belgrano* in Margaret Thatcher's war cabinet? Life was suddenly an adventure to be seized upon.

In Hammersmith, Raymond Land sat in a workmen's café watching a fried egg drip out of his sandwich. Leanne, his ex-wife, had taken their house, so he had moved into a rented top-floor flat off Shepherd's Bush Road, sharing the building with a bad-tempered Chinese pensioner, a cheery Latvian pastry chef, a pair of unbelievably shrill Brazilian dancers and a clearly deranged cockney landlady who changed the locks on a weekly basis and spoke like a character from an Ealing comedy.

This is what happens to people like me, Land thought gloomily. *This is where we wash up, the disappointed, in the last remaining transport caffs and laundromats, betting shops and old-geezer pubs, milling around like paddle-tubs on a boating lake waiting to be called in when our hour is up. Once I had ambition and drive. I should have done something important while I still had some hair. Why didn't I stand up for myself and make people take me seriously? What happened to the springtime dreams of my gilded youth?*

'You've got egg on your trousers,' said the waitress, taking his teacup.

Janice Longbright shook out her umbrella and entered the darkened hall of the Peculiar Crimes Unit, the first one in again. It was easy to get out of bed early when there was no one else in it. She ignored the video security system that had not worked since its installation, stepped over Crippen's litter tray and headed into the staff kitchen to put the milk away. While it was nice not to come across any severed fingers in the salad crisper, something that had happened on more than one occasion, she found herself wondering if the badly behaved Arthur Bryant of old would make a final reappearance, or if he would now subside into the darkness of his disorder, never to resurface as the appalling old man she had so long adored.

He'd tell me off for thinking like this, she reminded herself, making tea and settling at her terminal, determined to concentrate on today's subject: the last days of Lynsey Dalladay. Bryant had been right about the parents. They had been anxious to distance themselves from their daughter. It was as if by dying she had finally found a way to publicly blame them for the way she had lived.

She scanned Dan Banbury's summary of the crime scene. Only one set of footprints leading across the beach. No CCTVs covering the river. A lone homegoing witness who had heard a cry but thought nothing of it. Why? 'Because there's always someone screaming around here – the pubs were turning out.' *Fair enough,* she thought, *there isn't much to be learned from her death so the answer lies somewhere in her life.*

The phone log showed that Freddie Cooper had already called this morning to ask about the status of the case. She wondered if anyone had informed him about the paternity result, and called him back.

'I went down there,' he said before she could give him the news.

'Down where, to the river?'

'To the spot where you say you found her. I thought I might see something.'

'Like what?'

'Hey, I don't know. Something that would explain why he took her there. She liked the river. She couldn't swim. Maybe she wanted to go for a walk and asked him along for company. Maybe he was just a stranger and they got into an argument. She could be incredibly stroppy. He might have just lashed out—'

'Mr Cooper, she was shackled to the remains of a concrete post. It was premeditated. I'm sending you over a photo of the chain that was locked around her wrist. Take a look at it and tell me if you've ever seen it before. And we have your results back. You're not the father of her child.'

'I told you I already knew that.'

'We needed proof. You still don't have any idea where she went or who she was seeing?'

'She made new friends all the time, then dropped them.'

'You said she partied a lot. You also said she spent time trying to find herself. Did she belong to any groups?'

'She tried AA, a couple of religious things – those people who have the happy-clappy place in Finsbury Park – not a cult, but not far off. Some mystical societies, getting in touch with the elements and your inner child. When I first met her she told me she'd been a water goddess in a past life. I should have been warned off right then.'

As Cooper was keen to help, Longbright gave him a series of questions to answer and told him to call back. Dan Banbury arrived in a yellow plastic rain hood with a Mumsnet logo on the side. 'It's just started bucketing down out there. I had to borrow this from the missus,' he said, slapping it against the radiator.

'Did you have any luck with the chain?' Longbright asked. 'Cooper says she didn't wear one.'

'It's solid silver, not made here,' Banbury replied. 'There's a hallmark – 84, the outline of a woman's head and the initials PT. That's not someone's name, it's an assayer's mark that was stamped on imported Russian silver. There's also a little triangle – a delta symbol standing for "Moscow". The links can only be opened if you know the trick, so she had no chance of getting it off. It's quite old, maybe as early as 1920s. However, they're fairly common and can be picked up in jewellery markets around the world. The crescent moon makes it a narrower search. There's something else. The red bus, Golden Dreams, the one Mr Bryant mentioned, it just paid off.'

'I'm not with you,' said Longbright, correcting her notes from Cooper's conversation.

'The old man was right. It parks outside the Tower of London every weekend. It's an Anglo-Japanese company used by tourists from Tokyo and Kyoto, and of course they all have good cameras, Go-Pros, selfie sticks, you name it. I started running checks last night. They're all in the same hotel, and very helpful. I found a couple who went down to the water's edge late on Sunday night to take some shots. Look at what they came up with.'

He plugged a USB stick into the back of Longbright's screen and opened the file. The flashlit shots showed the foreshore and the glittering black water beyond. At a distance of about two metres into the water was a dark, ragged hump. To the tourists it would have looked like a rock, but Longbright knew from the position that it had to be Dalladay's body. It exactly matched Giles's shots from the following morning.

'They must have arrived there just after she'd drowned,' said Dan. 'There's no depth. You can almost see through the water. They were trying to take shots of themselves against the skyline with the selfie stick but you know how difficult it is to hold those things still. See what they got instead?'

Longbright spotted it at once. 'That's not possible,' she said. 'Those are her footprints?'

'Let's have a look.' He magnified the shot as much as he could. 'You can see that they're going the wrong way. They're leading down to the water's edge.' The photographs clearly showed a single track of trainer-prints going to the stanchion, and none coming back.

'Where the hell are the rest of the footprints?' asked Longbright. 'That sand looks soft enough to have picked them up. What are we dealing with, the Invisible Man?'

For once the crime scene manager was at a loss for words.

'You want to know how I think? It's very simple,' said Bryant, allowing his worn silver pocket watch to turn on its chain. 'Do you know why I keep this?'

'As your every move is a mystery to me, no,' said May,

leaning back in his chair. 'You told me it hasn't worked since the old king died.'

'And indeed it has not, which at least means it tells the correct time twice a day. It belonged to my grandfather on my mother's side. Look.' He picked open the back and revealed some tiny, illegible scrollwork. 'It was supposed to be presented to him for long service. They handed out a silver watch to any employee who lasted fifty years in the same government department. He started there when he was sixteen and left when ill health drove him out at sixty-five. But that was after forty-nine years and eleven months. So they said no, you can't have a long-service pocket watch, you weren't here for the full fifty years. My mother was furious. She put on her best coat, jumped on the first tram that came along and went up to Whitehall, where she had a word with his boss. She never told anyone what was said, but the very next morning my granddad was given the watch. On his way home after the presentation the old man dropped dead in the Whitechapel Road. You would have thought his heart had been wired to the lights in his office. The watch landed in the gutter and never worked again. My mother said she kept it to remind herself of what happens to London's invisible, loyal workers.'

May shrugged, puzzled. 'Well, that's a fantastically depressing story. Am I supposed to attach a moral to it?'

'The city rewards the ambitious and dumps on everyone else,' said Bryant. 'For half a century my grandfather did exactly what he was told, and at the end of it they tried to gyp him out of a cheap silver-plated watch. That's why my father never held down a steady job. He hung around the streets of Whitechapel doing a favour here and there, scoring a few bob whenever he was short of beer money. If you just keep your head down and do what's expected of you, you vanish and get less than nothing. If you want anything more, you have to stand up and make yourself visible. Our victim, Lynsey Dalladay – we know nothing about her so far except that she was "lost" and attractive and got pregnant. Do you see my point?'

'I want to say yes,' May began, 'but . . .' He waved his hands at the air.

'She wasn't ambitious, but she stepped in the way of someone who was. A pregnant girl in a skanky club with a history of unpredictable behaviour explains that she wants to keep her lover's child, and that's why he gets rid of her. She blocks his path and puts his future at risk. Do you understand now?'

May sat down on the edge of his desk, amazed. 'Do you know, that's the first time in all our years together that you've even come close to explaining how your brain works? I can see the kind of person we're looking for.'

'Exactly,' said Bryant with a shrug. 'I told you it was very simple.'

15

DUCKING & DIVING

The auditorium was over half full; not bad for mid-week. It had been built as a concert hall, then converted to a night-club, an African temperance hall, a recording studio, an Indian disco and now a council-leased community centre. The audience could see the new red curtains and gold paint-work coating an art deco sunburst, but if they looked any higher they'd spot the peeling paintwork on the ceiling and the damp patches at the back of the upper circle.

Cassie looked out from her position behind the mixing desk at the top of the hall and flicked the switch on the black plastic box at her hip.

'We need to run another sound check,' she said. 'I was picking up static every time your lapel moved last night.'

'There's no time,' said the voice in her ear. 'Just give me the rundown.'

'OK, who are you going to use as a spirit guide?'

'I thought I might switch between Hiawatha and Dr Millingen.'

'Who's he?'

'The physician who brought back Lord Byron's body from Greece.'

'How do you even know about something like that?'

There was a crackle as Ali fiddled with the earpiece. 'I read a lot about the English. You should try it sometime.'

'OK, which section do you want me to start with?'

'How about something easy near the front centre aisle, then we can skip further back and go for more detail.'

'All right, C-12, overweight female, red jacket, lives in Streatham, bad lower back. She's scared of having an operation on her spine. D-17, elderly female, grey sweater and scarf, Lewisham. She has trouble walking, left leg, probably related to a car accident she had a few years ago. E-8, middle-aged male, black leather coat, Deptford, thinks his grandson is on drugs – how many do you want to do in one go?'

'Let me try for six or seven. You can give me a prompt.' They had a signal for that: if he got stuck, Ali took two half-steps across the stage instead of a single full stride.

'OK,' said Cassie, 'let's take it up a notch. L-20, overweight male, pale blue shirt, started drinking heavily after his wife died and had to have his left leg amputated.'

'I can't promise his leg will grow back.'

Cassie laughed. 'No, but you could tell him to lay off the booze. Say that the Lord says—'

'I'm not bringing religion into it, Cassie. We had an agreement.'

'If you did, we could get a wider range of venues. I'm just saying, that's all. N-6, little boy—'

'I told you no kids. Keep the ages above forty.'

'All right, P-22, older female, fluffy pink sweater, worried that her mother's cancer has come back.'

'Give me a couple more.'

'A-9, middle-aged black female in orchid-print dress and big glasses, depressed because her husband Ronald died of a respiratory illness last month. Want to try a tougher one?'

'Bring it on.'

'Back row, end seat, I don't have the number. Young male, checked shirt, defensive, arms folded. His wife made him come along. He's been tweeting a lot about dental problems, either the bills or the work he's had done. Do you want that?'

'Do I have to look inside his mouth?'

'See if you can make him smile for me.'

'I'm on it.'

Ali took a deep breath, stepped on to the stage and raised his hands. The rounds of applause had been steadily growing over the past month. Their tour around the North Circular halls and concert venues was starting to attract regular followers. Cassie made a note to renegotiate their performance fee.

London has a unique quality that is hardly ever spoken of. If you look in the crowds and find someone who appears to be the most complete Londoner you can imagine, an almost parodic image of someone born within the sound of Bow bells or the clubs of Westminster, listen until you hear them speak and you'll often find they've been assimilated from a far-off place. The city attracts those who aspire to it. But listening to Ali gave away no clues to his origin. He was remaking himself so completely that no remnant of his past survived.

'I'm feeling a wave of pain here from somewhere in the third row,' said Ali, hovering his hand over the seats like a metal detector. 'The lady in the red jacket, you've come here from quite nearby today – Streatham, I'm guessing, because it's just a short bus-ride away? You can't go far, can you? You feel every jolt and bump in the base of your spine, right here.' As soon as he saw her nodding, anticipating his words, he pressed the same spot on his own back, sympathizing with her pain.

'This may not work but let's try,' he said, suddenly vaulting down from the stage with his legs together, landing so nimbly that the crowd gasped. 'Violet, is that your name? Don't be alarmed, it's not mind-reading. I overheard your friend sitting next to you – I wouldn't want you to think that I was cheating or making things up.' The crowd relaxed in approval.

Nice touch, Cassie thought. *He always tells me to remember they're not stupid.*

'But she didn't tell me about your pain, that's something I can feel in the air sparkling around you like a magnetic force. It's OK, I'm not a psychic and this is not mumbo-jumbo, I just deal in basic science. Neuroscientists from the Universities of Colorado and Michigan have been using functional magnetic resonance imaging to identify pain for years. Pain radiates out from the body and gives off heat, and some sensitive people can feel this heat. That's all, there's no mystery to it. But it's not the sort of thing doctors are interested in. You don't want the doctors to operate because you're frightened, aren't you? Tell me, why are you scared?'

He won't get anything out of her, Cassie thought. *She's shrinking in her seat.*

'It's because you're frightened of being left paralysed, aren't you? Was there someone else in your family who suffered? There was, wasn't there?'

Violet nodded shyly. *Of course someone suffered,* thought Cassie, *everyone knows someone who's suffered.*

'But let me tell you, the chances of that happening in such an operation are relatively small, and you compare that to the grinding pain you suffer all day, every day – and it's worse at night, isn't it?'

Another nod, more emphatic.

'It won't get better by itself, it will only keep getting worse – so which is worse, the fear of what probably won't happen, or the pain of what you know will?'

He's making it too complicated for her, she thought, *making her afraid of him.* 'Do something, Ali,' she said, 'you're losing her.'

Ali was one step ahead. Taking his left hand from the small of his own back he now reached forward, grabbed her arm with his right and pulled her forward, pressing his warmed palm over her spine. 'Can you feel that heat, Violet? I'll push down the pain for now. With my help you can take it away for a while but it will return, and when it does you must be brave and tell your doctor you'll have the operation. Will you do that for me?'

'Yes,' she said in a tiny voice, urged on by her friend.

'Louder, Violet, say you will do it.' Ali raised his own voice. 'Once it's out in the open you have to keep your promise.'

'Yes,' Violet cried out, and her friend applauded and Ali applauded and everyone else around her put their hands together, feeling the waves of positivity in the room.

He really is a fast learner, Cassie thought, pulling down the mouthpiece. 'OK, now head over to D-17, bad leg.'

Back in the present day, Max Wright came wading out of the Thames with a black plastic bag in his right fist. 'Sodding mask,' he complained, pulling the rubber seals free from his face. 'It's freezing cold down there and I've still got sweat dripping into my eyes.'

Dan Banbury hovered at the shoreline, anxious to help. He admired the Thames police divers intensely. 'You were down for nearly an hour,' he said. 'I don't know how you do it.'

'That's the longest I can go without losing the plot, mate. Nil visibility. Very disorienting. It's like wading through the contents of my littlest one's nappy.'

'You can't see anything at all?'

'Not surprising, is it? On days with a bright sun overhead you can see a bit, but not much.' Wright stamped some life back into his feet. His co-diver surfaced a few metres away and strode to the beach. 'The ground suddenly drops away as you approach the centre channel, and the flow increases sharply so you have to keep your wits about you. It's bloody hard work, concentrating on the floor while you're pulling in air.'

'But you got something?' said Banbury, eyeing the bag.

'Yeah. Let's get these things off first.' The divers began helping each other remove their harnesses.

'So what's actually down there?' Banbury wanted to know. 'I suppose everyone asks you that.'

'Oh, man, barbed wire, shards of wood, all kinds of sharp obstructions. Shopping trolleys, stacks of 'em. We pull one body a week from the river. You can bet there are plenty more tangled up in the centre of the channel that nobody ever finds. I never seem to get a Gucci Dive.'

'What's that?'

The other diver laughed knowingly. 'A body on the first sweep,' said Wright. 'It's just luck. I don't only do the Thames, you know. I did a job for your bosses, old Bryant and May, years ago. We were looking for someone in the Regent Canal. I did the King's Cross 7/7 bombings—'

'There was no water involved there, was there?' Banbury asked.

'No, but breathing apparatus was needed. It was like being underwater in the tube tunnels.' Wright and his partner had pulled off their suits now and were changing into the overalls they kept in their backpacks. 'I don't know what you were expecting us to find, but I don't think this is it.' He indicated the black plastic bag he had set down on the sand. 'Take a look.'

Dan Banbury pushed back his gloves and opened the bag. Sitting in the silt at the bottom was a male human hand like a fleshy crustacean, palm up, its fingers outstretched, pale and crablike. Banbury picked it up and examined the wrist. 'Neatly severed,' he said. 'The skin's very loose. The fish have had a good go at it. What do you reckon, two to three weeks' immersion?'

Wright pursed his lips, considering. 'Yeah, something like that.'

'Ever had just a limb before?'

'Oh yeah, loads of times,' said Wright matter-of-factly. 'More legs and torsos though. You know – dismemberments.'

'How far was it from the concrete post?'

'I reckon no more than three metres. You touch something

and you know it's worth investigating. It's almost like a sixth sense. I've got very sensitive fingertips. Mostly I'm looking for knives, so I have to go carefully. You don't want to get nicked with so much crap in the water.'

'It's bloody hard work to move through because you can't get a proper grip,' his mate added.

'There's a tattoo,' said Banbury, peering at the severed wrist. 'What's left of one, at least. I need to get this back to St Pancras.'

'Be my guest,' said Wright with a grin. 'Our bill will be in your inbox before you arrive there, knowing my boss. If you want us back to search for the rest of him, we'll be very happy to give you an estimate.'

16

SIGNS & PORTENTS

Arthur Bryant packed the last few strands of Ancient Mariner Rough Cut Naval Shag into his pipe bowl and tamped it down. The tobacco caught eventually, and blue smoke drifted to join the rags of mist that rose from the shadowed arches below, dispersing in the diluted sunlight.

'They saw it as the giver of all life, of course,' he said, puffing contentedly. 'The centre of organized society and industry. The great abbeys built bridges and supervised the cultivation of arable land here. They reclaimed the marshes and planted crops.'

Clenching the stem between his peppermint-white false teeth, Bryant placed his gloved hands on the balustrade and leaned over the side of Waterloo Bridge, looking down into the turbulent flow of the Thames.

'The spot where the river rises in Trewsbury Mead has always been regarded as holy,' he continued. 'The artist Stanley Spencer believed that immersion in its sunlit waters returned us to the pagan roots of Christianity. The river is continuity, of faith and inspiration and bloodlines. It's a boundary, a frontier, a defence.'

He took another leisurely puff. 'And as the monarchy had

a direct line to God the Thames was always held to be a royal river. The palaces were placed on its banks. Henry and Elizabeth both held pageants on the waters. For his "Aqua Triumphalis" Charles II was rowed from Hampton Court to Whitehall while being serenaded by the painted figure of Isis.' Bryant's fingers followed the pattern of snakelike ripples below. 'The Thames wasn't just used by royalty, of course. During the Great Plague more than ten thousand city folk sheltered on the waters, locked up inside their boats. But of course rats can swim, and it was said that people died at the oars, to be washed up on the tides over there. The rats were blamed for infecting them before they set out to sea as well, but we always seek to blame, don't we? The river was involved in the Great Fire too – people dived in to face drowning instead of being burned alive. Man-made machinery toppled the ancient gods, and industry polluted the sacred Thames. By 1827 its contents were so lethal that they had been branded "monster soup". During the Great Stink, when the windows of Parliament were left open everyone on the windward side was asphyxiated. But long after the factories have gone the river's still here, just as it will always be.'

'I like it when you're like this,' said May. 'On safe ground.'

Bryant turned around, his cornflower-blue eyes wide and distant. 'What do you mean?'

'Inside the history of London. It's where you belong, standing here looking out. But there are parts you don't know any more, Arthur. You think all the poisonous factories have gone, but what are those financial powerhouses doing? Belching out cash and rewarding their workers with privileges denied to the likes of you and me. It's invitation only now, and we aren't allowed in. The culture of civic-minded philanthropy we once had has been lost in the feeding frenzy of making money.'

'Oh, the frenzy was always there,' said Bryant dismissively. 'It's a cycle of growth and catastrophe. And actually, we can go anywhere we please. The Square Mile's trained monkeys don't frighten me. This city is my jungle gym.'

'Is that so?' asked May. 'When we last stood here you were saying goodbye to it.'

'I wasn't feeling well then.' He ran a hand across his hat. 'It comes and goes. I've been looking up medical precedents that might help me to understand what's going on in the old brain-box, and I think I've found a couple.'

'OK, what are they?'

'Do you know, I can't remember right at this moment, but I'm sure they'll come back to me.'

May sighed. 'Then I guess we'll have to get on with the investigation while we're waiting.'

'It's almost half ten,' said Bryant, checking his stopped watch. May had no idea how he could tell the time from it. 'Does that mean I'm to be imprisoned in the office for the rest of the day?'

'No – Dan is heading over to Dalladay's old apartment and thought you might like to be in on the search. Just this once.'

'That's more like it.' Bryant slapped his gloves together with satisfaction. 'You can let me take over for a while.'

May studied his partner objectively. What did civilians make of this rheumy, rumpled, pink and wrinkled figure dressed in clothes three sizes too large for him? A rare species of *Senex Londiniensis*, discovered somewhere between the stalls of Whitechapel and the sidings of King's Cross, struggling on between prostate and probate, becalmed and possibly embalmed, with only the crystalline gaze of his blue eyes to suggest the iceberg of his intellect – no wonder he was perpetually underestimated. Now, though, since the onset of his illness, people were already starting to ignore him – something May knew they did at their peril.

'Come on,' he said, giving in and offering Bryant an arm. 'Show me how it's done.'

*

The flat was in a graceful cream-coloured terrace on Denbigh Street, Pimlico, just behind the statue of the nineteenth-century master builder Thomas Cubitt. Dan Banbury was agitatedly waiting for them at the door. 'I started an inventory last night but haven't done the bedroom or lounge yet,' he warned, 'so don't—'

'Don't say it,' said Bryant, waving him inside the house. 'Where were you earlier?'

'Dredging the murder site,' Banbury replied, heading upstairs. 'Max Wright gave me a hand.'

'So he should do,' said Bryant, 'he costs enough.'

'No, he gave me an actual hand. Cut off at the wrist. Here.' He passed back a photocopy of the half-eaten tattoo. 'Any idea what that is?'

Bryant dragged out his trifocals and breathed on them. He studied the remains of a blue-ink pattern showing what appeared to be a stack of foreshortened bricks. 'Yes.'

'Yes, what?'

'Yes, I know what it is.'

Banbury stopped on the stairs, exasperated. 'Do you want to tell me?'

'No, I want to check it against an illustration in one of my books back at the office. It's a bit moth-eaten.'

'Fish-bitten, actually.'

'Then let me do some reconstruction first. Which flat are we heading for?'

'Here. Her parents bought her this place. She kept it on even though she'd moved in with Cooper.' The CSM led the way into a bare, expensively furnished open-plan lounge, as white, light and impersonal as a letting agent's photograph. 'May I?' asked Bryant politely, pointing at the next room.

'You've never bothered to ask before,' said Banbury. 'Are you feeling all right?'

'No, I'm not. So?'

'So can you go tromping through my floor grid leaving

sticky fingerprints all over everything?' He sighed. 'I suppose so. Go on, off you go.' He turned to May. 'It's like dealing with a child.'

'Have you turned up anything?' May asked.

Banbury rubbed his face. It was only mid-morning and he was already tired. 'Not really. She has a lot of very expensive clothes and virtually nothing in her current account. She stayed in the Ham Yard Hotel and the Soho Hotel in the last two weeks – we've got all her movements from the hotel room swipe cards. She ran up a few stiff restaurant bills and bar tabs, but it's hard to say who with. One waiter remembers a young man and a young woman, blonde – that's all. It's like trying to lay hands on ghosts. It'll take a while to get CCTV footage from the hotels because there's a lot of it to go through. I can see where she's been but I don't really get who she is.' He looked down at the opened layers of his technician's box and shook his head. 'All this equipment. It tells you everything and nothing.'

There was a crash from the bedroom. May and Banbury ran in to find Bryant sprawled on the floor, pieces of a giant china horse everywhere. 'I slipped,' he said, taking their proffered arms as he climbed off his knees.

'OK, I'll take over from here,' said May.

'No, there was something inside the horse's mouth,' said Bryant. 'I could see it, I just couldn't reach it. Fat fingers. This.' Unclenching his fist, he revealed a matt black card. 'I can tell you a bit about her now.'

'Like what?' asked Banbury, nettled.

'She was a binge eater and serial dieter, she wanted to be a mother, she hated her father, she tried yoga, meditation and prescription medication for stress, she had an addictive nature, she's travelled all over the world and was thinking of going to Peru, she felt she was a failure, wanted a baby and was thinking of getting a cat.'

Banbury stifled a laugh. 'Where did you get all that from?' He shot May a puzzled look.

'The books,' said Bryant, waving vaguely at the shelves lining the walls of the next room. 'They're the first thing you should always check. It's all in those volumes, from travel guides to self-help manuals.'

'How do you know they're hers?'

'Do you see any signs of a flatmate? And she has a silver library punch, one of those things that embosses the title page with the owner's name. Do wake up. Is it lunchtime yet?' He pulled a suppurating sardine and tomato sandwich from its paper bag and munched thoughtfully, filling the flat with the smell of vinegared fish. 'No one else has been here. It's all very curious. Who's the daddy, eh? Girls like this – how can they have so much and so little? She could have been anyone she wanted. She had money, looks, youth, and a great empty gap where her soul should be. The children of the privileged: it's as if some of them are handicapped from birth.'

'She might just have been not very bright,' May pointed out.

'She was smart enough to read all these,' said Bryant, indicating the filled bookcase. 'Hesse, Kafka, Marquez, they're signposts staked at different points of her young life. And there's one very interesting one I need you to test for prints.' He led the way back to the bookcase and pointed. 'That one. I don't want to touch it. Sardines.'

'Very thoughtful of you,' muttered Banbury, removing the volume carefully and turning it in his gloved hands. 'Greek mythology.'

'Check the bookmark,' said Bryant.

Banbury carefully removed the marker and turned it over. 'There's nothing on it.'

'No, you twerp, see what it's marking,' said Bryant, rolling his eyes.

'Prometheus.' Banbury scanned the pages. '"The mortal Prometheus tricked immortal Zeus into eternally claiming the inedible parts of bulls for the sacrificial ceremonies of the gods, while conceding the nourishing parts to humans for the eternal benefit of humankind." I don't even know what that means.'

'I thought you were a grammar-school boy? At a ceremonial dinner Prometheus placed two sacrifices before Zeus, one with the edible, juicy bits hidden inside a bull's stomach, and the other a bunch of bones wrapped in meat and fat. He tricked the god into choosing by looks alone. Zeus went for a superior exterior and got an inferior interior. Do you see what I mean?'

'No.'

'Prometheus taught him a lesson, that looks can be deceptive, and it's what's inside that counts. Zeus took revenge by hiding the fire Prometheus had brought. Then do you know what he did?'

'I'm sorry, Mr B.,' said Banbury, flummoxed. 'I'm all at sea here.'

'He chained Prometheus to a rock,' said May.

'What, so this girl marks a passage in a book, then serves someone a duff meal and gets chained to a rock in the Thames?'

'Good heavens, you don't have to take it so literally.' Bryant sighed. 'It's an analogy. John, you explain.'

'I think what Arthur means is that maybe she feared being punished by someone,' said May. 'She knew she'd done something bad. Hiding something inside – it could mean the pregnancy.'

'Well, if you're going to go by signs and portents you might as well make a pot of tea and sit here reading the grouts,' said Banbury. 'I'm a simple bloke, Mr Bryant, I go by bloodstains and fingerprints and DNA samples, not Greek myths.'

'I always had you down as an ideas man,' said Bryant, crestfallen.

'I am, but I need something a bit less conceptual to hang an idea on.'

'Then how about this?' Bryant held up the black card. 'It's

a calling card, maybe a company of some kind, just a name and a number. She kept it in the mouth of the statue by her bed, ready to call at any time.'

May and Banbury studied the card. There was just one word on it: 'MEDUSA'.

'Greek mythology,' muttered Banbury, thoroughly annoyed.

17

ACCUSATION & DENIAL

Cassie and Ali. Over time their names had become linked, but why? They had little in common but fitted together, even though there was something missing. They were not in love. They did not share pasts or friends – Ali had none – but had been paired for over a year and a half. And they were on the last leg of what they had come to refer to as the North Circular Tour.

The Great Hidini had been killed off, to be replaced by the Ministry of Compassion. They had spent the previous week at the Neasden Civic Centre in an auditorium that smelled of too many municipal dinners, in the most relentlessly boring part of London, and had moved on to the Rainbow Theatre, Finsbury Park.

The venue was steeped in legend. Here Jimi Hendrix had burned his guitar onstage in a carefully choreographed act of rock rebellion, making music history. Pink Floyd, Queen, Marc Bolan, the Beach Boys, Eric Clapton and Bob Marley had all performed in its art deco auditorium, but now the theatre was occupied by the Universal Church of the Kingdom of God, a Brazilian Pentecostal organization that had been accused of everything from extortion and anti-Semitism to charlatanism and witchcraft. That it continued to flourish in a North London suburb was typical of the area's tolerant attitude to race and faith.

It was their final show and they had, Cassie decided in retrospect, grown careless. That Saturday night, news of Ali's talent had spread far enough to pack out the hall and create a queue for returns. He had finely tuned the evening to provide a mix of showmanship, prediction, inspiration and magic. To stay within the Consumer Protection Act he never declared that he could heal, and avoided religious matters entirely. But that was why they came, of course, to be healed. He and Cassie both knew that. And if it was what they wanted to believe, who was Ali to stop them?

He wore a Savile Row suit these days, and had his own band. His singing voice wasn't strong enough to sustain a set, but he managed a few inspirational songs between the mind-reading tricks and promenades into the audience. Cassie still sat in the control room feeding him information about the attendees, preselecting them with the help of the girl they had hired to sell merchandise. It was she who listened while they talked to each other in their seats before the show, passing the information to Cassie, who could then run online checks and gather the information Ali needed to make his pronouncements.

Ali had pushed the boundaries tonight, telling one old lady she would walk again if she believed strongly enough and offered up a bigger donation than usual. They weren't allowed to solicit money in the venue but it went on, of course, and as they had data from the bookings system it was easy to hit the devoted for subscription fees and donations referred to by a variety of euphemisms. As they were unable to register for charitable status, Cassie had decided that they should launch a gift catalogue. She had already lined up someone who could make 'lucky' jewellery.

'You'll like this one,' she said, donning infrared glasses and peering over the maroon velvet edge of the balcony. 'R-14, female, striped tights, multi-coloured sweater-thing, bright red hair, tons of jewellery, looks a bit mad. Lives in Highbury, Islington. She just told the woman sitting next to her that she's a practising witch.'

'I don't want to finish this on a nutter tonight,' said Ali wearily. 'We had too many of them in on Tuesday and you saw how that went.'

'I've checked this one out. Her coven has its own Facebook page. She gets a lot of hits. It could open us up to a new market of off-the-scale gullible women.'

'I suppose it could close the evening with a bit of light relief. What else have you got on her?'

'She's got a dear friend who's very ill,' said Cassie, checking the notes on her phone. 'Alzheimer's.'

'I thought we agreed no incurables.'

'Just getting the disease right should be enough. Remember what we talked about; the secret to controlling people is letting them think they're controlling themselves.'

'OK – I'm going on.'

Maggie Armitage, Grand Order Grade IV White Witch of the Coven of St James the Elder, Kentish Town, jangled her jewellery as she fidgeted in the seat. She had spent her life being accusing of charlatanism, and recognized it in others. This fellow was billing himself as the founder of the Ministry of Compassion, but a few online checks showed that the ministry had only existed for four months, and when she searched for images of its founder she discovered a magician with the same handsome face and a similarly truncated history. He had a number of aliases, Ali Hidini, Ali Futuri and now Pastor Ali Michaels, a nice wholesome, comforting name.

She had to admit that Ali was very charismatic, bounding through the awestruck punters in his elegant suit, but only a few months earlier he had been peddling a clapped-out magic act around the provinces. There was clearly more money to be made here, gypping fearful old ladies out of their pensions.

She had filled in the request slip asking for Pastor Michaels to come and make predictions about her. Before he would deign to relieve her of her savings she had to give him her email address, tick a confidentiality box and waive her legal rights. After this she was entered into a lottery while his assistant presumably sorted through the candidates' online profiles to find the ones who had been a little too free with their personal information. Maggie had made sure she was indiscreet, talking loudly to the tiny old lady next to her while they waited for the show to start.

'What are you here for?' Maggie asked.

'Me? I'm shrinking,' the tiny lady replied. 'I want Pastor Michaels to tell me if I have a deficiency.'

'Everybody shrinks,' said Maggie. 'You don't need vitamins, you need lower cupboards.'

And now here came Pastor Michaels himself, dropping down into the aisle as the music picked up tempo. He bounced towards Maggie with his right arm outstretched, his gaze focused intently on hers. The spotlight slid from him to the white witch. She flinched in the glare.

'I'm getting a very unusual feeling from somewhere over here,' he told the audience. 'This little lady is a kindred spirit, I believe! You, madam, I can sense a cloud floating over you. Something dark and burdensome.'

Burdensome? thought Maggie. *He must have gone to one of those dodgy English schools behind Oxford Street where they teach students from very old textbooks.* She nodded piteously at him.

'You are worried for a friend – worried that he is losing his wits, that he has dementia, is that right?'

Maggie nodded again and considered dabbing away a tear, but realized she'd used all her tissues mopping up a spilled cappuccino.

'But there's something else about you,' cried the pastor, turning to the audience with his head tilted, as if trying to hear a distant radio. 'You – you also have the power! Is it true, do you have the same gift as me?'

'You're right, I do have certain abilities,' she said in a tiny voice.

'Speak up, madam, so that everyone can hear you.'

Maggie went for the Oscar, laying a hand on her throat and looking pathetic, a sympathy-gaining trick she had learned from Arthur. She beckoned at Pastor Michaels, summoning him to her.

Ali stepped closer.

Now, if you've ever had the pleasure of visiting the beautiful city of Hanoi, you'll know that the Vietnamese have a wonderful way with vegetable knives, which they make and sell at the river market. In fact, they've proven so popular that many of these kitchen implements have made their way around the world. One particular pair of scissors has tiny razor-sharp spring-loaded blades, and is used for cutting up herbs. They can be bought in Columbia Road for about a fiver.

As Ali bent down, Maggie stretched up to whisper to him and used the scissors she had secreted in her palm to snip through the slender white wire that extended from his earlobe into the top of his shirt. It looked like part of his throat-mike but was the transmission device that allowed him to toggle between his conversations with Cassie and his pronouncements to the audience. As Cassie found herself suddenly silenced, Maggie stood up and addressed the stalls.

'This man is a fake,' she said in a loud, clear and extremely authoritative voice. 'He and his assistant have been listening to your conversations and pretending to guess your problems.'

She turned just in time to see a pair of bouncers loping down the aisle towards her. 'Pastor Michaels does not have healing powers, he's a liar and a cheat and is stealing your money, and that's not even his real name.'

The audience sat there in stupefaction as the security staff seized her. *They don't care,* Maggie realized with a sinking heart. *I'm the crazy one, not him. It's not me they've paid to see. They'll do whatever he wants.*

'I'm terribly sorry, ladies and gentlemen,' said Ali, correctly gauging the mood of the auditorium, 'sometimes we do get non-believers in who try to trick us – and you – into leaving the path of our faith. But they cannot and will not prevent the truth from being told; that there is a world beyond our own and that if we can only open our minds and reach it, we can learn more than we will ever know here on earth, trapped in these too mortal bodies.'

Up in the box Cassie leaned forward, smiling in the dark. *Nice save,* she thought. Not that he'd ever lost them. The little white witch in the stalls had completely misjudged the audience. Cassie cupped her hand to her ear as the other line came through.

'What do you want done with her?' one of the security guards asked her.

'Take her outside, shoot her in the head and throw her into a skip,' Cassie snapped back. 'Have you been watching reruns of *Breaking Bad*? God, she's an old lady and a paying customer, there's no harm done. Apologize to her, make sure she's all right and offer her free tickets for another performance.' She cut the line and checked her watch. It was just as well that the show was coming to a close; she had no way of contacting Ali now. There had been no harm done but part of her wondered how much longer they would be able to get away with this life without going to jail.

It turned out that Cassie didn't have long to wonder. When she got home she found that Maggie Armitage had uploaded the footage she had secretly shot in the auditorium to her website, revealing Pastor Michaels's tricks of the trade, starting with footage of his assistant singling out the most vulnerable members of the audience and ending with close-ups of the bruises left on her arms by the two security guards who walked her out to the theatre foyer.

The video didn't go viral – it only got around four hundred

hits – but Ali Bensaud watched his career collapse over the next few days as venue managers ran background checks and cancelled his shows. At night he lay in bed wondering how things had gone so wrong. It seemed to him that his troubles had started on the day he'd convinced Ismael Rahman that they should escape and take their chances at sea. Watching his best friend vanish beneath the black waters had only driven him to greater heights of ambition. But London was not an apple ready to be plucked for the eating. The apples were on higher branches than he'd imagined, and now they had moved far beyond reach.

This time it was Cassie who found a way to reach them.

Arthur Bryant sat with the volume propped open at his desk, studying the illustrations as he munched the last squashed piece of his sardine sandwich. Lowering his trifocals, he peered closer until the tip of his snub nose was almost touching the paper. 'John!' he bellowed suddenly.

'I'm standing right here,' said May. 'You nearly gave me a heart attack.'

'I think it's a lighthouse.' Bryant stabbed at the page with his greasy finger. 'The tapering brickwork, and those things above it could be beams of light – it matches the drawing fairly closely, and that makes it a Russian prison tattoo. A lighthouse means that the owner spent time in jail. It's a reminder to pursue a life of freedom after a life of crime.'

'What, you mean by going straight?'

'No, I don't think so.' Bryant read on a bit. 'It can simply mean that from now on he'll stay out of jail.'

'The severed hand of a Russian prisoner,' sighed May, 'and the fingerprints aren't on a British database.'

'Unfortunately Putin's Federal Security Service isn't very free with its information these days. We can give it a try, but I wouldn't hold your breath.'

'Max Wright doesn't think we should get our hopes up about the hand being connected to the Bride in the Tide.'

'Don't call her that,' said Bryant. 'Point one, she wasn't a bride, and B – just don't call her that, all right?'

'Max thinks there are two other possibilities: that the switching current simply deposits random items at the reach, or it was thrown from the window of a building near the foreshore.'

'Maybe Dalladay's killer had used the spot as a dumping ground before.' Bryant closed his encyclopaedia of prison tattoos. 'That would suggest a gang slaying, which fits with the symbol.'

'You think someone with criminal connections at the Cossack Club fathered her child?' May asked. 'Is it worth staking the place out for a while?'

'I wouldn't have thought he'd be likely to go back there, would you?' said Bryant. 'I could go and talk to—'

'For the last time, I can't have you wandering around on your own,' said May firmly.

Bryant replaced the book on his shelf, between *WWII Carrier Pigeons* and *Farming Smocks of Somerset*. 'I don't want to feel like a hospital patient confined to a ward.'

'Then don't think of it like that,' said May. 'Make the most of it, Arthur. Do a Mycroft Holmes, run things from here without leaving the comfort of that ratty old armchair. Get us to do all the running about.' He had a sudden thought. 'Suppose Tower Beach *has* been used before? It's one of the few really secluded parts of the Thames Path. What if Dalladay wasn't the first? You can get access to every cold case going back over the last decade, you might turn up something.'

'Could you be any more condescending?' asked Bryant with a grimace. 'Perhaps you'd be happier if I sat here doing a nice jigsaw or taking the clock to bits.'

'Well, the case is sort of like a jigsaw if you prefer to think of it—'

Bryant threw a shoe at him. 'Go on, hop it,' he shouted. 'I will not be treated like a mental defective.'

'I think perhaps you're in denial about your situation,' said May.

'I'm not in denial, I'm in an extremely aggravated state of furious despondency,' Bryant barked back. *And I'll go where I damn well please,* he thought, waiting until the coast was clear before picking up his overcoat and hat once more.

18

BIRTH & DEATH

Arthur Bryant made two clandestine trips on Tuesday evening, and got an unwelcome surprise. First he went to visit Marion North in Chelsea, having been put in touch with her by his old friend Maggie Armitage. 'If you really want to talk to an expert on the sacred river,' she said, 'you need to talk to Marion.'

'Is she an academic?' Bryant asked.

'No,' Maggie replied, 'she's a rather glamorous New Age evangelist and property developer.'

'That's an unusual hyphenate.'

'She's also a crook, but she's very well connected and knows a lot about spiritual matters,' said Maggie. 'Let me give you her address.'

Cheyne Walk had long been the most fashionable street in Chelsea, thanks to its extraordinary roster of residents, which had included Whistler, Turner and Ralph Vaughan Williams, Henry James, Laurence Olivier and Mick Jagger. Big names still lived there, but they were no longer drawn by the nature of the light dancing on the water. They were there to say *I've arrived, I'm important, see what I can afford.* But in truth it was hard to know if there were any residents at all, so rarely did Marion see anyone coming and going. They had to exist, of that she was sure, but perhaps they were mere names in company registers held overseas, investors in prime real estate they had only ever seen on a website.

Marion North lived just beyond the walk in an ex-council flat on Cremorne Road, which veered away from the river and therefore became a less desirable location. She could see the back gardens and catch tantalizing glimpses of the river sparkling between the trees, but she might as well have been on Mars for all the good the proximity did her. Mrs North was a social climber, eaten up by the idea of getting on, and to be so close to so many rich and powerful people was a torture in which she luxuriated.

'So lovely to have a visitor,' said Mrs North, beaming her sunniest smile as she opened the door. She was small, neat and attractive, with gimlet eyes that missed nothing. She actually craned her head forward as she studied the elderly detective, noting the frayed lining of his oversized tweed coat, the hand-knitted scarf which appeared to have been knotted underneath his shirt and the darned hatband on his trilby from which protruded a ticket stub for a 1959 production of *Ruddigore*. As her eyes swept up and down, her smile lost a little of its effervescence. And those trousers – were there really pyjama bottoms sticking out from beneath them? She quickly invited him inside before anyone passing could see.

'Thank you for meeting me at such short notice,' said Bryant. 'Do you have a bin?' He pulled what appeared to be a sardine from his pocket. 'It fell out of my sandwich,' he explained cheerfully, handing her the fish.

Marion managed to conceal her revulsion beneath a determined smile, and offered tea. 'I have camomile, mint or elderflower.'

'Builder's will be fine,' said Bryant, looking around like a burglar casing the joint. 'And a biscuit.'

Mrs North looked flustered. 'I don't think we have—'

'Nothing fancy, just a custard cream will do to settle me. Gyppy tummy. Ta.'

Mrs North led him through to a front room that had enough dried flowers in it to choke an asthmatic. Bryant found himself in a hell of pastel shades, beige, soft olive and mauve. Locating a gigantic, dusty-pink armchair, he disappeared into it.

His hostess returned with a rough approximation of regular tea, acknowledging her visitor's social status by providing him with a mug, keeping a Spode floral teacup for herself. Of biscuits she found none. 'Before my husband and I divorced we travelled the world,' she said. 'We lived in Geneva – for our daughter's schooling, you understand – and were going to live in Cheyne Walk when we returned.' She was unable to resist a peep out of the faux lead-light window. 'But it transpired that he had debts and, well, one was forced into more straitened circumstances.'

'I wouldn't complain,' said Bryant. 'It's a nice gaff, this. Mind you, these old drums near the river get wicked damp.' Bryant did not enjoy the company of the upwardly mobile, and tended to exaggerate his use of the vernacular when he was in their presence. He could get quite jellied eels-ish if the wrong person wound him up, and there was something about Mrs North that wasn't quite right. 'As I explained on the phone, you know a friend of mine—' He moved a china Buddha back from his elbow, just in case.

'I wouldn't say "friend", exactly,' Mrs North replied, anxious to distance herself from Maggie Armitage. 'More of an acquaintance.'

'I understand she met you at a spiritualist's meeting.'

Mrs North shifted uncomfortably on her too-small chair. 'It was all terribly Victorian. I thought she was quite wrong about the medium, who was quite marvellous – but surely this isn't why you're here.'

'Maggie tells me you're a bit of an expert on certain elemental subjects, specifically the Thames.'

Mrs North set her teacup aside. 'If one is interested in matters spiritual it's only natural to study the elements. After all, water is their mother. It has the ability to purify itself, which is one of the requirements of motherhood, since life must begin in purity. Do you wish to take notes?'

'No, ta,' said Bryant, 'I've got a brain.' He flicked the side of his head.

'Right, well, er, water – moving water is spiritually pure. It calms and harmonizes. It is clear, yet contains all. It changes constantly, and can never be stilled. It is consciousness personified. No wonder we revere it.'

'You can freeze it,' said Bryant.

'I'm sorry?'

'You said it can never be stilled, but it can turn to ice.'

'Yes, but only to thaw and start flowing once more.' Mrs North's smile slipped a little. She was not one to be beaten by a common little policeman dressed like a rag-and-bone man. 'Please feel free to ask me anything. If I can't answer I'm bound to know someone who can – I know simply everyone. For example just the other day—'

'Why are rivers considered sacred?'

'They bring life. They *are* life. But as a rule they are not Christian. They contain deities, promote fertility and bring about destruction, so in that respect they behave like pagan gods and demons. There was a spot in the Thames known as "Black John's Pit" from which imps leaped forth to push the heads of children underwater. I've always thought that the indentations along Blackfriars Bridge look like pulpits, with a backdrop of pedestrians forming a moving congregation.'

Bryant tried the tea. It was awful. He didn't bother to suppress a grimace. 'If rivers are gods, do people make sacrifices to them?'

'But of course! All kinds of sacrifices were made to the Mother Thames, from sheaves of corn and loaves to money and animals, and thus the future was divined. The Thames possesses the power of hydromancy. Its roots are sacred. Even the tree that grows at its source has been worshipped for centuries.'

Bryant set the tea down and pushed it away. It was so weak that he could see through it even with milk in. 'I read somewhere that the Thames has its own saint.'

'Indeed, Mr Bryant, St Birinus, who converted the Saxons to Christianity by baptizing them in the river during the seventh century. And later, in the eleventh century, St Alphege, who was said to have parted the Thames and was beaten to death with ox-bones.'

'Well, nobody likes a smartarse.'

'There are many, many other saints, both male and female. Some of the men had their left hands cut off and cast into the river.'

'Oh?' Bryant perked up. 'Why?'

'To transubstantiate, to unite them with the water. This was the line where penitence crossed into punishment. The church was always a political body, and wherever there is water there is worship. That's why so many churches and abbeys line the Thames Valley.'

'What about this area?' Bryant dug into his coat and produced a crude map he had scribbled out on the back of a takeaway falafel menu. 'Tower Beach?'

'That's an area associated with St Mary the Virgin,' Mrs North replied without a moment's hesitation. 'Masses were held at Greenwich for the souls of mariners. Some of her churches are the sites of prehistoric settlements. One arch of London Bridge was actually known as Mary Lock. There were a great many monasteries built on the banks, and there are still more than fifty riverside churches dedicated to St Mary over the course of the Thames. Virgins bathed in its waters to become fertile.'

'So it's possible that a female might also be sacrificed to the river?'

Mrs North pursed her lips. 'Unlikely,' she said. 'The river is a giver of life.'

'But you said it also destroys.'

'It does, indeed. But it would have to be a male sacrifice.

The waters can only move in conjunction with the moon, which is of course the greatest female goddess.'

Bryant had the distinct sense that he would get nowhere further here. Mrs North was selecting facts that suited her own particular world view. He knew that the Reformation had all but destroyed the spiritual significance of the Thames, because of the dissolution of so many monasteries along its banks. The saints were replaced by the pageantry of monarchs, and then the commerce of maritime trade.

He mentally crossed out the line of inquiry. If anyone recalled the sacred origins of the Thames today, it was hardly likely they considered the Square Mile to be best suited for conducting such a ceremony.

'Take a look at this,' said Ray Kirkpatrick, the ursine head-banger who happened to be an English literature academic. They were standing in the conservation department of the British Library on Euston Road, a long white hall filled with wide, antiseptically clean tables and plans chests. Kirkpatrick raised the battered brown leather volume in his great paws, which were barely covered by a pair of white cotton gloves. 'Back in 1623 it went for about a quid. Seven hundred and fifty copies were printed. There are two hundred and twenty-eight left, one recently found in a Calais library. Most of the remaining copies are owned by bloody dot.com millionaires. Be careful with it.'

'May I?' Bryant goggled at the pages, as brittle as dried rose petals. 'A Shakespeare first folio. I've never seen one before.'

'Check out the dedications,' said Kirkpatrick, 'especially from John Heminge and Henry Condell, the actors who edited it.' He raised the volume and read aloud.

'To the great Variety of Readers. From the most able, to him that can but spell: there you are number'd. We had rather you were weighed; especially, when the fate of all bookes depends upon your capacities and not of your heads alone, but of your purses. Well! It is now publique, & you wil stand for your priviledges wee know: to read, and censure. Do so, but buy it first.

'They're making jokes and saying don't just stand there reading it, buy the bloody thing! Nearly four hundred years later and people are making exactly the same joke on their book jackets.'

'The Thames,' Bryant prompted his old friend once more. Kirkpatrick spent too much time working alone in the library stacks and was apt to drift off into its byways.

'I can't recall any direct Shakespeare quotes about the river, but there must be some. Most London books have something about the Thames in them. Are you sure this is the right way to be tackling a murder investigation?'

'Why have you got this out anyway?' asked Bryant.

'Running repairs, innit? We had the Magna Carta in here for treatment against mites last week,' said Kirkpatrick, sounding like a cabbie mentioning a celebrity fare. He scratched about in his voluminous beard and dislodged heaven-knows-what in the way of breakfasty residue. 'Now *that's* a Thames document, signed on the river itself, at Runnymede. The Thames is central to all London history. What about Dickens? There's a whole book on the subject: *Dickens's Dictionary of the Thames, 1887.*'

'Which Charles Dickens didn't write,' said Bryant dismissively. 'His son banged it out. Unfortunately he wrote like a tea merchant, which is what he was. He died with just seventeen quid to his name. Dad had cut him out of the will for marrying a barmaid. Don't try and test me.'

'Sorry.' Kirkpatrick laughed and shook his great head, which reminded Bryant of the stone bust of Karl Marx in Highgate Cemetery. 'I heard that you were losing your marbles, but you seem pretty much all there to me.'

'Let's not talk about illness, it's as boring as looking at

photos of babies,' Bryant responded. 'I've got a problem.'

'Of course you have, that's why you're here.'

'A drowning.'

'Whereabouts?'

'In the Thames Tideway.'

'Oh, come on, Arthur, the tidal reach stretches all the way from Teddington Lock. Can't you be a bit more specific?'

'Only if you keep your fat mouth shut this time,' said Bryant, indignant. 'Remember when I told you about the Shepherd's Market black sausage scandal? "In the strictest confidence", I said. I had half a dozen blokes armed with nail-studded cricket bats threatening to make me the mystery ingredient in their catering packs, all because you talked to someone in a pub.'

'All right,' sighed Kirkpatrick, holding his thick fingers over his heart. 'I swear not to tell a living soul. Who's brown bread?'

Bryant explained the situation. 'Normally you look for motive and opportunity among those closest to the deceased, right? So far we're getting nowhere with that. In this case it's the location that's puzzling me. Why the Thames, why Tower Beach? There are some obvious answers – the seclusion and lack of cameras – but I can't shake the feeling that there's something else. The location. The river must mean something.'

'Of course, Chuck Dickens wrote a load more about the Thames,' said Kirkpatrick, rolling his chair over to the nearest monitor and flicking open the digitized works. 'At the start of *Bleak House* he speaks of "Chance people on the bridges peeping over the parapets into a nether sky of fog, with fog all round them, as if they were up in a balloon, and hanging in the misty clouds." But most obviously, he speaks of the Thames throughout *Our Mutual Friend*. Towards the end of his life Dickens was heading into some pretty dark places. His marriage had fallen apart, his friends were disappearing and none of the things that fired his lifelong anger had changed since he'd begun writing. London's grinding poverty was still all about him, and the ambitious were climbing on to the backs of those less fortunate to reach the top. *Our Mutual Friend* is Dickens's last complete novel, and it's about shit. Making money from it, to be precise. It's a book about ambition in London, turning waste into gold, and of course it starts with a corpse being dragged from the Thames between Southwark Bridge and London Bridge, like something from a horror film. But parts of the book are also a bloody good laugh. And the river courses through it, flowing and swirling and frothing around the characters, befouling everything it touches. Once it had been something pure and fresh, but after the Great Stink of 1858 it became the personification of misery and death. The Thames was a signifier of class, too. Its upper waters, where higher society resided, were far cleaner than the lower reaches. It affected everyone. Even the railway arches that scar South London were put there because the river had turned the land to marshes.' Kirkpatrick shook his head again. 'Is it such a surprise to find one more body there?'

'A sacrifice, no,' said Bryant, 'but a murder, and in such merciless circumstances . . .' He searched about for his hat and jammed it on his head. 'I wish I could say you've been a great help, but it feels like every step forward I take involves another step back.'

'Then you're behaving like the Thames itself,' said Kirkpatrick, giving a great bellow of a laugh. 'You're just another courtier to the tides and the moon.'

The tides and the moon, Bryant thought as he headed home. It had gone 8.00 p.m., and as his flat was just across Euston Road and the weather was clement, he decided to walk back.

He had only got as far as Bidborough Street when the bomb went off.

19

LADDERS & SNAKES

'Oi, you, don't just stand there, get to a bloody shelter!' shouted the man in the green tin helmet. The fat little ARP warden was pointing right at him. Bryant had been planning to cross the road and cut through to the alleyway connecting the two grey halves of Cromer Street, but when he looked up it had gone, blasted away in a great tumbling torrent of tarmac, bricks and plaster. Flames flourished at the mouth of a shattered gas pipe, sending shafts of saffron light through the smoke, painting the street in the colours of hell.

Bryant looked down at his coat, his trousers, his boots. He was covered in dust but didn't seem to have been harmed in any way. The siren soared and dipped as the warden ran over to him. 'Didn't you 'ear what I just said? You want to get your bloody head knocked off?'

'What's the date?' asked Bryant.

'The date?' The warden looked nonplussed. 'Friday.'

'No, what month? What year?'

'You sure you ain't been hit? It's the fifteenth of November 1940. Leicester Square an' Charing Craws 'ave bin knocked flat, and now the bloody Luftwaffe's coming up 'ere.'

'I love your accent. Leicester Square's gone?'

'Saw it wiv me own eyes,' the warden told him, "Itler sent 'is bully boys down St Martin's Street and now it's just a bleedin' great 'ole in the ground. Cripplegate's vanished, the 'ole neighbourhood gawn up in smoke. An' so will you be if you don't get back up to Euston Station.'

'I don't think I will,' said Bryant. 'I just live over there. I think.'

'Gawd, it's allus the old'uns who give me trouble,' complained the warden. 'If you're worried about picking up a shelter infection, don't be, they've sprayed the 'ole place wiv antiseptic.'

'So many beautiful buildings,' said Bryant sadly. 'They all went, didn't they?'

'Dunno abaht that,' said the warden, taking his arm. 'They blew up the Ring at Blackfriars so there won't be no boxing there for a while. That should please my missus.'

'The Luftwaffe – they're waiting for a bomber's moon so they can see their way into the heart of London.'

'Bloody right they are, the pilots are following the moonlight on the Thames – we're being betrayed by our own bleedin' river.'

'They'll bomb Leicester Square again, you know,' said Bryant as they moved out of harm's way. 'The worst raid will be on the sixteenth of April, 1941. There'll hardly be anything left of the West End after that.'

'How do you know so much abaht it? You don't look like a fifth columnist,' the warden said. 'Hang on, where do you think you're going? Wait!'

But Bryant had walked off, skirting the edge of the great smoking crater, trying not to breathe in the bitter stench of burned tar, gas, varnish and wood. Across the road one side of a building had fallen away, turning it into an opened doll's house. *I can't be hurt because this isn't happening,* he thought. *I'm only here inside my head, so I must stay on the pavement – who knows where I'm wandering in the present?*

As he approached Euston Road, he saw the chaos that had

been caused by the raid there. The area was blacked out, of course, but fires burned on either side, marking the sites of bombs. The building next to the Quakers' Society had collapsed into a pile of bricks, as if a petulant child had kicked it over. A group of well-upholstered ladies were standing in the little Quakers' garden beside it, waiting for instructions.

'I say, I don't suppose you have a ladder about you, do you?' called one of them, patting the dust from her sleeves. 'Only the front door got blown in, so we'll have to use the upstairs window.'

'Has anyone said whether it's safe to go back inside?' asked another, a matronly lady who bore a remarkable resemblance to the actress Margaret Rutherford.

'I don't see why not,' said a third. 'We'll be safer with the Quakers than over at the station.'

'We have to get back in because the Reverend Peabody is still inside and he's stuck in a folding chair,' the first added, turning back to Bryant. 'He was giving a most enjoyable talk on the history of the Thames.'

'I'm afraid I don't have a ladder,' said Bryant. 'Don't you think you'd be safer at the station?'

'There have been bombers over London every night for two and a half months now, young man,' said Margaret Rutherford. 'If one waited for them to finish, one would never get anything done.'

Young man? thought Bryant. *Blimey.*

'The Reverend Peabody says the most frightfully shocking things,' another of the ladies confided. She was covered in little pieces of mortar and sported a preposterous feathered hat. 'He says they should put another girl inside London Bridge.'

'What does the Reverend mean?' Bryant asked, puzzled.

'Well of course the Romans started it,' said the lady with the hat. 'Human sacrifice, I mean. Putting a *virgin*' – she mouthed the word to protect the delicate sensibilities of the others – 'inside the bridge to consecrate it. The Reverend says that whenever the bridge was rebuilt they did it again.'

'Do you believe it?'

'No, of course not. This is England, for heaven's sake, we don't tamper with our virgins, we leave that sort of thing to foreigners.'

'You're wrong, Muriel, quite wrong!' said the most rotund lady. 'Somebody really should make a sacrifice to the river, trinkets perhaps, just to be on the safe side.'

'You do talk nonsense, Lavinia,' said Muriel. 'Why on earth should anyone do that?'

'Because it's the river that's guiding the bombers directly to us.'

'It's the moon that's doing it, not the river,' Bryant reasoned as an alarming series of thuds sounded in the distance.

'They're the same thing,' cried Lavinia impatiently. 'Don't you see? The moon and the waters are female. Betraying women! Betraying London!' And with that she led the little group back inside the Quakers' House.

'You're sure he's OK?' asked John May. He had been leaving the PCU when the call came through.

'I think he's fine,' said Alma Sorrowbridge. 'He found his way back all right but he's still a little bit confused. It was another hallucination. He says he thought he was in the Blitz.'

'But he's all right now?'

'He's just put away two slices of ginger sultana cake and a pint of tea so I think he'll live,' said Alma, 'but you really can't let him go wandering again.'

'It's my fault,' May admitted. 'We had a bit of a miscommunication here. Keep him there, can you? Lock him in his room if necessary. Call me if there's a problem. I'll be there in the morning as usual to bring him to the unit. He'll drive you mad if I don't.'

'He's driving me mad right now. I'm going to tell him to turn down those Vera Lynn records. We've had "Bluebirds over the White Cliffs of Dover" four times in a row, and before that, "London Bridge is Falling Down".'

In the seventeenth century, Nine Elms still had its eponymous riverside trees. The area was swampy and miasmic during high tides, when the Thames overflowed into it. The marshes were drained and filled with stones and factories; a gasworks and a locomotive depot arrived, remaining until they attracted the attention of German bombers. Now, after decades of dereliction, the area was starting to rise into something approaching cohesion. Covent Garden Market relocated here, Battersea Power Station was being restored (albeit for the pleasure of the wealthy 1 per cent) and the American Embassy was building a moated fortress at its riverbank. But for the time being there were still ugly, desolate pockets beyond the reach or interest of pedestrians.

The Thames might have been turbulent in its olivine depths, but its surface was smoothed by the onslaught. Overflowing drains led to outlets in the riverbank walls, cascading torrents of water on to the foreshore.

The falling rain was incessant and pernicious. It glossed the empty road beside the river, haloed the street lamps and pooled on Janice Longbright's black PCU jacket, spitting icy droplets down the back of her neck. She tried to check the address on her phone but the rain obscured its screen.

Turning to get her bearings, she spotted the sign that read 'Medusa Holdings', one of five companies sharing the nameboard beside the floodlit truck depot. The big hauliers moved vessels ranging in size from three to sixteen metres, while the dry-bulk pneumatics shifted salt, gravel, sand and cement to building sites across Europe. Beneath the glare of metal halide lights they trundled past the detective sergeant as she stepped across ditches, crossing the tarmac yard. At the back of the depot, the lorries manoeuvred their way into berths like exhausted prehistoric beasts.

Longbright found the main office in a blank brick building

near the front entrance. The counter clerk ignored her until she laid down her badge, then merely looked annoyed.

'It's OK, Leon, I know her,' said a familiar voice. She turned to find Freddie Cooper on the stairs. 'Longbright, isn't it? What are you doing here?'

She had forgotten how dissolutely handsome he was. Now she understood his line in sharp suits; it made him stand out from the drivers, otherwise he might have been mistaken for one. He was a throwback to an earlier era, unreconstructed man, a vanishing breed.

'It seems you're back on our radar, Mr Cooper. We found your calling card in Lynsey Dalladay's flat.'

'I imagine you did,' said Cooper. 'When she was by herself she suffered from night panics. She was incapable of finding numbers on her phone so I gave her the card and told her to call me any time of the day or night. Do you want to come up?'

He led the way to a steel platform running the length of the building. From here Longbright could see the full extent of the truck operation below. 'Are these all yours?' she asked.

Cooper looked out over the lumbering lorries. 'No, I have a fleet of ten at the moment, but I'm expanding.'

'So business is good?'

'In this climate you can never tell. That's why I diversify into other markets. I have to stay one step ahead.'

Longbright watched one of the drivers dropping down from his cabin. 'Where do they go?'

'Right now they're delivering engine parts from factories in the Midlands to the south coast. Our safety certificates are all up to date, if that's what you're wondering.'

'I'm not here for that,' said Longbright. 'I'm just following up every lead we can think of, Mr Cooper.'

'So you're not getting anywhere. I assume you went to the Cossack Club.' He smiled darkly. 'If you can understand why she would want to work in a dump like that, maybe you can let me know. It's not the sort of place that's kind to women. Still, you're the detectives, you should be able to figure it out.'

Longbright turned to face the entrepreneur. 'It's not our job to understand why people do the things they do, Mr Cooper. Even the well-intentioned ones can end up lying, and the best lies come when they're finally convinced they're telling the truth.'

'Then your job is to make sense of that, isn't it?'

'People omit truths in order to ease their pain. We have to get the full story so that we can decide what to do.'

He looked at her levelly. 'And what you decide changes lives.'

'It's not always possible to know if you've made the right decision. Sometimes it's hard to tell if a crime has been committed at all. People can hurt each other without breaking laws. We're very good at finding ways to punish ourselves. I think Ms Dalladay was doing that.'

'So you're applying a bit of cod-psychology to poor old Lynsey now, are you? She was a bitch, did I tell you that? A self-centred flower-child born fifty years too late. She went looking for herself and found there was nobody inside.'

'She found you,' said Longbright. 'That didn't help, obviously, given the amount of cocaine you keep lying around the house. Were you actually hoping we would bust you? Right now we're after bigger fish.'

Cooper turned to face her. 'So why *are* you here? I told you I'd call if I thought of anything else. There's really not much more to say about Lynsey. She made bad choices.'

Longbright raised an eyebrow. 'I'd say somebody else made the choice for her, wouldn't you?'

Cooper checked his watch and let her lead the way back down from the platform. 'Is there anything I can do for you before you go?'

'Yes, the name – Medusa. How did you pick it?'

Cooper laughed. 'I bought it off the peg. It's cheaper to buy a bankrupt holding company that's already set up than to start from scratch. I'm just a capitalist trying to make a living, and you're looking a bit too hard, Longbright.'

'Maybe, but I've not finished looking yet,' she said.

'You know, you're a handsome woman.' He bounced to the bottom of the stairs, moving closer, examining her. 'What's the attraction of a job like yours? Dealing with the scum out there on the streets? Does anybody ever thank you? Do you go home alone at night and wonder why you bother? Do the people you try to help ever do anything except hate you?'

'I don't expect anything from them so I'm never really disappointed,' she said. 'The work suits me.'

'Then maybe my job isn't so different from yours,' he said.

'Thank you for your time, Mr Cooper. We may see each other again.'

Longbright stepped back into the night drizzle. When she glanced back she found him motionless behind the glass, still watching her.

20

START-UPS & NEWBORNS

And so for Ali and Cassie we arrive at the present year, and a further refinement in the couple's plans. This time, Cassie had decided the course they would take.

The St Alphege Wellbeing Centre was situated in a converted boathouse that had belonged to the Chelsea Rowing Association, which had been closed down after the council found asbestos in the ceiling. It had been rebuilt and transformed into a lacuna of tranquillity in SW1, which was already considered to be one of the most elegant and expensive quadrants of the metropolis.

At first there were spa treatments and yoga classes, but the business was poorly run and failed. Determined to find a new way to use Ali's persuasive charms, Cassie took over the lease from the old owners and set up a company called Life Options, launching a new schedule of courses that required no teaching qualifications in order to comply with local laws.

As soon as Ali started leading the new classes she knew their fortunes were finally made. He radiated the kind of charisma that made people stop talking and pay attention. With lifestyle coaching he found himself on firmer ground than magic or ministries. It helped that he was over six feet tall, lean and lightly muscled, so that he appeared to practise what he preached. He was the very picture of wellbeing.

'We don't have to lie to people, we can make them feel better,' said Ali. 'It doesn't have to be based on science, just common sense, dressed up a little. Think of it as psychological folk-art.'

Ali adopted the alias of Thornberry for his new customers. He'd come across the name in a peculiar magazine called *The Tatler*, which seemed to be about rich people who thought it was the 1800s, and decided that the name carried the right connotations of Englishness. He worked from scripts that the pair developed in the evenings, but soon created his own courses, from exercise and diet to mental clarity, stress reduction and emotional stability, then spirituality, astrology, crystal healing and meditation.

As usual, he absorbed everything he read and quickly learned how to put his new knowledge into practice. Ali hired life coaches working freelance on a per-client basis. He gave them template scripts that added layers of parapsychological double-speak, preaching the kind of life-affirming, positive, undemanding lessons their well-heeled clients were prepared to accept. Most of their repeat visitors came from the wealthy environs of Chelsea, Fulham, Putney and Chiswick. After one visit over half of them signed up for further complementary courses.

A macrobiotic café was opened, then a shop selling lotions, candles, mineral salts, healing stones, pots of earth from sacred sites, CDs of ethereal chanting, whale noises downloaded from the internet and magical luck-bringing paintings.

Cassie now needed proper funding, but couldn't go through a bank. Instead she found a backer for the centre through the LinkedIn website. Freddie Cooper was a smooth-talking entrepreneur who ran a road-haulage business in Nine Elms. Flushed with success right from the start, Cassie had visited their backer at his house in De Beauvoir and discussed the possibility of opening a chain of Life Options wellbeing centres. She explained that they couldn't attract too much attention because none of their experts had qualifications. What would they be able to get away with selling in their shops if they expanded? The outlay wasn't enormous and the potential rewards were huge. Cooper knew a good thing when he saw it. He agreed to put his money down on the condition that Life Options kept to its proposed roll-out schedule, and he drew up a private contract between the three of them.

While Cassie handled the bookkeeping, Ali charmed his way through swathes of wealthy West London women, talking about spiritual fulfilment, music therapy, astrological alignment, sexual healing and the abandonment of guilt, shame and negative energy. Although he had learned all of the terms, he still did not know all of their meanings.

'Remember to keep the messages simple,' Cassie warned him. 'People will fill in the blanks themselves. You don't have to say anything that can stand against you in a court of law.'

At first, whenever the questions became too specific, on dietary requirements, say, or the disadvantages of taking prescription medication, Ali danced around the topic and delivered calming platitudes, but after a while he became less cautious and began making the kind of recommendations his clients were anxious to hear. He grew into his London persona as a plant takes to wet soil and sunlight.

'How do you do it?' Cassie asked once. 'The way you speak, the way you move and behave – no one would ever know . . .'

'I watch and listen,' he said simply. 'My old life is always with me, but you can put it away. You can be someone else.'

This, he could see, was what being an ambitious Londoner was really all about. He listened to what the Prime Minister and the Mayor had to say about people who helped themselves, and resolved to reach his maximum potential. Realizing that he would never be treated like a true insider, certainly not the kind who appeared in the pages of *The*

Tatler, he decided to become the man who would tell those on the inside what to do.

The money rolled in. The clients adored him. He and Cassie rented adjoining flats in one of the better streets in Chiswick. Suddenly they were leading charmed lives. It seemed as if nothing could go wrong.

Then came the third week in November, and everything began to fall apart.

Arthur Bryant looked out of the living-room window at the rain cascading into the centre courtyard of his apartment building. 'I'm missing something,' he said.

'You always say that whenever you're on a case.' Alma was seated at the table addressing cards to her fellow parishioners. She was forever organizing outings and charity collections for her church. The flat looked more like an Oxfam shop these days, with trays of lurid iced cakes ready for dispatch to fundraising teas and boxes of second-hand clothes awaiting shipment to refugee camps. Alma had always been a large, expansive woman but now as she started to shrink her kindness expanded to fill the rooms. Bryant had managed to keep his quarters sacrosanct, although he noticed she had tried to sneak a crucifix on to his bookshelves. He said nothing, but turned it upside down. She got the message and removed it.

'No, I don't mean the case – although I'm definitely missing something there, too,' he said with a sigh. 'The hallucinations are some new side effect of my deteriorating mental processes. Where am I while they're happening? Am I just standing in the street with my mouth open, easy prey for muggers? Am I wandering in the middle of the road liable to be crushed beneath juggernauts? Do I just sit down on a bench and go to sleep? What happens when these states of mind come on?'

'God is granting you visions,' said Alma simply. 'He'll protect you until he makes his purpose known.'

'He can't protect me from the wheels of a number seventy-five bus. I need John for that. I almost wish I had your faith. Wait a minute, what do you mean he'll protect me *until* then? What's he going to do afterwards?'

'That's for Him to decide. He may choose to fold you into His bosom.'

'Oh, that's charming. You lot have got all this worked out, haven't you? If I live it's because He has a higher purpose, and if I fall off my perch it's because I'm answering His call. As I'm not planning to assume room temperature just yet He'll have to get on with something else for a while, cause a few famines and start some new wars until I'm ready. I've got work to do.'

'Oh, that poor girl,' said Alma, setting aside her cards. 'The one who was drowned. Is that the case you're working on?'

'You know it is,' said Bryant irritably, 'I told you all about it yesterday.'

'Yes, but I only listen to about a quarter of what you say.' She thought for a moment. 'Perhaps a fifth. Are you getting anywhere?'

'I'm not about to tell you, am I? It'll be all round your church by this evening.'

'Mr Bryant, I'm shocked you should think that. You know I never talk to my ladies about you. I haven't dared to mention your name ever since you accepted their offer to deliver the weekly sermon.'

'I don't see why that should have upset you,' he huffed. 'It was about God.'

'Yes, but it wasn't about *our* God, was it?'

'I didn't expect them to be so proprietorial. I thought they'd be interested in hearing about a different belief system.'

'You frightened the life out of them. All that stuff about biting the heads off monkeys and burning people to death.'

'Very well, to answer your question, so far we've utterly failed to find out anything useful at all. Why?'

'It's just that I saw her picture on the news and thought it was funny it should have happened on that spot.'

Bryant turned, intrigued. 'What do you mean?'

'My mother told me she used to see the vicar of All Hallows conducting services right on the beach there, after the church was damaged.'

'What sort of services?'

'Hymns and readings – and baptisms, she said. It makes sense, doesn't it? The Black Friars and the White Friars were just a bit further along, and they used to conduct ceremonies beside the Thames, didn't they? You know – the monasteries. I know most people think it's dirty and dangerous, but if you have faith the river is life. It can wash away your sins. I was just thinking, she'd sinned, hadn't she?'

'How do you mean?'

'By getting pregnant out of wedlock.'

'Good Lord, it's not the 1950s. So you think someone was trying to purify her in a sort of perverted baptism ceremony?'

'I didn't say that, Mr Bryant. I suppose it was just the idea of babies and water. The unborn and newly birthed are innocent even if the mother isn't.' In the kitchen the oven pinged, so she struggled to her feet. 'Would you like some cabinet pudding?'

'Only if I can get my teeth in first,' said Bryant. 'You always leave the stones in the plums.' He rose and set off in search of his dentures. He kept several sets in order to cope with the inconsistencies in Alma's cooking. On the way he grabbed a pencil and paper. *The innocence of the newborn absolves the sins of the mother,* he thought. Then: *There's someone I have to see.*

Looking through his reference books, an idea had begun to form about the uniqueness of his condition, and once it had taken root he knew it would not be shaken off without thorough exploration.

21

RUN & SWIM

James Crawley hated his sedentary job, but since he worked as a risk assessor in a government office on Millbank he was doomed to a life of sitting in meetings, sitting behind his desk, sitting in the canteen at lunchtime and generally – sitting. As he lived in nearby Vauxhall he had recently started running to work, pacing along any path that still ran close to the river to finish at Lambeth Bridge.

His exercise regime had its good and bad points. The downside was that he frequently found himself running in squalls of rain driven in by the river winds, and on fine, mild days the air pollution from Westminster's traffic was suffocating.

On Wednesday morning he discovered another bad point; you might accidentally be confronted by a corpse. At first he thought a workman's tarpaulin had blown off the bridge and become entangled in the steel rafters underneath. But tarpaulins didn't have feet, and this one was hanging by them. When he touched the tarpaulin it slid away to reveal a man in a grey boiler suit, his arms dangling down on either side of his head, almost invisible in the shadows.

As a risk assessor Mr Crawley should have been able to

work out the odds of such a bizarre accident occurring – for that's what he assumed it was, because what else could it possibly be? Down here, beneath the thrum of the traffic and the warbling of pigeons, was one of London's lonely recesses. It was a spot where the dankness of the Thames could permeate your marrow and any vile deed could pass unnoticed.

Mr Crawley called an ambulance rather than the police, figuring that the workman might still be alive, in which case he would require urgent medical attention, but the police and the ambulance crew arrived at the same time. The assessor gave his name and address, then headed back to the Economy-Plus 2-Lever Lumbar Support office chair he had lately grown to despise. His strange discovery became just another anecdote to be trotted out in public houses, the gristle upon which Londoners daily fed and thrived.

It was 7.53 a.m. on Wednesday when John May arrived with Dan Banbury and an ambulance from St Thomas' Hospital. Banbury had caught the incoming call because he had gone in early and reset his incident parameters to prioritize anything unusual happening on or around the Thames foreshore between Hammersmith Bridge and Tower Bridge.

Even as the EMTs were cutting the body loose and lowering it on to the stones, May knew it had a connection to the discovery two mornings earlier on Tower Beach; the workman was missing his left hand and the cauterized stump of the wrist showed the frayed upper edge of a tattoo.

The pair followed the body to the St Pancras Coroner's Office, then ran through their notes in Rosa's room while they waited impatiently for Giles Kershaw to carry out a preliminary examination.

Giles finally called them in, booting a plastic bucket across the floor until it was positioned under the worst of the leaks. 'This place is falling apart,' he complained. 'We need a new roof.'

'Why don't you have a word with one of your friends in high places?' May suggested. 'I'm assuming you still have the Chancellor's ear.'

'Not so much these days, since I stopped going out with his niece,' said Giles gloomily. 'I think the initial thrill of hanging around a mortuary at night wore off. She said I smelled of death. Not terribly conducive to a relationship.'

'If you really want to prove yourself useful, couldn't you start dating the Metropolitan Police Commissioner's grand-daughter or something?'

'As surprising as it sounds, John, I'm not seeking career advancement, I'm looking for a soulmate.'

May sighed. 'That's very selfish of you. Right now we could do with all the help we can get. Arthur's illness has become a lot more serious, Raymond couldn't organize an egg-and-spoon race and the rest of us are just trying to keep things together.'

'Other police units get financial and psychological support,' said Giles, placing a friendly hand on May's shoulder. 'They have systems in place for coping when a senior team member drops out. Why don't you?'

'Are you kidding? Nobody outside knows that Arthur's working on the case. They've been told he's on compassionate leave. And we still have nothing.'

'Then maybe I can help,' said Giles. 'Dan, perhaps you can assist? Come with me, you two.' He led the way back to the mortuary and started to pull open one of the body drawers. 'Do you mind taking a shufti? Or is it a bit early in the day? He's not in terribly good condition.'

Giles and Dan eased out the tray. The drawer's runners squealed appallingly, as if the corpse did not wish to have its dark sleep disturbed. 'What we have here is a short, stocky male of mixed race,' said Giles, 'late thirties, heavy smoker. He appears to have died about three weeks ago, which accounts for his poor state, and as you can see he's missing his eyes and his left hand.'

'You think it's the same—'

'Oh yes, we have a perfect fit.' Giles pulled open a Mylar envelope and carefully lifted out the missing appendage, laying it next to the corpse's grey wrist-stump. 'It wasn't the result of a medical procedure, but nor was it an industrial accident. I'm pretty certain a sharp knife was used to sever the tendons and cut through muscle and tissue, but the bone separation is quite clean. There are no chips or splinters in either section of the wrist. The saw-marks are short, indicating a short blade.'

'So it was done deliberately but not by a surgeon?'

'I suppose it would be consistent with torture or punishment. I can't think of a normal situation that would result in something like this.'

'That stump – he didn't bleed to death?'

'No, the severance looks as if it was sealed. It's likely that it occurred some time before his demise,' said Giles. 'He quite clearly drowned. There's still evidence of mucus in his air passages, distension of the lungs, plenty of burst blood vessels. He tried to breathe. I'd hoped to find ventricular diatoms, bruises on the arms and the neck, but it's a bit late to find signs of a forced drowning.'

May turned to Banbury, who was digging around in his backpack. 'Do you think he was killed at the bridge, Dan?'

The CSM found his notebook and stepped closer, examining the body with interest. 'I think someone wedged him up in the rafters of the bridge and hoped he'd just stay there until he'd rotted apart or the seagulls had finished him off. The birds would have taken his eyes first. He was drowned and put up there immediately because his overalls were still wet. They shaped themselves to their drying position, which largely held him in place. Eventually he decomposed sufficiently to fall off his perch, but his boots got caught in some cabling.'

'So someone hacked off his hand, then managed to stow

him up there,' said May, puzzled. 'The bridge rafters have to be ten or twelve feet above the top of the shoreline.'

'I've done your work for you on that one,' said Giles. 'A scaffold platform had been left there after the council carried out some rust-proofing. It was removed some time during the third week in October.'

'The tattoo. Could you?' May pointed to the wrist. Giles carefully added the hand to it. Now the complete design could be seen, but it wasn't a lighthouse, as Bryant had suggested. It appeared to be a bulbous head with protrusions crushing a stack of bricks, but it still wasn't clear. 'Could the hand have been severed earlier to hide the tattoo and delay identification?' asked May.

'A bit of a melodramatic notion,' said Giles, who was used to such things from the PCU. 'More likely he was punished for being a naughty boy, then sent for a swim.' He covered up the corpse.

'Why was the hand so far away from the body?'

'That might be to do with the tides,' said Giles. 'It used to be said that a body thrown from one house in the Thames would be picked up and scavenged by another. There's a further possibility.'

'What's that?' asked May.

'Assuming the amputation and the drowning were carried out on different occasions, it might be that the hand was removed and chucked into the Thames at Tower Beach simply because it was expedient to throw it from a spot in that area. It was only because we were searching the Dalladay site that we found it.'

'Maybe getting rid of the hand was a trial run for dumping Dalladay,' said May. 'Which would mean that the two events are connected. Arthur would love that.'

The coroner had not been able to avoid noticing that there was something odd about Mr Bryant's reactions lately. They seemed delayed and unfocused. He would start suddenly, as if being reminded of his duties in the present. But as he continued to be spoken of as if he was still a fully functioning member of the unit, Giles decided to keep his counsel. At some point, May would be forced to acknowledge the truth; that his days of working with his old partner were finally over.

22

GLOOM & DOOM

Arthur Bryant was getting better at evading his keepers.

He slipped out of the PCU by keeping to the edges of the stair treads and using the two Daves to create a distraction, which wasn't difficult as one of them was under the floorboards hammering on pipes like a tunnelling POW who'd made a wrong turn and the other was on the phone to his girlfriend while trying to light a cigarette with a blowlamp.

Bryant made his way through the rain to St Giles-without-Cripplegate in the Barbican. A church had stood on the site since 1090. The name referred to one of the gates through the old City wall, which had been built in Roman times to protect the settlement from attackers. The area of Cripplegate had once boasted residents of great importance, but the entire neighbourhood vanished in a single night when in 1897 an ostrich-feather warehouse caught alight.

St Giles was one of the few remaining medieval churches in the Square Mile and, unusually for London, was still used by a local community. Bryant had gone back on the promise he had made to himself and had arranged to meet Audrey Beardsley, a historian currently working with the British Geographical Society. They had met by accident several years earlier at a conference centre in Berlin. Bryant had gone to the toilet during a talk on the Würzburg Witch Trial of 1626 and had taken the wrong door back, only to find himself attending a Punjabi wedding. It was not the first time he had made such a mistake, and not the worst, which was erroneously projecting a film entitled *Autopsies: What Can Go Wrong?* to a darkened classroom full of terrified toddlers.

Beardsley's spectral figure appeared on the steps of the church. As thin as a cherry tree, as pale as paste, as exsanguinated as Mina Harker, she looked as if she might not make it to the end of the week. 'I'm glad you wanted to see me today,' she said, shaking Bryant's hand with an icy claw. 'It's best not to leave it too long with me. I'm on the way out. The doctors gave me three months.'

'When was that?' asked Bryant.

'Three months ago. Dying is a pain in the arse. Quite literally, in my case. I've had the chemo and the radio but it made no difference. And even if I do go into remission it'll only come back at some point. There's no point in starting *Bleak House* now. Your Janice Longbright brought me a kitten to cheer me up but it got run over. I mean, what's it all for? What are we here for? My hair's coming out in clumps. Look.' She grabbed a dry grey tuft and pulled, unfurling her fist to release a fall of follicles. 'I tried a wig but it made me look like Shirley Bassey. Look at you, though, the very picture of health. How are you?'

'Oh, I'm losing my marbles,' said Bryant cheerfully. 'I've gone totally East Ham. One stop short of Barking.'

'I thought you had a very fine brain,' said Beardsley.

'Yes, and shortly it'll be in a jar at the Hunterian Museum. My disease is incurable and getting worse by the day. I haven't quite started taking my plate out in public but it can't be long.'

'I guess that puts us both in the same boat.' Beardsley shook her head so violently that Bryant thought he heard her teeth rattling in her skull. 'It seems such a waste, doesn't it? We spend the whole of our adulthood accumulating specialist knowledge, forgoing the opportunity to have normal lives, and for what? To die without passing it on.'

'But didn't you write a book about the Thames?' Bryant asked. 'That's passing it on.'

'Do you really think any one of them cares about such things now?' Beardsley gestured towards the unwary residents of the Barbican going about their daily lives.

'Yes, I do,' replied Bryant. 'Somebody somewhere will share the same passions. They'll want to use the information you leave behind.'

Beardsley sniffed. 'I fear for today's teens. I look at them sending pictures of their dinners to each other on their phones and wonder what happens if they ever find themselves in a bookshop. They probably think they've accidentally gone back in time. I wish I had your positive outlook. I'm more a glass-three-quarters-empty kind of person.'

'Then share your knowledge with me,' said Bryant. 'I need your advice. Maybe I can put it to good use before either of us goes. Is there somewhere we can sit?'

They found a café across from the entrance to the church, on the other side of the fountains, and settled at a table by the window. Audrey lowered herself with a wince.

'Is there anything you can't have?' asked Bryant, ordering.

'At this stage? With my insides? The most I can manage is the odd mouthful of bircher muesli. A weak mint tea will be fine. And some cáke. And perhaps a sausage roll.'

A Polish waiter shot over and took their order with smiling efficiency. While they waited, Bryant did his best to outline the case.

'Interesting,' said Audrey when he had finished. 'So you know it's considered a holy river. Anything with the word "Temple" in it, from locks to tube stations, is a sign that the Knights Templar were there.'

'So I believe.'

'Therefore baptism makes sense, even the baptism of an unborn child. But you say she was chained to a rock, which suggests sacrifice. The Thames is considered the spirit of London, its principal avenue, yet most of us take it entirely for granted. Technically speaking, it was always beyond the jurisdiction of the City.'

'What do you mean?'

'It's not policed in the same way. So few people use it now. And it's lost its distinctive smell, have you noticed?' Audrey scratched at her head, then checked her palm as if daring anything else to fall out. 'The odour was of tar and rope, but mainly from hydrogen sulphide caused by lack of oxygen. In Victorian times there were so many chemical reactions going on in the water that it actually heated up.'

'It's not the condition of the river I'm interested in but what it stands for,' Bryant pointed out as the waiter returned with a mound of food. 'It may help me to understand why this young woman was so brutally killed.'

'A bit of an unorthodox way to investigate a crime, isn't it? What about witnesses and fingerprints and DNA, things like that?' The academic crammed a doorstop of sponge-cake into her mouth.

'It's not how I do things,' said Bryant simply. 'We're assuming she was killed because she was pregnant, but why in such an odd fashion? We also found a man's severed left hand nearby. Any ideas about that?'

Audrey sluiced the cake down with tea. 'This could be hotter. I know there were votive ceremonies connected to the Thames but those took place in Celtic and Roman times.'

'What sort of things were offered up?'

'Mostly small animals, bronze bowls, weapons and helmets, gold coins and figurines with amputated limbs. The waters were meant to transport heathen idols to hell. They were often found around the bridges – after all, there are twenty-four of them, and London Bridge is the oldest. It got so overcrowded with horses and carriages that in 1733 they put up "Keep Left" signs, which is why Britain still drives on the left.'

'Offerings,' Bryant reminded her. 'You were saying.'

'Ah yes. In the sixteenth century witches' bottles were thrown into the tide at Southwark to ward off evil. And of course, there were always severed heads to be found, right through history.'

'I thought they were just placed on tall poles at London Bridge.'

'Oh no. We used to believe that the soul lived in the head, not the heart, so it was a way of sending someone to the underworld. Decapitations occurred around the site of the old Billingsgate fish market, just down from where you say you found the body. We probably get the name of the market from Belinus, one of the great gods of the Thames. And less than twenty years ago around fifty decapitated skulls were found in one of the Thames's tributaries, the River Lea. The heads on Traitors' Gate were stuck on pikes thirty at a time.'

'I assume they were put there to scare visitors into behaving themselves.'

'Not just that. The Thames was once considered to be a pathway to heaven. Of course, as it filled with industrial waste it became associated with hell. Corpses always beached at Dead Man's Stairs in Wapping. And as the Thames comes around the Rotherhithe Peninsula – the wiggly bit – most bodies and parts still get washed up at Limehouse.'

'Why is that?'

'The river has strange turbulence. There are hidden currents, whirlpools and maelstroms that can suck you into the depths in seconds. It was always treacherous to cross. Ferrymen and passengers drowned trying to shoot the rapids beneath London Bridge.'

'Yet we encouraged children to swim from Tower Beach,' said Bryant, amazed.

Audrey appeared not to have heard him. She sucked her teeth and stared grimly into her tea as if expecting to find something dead floating in it. 'That's part of the London paradox,' she said. 'There were always scaffolds set up on the

Thames or on its tributaries – at Dagenham and Millwall and Greenwich, the Hanging Ditch at Blackwall and the gallows at the mouth of the Neckinger, which means "Devil's neck-cloth", slang for a hangman's noose.'

'Why build execution docks on the river?'

'There could be a prosaic reason: the height of the gallows above the water. Or it could be something more spiritual, the idea that the water takes the soul out to sea. The Thames has always been used to dispose of bodies. Back when there were houses built out over the water's edge it was said that certain taverns had trapdoors opening directly into the water. Dismemberment and despatch, all in one. In late Victorian times, body parts washed up at a tremendous rate, arms, legs, torsos and innards.'

'That's a cheery thought,' said Bryant, now feeling thoroughly depressed. He looked at the purple *Osteospermum* standing in its little vase on the table and fancied that the academic could wither it just by reaching out and brushing it with her fingertips.

'Yes, it's a catalogue of death and disaster,' Audrey added for good measure.

'I remember the sinking of the *Marchioness*,' said Bryant. 'Nineteen eighty-nine, wasn't it? Fifty-one drowned.'

'There was a worse case: the *Princess Alice* pleasure steamer went down at Gallions' Reach in 1878, drowning some seven hundred souls. But that wasn't the most awful part of it. An hour before it sank the river's sewage outfall pipes had opened, pumping millions of gallons of excrement and oil into the Thames. The corpses came out so black and slippery that they couldn't be cleaned. Some of them exploded. One of the few survivors was Elizabeth Stride. She lost her entire family and turned to prostitution. She became Jack the Ripper's third victim.'

'Well, thank you for that,' said Bryant. 'I'd love to stay and chat longer but I'd end up killing myself.'

'And another thing,' said Audrey, waving a bony digit at

him. 'The river's blackness attracted suicides. Its Celtic name was "Tamesas", meaning "dark water". The watermen said that women floated face-up, men face-down. Waterloo Bridge was the most famous lovers' leaping spot. So many people jumped to their deaths that there was a special boat moored by the bridge to recover the bodies. No wonder people came to believe that the river was haunted.'

An idea began to form in Bryant's head. 'Are they supposed to occur at any particular time of the year, these deaths?'

Audrey chased the last scraps of sausage roll around her plate. 'There have always been more at this time of the year than any other. It's hardly surprising. The darkness of winter is associated with depression. There are still as many unexplained deaths on the river as there ever were. People come here from all over the world with high ambitions, and when they fail the Thames calls to them. It'll be us next. Nattering away like this one minute, then suddenly becoming part of London's sediment.'

Bryant's thoughts were in turmoil. No matter how hard he tried to employ cold logic, the ghosts of the Thames took up the reins of his imagination. 'I have to go,' he said, rising. He reknotted his ratty green scarf and pulled his hat down over his eyes. 'Audrey, I think you've certainly cleared up one thing for me.'

'Really?' sighed the historian, almost disappointed to have been of use.

'Yes, I've realized something – that even though I walk in the Valley of Death, I shall do so armed with a pint of beer, a pork pie and a Batman comic. I can't help it, Audrey, I'm just a naturally optimistic person. You should try it some time.'

Bryant released himself back into the vibrancy of the city with relief, for he had come to understand that in the midst of winter there was within him an invincible summer.

23

RAIN & SPEED

It would be wrong to think that the staff of the PCU were merely drifting about like flotsam, lost in a sea of academic misinformation. For the last two days the unit's three detective constables, Colin Bimsley, Meera Mangeshkar and Fraternity DuCaine, had been conducting witness interviews and logging data searches, recording conversations, filing evidence, cataloguing information and carrying out door-to-doors.

They did not perform the duties of their pay-rank but often worked at higher levels, having long refused any promotion that would remove them from daily contact with the public. Ground crew got their hands dirty; it meant that when a case began to break, they weren't stuck upstairs in PowerPoint presentations. While autonomy within the PCU insulated them from Met policies, it didn't stop them from being placed on bin duty, overnight surveillance or so-called 'nuisance runs' if Janice Longbright thought it would benefit an investigation. There were still times when Meera felt like walking out and getting a job in a bakery. *Just once,* she thought, *it would be nice to make something attractive for a living, to bring people pleasure, to go home smelling of strawberries and warm bread, instead of this.*

This being the rotting cabbages at the bottom of a skip beside Lambeth Bridge, where they were bending over in the sifting rain, searching for anything that might give them a lead on the drowned, amputee workman. It was unlikely that they would find anything after so long, but it was worth a try. Fraternity was talking to office workers in the nearby buildings, leaving Meera and Colin to grub about in rubbish and poke through the undergrowth beneath the bridge.

'I don't know what you're complaining about,' said Colin. 'Someone's chucked away a rabbit. This would make a nice fur collar.' He was holding up a length of sodden pelt in one gloved hand.

'Can you put that down? You're actually making me sick.' Meera was seesawed over the edge of the skip trying to reach its murkiest recesses. 'I can't believe I'm doing this again. I thought we were finally getting somewhere.'

'I did too,' said Colin. 'When you put your head on my chest the other day and held me for the longest time, and it felt as if—'

'I meant with the case,' she snapped. 'A poor little rich girl, hanging out with a few rough geezers in a Dalston dive bar, sounds like a recipe for disaster to me. Then this one pops up. Why are we here? There can't be any connection.'

'What, you mean beyond his chopped-off hand appearing near her body?'

'Yeah. Bits of people turn up all the time.'

Colin looked over to the line of police boats moored a few metres offshore, beneath the abutment of the bridge. 'My granddad worked as a lighterman down at the Pool of London when he was in his early twenties,' he said. 'He reckons there were all kinds of weird superstitions about the river. Like, if you pulled a body out of the water and gave it a proper burial, you were cheating the Thames of a soul and creating a ghost.'

'He sounds like a laugh,' said Meera, levering herself further into the skip to pull aside a disconnected washbasin and a box full of taps.

'So if you think of the Thames as a person,' Colin persisted, 'it's like it deliberately directed its currents to wash this bloke's hand up right beside the girl's body, so we'd connect the two events and solve the case. Like it's helping us. They call them "strange tides", when things wash up somewhere they're not supposed to.'

'You don't half talk some toss sometimes,' said Meera. 'I'm stuck.' She had teetered too far forward and was about to fall into the rubbish.

Colin knew how she would react if he put his hands around her waist, then thought: *Sod it,* and grabbed her just as she tipped over.

For once Meera did not complain. He set her upright and was about to dust her down before he realized that would be a step too far.

'What?' she said as he stared at her. 'Have I got something on me?'

'It's just—' Colin swallowed. 'You're still beautiful, even when you've been in the bins.'

'Cheers. I'll file that under Compliments I Never Want to Hear Again.'

'It's just that ever since that night—'

'Colin, give it a rest,' she snapped, then caught herself. 'I just ended my engagement. Give it – some time.'

'Yeah, sure, fair dos, no worries, understood.' He looked up into the darkness of the bridge rafters. 'Dan already searched down below, right? He never misses anything. But he couldn't have gone up there. He's too short to reach.'

Before Meera could stop him, Colin had scrambled up into the corner where the underside of the bridge met the road and was climbing from a drainpipe on to the girders.

'Think you should be doing that with your spatial awareness issues?' Meera called up.

Colin flicked on his torch and shone it around the joists, dislodging a number of diseased-looking birds. 'It stinks of

ammonia up here,' he shouted back. 'There's bits of his overalls still stuck to the girders. Hang on.'

Meera waited while her partner grunted and clattered
around, finally swinging back down in a spray of dried
seagull waste and cascading filth. 'I'm surprised he didn't fall
off his perch earlier,' said Colin.

'You smell of dead people and pigeons,' Meera replied

Colin grinned. 'You smell of cabbages. Now we're even.'

Neither of them saw the shape that divorced itself from the
shadows until it was too late. Colin was suddenly and
resoundingly gonged across the back of the head with a
shovel. He fell forward on to the beach.

Meera ran into the murk beneath the bridge, unsure of
what she had just witnessed. As the figure floundered out
into the water she ran across the stones after it.

Colin pulled himself up on to one knee. 'Meera, don't!' he
yelled, fumbling for his radio. Fraternity answered his call for
assistance.

Bimsley's head was used to being hammered at his boxing
club, so being hit with the flat of a shovel did little more than
make his ears ring. He told Fraternity to get back as quickly
as possible, but his call was drowned out by the start of an
engine. Colin's assailant had climbed into one of the police
launches moored offshore.

Fraternity came running down the steps, passed Colin's
pointed arm and charged straight into the water without
stopping. He made a grab at the launch but was only able to
seize the tarp that partially covered it. There was another
launch right behind, and without a second's hesitation he slit
the canopy with the blade of his Swiss army knife and hauled
himself into the driver's seat. A moment later the second
engine roared into life. Meera was still wondering how this
was possible when he pulled away.

Colin was up on both feet but wavering. 'What does it take
to bring you down?' asked Meera, amazed. He was pointing
at the launches, trying to speak. She knew what he wanted.

'You're not going anywhere,' she warned. 'Not until you've had that checked out.'

'Where the hell did they get keys?' Colin asked, staring after the boats.

'I don't know about the other guy but Fraternity used to be with the Marine Policing Unit,' Meera replied, looking back at the two launches as they headed out into the middle of the river. 'He knows what he's doing.'

'Headache,' said Colin, falling back on to the beach.

Fraternity might have known what he was doing, but he had never piloted a launch unsupervised. This was not a state-of-the-art blue and yellow; those had tall cabins and bristled with technology. This was a decommissioned training cruiser, but it still had some kick.

He brought it up to speed as they passed Victoria Tower Gardens heading towards the Houses of Parliament. A moment later Meera was in his earpiece explaining what had happened.

'He must have experience,' Fraternity shouted back. 'He had the ignition key-code, and these things are light – they're tough to steer against the current. But he doesn't know the river, he's going the wrong way.'

'What do you mean?'

'He's fighting the tide and heading into a busy area. He'd have been better turning around and making for Putney. There are serious undercurrents around the bridges.'

Fraternity tried to keep the rain out of his face and an eye on the boat in front. All he could see was the back of a black plastic raincoat with its hood up. The launch was veering away from the Houses of Parliament, which meant that its pilot knew about the anti-terrorist stakes that prevented boats from coming close without permission. Only the tips of their yellow pennants could be seen near the river's surface, and then only when you were right on top of them.

The wake of the launch swung underneath his bows, nearly

wrenching the wheel from his hands. There were obstacles ahead: Westminster Pier to the left, the London Eye to the right, the *Tattershall Castle*, a pub-cruiser moored off Victoria Embankment, just a little further on. Rain punched into his eyes, combining with the spray from the wake in front.

He needed to cut inside and overtake, but the powerful current was dragging at the launch's steering. The intercom was locked, so he tried the siren to draw any other marine units in the area. There was a staff of nearly eighty working out of Wapping – somebody had to be around.

The boat ahead showed no signs of slowing down, which was bad for both of them. Too many deaths on the Thames were caused by private craft colliding with commercial vessels.

They were approaching one of the trickiest sections of the river. Three crossings clustered next to each other. The misted struts of Hungerford Bridge and the two Golden Jubilee Bridges rose through the rain, then Embankment Pier on the left, Festival Pier on the right, plus various slow-moving river buses, cruise boats and barges, some crossing from one shore to the other, all in the lowered visibility of the downpour. Fraternity had been raised in a West Indian Christian community, and although he was no longer a believer he felt like touching the gold crucifix he still wore beneath his shirt.

The other launch swung hard to port and he only just managed to avoid punching into its wake. Thames regulations were the opposite of those for road driving, and required users to stay right on the river. Now he was being forced over, out into the central channel and the lane of the opposing river traffic. Worse, the dark columns of the pier were dead ahead. His opponent was pushing closer, seizing the advantage.

Fraternity was forced to throttle back as the first launch powered forward. There had to be another way around.

A river bus was turning, churning the water into a greenish plume around its stern, blocking access. The next pier was connected to the shore by a walkway held aloft on thin iron stanchions. There was space enough to get the launch through to the other side, but he would not be able to see the struts until he was almost upon them.

If I make it through this, thought Fraternity, *I'll stay on dry land for the rest of my life.* He accelerated, preparing to cut under the walkway. He knew the metal pillars were hard to spot because they had recently been painted deep green. He stood up, leaning forward, trying to see them. He thought about closing his eyes and hoping for the best. The pier was approaching at tremendous speed. A handful of startled tourists began clearing the walkway as he came near.

The pylons loomed out of the rain just as he was almost upon them. They appeared a lot closer together than he remembered. One was dead ahead. Fighting to correct his path, he oversteered and caught it on his port side. The grinding of iron pillar and fibreglass hull sounded bad, but a moment later he was through the pier and out, drawing parallel with the other launch. He tried to see the pilot's face, but rain and speed denied him a clear view.

Between the golden eagle of the RAF memorial on the north bank to the London Eye on the south, the Thames was suddenly filled with small craft and tourist boats. They were hitting the city's single most crowded marine crossing-point. Everywhere he looked there were river vessels of every size, shape, power and colour. Half a dozen skiffs were filled with schoolchildren, for God's sake.

The launch beside him took the only option possible, fantailing into the tightest U-turn it could manage. Enveloped in a blast of horns it looped to starboard against river rules, still making the turn too wide. Its pilot had not allowed for the incoming powerful current, which broadsided his launch and slowed it down.

Fraternity could see what would happen; the boat would be forced between the barges and the great wall of the embankment. He swung to port, powered up and came in from the other end, blocking its path. There was a rasp of steel and stone from the pursued boat as it hit a buttress protruding from the embankment wall.

Fraternity was only just able to come to a stop before meeting the same fate. The other vessel rocked heavily as the man he had been chasing leaned out to reach the river wall. As the boat moved away beneath him he lost his balance and was dropped into the water.

The DC knew that if he dived in as well he would lose his only advantage. He came alongside the panicking man and signalled to him. The launch was still turning and grinding against the wall. The suspect thrashed in the water as it backed on to him, its spinning propeller now a lethal weapon. As it bore down on him he disappeared from view. Fraternity brought the launch around and grabbed the lifebuoy attached to the boat's hull.

He thought he had the situation under control until he saw the blossom of crimson in the brown water; the object of his pursuit had been sliced by the roaring blades.

24

TOSHERS & MUDLARKS

On Wednesday afternoon, King's Cross was scabbed with clouds the colour of dried blood. As a rainstorm of apocalyptic proportions broke, the two Daves went running for buckets, knowing that the downpour would expose a number of flaws in their window repairs.

'Well, if it isn't James Bond,' said Janice Longbright as Fraternity dripped all over her desk. 'Do you want me to give you a rough estimate of the damage bill?'

'I was trying to save someone's life,' said Fraternity, struggling to get his soaked boots off.

'Your suspect came in DOA. It wasn't your fault.'

'I know that,' said Fraternity quietly.

'Do you want to know who he was? Bill Crooms, fifty-six, an engineer from Manchester down on his luck, staying at a Travelodge on the Euston Road, paying his bills in cash.' She checked her screen. 'Chalk another one up to Old Father Thames. We've got an ID for the body under the bridge, too. Dimitri Gilyov, forty-seven, engineer, born in Fryazino, which is supposedly to the north-east of Moscow, although I couldn't find it. While I'm waiting for further information, read and sign please.' She handed him several pages.

'What's this?' Fraternity asked.

'Your insurance waiver. Don't worry, there'll be lots more paperwork after your interview with Barbara Biddle.'

'Who's she?'

'New internal investigations. It shouldn't be too adversarial. Charing Cross Hospital's Emergency Medical Team say Crooms suffered a massive myocardial infarction. Not his first one. This time he died instantly, thanks to a combination of factors: the stress of a high-speed pursuit and a plunge into freezing water. The head wound probably came just after and finished the job. He had a stratospheric alcohol level in his bloodstream.'

'So I'm off the hook?'

'Not quite. We have to argue that his death wasn't the direct result of police intervention but a consequence of him fleeing the scene after assaulting an officer, which means it'll be treated as misadventure pending further investigation.'

'Surely if he died in the river the matter should go to the Wapping Marine Policing Unit,' said Bryant, appearing in the doorway. He gave his Lorenzo Spitfire a thump and dug for his tobacco pouch. 'They get the corpse but not the case.'

'Can you not knock your pipe out on my lintel?' asked Longbright. 'I'm about to copy them in on Fraternity's statement.'

'Give them more information than they know what to do with.' Bryant made a horrible draining noise on his pipe and squinted through the barrel. 'They pull a hundred bodies out of the water every year so they'll be thrilled to receive tons of extra paperwork. Their job's tough enough as it is. Ask Fraternity here.'

'Yeah,' Fraternity confirmed, 'I saw some stuff dragged out of the mud that I'd rather forget. And it was always cold out on the water, even on sunny days. They're a hard bunch.'

The Marine Police Force had been founded in 1798, and was the oldest in the world. At that time the Pool of London was so congested that ships waited up to two months to leave, so two hundred men armed with muskets, pistols and swords fought the night plunderers and river pirates who pilfered cargo. They wore nickel anchors on their reefer jackets and eventually became the Thames Division of the Metropolitan Police. DC DuCaine had trained with them for six exhausting, freezing weeks.

'They're not happy about you commandeering one of their launches,' said Longbright. 'Where did you get the ignition code?'

'The old boats just have a key,' DuCaine explained. 'We were issued with them during training. I never returned mine.'

'What, and you just happened to have it on you?'

'It's got a really cool anchor on it. I use it as my key ring.'

'I imagine they might want it back now. What about his?'

Fraternity blew his nose noisily. 'No idea. He certainly didn't know the river, that's for sure.'

'Did you know it's where we get the term "police station" from?' said Bryant out of the blue. 'From the Marine Police Force. If a craft is "on station" it's anchored. And "on the beat" – that comes from the beating of oars in river police boats.'

Longbright looked at the man she had known all of her working life in puzzlement. Today he was back to his usual infuriatingly random, lateral-thinking self. Yet he had failed to attend his appointment for a new MRI scan and was flagrantly disobeying orders to stay put.

'Connections,' Bryant continued, 'where are they? Crooms and Gilyov were both engineers. Did they know each other? Were they friends, did they work together, live in the same area?'

'Until two months ago Crooms was doing contract work as an automotive mechanic based out of Dubai,' said Longbright. 'We've got nothing on Gilyov except that he was born in Russia and was carrying out electrical work here in London for corporate clients. His last employer says he failed to turn up for work three weeks ago.'

'Nobody reported it?' asked Fraternity.

'What, electrician fails to turn up for job?' said Longbright. 'Are you having a laugh?' She checked her screen. 'Gilyov has no family here. Like Crooms he was broke and living in a cheap hotel. Dan is covering both sites.'

'Then maybe they've got nothing to do with Dalladay,' said Bryant, 'and Gilyov's left hand just happened to wash up near her body.' From a man who spent most of his time trying to join together disparate events, this was an atypical remark.

'So we go back to concentrating on Dalladay?'

'I didn't say that they weren't associates, Janice,' Bryant warned. 'Just that they weren't directly involved with the drowned girl.'

'I'm sorry, I'm confused,' said Longbright. 'If they had nothing to do with Dalladay, what connects them?'

'Why, the river, of course,' said Bryant, waving his pipe. 'And it's going to help us find out what's going on.'

'I wish I had your faith,' said Longbright, 'but it's a bit like expecting the pavement to tell you why a bloke was stabbed on the street.'

'Exactly,' Bryant agreed, lighting his pipe.

Out in the corridor, one of the Daves was rehanging a grim sepia painting of a scowling, top-hatted Sir Edward Henry, the police commissioner who had introduced fingerprinting and police dogs. 'The old man's back on form, then,' he told Meera. 'He's in there arguing with everyone. I don't know why he wants this ugly old git put up on the wall. Is it valuable?'

'It's crooked, like you, and it's history, which is what you'll be in a minute if you don't watch it,' said Meera.

John May opened his office window and coughed out of it. Bryant's pipeful of Ancient Mariner Mentholated Rolling

Tobacco was filling the room with pale green smoke. Some months earlier, May had been forced to take the batteries out of the alarm to stop it from constantly blaring out through the building. *I'm a victim of passive smoking,* he thought, *and passive lunacy. He poisons me with his tobacco and fills my head with miscellaneous rubbish.*

'What snakes through the heart of this investigation?' Bryant continued, unconcerned about whether anyone was listening to him. 'The Thames. The Silent Highway. Liquid history. Think about the crimes that have been committed on it, in it or beside it, the livelihoods that depended on it, all the dock complexes, London and St Katharine's, Surrey Commercial, India and Millwall, the Royals and Tilbury. Between them they took up an area of three thousand acres. Thirty miles of quays and dry docks. Think about the toshers, the mudlarks, the scuffle-hunters, the lumpers—'

'Nope,' said May, 'it's gone.'

'What?'

'The signal.' He rotated an index finger at his forehead. 'The decoding apparatus that translates your transmissions from gobbledegook into something my dullard brain can process. Who are these people you're on about, and of what possible use are they to us?'

'It's simple,' said Bryant, warming to his subject. 'Toshers were sewer-hunters. They worked the outlets at the edge of the Thames, trudging through the glutinous mud with eight-foot poles that they used to extricate themselves. They were after copper mostly, but iron, rope, bones, anything they could use or sell. They had names like One-Eyed George and Short-Arse Jack, and sometimes they found gold sovereigns, silver cutlery, jewels and necklaces that had belonged to the brothel-ladies of Southwark.'

'OK,' said May slowly. 'And mudlarks?'

'They were lower down the scale. They lived in tunnels or on the foreshore itself. Wretched old women clad in rags, fighting off rats to hunt for dropped copper nails and tools.

Scuffle-hunters pretended to look for work in the over-crowded docks, causing fights so that they could steal imported items and hide them in their long aprons. And lumpers—'

'All right, I get it, but listen to me, Arthur, you do under-stand that it was all a long time ago, don't you?'

'Yes, of course,' his partner replied irritably. 'I'm not an idiot.'

'There's no Pool of London any more. These people don't exist now. The Thames merely provided Dalladay with the manner of her death, so all of these potty facts you trot out are of no use. They're just local colour. If you put them in your memoirs an editor would write "irrelevant" beside them in red ink and make you cut them out.'

'Exactly, which is why they're so important,' said Bryant. 'It's the irrelevancies that lend us an understanding of the world.' He raised his forefinger. 'Here's an interesting fact.'

May groaned.

'When the BBC needed to re-use videotape in the 1960s they had to decide which programmes to wipe. They kept the Shakespeare productions and taped over the "irrelevant" modern dramas. Guess which would have been more useful to us today? Here.' From beneath his desk he dragged a length of chain and dumped it on to his blotter.

'Is that what I think it is?' asked May. 'The reason why we have evidence bags is to stop you sticking your fat fingers all over things.'

'The connection between Dalladay's wrist and an iron ring set in a slab of concrete,' said Bryant. 'Dan couldn't find out anything else, but then he was looking for relevant facts, where and when it was purchased and so on.'

'What's your point?'

He held the chain high and twirled it. 'What do you think of it?'

'What do you mean? It's a spivvy silver chain with a silver moon on one end.'

'But it's not hers. It's an Arabic man's neck-chain, John. You just don't see it as one because it's not an English style of male jewellery. The links are old but the one that opens is modern. Maybe the original was broken so someone repurposed it. If the killer didn't want her to escape, why not use a proper chain and padlock with a key, then throw the key away?'

May found himself growing exasperated. 'I don't know, Arthur. Maybe he was improvising.'

'Try again. Who would wear something like this now?'

'I don't know – someone who likes old jewellery—'

'But not a collector. Look at the scratches and dents on it. So it has sentimental meaning rather than monetary value. Someone changed the lock – why? So he could give it to a girl? Or did it belong to a *she*? Dalladay was pregnant but by whom was she loved?'

'I don't see where you're going with this,' said May, waving away smoke.

'What did I tell you about the river? The Tamesas, the Dark Water. It attracts suicides. I think she killed herself.'

'That's ridiculous,' May exploded. 'No one in their right mind—'

'She wasn't in her right mind, was she? That's why there was only one set of footprints going towards the tideline, and why no one saw her – because if they did, all they saw was a girl walking along the shore. What if she acted on the spur of the moment and used the chain from around her own neck? It bothered me right from the start that only her left wrist was tied. Try locking this with your hands held together; it's almost impossible.' He hefted it in his palm. 'What do we know about Dalladay, really? That she was an easily influenced young woman who failed to find her place in the world. She was frightened she was going to change her mind about committing suicide, so she chose a method of death that took away the option of escape.'

'Wait – if it really was a suicide that means there was no

murderer, and *that* means this other thing, the drowning of Dimitri Gilyov, isn't related.'

'Oh, I didn't say there wasn't a murderer,' said Bryant with a mysterious smile.

25

MOTHER & DAUGHTER

It seemed like a lifetime ago since the crazy witch-woman in the Rainbow Theatre had foiled Ali's communication system with the aid of a pair of scissors. Much had happened since then. Cassie had always known that the faith-healing racket would turn out to be a waste of time and resources. The problem, she knew, was that they'd had no way of tapping into the ministry's congregations. Most of those who'd attended Ali's events came because they were lonely and credulous, and they were usually so short of cash that the Ministry of Compassion had struggled to sell so much as a T-shirt after each show. Finsbury Park wasn't America, where the tradition of evangelism had deep roots within communities and the congregations had deeper pockets.

Cassie was worried. She rarely turned to her mother for advice, and doing so made her feel uncomfortable. She checked her watch and knew that Marion would be entering the restaurant right now. Her mother was always on time. Today she was dressed entirely in purple, which was unfortunate because she clashed horribly with the orange leather banquettes.

'I don't know why you had to pick this place, darling,'

Marion said with distaste, settling herself gingerly. 'No one would be seen dead in here.' She had missed the point; Cassie had chosen it precisely because it was unfashionable. The only diners were a group of dough-faced Russian men hammering vodkas beneath a vast golden chandelier.

'I'm not here to network, Mother,' replied Cassie. 'I couldn't talk to you at the centre.'

'Why, do you have a problem? I thought you were both doing very well. I haven't been able to open a magazine this month without seeing the pair of you smiling out.'

'As usual you're exaggerating.' Cassie poured herself water and gave her mother wine. 'We've had three mentions, not exactly in-depth pieces.'

'Lifestyle magazines are terribly important to your potential clients,' said Marion, accepting the glass. 'Have you looked around the Thames Valley lately? All those grand riverside mansions full of social-climbing foreigners? Being English is a commodity that they want to buy into. They'll always be outsiders, of course, but they can at least enjoy the illusion. And setting up a place like Life Options is a part of that.'

'Ali isn't English,' Cassie reminded her.

Having erased her own background details many years ago, Marion waved the thought aside. 'No, but he gives a very good impression of being so. They always do, the intelligent migrants, and Ali plays the game well. Remember Mohammed Al-Fayed? The poor little shopkeeper thought if he spent enough he'd become respectable one day. He genuinely didn't understand why the establishment considered him vulgar.'

'Ali doesn't have some outdated dream of being English. He just wants to make money.' Cassie called over a confused-looking waiter. She did not want to spend the lunch justifying her partner's motives.

'English property is so desirable these days,' said Marion wistfully. 'The wives are stuck at home with the children and their nannies, bored out of their minds. They don't care what they spend their money on so long as it fills up their afternoons. I should know. You should see how much my premium phone lines bring in these days.' She briefly engaged the waiter's attention. 'Just a green salad.'

Cassie had always known that her mother did not really believe in the pseudo-spiritual books she sold. Perhaps she had at first, but these days her website and cable show shifted tons of junk jewellery, lifestyle-enhancing potions and lucky gemstones, even exclusive 'magical' artworks that were supposed to bring their owners wealth and good fortune. They were painted by gangs of children in India because HM Revenue and Customs weren't interested in glittery daubs from ten-year-olds, bundled in cheap brown paper and posted to a school where Marion collected them, repackaged and resold them for increasingly absurd amounts.

'What's your financial situation like?' Marion asked after the waiter had departed. 'Is your cash flow OK?'

'The expansion plans are on schedule and we've revised our projections upwards. Freddie is fully on board, although I don't think he understands the extent of his liability. He just reads the bottom line on his loans.' Cassie pulled a copy of *Hard Press* from her bag and slipped it across the table to her mother. 'I need to know if you've seen this.'

Marion examined the article. 'I read something similar in the *Evening Standard* last night. Who is she?'

'Her name is Lynsey Dalladay. She's enrolled as a client at the institute. Freddie introduced her.'

'So what? You must have hundreds of clients by now.'

'After the news got out about her death I checked which courses she was taking. She only signed for the ones which were led by Ali.'

Marion's Botoxed brow furrowed as far as her nerve endings would allow. 'I'm sorry, darling, I don't see what you're driving at.'

'Read the rest of the piece,' she suggested. 'Lynsey was pregnant.'

'Oh God.' She put her nails to her cheek.

'Last night Ali told me he'd slept with her. He said she kept hanging around and suggesting they go for a drink—'

'And what, the poor provoked man didn't have the will-power to turn her down? What did you say?'

'We had a fight about it. I told him I'd continue to handle the schedules and the accounts and that we would still be partners on the condition that he stayed away from the clients in future.'

'So you're not – together?' It pained Marion to ask anything personal. 'You know I never pry.'

Cassie turned over a fork, refusing to catch her mother's eye. 'I suppose I was infatuated at first. He was unlike anyone I'd ever met. But things change when you work together.'

'What did he have to say for himself about this girl?'

'He said he could see into her soul.'

'I thought he only believed in making money.'

'So did I. He promised to keep more distance between himself and his pupils.'

'And it only took a death to wake him up to that? You're on to a very good thing here, Cassandra – we all are. He can't make it work without you, and you can't do it without him.'

Cassie leaned forward, lowering her voice. 'You're missing the point. The girl is *dead*. She'd been staying with him.'

'Ali? Why?'

'She left Freddie. Ali agreed to put her up for a few days. She has other places to stay, but she asked to be with Ali.'

'When was this?'

'A couple of weeks ago. He said she didn't come home on Sunday, so he assumed she was at her own flat. She has a history of not sticking around. One of the courses she was taking involved going down to the river's edge, specifically near the stretch of water where she was found.'

Marion's eyes widened. 'My God, you don't think Ali did it?'

'I don't know. How can I know something like that? Hell, I can't afford to believe he did. What does such a person even look like? I don't understand her state of mind. What if she threatened him? She could have wrecked everything.'

'You're talking about—' The word *murder* stained the air between them. 'How long is it going to be before the police uncover the connection between her and the centre?'

'I don't suppose it's the most obvious lead to follow up, but it won't take them long. They'll want to talk to Ali.'

'And what if they ask him to take a paternity test?'

'I've done some checking online.' Cassie took out the small leather notebook she always carried and opened it. 'They'll need what's called a court-admissible test, where the collection of samples is carried out through a controlled chain-of-custody procedure – it requires a third party to act as a witness and to verify the authenticity of the samples. It's almost impossible to cheat because the swabs will be taken by a qualified medic. The only thing that can go wrong is if the swabs are contaminated.'

'Wait, stop this.' Marion made sure the waiter wasn't within earshot. 'You're talking about breaking the law. I mean *really* breaking the law.'

'I'm just trying to explain what we're facing,' said Cassie.

'You mean after all your years of hard work it could blow up in your face, just because Ali isn't able to resist the advances of some stupid lovestruck girl?'

'I'm just saying that we have to be aware of what could happen, that's all.'

'Have you spoken to that ghastly little money-man to see what he thinks?'

'Freddie told me the police have already been to see him. Obviously they uncovered his connection to Dalladay at once, and he had no reason to lie to them. He mustn't find out that Ali's the father. If he gets wind of anything involving the police he'll pull the plug on us. We can't afford to have any kind of scandal attaching itself to the centre. Freddie's not too bright but he's got a sixth sense about business opportunities. If he thinks there's going to be trouble he'll pull out his stake and vanish, and we'll be left twisting in the wind.'

'So what are you going to do?' asked Marion.

'Me?' Cassie looked surprised. 'You're in this as well.'

'I'm just one of the resident instructors – what do you expect me to do?'

'I don't know. We need some kind of a game plan.'

'You've got to protect your asset,' said Marion. 'Whatever he's done, you have to make sure it never gets out.'

'How do I do that?' At moments like this Cassie took her mother's advice. Marion was a survivor.

'First you have to totally disconnect yourself from this girl,' she said. 'Go through every piece of paperwork you've got and make sure there's nothing that could get either of you into trouble. The centre has to be clean. I may have to take a few of my products off the shelves. And as soon as you've done that, talk to Ali and brief him. He has to understand the devious ways in which the British police can work.'

'What do you mean?' Cassie asked.

'I already had someone from an independent unit visiting me,' Marion explained. 'A funny little old man asking a lot of peculiar questions about the Thames. I tried to find out what he actually wanted but he wouldn't be pinned down. At first I thought he wasn't all there, but now it looks like he was playing a much smarter game. The police are very fond of sending round people like that. They'll try to catch you both off your guard.' Marion thought for a moment. 'You need to find a way of controlling Freddie Cooper. He has to be kept away from the centre, so maybe he only gets his information via you from now on. Hold any future meetings off-site and limit his channels of access. And let me do some checking on Ali. He won't be expecting me. If I think he might have had a hand in this girl's death, we'll decide what steps to take next.'

Marion North had a sharp, analytical brain. Cassie knew that if there was anything unpleasant to be discovered, she'd find it and know exactly how to use the knowledge.

26

EBB & FLOW

Freddie Cooper stood at the river edge and looked down. The tide was at its highest point, so that when a police launch passed it sent water on to the flagstone walkway. 'I've been trying to talk to Ali all day but I just keep getting his voice-mail,' he said. 'Do you know where he is?'

Cassie was walking back from lunch when she took Cooper's call. She tried to sound calm. 'He's taking classes today,' she replied. 'One of our instructors didn't come in this morning. You can tell me anything you'd say to him, Freddie, you know that. In fact it's probably easier to go through me. I'm handling the business plan.'

'I wanted to let him know that the money made it through the transfer and is now in your account,' said Cooper. 'When are we going to go over the plans?'

'How about this weekend?' Cassie knew that Cooper was anxious to start the franchise roll-out as soon as possible. He had already told her that every day they waited was a day's profit lost. He was hungry, and that made him eager to extend credit to them. 'Where are you?' she asked.

'In Greenwich, seeing my little boy.'

'Oh, I didn't know you had—'

'Yeah, his mum and me, we got divorced when he was three. I came down to the river. I can't stop thinking about her, Cassie. The police don't seem to be any further on than they were two days ago. I told her about the centre. Was she taking any of the classes?'

In the middle of Notting Hill, Cassie stopped on the pavement and held her breath. It was imperative that Cooper did not make the connection. If he did, he'd realize that the police would be interviewing Ali in the near future. The Life Options brand was a cash cow, and if everything went according to plan there would soon be one in every major city in Britain. It needed to be rolled out smoothly. There was too much at stake for anything to go wrong now.

'I don't believe she was taking any,' she said, trying to sound as relaxed as possible. 'I can check if you like, but I'm pretty sure—'

'There's no need,' said Cooper, to her relief. It didn't sound as if he'd realized the possible consequences of his question. 'I should let you get on. Tell Ali the good news about the money, and I'll see you at the weekend.'

Cooper rang off and went back to staring into the olivine water as the wake of a passing tourist boat sent waves to shore. He tried to think everything through. The latest tranche of his invested cash had been sent to the Life Options account. It looked like smooth sailing from here.

'Why don't you let me get that?' asked May, watching with trepidation as his partner stood on one leg at the top of his library steps, trying to reach a box on top of his bookcase.

'I'm barmy, not paralysed,' Bryant snapped. 'And I feel eerily back on form today, so watch it.'

'What are you trying to reach?'

'Spoons,' said Bryant through clenched dentures. 'I electroplated some and put them up here where no one could get at them. They were the control part of the experiment, obviously. I buried the others in my window box. I have this theory that— Ah, here they are. Now I just need to compare the two sets.'

Half a dozen silver dessert spoons bounced off Bryant's head and clattered to the floor. He nearly lost his balance, but managed to hang on to an enormous leather-bound book that slowly divorced itself from its placement in the bookshelf. 'That's a piece of luck, just the thing I was looking for,' Bryant had time to say before the book came free, sending it and him flying. He landed on his armchair, but the book split its spine and cascaded pages all over the room. Along with it came several other volumes, including *Penny's From Heaven: Girls Who Returned from the Dead*, *Behind You!: Famous Pantomime Ghosts* and *The Encyclopaedia of International Shoes* (missing one section: 'Espadrilles–Estonia').

May bit his tongue and resisted the temptation to yell. He couldn't tell if Bryant was being his usual eccentric self or if his mind was taking another left turn into Narnia. 'Next time, just ask me to help you,' he said testily.

'I was looking for one of the volumes of my Dead Diary,' Bryant explained, struggling back out of the armchair. He had long kept daily files of all those who died in suspicious, inexplicable or unusual circumstances in the Greater London area, but several of the earlier volumes had become unusable. Crippen had been sick in one and another had become impregnated with potassium chlorate, which made it unstable and highly explosive.

With a sigh, May helped him gather up the pages and reassemble them. 'There's a section somewhere on unattributed deaths occurring in disputed jurisdictions,' Bryant explained. 'Obviously, that includes the Thames.'

'I don't understand why you think the river is so key to this,' said May.

'There are two answers to that.' Bryant shuffled his loose pages back into shape. 'One, London has become the most observed city in the world, and the only place where a killer may now ply his grisly trade unseen is on the river and its shores. It gives him free rein to work anywhere within seven counties along a two-hundred-and-fifteen-mile length, from the Thames Head in Gloucestershire, at its reaches, on any of eighty islands and around any of forty-seven locks, all the way to the Sheerness estuary, which is five miles across. Arguably he could go further to Whitstable, eighteen miles across, but I start to count that as open sea.'

'OK,' May agreed, marvelling at Bryant's continued ability to marshal figures. 'What's the other answer?'

'OK, Point B is slightly more esoteric. The Thames holds the collective memory of the city and all its dwellers, and there's a long history of belief in the idea that it's a sacred river granting death and rebirth. If someone as vulnerable as Lynsey Dalladay came to believe that this was true and she really thought she had wrecked her life, she just might be persuaded to kill herself in order to attain rebirth and a fresh start.'

'You mean persuaded by someone else.'

'Yes, someone powerful enough to have a hold over her. We have witness statements from Freddie Cooper and Joe Easter, the barman at the Cossack Club. They both stated that she wished she could wipe the slate clean and begin her life over again. Do you think that's feasible?'

'When you put it like that, yes,' May agreed. 'There's precedent for it. Jonestown Syndrome.'

'Good.' Bryant slapped his hand on the huge unkempt tome before him. 'So now I want to look through the Dead Diary and see if there's anyone else who might fall into this category. Surely the best way to murder someone is to first persuade them that their life is worthless.'

'Why do I always underestimate you, Arthur?'

'We inhabit slightly different worlds, that's all. You're like the spoons that were up there, the control part of our grand experiment.' Bryant began pulling out selected pages and laying them on his desk. 'All right, off with you and let me be for a while. This will take the rest of the day and the best part of the night.'

'How is he?' May came out to find Raymond Land wringing his hands in the hallway. 'I heard a lot of crashing about.'

'Well, he seems quite normal,' said May, pulling the door to behind him. 'I mean in his abnormal way.'

'Why, what's he doing?'

'Going through historical files. And examining spoons.'

'Oh. So he really *is* back to normal, then. I wonder how long it will last this time.' He saw the crooked painting of Sir Edward Henry on the wall and flinched. 'God, that's not one of his relatives, is it?'

'Arthur's safe so long as he stays in there,' said May, 'but there's no way of telling how long this current mood will hold.'

'I wish I knew what was going on,' Land complained. 'Three bodies pulled out of the river in three days: it's not exactly our finest moment, is it?'

'The Dimitri Gilyov killing may not be connected,' May pointed out, 'and Crooms's death was Misadventure. There's no reason to suppose he even knew Gilyov. He could have been set up.'

'What do you mean?' asked Land, confused.

'For all we know someone may have sent him there to check on the site. It crossed my mind that it may have been a drop-point for drugs, and that Gilyov was part of a deal that went bad. That could be an entirely separate situation.'

'I hate it when things get over-complicated,' Land complained. 'What am I going to tell Darren Link?'

'Don't tell him anything,' May advised. 'As far as he's concerned we're still following leads and making progress.'

'Couldn't you do it? He's on his way here right now.'

'I'm afraid this one's yours,' said May, checking his tie in the hallway mirror. 'I'm off out.'

Land was aghast. He pointed back at the door to the

detectives' office. 'You can't leave me with Link and your partner. Is he even safe in there?'

'Just so long as you keep the doors and windows shut.'

'Where are you going?'

'To see Freddie Cooper. He called to say he's remembered something that might be of use.'

'Couldn't you do it later?' Land pleaded.

'His office isn't far away. I'll only be a few minutes.' May raised a firm fist. 'Put your foot down, Raymond. Be resolute. Don't let Link bully you.'

'He always did when we were at school together,' muttered Land. 'He used to hit me around the head with a sock full of conkers. I joined the force to get away from people like him.'

But the hallway was empty; May had gone. Land stepped around the fresh hole in the floorboards created by the two Daves and found Crippen looking up at him with wise eyes.

'And you're no bloody help either,' he said, returning to his office to prepare for the worst.

Freddie Cooper had a floor of an unrestored building on Shaftesbury Avenue just past Cambridge Circus, where fully grown plane trees shielded the windows of the upper levels and dappled the pavements in summer. Even in November they sheltered the route and helped pedestrians to forget the vast new development that stood there.

The ward of St Giles was one of London's peculiarities: opaque, forgotten and remarkably unchanged for most of its life. Its High Street had seen the Roman army march down it to the City of London. In the Middle Ages its best-known public house, the Angel Inn, which stood beside the equally venerable St Giles-in-the-Fields church, had served as the last watering hole for those to be hanged a mile west at Tyburn Tree. The church, the pub and the street survived, but now they had been rendered even more invisible opposite the 134,000 green, orange, red and yellow glazed terracotta tiles that covered Central St Giles, the towering development newly wedged into this unphotogenic corner of the West End.

John May turned up his collar and hurried across its rainswept plaza, locating Cooper's address in the surviving terrace over the road. The entrepreneur met him in a dank grey lobby and guided him to the lift. On the top floor a staircase extended to the separate part of the roof.

'I didn't want to touch anything,' Cooper said, leading the way. 'My folks owned this building back when the street was really run down. I held on to the flat after they sold the rest. Lynsey didn't like the house in De Beauvoir. She spent her life shuttling between properties, unable to settle. She didn't really have a base.'

They had reached the end of a bland pastel office corridor. Cooper pushed open the pale oak door to reveal an unchanged part of the original structure. A hall of bare boards and stripped brick opened out into a gaudily decorated living room with windows overlooking the tops of the plane trees.

'She kept some of her stuff here,' he explained.

May looked around. 'Why didn't you tell us this earlier?'

Cooper looked amazed. 'Why would I want to tell you everything? It didn't seem important. Anyway, I assumed she'd been at her own flat, but I think she must have come here to get some clothes 'cause one of her bags is missing. She left bags everywhere.'

'So what made you change your mind about contacting me?'

'I was down by the river earlier, thinking about what she said – something about wishing the river could take her out to sea. She talked so much, I didn't listen most of the time.'

He led the way to a small bedroom with built-in wardrobes, opened one and pointed down. In the back was an expensive black leather travelling bag. May looked about, found a shoe-horn and lifted the bag out by its handles. 'May I?'

'There was a canvas holdall too. I have no idea what she stored in any of them.'

May removed a neatly folded handkerchief and used it to

pull open the top zip. Inside was a jumble of unironed clothes, shoes, make-up bottles, cigarettes and a smaller case stuffed with paperwork, which he took back to the lounge table and carefully laid out. His show of keeping his prints away from the collection was performed mainly for Cooper's benefit.

There were receipts from the Cossack Club, torn-up bank statements, a couple of sketchbooks filled with unfinished spidery drawings, as if she had suddenly lost interest in them, and a plastic folder of what appeared to be coursework.

Unclipping it, May read for a minute and held the top page by its edges. 'Life Options – what's that?'

Cooper squinted at the heading. 'It's a new company, like a spa, holistic stuff, not my sort of thing but it's already making good money. I'm funding their expansion. We're planning to roll it out as a national chain next summer.'

'And she went there, did she?'

'I don't know. I guess so.'

'What, you really don't know or you don't want to tell me?'

Cooper gave him a dry look. 'I think she was planning to enrol there.'

'So you told her about the place? She didn't just happen to pick up a brochure for a company you're investing in?'

'I guess I must have said something. I'm not good with details.'

'It looks like she was thinking of taking an awful lot of courses,' said May, flipping through the pages. '"Energy Attunement for Spiritual Development", "Emotional Healing", "The Healing Power of Crystals", "Enneagrams & Metaphysical Communication", "Chakras & Auras", "Inner Child Rehabilitation". It's starting to make sense now.'

'What do you mean?' asked Cooper, looking over his shoulder.

'These are expensive sessions. Maybe hostessing at the Cossack Club paid for them. Did you give her money?'

'I tried but she wouldn't take it. She didn't tell me she was planning to take all this stuff.'

'You never talked about what she did, where she went?'

'I'm not one of those blokes who talks to birds, OK?' said Cooper. 'She never told me much about anything.'

'She talked, but you didn't listen.'

'Yeah well, she didn't make a lot of sense. Of course I feel bad about what happened.'

'Mr Cooper, I've done some checking on you,' said May. 'You weren't exactly sitting at home pining while she was disappearing for days at a time.'

'Of course not,' said Cooper. 'I move in a lot of circles, attend a lot of social events.'

'We're not talking about black-tie stuff.'

'No, more like bars and clubs, hanging out with the right people.'

'Why?'

Cooper looked puzzled. 'What do you mean, why? What kind of question is that? To raise money, to move it around, to find investment opportunities—' He was at a loss for words.

'And that makes you happy.'

'I don't understand what you're getting at.'

'I mean here was a beautiful girl you say you were in love with. She goes off the rails and you don't prioritize her welfare.'

Cooper smirked. He looked like a schoolboy sharing internet porn. 'She was hot but she wasn't going to be around for ever, if you know what I mean. There are plenty of others ready to take her place.'

May tried not to judge, but he really did not like Cooper. London was full of shapeshifting wolves who never dreamt of taking regular work when there was easy prey around. He held up the wad of papers. 'You honestly think there's money in this company? Selling fantasies?'

Cooper ran a hand through his hair. 'I see the bottom line. Their business plan makes sense and the time is right. There's a Middle Eastern guy who conducts the courses. He could sell anything to anyone. He has a business partner, a woman with a head for making money. I like her; she thinks like a bloke. They have a very franchisable brand. Word's getting around, so they need to roll it out fast.'

'How much are you in for?'

Cooper shook his head. 'Everything, man.'

'You know I have to check them out.'

'Hey, I showed you her stuff because you said you wanted to know where she'd been, that's all. Don't drag me any further into this.'

'Let me make it simple for you,' said May, stepping closer. 'You have no way of explaining why a woman with whom you were intimate died. Her family and friends have no explanations either, but everyone seems to think it was inevitable that something bad would happen to her. Perhaps we should just leave it there . . . What do you think?'

Cooper shrugged. 'I don't know what to say to that.'

'How about telling me you're angry?' said May. 'If it was my girl I'd want more than justice – I'd be ready to kill someone. But I'm not you, I'm a public servant. I wait for bad things to happen and try to stop them from happening again. That's how it works in my world; you can be walking over a bridge when someone coming the other way decides to throw you off. I only get the call after you've drowned. Wouldn't you want me to take someone down for it?'

'Some people bring bad karma on themselves,' said Cooper. 'You didn't know her. It was like she deliberately used up all her options.'

'So there was nothing left to do but die?' May shook his head. 'You of all people should understand the difference between victims and predators. Sometimes it's hard to tell which is which. Last year I heard about a woman in King's Cross whose husband beat her up nearly every Saturday night. She wouldn't leave him or go to a refuge. He thumped her so hard with a saucepan that he broke the handle off, then sat next to her body eating pizza and watching football for the next three days. She nearly died. In his defence he said she'd told him that she didn't deserve any better. Victim status is learned from family members during childhood. If it isn't stopped it just gets passed down.'

'You think I don't know anything about victims?' asked Cooper hotly. 'You should have met my folks, man. They're dead now, and good riddance. And maybe you should talk to Lynsey's parents. See how caring they were.' Cooper held his gaze with calm arrogance.

'I will, and then I'll talk to this wellbeing place. If anyone there is connected to the case in any way you may find yourself with a bad investment on your hands.' He held up the schedule. 'I'll hang on to this.'

On his way out, he called Longbright. 'Janice, see what you can dig up on a health spa called Life Options, based in SW1. Dalladay was signing up for courses there.'

27

WATERS & VAPOURS

For a minute Arthur Bryant entertained the notion of knotting sheets together, but the only bed linen available was in the Evidence Room and had belonged to Coatsleeve Charlie, the bogus butler of Belgravia, and the last thing Bryant wanted to do was muddy this story's flow with an apocryphal and highly libellous tributary. So he just put on his coat, switched his slippers for boots, pocketed his sandwiches, knotted his scarf over his nose and crept out of his office as soon as Longbright was called to a meeting.

'You off out again, Mr B.?' said one of the Daves, sitting on a camp stool by the hole in the floor brewing coffee.

'You haven't seen me,' said Bryant, waving his hands in an ethereal fashion. 'I'm here in the building somewhere but you're not sure where.'

'Do you want one of us to come with you?'

'There wouldn't be much point,' Bryant replied. 'What's the other one going to say if Janice asks where I am?'

'Well,' said Dave One, pointing to his mate, 'he always lies but I always tell the truth. So if she asks him where you are, he'll say that I said you're in the building. And if she asks me where you are, I'll say that my mate says you're in the building. So it's a win-win.'

'But one of you will be out,' Bryant reminded him.

'Yes, but it won't make any difference which of us is out.'

'Yes it will,' said Dave Two.

'You two are wasted here,' said Bryant. 'You should apply for the CID.'

As he moved through the sifting rain across the grey striped concourse of King's Cross Station, munching a last triangle of sandwich (fish paste and banana chutney), Bryant considered suicide. Not his own, for he had lately become far too cheerful for such gloomy thoughts. Rather, he was thinking about suicide and water. The Thames was not Lake Windermere, placid and depthless. It was a hazardous, occluded and somewhat repellent maelstrom, not perhaps at its shoreline, where he was now convinced that Lynsey Dalladay had lost her wits and taken her own life, but certainly in its main channel, where for all he knew the engineer Dimitri Gilyov might have chucked himself, although that would hardly have explained how he came to be lodged in the struts of a bridge.

The Dead Diary had made him think of all this. In its pages he had found reports of other strange deaths: drowned bodies pulled from the depths in unusual circumstances. There was the Olympic swimmer who waded into the high tidewater at Rotherhithe and never came out, and the Japanese couple crossing Tower Bridge on a sightseeing tour who somehow managed to fall in together and drown. These were high-profile cases with national attention that yielded rational explanations: the swimmer had discovered he was suffering from motor neurone disease, and the Japanese pair had fallen after climbing out on to one of the parapets to photograph themselves with the tower in the background.

But there were other, quieter deaths that barely scratched a rune-mark on the stones of the city. In September a well-off middle-aged lady from Chiswick named Angela Curtis had jumped into the waters at Hammersmith for no apparent reason. Bryant's attention had been drawn by the fact that the profile on her police report bore a remarkable similarity to that of Lynsey Dalladay's. Mrs Curtis had wedged her foot under a rock, either accidentally or in an effort to prevent herself from changing her mind about suicide. She had recently divorced and moved in with her daughter in Oxford, but the daughter now worked in Great Portland Street, managing a dress company called Coco Bean.

Bryant took the Victoria line to Oxford Circus and walked back to the company's wholesale shop. When he entered, stepping carefully between white-lace bridal gowns, two young women so thin that they resembled praying mantises came forward to shoo him out.

'No no no,' said one briskly, 'if you're here about the bins we've had them taken off the pavement.'

Bryant removed his PCU card and held it at arm's length to ward them off.

'Oh, I'm frightfully sorry,' she said, reading it. 'There was a tramp here last week going through our rubbish—'

'And you thought I was a paraffin,' said Bryant, irritated. 'Next time I'll wear my Chanel. Meanwhile, I'd like to speak to Jade Curtis. Is she here?'

'I'll get her,' said one of the mantises, beating an awkward retreat.

They sat together at a tiny white plastic table in the back of the store. Although the room was overheated, Bryant felt an odd chill. Jade Curtis was a pleasant-faced ebony-haired woman in her late twenties who looked as if she hadn't slept well for six months.

'I blame myself for not taking control of the situation earlier,' she said. 'When someone you love dies like that, well, of course you examine the past. If there's anything you can tell me—'

'I'm afraid I'm not here with answers,' said Bryant. 'I'm

working on a case unconnected with your mother's death.'

'Then I don't understand—'

'At least it seems to be unconnected,' Bryant added hastily. 'It may be nothing, but if you could hear me out? I understand that your mother underwent psychological evaluation sometime after she went to live in Thailand?'

'How could you know that?'

'I checked her medical records.'

'I thought doctors couldn't talk about their patients.'

'Your mother's death required an inquest. What did she do while she was in the Far East?'

Jade ran a piece of silk material over her fingers, back and forth, a nervous habit. 'She was always very driven. She staged fashion events around the world, and the pressure eventually got to her. After my father left she moved to Phuket and lived there for a while. When she returned she suffered a nervous breakdown. She was put on medication to prevent any further episodes, but the regime was difficult because it made her put on weight. She tried every alternative therapy under the sun to replace the pills, but nothing worked. She was very unhappy about that.'

'You think it was enough to make her want to kill herself?'

'I talked to her doctor and he said no. But I know that without her meds she became very depressed.'

'What actually happened on the night she died?'

'She went out with her dog, a Staffordshire bull terrier – she often walked it late. She would drive to the towpath on the south side of the river at Hammersmith. The police thought she might have slipped and fallen in but there were no unusual marks on the bank. And there was a big flat rock on her foot. The police said she'd placed it there. I don't under-stand. How could this have a bearing on any other case?'

'Would you say your mother was a pragmatic woman?' asked Bryant.

'Very much so. Why?'

'It's just that she did some things which were out of character.' He checked his notes. 'Joining an anti-capitalist protest group, travelling alone around Greece, becoming a Buddhist. Would you say she felt lost?'

'No.' Jade shook her head. 'She just wanted to try all of the things she couldn't do when she was still with my father. She was a happy woman, full of passions and interests.'

'Could you give me the name of her doctor?' Bryant asked. 'I'd like to know a little more about her medication regime.'

'I can do better than that,' Jade said. 'I have all her pills right here, together with her medical notes. They were just returned to me. I didn't know what to do with them.' She rose and came back with a clear plastic bag. 'Please take them if you think they'll help you in any way. Just let me know if you find anything. I loved her very much.'

Bryant made one more stop before heading back to the unit. The last time he had met Darcy Sarto he had spilled a glass of Rioja down Sarto's shirt at a book launch, not because the room had been crowded but because he wanted to shut him up. Sarto was an absurdly arrogant self-styled expert in the lore of London, about which he wrote a great many preposterous and fanciful doorstops, but Bryant realized he might have some information to share, so he called ahead and made his way to Biblio, the grand literary club in Whitehall where Sarto hung out with his chirruping acolytes.

The porter was clearly not happy about letting the detective inside. 'Are you here for dinner?' he asked.

'No, I've had me dinner, it's nearly time for me tea,' said Bryant, just to prove his working-class credentials. 'I'll see myself up, I know the way.'

He passed between a pair of intricate ceramic-tiled pillars and made his way to the first floor, past marble busts of forgotten statesmen and dun-coloured paintings of high-collared noblemen, heading for the club bar, where he knew he would find Sarto.

'I suppose you know it virtually has its own weather system?' said Sarto, swilling a brandy glass that looked as if it had been grafted on to his hand some time during the Thatcher years. His appearance had been described by desperate interviewers as 'Pickwickian', 'Falstaffian' and plain 'portly'. A handful of other armchairs in the clubroom had occupants who ruffled themselves and resettled every now and again, rather like bats in a cave. 'There's a breeze that blows across the river unlike anywhere else,' Sarto explained. 'London's winds are generally westerly but not on the Thames, where it's south-west, stronger and colder than on the shores. In the eighteenth century it was infamous for plucking wigs off.' He released a series of short, sharp laughs that sound like geese being shot. Several bats fluttered disapprovingly.

'Have you written a book on the subject?' Bryant asked.

'Oh, probably.' Sarto twirled his free hand airily. 'Who can honestly remember all that one has done? I probably won an award for it. I'm getting you a brandy; you look as if you need it.' An ancient waiter crept out of the gloom, took the order and retreated. 'Where was I?'

'Wind,' said Bryant.

'Ah yes.' His thoughts changed direction. 'The Grand Order of London Druids believe the Thames encourages death in order to start over again, an idea that recurs through the history of the river. Like all mystic landscapes it starts life in a sacred form and eventually becomes corrupted. In the case of the Thames it was exploited by industrialists, its magic destroyed by the pollutant of greed. But that doesn't stop some people from believing that it still brings death and rebirth, the core of any sacred belief. I remember Margaret Thatcher once said to me—'

'Yes, your book about Mrs Thatcher is on my list,' said Bryant. He thought it best not to say which list. 'The Thames is just a river. Why would people think it could grant rebirth?'

'Because its nature is akin to religion. You can't trust the Thames any more than you can trust God, and like God it knows how to stage a good disaster.' The waiter crept back in, set down the brandy and crept off. 'It washed away London Bridge with sweeping high tides that swallowed men and cattle, and burst its banks century after century. It could rise twelve feet in five hours and drown passers-by strolling on main roads. On a bitter January night in 1953 a great cliff of water moved up the Thames and drowned many in their beds, including, if I'm not mistaken, your great-uncle Charlie. He *was* living in the slums of Deptford, was he not?'

'Yes, he was,' said Bryant, thinking back. 'How would you know about that?' But he already had the answer to his question. Sarto made it his job to know about anyone who threatened his supremacy, and the detective was the only man who knew more about London than he did. The difference was that Bryant wore his learning with humility. Sarto had a fine mind that had been led astray by the sound of his own voice.

'I'm surprised to see you still working,' Sarto was saying now. 'Doesn't it bore you? Surely you'd be happier at home putting your feet up? It will never really change, you know. London will continue to appal and amaze in equal measure. Although murder is disappearing in the capital, isn't it? It always struck me as such a Victorian conceit.' He gave a theatrical shudder.

'I'm sorry you think murder is unfashionable,' said Bryant, 'but unexplained deaths still occur every day. Most go unnoticed, but when aggregated they create unrest. The city isn't quantifiable in mere numbers, Darcy. Ill humours arise; distrust of public services and corporations, disillusionment with one's fellow man. That's why the PCU still exists. You saw what happened during the banking riots. London is a place of vapours and residues. They have to be dispelled before they're allowed to infect the population.'

Sarto grimaced. 'You sound like a sanitary engineer sprinkling Harpic around a lavatory bowl. Arthur, you really should raise yourself from the gutter.'

'I was born in the gutter,' said Bryant, rising to leave. There was no point in talking to any more experts about the river. Back at the unit the rest of the staff would be data-trawling, analysing evidence, creating spreadsheets and cross-checking statements. May had been right; it was the only way to solve a case like this. Bryant couldn't help being naturally drawn to wilder suppositions, but the Thames had misled everyone who studied it.

Making his goodbyes, he replaced his hat and stepped back into the drizzle. It was now Wednesday evening, and approaching the moment when everything began to go terribly wrong.

28

CHARMS & BRACELETS

'I don't believe it,' May called to Colin Bimsley. 'He's gone again. Is somebody helping him to escape? Did he slip past you?'

'No, I thought Raymond was looking after him,' said Bimsley.

'So did I,' said May, 'but I can't find either of them. Raymond's not answering his mobile.'

'Mr Bryant's tracker is on his desk,' said Dan, emerging from the detectives' office. 'I thought he might leave it somewhere so I sewed another one into his overcoat.'

'So you've got him?' asked May, relieved.

'No, I've got his overcoat.'

May ran his fingers through his hair, thinking. 'He could be anywhere. Take Meera and Fraternity with you and check around the block. I'll call Alma and Maggie – maybe they've spoken to him.'

'What about King's Cross Station?' asked Banbury. 'He often goes there when it's raining because it's under cover.'

'Good idea,' May said. 'This is the last bloody time. If I find him in one piece I'm going to lock him in his bedroom and throw away the key. Alma can slide his dinners under the door. He likes dover sole and pizza, he'll be fine.'

Arthur Bryant found himself at the station, but it wasn't King's Cross. It was Victoria. And that wasn't the only odd thing; the electronic dot-matrix destination board above his head had been replaced by one with green wooden slats that clattered as they rolled over to reveal the routes. The taste of Sarto's awful brandy had seared his mouth and he looked around for a coffee shop, but there was only an ancient WHSmith stand surrounded by porters pushing a convoy of two-wheeled trolleys. In front of the platforms, stacks of rectangular brown leather suitcases were piled in geometric mountains.

Bryant pulled his scarf free and looked up. Everything was brown; the walls were streaked with dirt and the glass roof was sepia with soot. Some of the men wore belted overcoats, baggy pinstriped trousers, trilbies and bowlers. The women were in short flared jackets and odd little hats that clenched their perms like skullcaps. The headlines pinned to boards outside the paper shop were all about the coronation. 'The Radiant Hope Of Millions', read the *Evening Chronicle*; *1953*, he thought, *that's odd*.

At Platform 3 he was ushered through the barrier and a blast of steam momentarily blinded him. When it cleared he found himself confronted by a polished green train with brass door handles and three separate classes. For a moment he wondered if he'd drifted on to the set of *The Railway Children*, but there was no Edwardian elegance here, just the charcoal coats and crumpled collars of a city still feeling the after-effects of a world war.

He dumbly followed the ticket number, stamped on thick pale green cardboard, then climbed up and entered a corridor, settling himself in a first-class carriage. The single compartment had six smartly upholstered seats with white antimacassars and red leather armrests. Above four of them were framed rectangular paintings of British holiday destinations. Over the centre seats were two gleaming bevelled mirrors.

No other passengers arrived to take up the other places in the compartment, and the train pulled out shortly after he was settled. The grey factories of South London were pocked with so many overgrown bomb sites that it looked as if the remaining buildings had been left behind as a provocation.

He was shocked at how suddenly the city ended. The switch from town to countryside happened moments after leaving Clapham Junction. *I am dreaming,* thought Bryant; *let me dream some more.* He felt tired and cold and closed his eyes, allowing his head to loll against the antimacassar as the rhythm of the tracks matched the beating of his heart.

He woke up in Brighton. It was a bright sunny morning. Light streamed in through the terminal's dusty brown canopy. *How long was I asleep?* he wondered. The train stood at the buffers, fifty-three miles from London.

He was in for another shock when he alighted and left the station, for time had rolled further back with the passing of the miles. It was no longer winter but high summer. The street outside was covered in red and yellow flags, but not to mark the coronation. Now he was surrounded by men in straw boaters, bright red blazers and baggy white flannels. The ladies wore fussy full skirts of white calico. He knew Brighton well and headed for the seafront, as every visitor from London was predisposed to do. An immense floral clock bore a date picked out in peonies: 1887. *Queen Victoria's golden jubilee,* he thought. *Well now, I wonder what this is about?*

There were a few motorcars, unwieldy and seemingly all built along vertical lines, but they were far outnumbered by coach parties disembarking from horse-drawn charabancs while an astonishing assortment of local men fussed around them, hired to help water the animals and lug wicker hampers on to the beach.

Brighton was as yet unruined. There were still two piers; the West Pier had not burned down. It ended in a great square promenade, and looked more sedately elegant than its brash counterpart. *Why am I here?* he wondered. *Is it simply a random hallucination, or am I supposed to learn something from this?*

Oddly, Bryant did not look out of place in the slightest. Sartorially challenged at the best of times, his wardrobe looked to have been purchased secondhand somewhere between the invasion of Poland and the first season of *Monty Python*, incorporating elements of both events. In Victorian Brighton he simply looked like a gentleman of the road. Thanks to the fact that he always had a few coppers in old money somewhere about his person, he was able to buy a plate of cockles. He decided to enjoy the experience.

It's hard to say what took him to the Hall of Varieties at the end of the Palace Pier but it probably wasn't the bill of fare, which included Beryl Flynn, the Lancashire Contortionist, Horace Allcock, Derby's Finest Female Impersonator, and Walter Wainright and His Cheeky Otters. Sandwiched in between these acts was the resident compère. Dudley Salterton was a Yorkshireman who did a Mr Memory act and some ventriloquism with an eye-rolling sailor dummy called Barnacle Bill. He dyed his hair ginger and stopped removing his stage make-up after his wife died, until it finally gave him a skin disease. He came from a long line of entertainers and used to work with his wife at the intermission, threading balloons through her neck. He tried it with a sword for a while but she hated going on stage wearing a bandage.

'I've not seen thee for a while,' said Salterton. 'Not since you were a wee lad. My, you've put on some years.'

'No, that was my father,' Bryant explained. 'I'm Arthur, his son. He said you died before I was born.'

'I'm not surprised with my dicky colon. It's the diet. You get right fed up with boarding-house rissoles. What do you do?'

'I'm a detective.'

'Then you're someone to notice.'

'Do you want a cockle?'

'No, son. There's summat in them that builds up in me system and I can't afford to get caught short onstage. I'm assuming you're not here for the air.'

'Is that you doing your mentalism act?' asked Bryant. 'Or a lucky guess?'

'Neither, lad. Human nature. Your dad was never one for visiting out of friendliness.' Salterton scratched at his nose, removing a chalky teardrop of panstick. 'I don't do me mentalism any more.'

'Why not?' Bryant moved his plate of cockles away from a seagull that was hovering in sinister proximity.

'I haven't got the looks for it. Time marches on, and soon it marches over your face.'

'I don't understand. Surely all you need for your mind-reading is a good memory.'

'I can see you've never trodden the boards.' Salterton sighed. 'It's got very little to do with the brain, has presti-digitationary gubbins. What do you know of hypnotism?'

'Not much,' said Bryant, popping a cockle in his mouth and chewing ruminatively. He'd under-peppered them. 'From the Greek god Hypnos, presumably.'

'You presume correctly. But it were a term first coined by a Manchester surgeon forty-six years ago.'

'You mean in 1841, assuming this is 1887.'

'Hypnosis,' said Salterton, rolling the word around his mouth. 'What is hypnotism, really? Misdirection? Magic? Suggestion? A special state of mind? If you think of a lemon you can make yourself salivate. If I say the word "lemon" will it produce the same effect, or is that just neurolinguistic programming?'

'Steady on,' said Bryant. 'That won't be invented for another eighty-odd years yet.'

'I do beg your pardon.' Salterton craned forward alarm-ingly. 'Shall I tell you about those times I picked someone from the audience and got them to reveal a secret to me? I chose them because I looked for signs of gullibility, an eagerness to be deceived, a certain summat' – here he dappled his bony fingers around his face – 'that suggested they were happy to be in on the act, going along with me to be gulled, because back then I were a handsome, confident young fellow holding them in the palm of me hand. I had *charisma* – and that's not a new term; it means "the gift of grace". My mother used to call it *allure*. Those folk in the auditorium, they hoped some of it would rub off on them.'

Bryant flicked a cockle at a passing dog. 'You think some people have a natural ability to control others?'

'I think some people have the ability to make others *surrender* to control. To become complicit. There's a difference, lad.'

'And you knew you had that power.'

'Aye, for a while, yes. I capitalized upon it. I could be found on the billboards with lightning bolts flashing from me eyes. But when the petals fell from this rose, the public took a second look at me and no longer wished to assist in the deceit. In short, I got old. You know what they say a pretty young girl can do? *Anything she pleases.* Only they never realize it, of course, or if they do they must doom themselves.'

'It's not the same in our time,' said Bryant. 'Everyone thinks they're the bee's knees.'

'What I'm saying to you is, I attracted audiences not because of what I said or did, but because of who I was. Not how I was born but who I thought I could become. I created *meself*. I wore a special suit and shoes with raised heels. I tanned on the beach, brilliantined me hair and bleached me teeth, and I dazzled them. Do you see?'

'No, not really,' said Bryant honestly.

'There are two tricks to fooling people, laddie. One is to make yourself invisible. The other is to be the most visible fellow in the room.'

'I don't see how this helps our investigation,' said Bryant, emptying vinegar from his plate into the sea.

'No, but you will in the century after next. Because you're wrong; underneath all the nonsense people never change. What you *think* you see is what you see. See?' Salterton arose with an audible crack of the knees. 'I weren't bamboozling them with my cleverness. I'm not that smart. They just liked t' look of me. I was all "gawk, tousle and shucks", as we say round our way. The trouble with you is, you always think murderers are clever. Truth is, most of 'em are as slow as a tortoise.' He checked his pocket watch. 'It's nearly intermission; I must be getting on. I'm producing coins out of kiddies' ears in the foyer. Sometimes they get stuck right inside and I have to use me rubber tube. The parents kick up a fuss but it's better than doing nowt. You have to keep working when it's in t' blood.'

Bryant rose also. The sun had vanished behind a lone cloud and it had grown suddenly cold.

'One other thing,' said Salterton, looking back. 'Spoons. You're on the right track, but don't be too diverted by the spoons. Think about them lads and lasses in t' Congo. You gave that book to Dr Gillespie.'

And with that the ancient performer vanished through the swing doors of the variety hall, leaving Bryant alone on the pier.

Well, this is an interesting development, he thought. *My hallucinations seem to be leaving me cryptic clues.* For a minute he looked through the planks and watched the green waves crashing far below. Then, pulling his scarf more tightly around his throat, he headed back to the seafront.

When he awoke, somebody called the police.

'He's all right, he's not far away,' said Raymond Land, cutting the call. 'There's some kind of theatre at the back of King's Cross Station. They're doing a version of *The Railway Children.*'

'I should have thought of that,' said Fraternity DuCaine. 'They've built the stage around a railway siding and a real old-fashioned steam train comes in during the show.'

'An usher found him in one of the carriage compartments,' said Land. 'He timed his escape well. I only nipped out to buy some socks. He says he doesn't remember anything. John, can you go over and get him? If he cuts up rough stick him in bracelets if you have to, just don't bring him back here. Take him home and call the doctor. This has gone far enough.'

'I'm on my way,' said May, grabbing a coat.

'How did he get out?' Land demanded to know. 'I knew we should never have let him come back.'

'We were supposed to be watching him,' said Longbright. 'I didn't see his door open. We've been busy. We don't have Jack any more, and with Colin, Meera and Fraternity out on rounds there aren't enough of us here to provide proper cover.'

'It's taking a toll on all of us, Janice,' said Land. 'I had to cancel my watercolour course two weeks ago. Thirty quid down the drain. It's about quality of life, not just the ackers. I get a nervous rash if I don't sit myself behind a piece of Daler board at least once a month.'

Janice decided to ask the one question no one else had dared to broach. 'What are we going to do without Arthur? There's no unit without him.'

'Do you really think so?'

'Yes, of course.'

'Then it'll be our job to prove that's not the case. We're a unit, not a one-man band.' Land didn't sound as if he believed himself.

'I understand, but he lifts us to another level, you must see that,' Longbright persisted. 'Nobody else thinks like him, not even John.' The argument, she realized, was pointless. Right now it would probably suit Raymond to get the unit closed once and for all and take the redundancy package, but what about the rest of them?

She could see what was about to happen. With Arthur out

of the way, Darren Link would set spies in their midst to gain the intelligence he needed, and the rest would be a mere formality. This situation had been building for months. For the first time she started to think about getting out, and what she would do in the aftermath.

29

ATTRACTION & INDUCTION

Alma Sorrowbridge had wrapped Bryant in a tartan blanket and placed him in front of the electric fire so that he looked like a crofter who'd just returned from a long day of peat-cutting. She attempted to dry what little hair he had with a towel, but he irritably shrugged her off. The night was one of secret rain, a London speciality, where you couldn't see the rain falling but knew it must be because the roads were shining.

May shook his head as he accepted a mug of tea. 'I can't ask them to take you back, Arthur. I know you'll just bolt again the second we take our eyes off you. Where did you think you were going?'

'Brighton, back in time,' muttered Bryant miserably. 'Old Gillespie warned me about hallucinations but he couldn't explain why they might occur. Now I think I know.'

'So what do you think is happening?'

'My subconscious has gone into overdrive. I'm not sharp enough to handle the case because of my memory loss, so something below my level of consciousness has awoken to try and help me deal with it.'

'That would mean these delusions are there for a purpose. What did you think you saw?'

'This time? I met up with an old family friend. He was an entertainer on the pier, a magician like his father and grandfather before him. They all kept the same stage name. Actually, I think it must have been Dudley's grandfather that I met up with.'

May sniffed. 'You smell of vinegar.'

'I had a plate of cockles.'

'No you didn't, you were asleep in a train that was being used as part of a stage production, just around the corner from the PCU,' May pointed out. 'You had some old money in your pockets.'

'Yes, I sometimes do.' Digging into the pocket of his dressing gown, he produced a half-crown and a packet of sweet cigarettes.

'Exactly what kind of conversation do you think you had with this magician?' asked May.

'That's the odd part. He talked to me about the days when he started in the theatre, as if he was telling me some kind of secret that has a bearing on our investigation.'

'What did he say?'

'He said he attracted people not because of what he said or did but because of the persona he adopted, and that his real character always found a way to resurface. Something like that. I don't think I've been asking the right questions. These fantasies are trying to drag something out of me.'

'So you're manipulating them, like lucid dreaming. Your brain's not giving up without a fight, is it?'

'It's what I trained it to do for so many years.' Bryant hugged his tea mug. 'It's one of the reasons why Raymond has never understood me. He thinks I come out with reams of spurious, random tosh just to annoy him.'

'Well, you do.'

'Of course, but I'm processing information. You once said I'd forgotten more than most people knew and you're right. When a case demands it I have to dig up that data again. But finding it and then knowing how to employ it – that's the problem.'

'Then write it all down,' said May. 'Try to make sense of these – events.' He checked his watch. 'Arthur, I can't stay.'

Bryant's eyebrows rose. 'Are you going back to the unit?'

'No, it's not official business. It's just something I have to do alone.'

It wasn't like May to be secretive. Bryant had an uncomfortable feeling in the pit of his stomach. 'So I must remain here under lock and key,' he said.

'Raymond won't have you back at the PCU,' May warned. 'You can see his point. You could have walked under a train in St Pancras Station. If, as you say, these episodes replace the real world with something from your imagination, we have no way of knowing where you might end up next. Look at all the books you've got here. You can still work.'

'And if I want to go out I must be accompanied at all times, like a baby.'

May shot a beseeching look at Alma. 'Don't worry,' said the landlady, patting Bryant's arm, 'I'll be here for you.'

Bryant folded his arms in disgust. 'If you think there's a future that involves you spoon-feeding me tapioca pudding and taking me to church jumble sales, kindly open the oven door and put a cushion inside.'

'Alma, he's all yours,' said May, rising. 'I'll call you tomorrow to check that he's OK.'

'He'll be fine,' Alma assured him.

'You're talking about me in the third person now!' bellowed Bryant, horrified. 'I'm still here, you silly old fools!' But May had closed the door behind him and Alma had gone back to her stove.

Janice Longbright had changed out of her black PCU sweater and donned a flowery 1950s cocktail frock she happened to keep in the evidence room. *After all,* she decided, *it's an exclusive treatment centre, and if I have to work outside my regular hours I might as well get some enjoyment from it.*

She checked herself in the mirror. *'Zaftig' isn't the look I was going for,* she thought with a sigh. *I was thinking Joan Collins, not Phil Collins.*

The white clapboard frontage of the old St Alphege Centre was bordered with dwarf conifers and olive trees, and surrounded by African daisies in tubs. There was no sign of *wabi-sabi* here; the shrubs still bore their nursery price tags and a shiny new brass plaque engraved with the Life Options logo aimed to suggest heritage and elegance.

Facing Dolphin Square and marooned in a strangely unappealing stretch of the Thames, the former boathouse had been manicured to appear discreetly expensive, the sort of venue where you might find Gwyneth Paltrow and the Prime Minister's wife covered in cucumber slices.

I can't wait to put this through on my expenses, thought Longbright, looking up at the ivy-hung window boxes as she got out of the taxi. She was greeted by a young woman in a white collarless shirt and a man's black suit. 'You must be Mrs Forthright,' she said without need to refer to a chart. 'We have some spare spaces tonight. The rain has caused some cancellations.' She cast a disdainful eye over Longbright's dress – nobody wore summer colours in November – and ushered her to the counter.

Longbright had used her mother's maiden name for the booking. The young woman smiled at her distantly. The detective sergeant recognized the look; it was the kind ground staff gave passengers when they were scanning their passports.

'I'm Laura, your induction guide,' said the concierge, checking her watch. 'The introductory session begins at half past. Would you like to go straight through?'

'We have five minutes,' said Longbright. 'The gentleman giving the introductory talk – is he the owner?'

'That's right. Mr Thornberry set up the wellbeing centre with his business partner, Ms North.'

'Cassie North?' asked Longbright, attempting to look

delighted. 'I just saw her in *OK* magazine. She's very glamorous, a good advertisement for the centre.'

The young woman made a faint non-committal noise that
suggested she didn't entirely agree. 'She normally takes the
inductions with Mr Thornberry, but she has meetings tonight.
I'm sure you'll get to talk to her in due course.'

'Will there be many of us?'

'We like to keep the induction classes small. Mr Thornberry
and his team prefer to conduct one-on-one sessions wherever
possible in order to tailor treatments to individual needs.'

Longbright checked out the photographs of the instructors
pinned to the wall. She stopped before one headshot and took
a closer look, then backed up to the shot of Cassie North.
Same surname, she thought, *family resemblance.* 'Marion
North? Is she Cassie North's mother?'

'Yes. Mrs North is currently taking classes on the astrology
of finance.'

'I didn't know there was such a thing.'

'The induction is about to start so I can explain all the
courses and give you a tour of the facilities afterwards. Shall
we go through?'

Longbright was led into a very white lateral rectangle filled
with tropical flowers and laid out with fifteen bright red
seats. The inductees fitted a very particular demographic.
They reminded Longbright of country houses, elegant, stately
and expensive to maintain, but awe-inspiring to casual visitors. The detective sergeant did not belong in their world.
She couldn't imagine having days that were empty enough to
allow for perpetual refurbishment.

The concierge directed them to turn off their phones, but
Longbright had long ago mastered the art of sneakily firing
shots without appearing to move a muscle. There appeared to
be no CCTV in the room, which was helpful. These were
tough, intelligent women who would not take kindly to inva-
sions of privacy, especially if it included baring their souls to
a therapist.

'Well, *you're* an unfamiliar face.' The languorous, well-preserved woman sitting next to her raised huge dark glasses and blatantly examined her with tiny staring eyes. 'I'm loving your dress. That's a 1950s original Balenciaga, isn't it? Wherever did you find it?'

'It was my mother's,' Longbright explained.

'I'm Anna Marshall.'

'Janice.' Longbright shook the proffered hand. 'Isn't this the induction?'

'Yes,' said Marshall, 'but it's my third time.'

'I don't understand.'

'I just love watching Ali turn on the charm.' Marshall gave a knowing smile.

'You think he's good, then?'

'Darling, I've been on dozens of nutrition, diet and holistic wellbeing courses and he's by far the most intriguing instructor.'

'So you think he gets results?'

'Oh, I imagine he can get whatever he wants,' said Marshall, her button eyes shining in anticipation.

'But the courses—'

'The *courses*.' Marshall swept the idea aside with a clatter of bangles. 'They're exactly what you'd expect. I mean, they're never very different, are they? Far too much guff about energy lines and chakra-balancing – personally I find Chablis and Xanax does the trick just as well – and they gouge you for the beauty products, but who doesn't?'

'I thought it was about initiating change,' Longbright said, quoting the brochure.

'Good Lord no. I mean, if you want to lose weight cut out sugar, and if you want to calm down read a book. It's not rocket science, is it? Nobody signs up believing they're going to change.' She seemed to lose her train of thought. 'I spend an absolute fortune here,' she finished vaguely.

'So, what gives this place the edge?'

Marshall lowered her dark glasses and sat back in her chair. 'You'll see,' she said. 'Here he comes.'

Longbright smelled vanilla, cedar and something darker as the door behind them opened.

'Is that it?' asked Fraternity, sitting on the corner of Longbright's desk later. 'A bit of sex appeal? You, of all people – you fought harder for liberation than anyone and all it takes to undo decades of advancement is biceps and a cute smile?'

'It isn't like that,' said Longbright, briskly flattening out her notes and starting to type them up. 'You wouldn't understand. He has showmanship. He plays the room. He understands women. He's charismatic and responsive. He talks you through the courses and then does individual assessments, and you probably don't notice you've just lost two hours and two hundred nicker.'

'You're saying they all fall over and open their wallets because someone in a tight T-shirt waltzes into the room to sell a bunch of beauty courses.'

'I'm saying he's a fake, Fraternity. They know it and he knows it and it still doesn't matter, because he gives them value for money and makes them feel good about themselves. Like taking a younger lover, without the nuisance factor. Which means he's on to a real winner.'

'So what happened after the induction session?' Fraternity asked, intrigued.

Longbright watched the women filing out of the room, happy and lost, as if they'd been stunned to discover that they'd been left fortunes by forgotten relatives. Ali's effect on them was extraordinary, and even she had proven less immune than she'd expected. But now that the main attraction had disappeared the feeling of euphoria quickly wore off, so she set out to search the private rooms.

She knew that at this stage it would take time to get a

warrant for the centre, so a little clandestine snooping was called for. Ali's partner, Cassandra North, was away from the building, so it seemed logical to start in her office.

Longbright waited until a gaggle of white-robed women had passed along the hall and started checking the names on the doors. *There are no locks anywhere,* she thought, *but why would there be? It's a spa, not a prison.*

She found an office door marked 'North' but the room didn't feel as if it belonged to a company director. There were astrological charts above a treatment table, jars of herbal essences, a display of what she took to be semi-precious gemstones, a yoga mat, incense holders and some sparkly paintings that looked as if they'd been produced by ten-year-olds. A framed photograph showed Marion North and her daughter on horses somewhere in the Thames Valley.

Someone was coming. She heard a man's footsteps in the hall, and quickly tried the only other door in the room. It turned out to be a supply cupboard into which she barely fitted. Vowing to lose weight as she pulled the door closed, she heard the voice that had just addressed a roomful of enraptured clients.

'Slow down, I don't understand what you're saying. Just tell me . . . Really? You think now's a good time? I could do with you here, Cassie. Mrs Busabi's going crazy because she didn't get her appointment today, and you know how much she's willing to – Yeah, I can get your mother to give her a free treatment but I'd rather you were here to – Well, get back here as soon as you can . . . No, it's more important that you're here right now.' And then he was gone and the room was silent again. Longbright let herself out, waited until the coast was clear and checked the rest of the rooms.

Cassandra North had left her office computer in sleep mode, but it was password-protected. Her printer had a stack of Excel spreadsheets in its tray. Longbright took a chance and went through them with one eye on the door. The pages covered course schedules for three weeks back and one week forward. In the fortnight before her death Dalladay had signed up for almost every course Ali hosted, but one class in particular caught Longbright's eye. She was still reading the schedules when the footsteps returned and stopped outside. Folding a page into her pocket, she was forced to run to another cupboard. This one had a handle that refused to turn. Behind her the main door was starting to open.

The receptionist entered the room and froze when she found Longbright standing beside the desk. 'You're not supposed to be back here, Mrs Forthright,' she said sharply.

'I'm sorry, I got a bit disoriented when I came out of the induction. Mr Thornberry has a very powerful effect on people, doesn't he?'

'A lot of our clients say that.' The receptionist's professional smile slipped back into place. She took Longbright's arm with a firm, steady hand. 'I'll give you that tour now, shall I?'

'What have you got?' she asked Fraternity. 'North won't be able to tell you've hacked her account, will she?'

'Trust me, nothing will show up.' Fraternity checked his screen. 'Looks like North and Dalladay were pretty close; there are a lot of chatty emails going back and forth between them. Dalladay was taking one-to-one extra-curricular classes. They're twice the cost of group sessions. Specifically, this guy Ali is teaching a course called "The Sacred Power of Rivers". Any idea about that?'

'Not a clue.'

'She was booked for six sessions, two a week, and was less than halfway through. She had one arranged for last Sunday night. The night she died.' The young PC checked the Life Options website and found no mention of it. 'There's nothing here.'

Longbright winced at the thought. 'It seems a bit unlikely that a holistic health centre would be mixed up in this, don't you think?'

'Mr Bryant never seems to worry about whether it's unlikely,' Fraternity replied. 'He'd see that phrase "sacred river" and run off with it.'

'Then we'd better think like him,' said Longbright.

30

SINKING & DROWNING

Bryant was restless. The room was overheated. Alma's steak and kidney pudding lay heavily in his stomach. Feeling miserable and sorry for himself, he had gone to bed early and had now awoken at the wrong time. The duvet kept sliding to the floor with spiteful deliberation. He had somehow managed to turn himself around inside his pyjamas. Exasperated, he sat up and checked the time: 10.47 p.m. There was no point lying there staring at the ceiling, his brain racing. He decided to get up and work.

Locating a pad of foolscap and a fountain pen, he began making notes. Outside the secret rain was making the dullest surfaces glisten. In weather like this even the most trampled patches of Central London were capable of sprouting moss. Walls darkened, pavements turned green and drains blocked. It was as if the pervasive damp sought to breed more adaptive life forms. Restless, he turned the radio on. An announcer was warning that the Thames barrier had been lowered. The tide was unusually high tonight and low-lying parts of the city were at risk of flooding. A cyclist had come off his bike in a deserted part of Canary Wharf and had drowned in the shallow lake that had formed by the side of the road. The spirits of the river were abroad, Bryant decided. It was a bad night to be out.

He forced himself to think about the logistics of the case. They had assumed from the start that Dalladay had been chained in the Thames because it was an unmonitored spot. Along the sixty miles of north-side pathway following the river through the city, starting by the Prospect of Whitby, the oldest river tavern still standing, were alleyways hemmed with tall, spiked fences, coils of razor wire and security cameras. Corporations were required to allow public access but had made it almost impossible for anyone to gain entry. In place of the promised pathway lay a patchwork maze of obstructions cloaked in municipal ambiguity. The riverside developers acted as if they owned London's best views, hiring security guards to intimidate anyone who tried to exercise their legal rights. Therefore choosing the spot for its secluded inaccessibility showed premeditation and planning.

If Dalladay was despondent about being pregnant, why did she not choose to terminate? The doctor's report suggested she was not unhappy at all. So why would she have killed herself in such a bizarre fashion? She had a predilection for self-mythologizing and was in a confused state, so she might have attempted a rebirth ritual, casting her old spirit into the waters in order to return anew. Either that or she wanted to hurt someone, to say: *You made me do this.* Given what he knew about her, neither solution seemed likely, but who could fully appreciate her state of mind?

Stay at home and go through your books, John had kept telling him, but how could they help? There was no more room for books in Bryant's office. His bedroom and the lounge he shared with Alma had shelves bellying with the weight of obscure tracts, catalogues, indices, files, novels, magazines, paperbacks, reference works and manuals. He looked at the bifurcated, sundered, foxed and otherwise buggered-about-with volumes and his heart sank. Could this sad little archive really be of any use in uncovering the reason for a young woman's death? He knew he had to keep his mind occupied or he would sink in its churning currents.

'Keep at it, you stupid old fool,' he said aloud. 'What else can you do?'

Approaching the first of the shelves, he cracked his knuckles and set to work.

Longbright rubbed her eyes and checked her watch: 10.47 p.m. She fantasized about a microwaved toad-in-the-hole. It was either that or macaroni cheese, which she hated. There was nothing else in the PCU kitchen cupboard except cat food and a litre bottle of slivovitz with 'Toxicity test – Don't Drink!' written across the label in Bryant's hand.

She couldn't leave Fraternity collating reports by himself. Raymond Land had cited a migraine and beetled off home, Dan was going over data with Giles, Meera and Colin had been sent back to Lambeth Bridge by John. Speaking of which, where was John? She'd tried calling him, but his phone went straight to voicemail.

She and Fraternity had finished filing statements from Dimitri Gilyov's most recent workmates, and they repeated the same mantra: he was a good worker who kept to himself, he wasn't a man you crossed, and there wasn't anything more to say about him. Gilyov had sometimes worked in tandem with another engineer, Andrei, who said that Gilyov had a vile temper but didn't drink any more – that last word had been stressed with a certain ominousness – and tried to keep his nose clean these days. There were hints of past tragedies, but Andrei didn't seem too sure of his facts because Gilyov never confided in anyone. He kept his male friends at arm's length and if he wanted female companionship he hired it.

Longbright wandered into the common room and took another look at the whiteboard. The St Alphege Centre had come up clean too. There was nothing in the Life Options accounts that smelled bad. They weren't in financial trouble. Far from it; judging by their press coverage in the past few weeks investors were likely to be beating down their doors. North's mother was a bit of a character, a New Age therapist with a midnight cable TV show and a line of crappy-looking jewellery. Her daughter was more of a mystery, a finishing-school dropout who had somehow hooked up with Thornberry and set about turning him into a brand.

Unsurprisingly, there was no Alistair Thornberry on the electoral register. Ali looked to be of Arabic descent, in which case his name made more sense. His web presence had been so carefully controlled that she wondered if he'd used a company to eradicate past misdemeanours and have his auto-complete searches deleted. Maybe someone like Reputation. com had cleaned his cache and eliminated all earlier photo-graphs. The right to be forgotten was now legally enshrined, so the practice made good business sense.

She thought about Ali. Given his Middle Eastern features, there was a chance that 'Thornberry' might have fled from conflict at some point in the past. She ran a check through London GCHQ and Interpol but nothing was immediately apparent. She also talked to Cheltenham and Scarborough, but drew blanks in both security outposts, which meant that either he was an illegal immigrant operating under a new identity, or he had changed his name and they simply had no records on him because he had never done anything to war-rant their attention. Without a valid reason to connect him to the case, a deep search would require higher approval and take several days.

Not that she ever trusted GCHQ to tell her the truth. On the few times she had visited their red, white and purple offices, which reminded her of a mall in a motorway service station, their officers had treated her as if she was on a school trip to learn about democracy.

Back at her screen, she uploaded the headshots she had surreptitiously taken at the centre. They showed a man in his late twenties with aquiline features and slightly imperfect teeth, his musculature accentuated by a tailored midnight-blue suit. Dan had facial recognition software so advanced that no one else knew how to operate it. If he couldn't find out who Ali Thornberry was, nobody could.

Beneath Lambeth Bridge, Colin Bimsley stumped along the shoreline with a polystyrene tray of cod and chips in one hand. 'If someone jumps out of the shadows and clouts me with a spade again I'm going to be well manked off,' he said, through a mouthful of batter.

'That's not very likely, is it?' said Meera, chucking a pebble into the shallows, 'seeing as he's in the salad crisper, thinking about what he wants on his headstone.'

'It has to be someone who knows the river,' said Colin, peering up into the dark. 'You can't see that girder from the road above. You can barely see it from down here. Everything looks different from the water. But who'd spot that?'

'River police,' said Meera.

'What, you think it's one of ours?'

'That's just it, though.' She threw another stone. 'They're not, are they? They're a law unto themselves. Have you ever had a drink with one?'

'Nope, but that's because nobody wants to drink with anyone from the PCU, not even Community Support. The river boys won't. They threatened to duff Fraternity up over his little boating expedition. And they took their key back.' He bit the end off a pickled wally. 'They told him to stay away from the water in case he suddenly discovered he couldn't swim, which was thoughtful of them. I think he lost them their no-claims bonus.'

'We're wasting our time here. Nobody's going to come back now that the body has been removed.' Meera looked for a good skipping stone. 'What about the other bloke?'

'What, Bill Crooms? Janice thinks he might have known Gilyov from one of the river pubs like the Cutty Sark Tavern or the Yacht. They still get a lot of river people. I mean, it could be anything, couldn't it? Maybe they were both in a

Scrabble tournament as children or poked each other on Facebook. D'you want some of this wally?'

'I'd rather drink my own sick, thank you.' Another stone cracked off a bridge stanchion and slapped into the water. 'If the Dalladay and Gilyov deaths are part of the same case, how are *they* connected? You know the problem with this whole investigation?'

'You're about to tell me, aren't you?'

'It's a serpent with its head cut off.'

'What do you mean?'

'The old man! He's gone off to Storybookland and we've got no one in charge. John only works well when he's half of a team. You must have seen the change in him this week, it's horrible to watch. He's never had to handle the whole thing alone before. I'm getting my CV sorted.'

Colin looked up, startled, half a chip hanging from his mouth. 'You wouldn't jump ship, would you?'

Meera wiped mud from her hands. 'What choice have we got? Bryant's not going to get better and now that he's been told to stay out of the unit he'll go downhill fast, like teachers do when they retire. You should be looking around because there's not going to be much of a redundancy package. We'll be offered LOTs in the Met.'

'Lots of what?'

'Lowest On Totem. We didn't take promotion, did we? We're back to square one, you and me.'

'At least we still have each other,' said Colin, removing a fishbone from his teeth and flicking it into the water.

'Oh yes, thank goodness I have that to cling on to.'

'You're being sarcastic, aren't you?'

'Yes, Colin, I am being sarcastic.'

'I'll tell you what, I'll do a deal with you.'

'What, not another one of your special offers? If the PCU comes through you'll take me to Chopsticks of Fury on Kingsland High Road for a mystery-meat chow mein?'

'I thought you liked it there.' Colin looked crestfallen. He shoved his fish tray into a paper bag and carefully placed it, rather disgustingly, Meera thought, in his jacket pocket.

John May alighted at Temple Station, walking out on to the Thames side of Victoria Embankment, one of the last dark, green, quiet spots in Central London. He knew he must be crazy to have agreed to the meeting, but it was too late to turn back.

There were no pedestrians to be seen in either direction. May was reminded of old post-war films about London, where the roads were devoid of traffic and the number of pedestrians in any shot could be counted on the fingers of one hand. He checked his Timex: 11.10 p.m. She was already ten minutes late.

The Thames was higher than he had ever seen it. Its waters slapped the wall just below the railings. Leaning over, he could see one of the conduits from the underground River Fleet emptying itself as earth-darkened run-off poured down from the hills to the north. The lions were partially submerged.

He glanced at the ropes of lights on the opposite bank, thinking about leaving, but when he looked back a taxi was drawing away and there she was, running across the road towards him. *I really can't believe I'm doing this*, he thought, preparing to hold her in his arms.

At midnight, under a railway arch at Finsbury Park Station, one of the few that had been too angular and ugly to be sold off to developers and stuffed with minuscule luxury apartments, a strange turnip-shaped woman, ragged and filthy, uncoiled herself from an upturned blue Nissan and lowered her boots into a puddle in order to note its increased depth. Delighted by the result she dabbled her feet in the water like a duck, then hammered them up and down, splashing and thrashing with laughter.

'It's coming, Arthur,' she roared into the rain. 'I warned

you about the powers of death and rebirth before, but you wouldn't listen. Last time it was fire, this time it's water. London is at the mercy of the four elementables. The sea levels are rising. The lions are drowning! The river must give up its dead. You proved yourself once – it won't be so easy to do it again. You should never have married me and got me stagnant with your child. We'll be together again soon, just you wait and see!'

A pair of passing constables stopped to watch her for a minute, rolled their eyes at each other and kept moving.

As Esmeralda the tramp released another peal of shrieks the rain suddenly made itself visible, pounding on the chassis of the wrecked car. The sound of laughter and thunder was lost beneath the rumbling of the passing trains.

31

VICTIM & CULPRIT

The boys hadn't exactly stolen the bright orange dinghy, but nor had they got permission to use it.

Mitesh's brother had left it in his shed when he went off to Afghanistan, and when he came back he had lost his old enthusiasms. Once he would race to the coast to take the dinghy out, but now he stayed indoors playing video games and hardly spoke to anyone, so Mitesh and Bhavin had quietly removed it along with the pump and headed for the Thames without telling their mother. They went to the first set of steps beyond Tower Beach because the water was higher than they'd ever seen it, and they thought it would be easier to get into the river from there.

They hadn't given much thought to getting out again.

Bhavin was twelve. Mitesh was eleven.

Right from the first, Bhavin knew they were in trouble. The current snatched at their oars, the paddles of which were made from thin plastic and bent alarmingly. When they entered the water the tide had been on the turn. Now it started to draw them out. The dinghy had no steering other than its oars, and proved too skittish to control. It now seemed likely that they would be pulled into the main deep-water channel.

'This was a dumb idea,' Bhavin said. 'Look at all the rubbish that was floating against the wall – it's getting sucked out.'

Mitesh tried to see what was ahead, but away from the lights of the embankment it was much darker than he'd expected. The water smelled of dead plants and something earthier, like graveyard soil and mould. 'It stinks down here,' he complained.

'That's 'cause the other rivers are emptying in – see them pipes along the embankment? Water and dirt, man, 'cause of all the rain. We don't want to get sucked in under one of those.'

'I wanted to go under Tower Bridge,' said Mitesh. 'These oars are crap.' They weren't unduly scared because they had no real idea of the danger they were in. The orange dinghy was caught in an eddy and swung around like a fairground car. It lurched so violently that for a moment Bhavin thought they were going to overturn.

'We can't go to Tower Bridge,' he said. 'The river widens after that – we'll never get back.' He knew it might already be too late. The ominous tide was now dragging them in that direction, and the great plain of water that lay just ahead was starting to look dark and frightening.

Neither boy was prepared to give in. To do so would be to lose face, so they joked and made light of it while pushing the flimsy oars ever deeper. Bhavin looked past Mitesh's shoulder and grew afraid; something immense and black was coming towards them, and the little dinghy had no lights.

The barge was low in the water and approaching at speed. For a moment it seemed as if it would plough right over them. There was no way out of its path. Then it had slid past and the wash propelled them back towards the shore wall. The stairs were suddenly ahead, partly submerged beneath the dinghy. Bhavin tried to grab at a stone outcrop as they passed, but leaning out brought him down so low that he brushed the icy water. The face that surfaced beneath him was white as china, its eyes staring wide, its black mouth open in a silent scream.

It was not an arrest as such, more of an accompaniment, but it was required by law for any serious crimes suspect. It occurred just after dawn on Thursday morning in the narrow empty street of Shad Thames. The officers were young and from the Met, and were embarrassingly apologetic. After all, the man they had come to collect had far more experience than either of them, but thankfully he had the good grace to allow them to go through the process without interrupting.

Colin Bimsley, who monitored police calls while he was on the running machine at his gym, was the first to pick it up. He was so surprised that in straining to listen he stood still for a moment and shot off the end of the moving belt.

Word spread fast and messages flew back and forth. Some offered help, but there was plenty of *Schadenfreude* mixed in with them. Raymond Land turned up at the PCU without his tie, a sure sign that he had been told the news and had rushed to get there. By the time the rest of the team arrived even the two Daves had somehow discerned what was going on, in the way that electricians, decorators and plumbers always manage to, and were interjecting with helpful ideas as they trailed more cables across the floor.

'I had a cousin in the force,' said the swarthier and more luxuriously moustachioed of the Daves. 'He got banged up on a charge of receiving stolen goods. He explained how he couldn't have done it 'cause he was in Eyebeefa at the time, but they still prosecuted him.'

'Miscarriage of justice, innit,' said his mate.

'Miscarriage, exactly. It would have been all right but he got done for armed robbery in Eyebeefa and tried to say he was in London, which didn't really work out.'

'Couldn't they have just checked his passport?' said the other Dave.

'Yeah, there's that as well.'

'Get on with your work before I electrocute you,' said Land, standing by the wall switch. He turned to Longbright. 'Where is he now?'

'In the interview room,' said Janice. 'I can't do this. You'll have to do it.'

'Let me go,' said Fraternity. 'I can be just a messenger. It'll be easier.'

Land wavered. 'I should be there.'

'Sod it,' said Janice, 'we'll all go.'

So they trooped up to the new temporary interview room, which was still being used as a cupboard for stationery supplies and cleaning equipment, and then crowded at the door while Raymond Land went in.

'Hello, John,' said Land, clambering over a mop and bucket. There was no room for a desk and only two orange bendy chairs, so he and May had to sit with their knees touching. 'I'm really sorry about this.'

'You're only doing your job,' said May. 'It's weird, though. I've never been arrested before. You do realize it's a mistake.'

'Yes, of course,' Land agreed, 'but I have to suspend you pending a full investigation. I can't change the rules.'

May looked up at the dim bare bulb hanging down from the ceiling. 'This isn't going to work as an interview room, even temporarily.'

'I know, but we can't move downstairs until we've figured out what to do with that sarcophagus-thing in the basement.' Land felt he should obey the formalities. He glanced down nervously at his notes. 'How much did the Met boys tell you?'

'Just the bare bones,' said May, filled with a terrible sense of foreboding. 'That a woman's body has been found and that I'm officially a suspect.'

'Let me see if I can shed a little light on this.' Land squinted at the page. 'I can't see my own handwriting.'

'Her name is North,' Longbright said, sticking her head around the narrow doorway.

'That's right, Cassandra North,' said Land. 'Her body was discovered a little after eleven p.m.—'

'No, not Cassandra – Marion North,' said Longbright. 'She's Cassandra North's mother.'

'Er, that's right,' said Land, tipping his single page beneath the bare bulb. 'She was in the river. A couple of kids had taken a dinghy out because of the high tide and found her floating near the stairs at Tower Beach a little after one a.m.'

'Marion North,' May repeated, stunned. 'It can't be.'

'The kids were out by themselves on the river,' said Longbright. 'They got a bollocking from their parents, but finding a dead body will probably give them credibility at school. North's been taken to St Pancras. Giles is already on it. First indications are that she was strangled and dumped a short while before the kids arrived, just before midnight.'

'That's just a few minutes after I saw her,' said May, his heart sinking. 'My God.'

'You mean – you did actually meet up with her?'

'She needed to see me.'

'Do you want to start at the beginning?' Land untangled himself from the chair. 'Can we go to my office? The smell of disinfectant is doing my head in.'

May followed the others in a daze. The thought immediately entered his head that he was somehow responsible. What could have happened?

They reconvened in Land's room and now everyone attended, with the result that the two Daves had to man the phones again.

'I first met her seven or eight years ago,' May began. 'Maggie Armitage introduced us. Her husband had walked out on her and she was very bitter about it. She seemed smart and had a good head for business. I went out with her a couple of times.'

'I don't remember you saying anything,' said Longbright. 'Do you remember the exact date?'

'No, but I can probably work it out. I don't think I mentioned it to anyone at the time.'

'Why not?'

'I suppose I knew it wasn't going to work out between us. We were completely incompatible. She loved parties and hung out with a bunch of social climbers. I didn't like her friends and she couldn't bring herself to tell anyone what I did for a living, so I stopped calling. She was pretty upset. I hadn't really noticed that she was keener than me. I felt bad about it but we weren't suited for each other, and I didn't want it to get serious.'

'So how did you get in touch again?' asked Longbright.

'After Arthur visited Angela Curtis's daughter yesterday, Marion contacted me through Twitter. She remembered I was at the unit, and said she needed to talk to me about something.'

'Wait, back up – Angela Curtis, who's she?' As usual, Land had been kept in the dark about Bryant's side trips.

'She drowned herself in the Thames,' May explained. 'Arthur came across a report of her death in his Dead Diary. He's started keeping track of anything that happens around the river and discovered she'd been enrolled in Life Options courses that Lynsey Dalladay had been attending. Curtis's daughter knows Marion North because she runs courses at the centre.'

'Hang on, you mean this daughter phoned your – friend – and told her she'd been visited by Bryant?'

'Yes. Marion North said she'd also had a visit, and called me.'

'Then what?'

'We were all working late here last night. Marion said she was going to be in the West End later so I agreed to meet her when I finished. I went home to change first.'

'Why did you need to change?'

May gave his boss an old-fashioned look.

'Please tell me you weren't thinking about sex at a time like this?'

'No, Raymond, I had been to see Giles earlier in the day, I smelled of his damned chemicals and wanted to change my shirt, OK?'

'What did she tell you on the phone?' Land asked.

'She said she was worried about her daughter Cassie. She needed my advice, but given that we were suddenly getting close to her on a professional basis she wanted to keep our meeting confidential. She was always very concerned about appearances.'

'What on earth did you think you were doing, talking to someone involved in an investigation, even tangentially?' asked Land.

'I felt I owed it to her,' said May sheepishly.

'Had you ever met her daughter?'

'No, at the time I met Marion the girl was mostly living with her father.'

'So you met up with her – what time was this?'

'We said eleven p.m., but she was a bit late. She'd been to a networking supper and it overran. She was at the Holborn Dining Room so I suggested meeting down by Temple Gardens, near the tube station, because we wouldn't be seen there. Only I forgot that Temple is almost impossible to reach from Holborn tube, so she had to get a cab.'

'She turned up, and then what happened?'

'She told me her daughter was in trouble, that she could go to jail. She wanted my advice.'

'Did she say what kind of trouble?' Longbright asked.

'She was worried that Cassie might somehow be implicated in the investigation.'

'Why would she think that?'

'Cassie was friends with Lynsey Dalladay. Marion felt it was only a matter of time before we – that is, Arthur and I – came knocking on her door. She wanted to know what she could do about it.'

'You must have known at that point that you weren't in any position to give her advice,' said Land.

'What did you say to her?' Longbright asked.

'I said she had to be completely honest with us. I offered to go down to the institute and talk to her daughter privately.'

Land shook his head. 'Against any kind of ethical logic. Great.'

'Don't talk to me about ethics,' said May. 'You just had Janice breaking into Cassie North's office without a warrant.'

Land was indignant. 'That's different. It's the sort of thing your partner does all the time and I never hear you complaining.'

May sat back and folded his arms. 'OK, I met up with someone I shouldn't have.'

'Just after you met with Marion North she was strangled and thrown in the river near the spot where you met her. Her body was on the shore where we found Dalladay.'

'How do you know she was strangled at the same spot?'

'The taxi driver remembers that North hailed him in Holborn and asked him to take her to the Victoria Embankment, but he couldn't turn around and had to leave her on the other side of the road. He thought it was a funny place to drop someone, but she said she was meeting a friend. That would be you.'

'So how did she end up so far downstream?' May asked.

'Bryant's been measuring the tidal speeds to see how long it takes bodies and their various separated parts to get from one reach of the river to the next, except we won't let him out to do any practical experiments.'

'She could have walked further along after meeting me.'

'It's a long walk. It would have taken her a while.'

'And she was on Tower Beach?'

Land checked his notes. 'Yup, and no footprints around the body, just like Dalladay. Not chained up this time, but she had exactly the same kind of contusion, although it was further down in her right shoulder, and a lot deeper. So tell me, what did you do after seeing her?'

'I left her there on the embankment, waiting for a taxi,' said May. 'The street was deserted. Anyone could have come along.'

'It wasn't very chivalrous of you,' said Land. 'I thought you always escorted ladies home.'

'Not this one, trust me, you wouldn't,' said May. 'She's very independent. I mean, was – she was always in control.'

'Well, she lost control of the situation last night,' said Land. 'She was strangled with your red scarf.'

The revelation brought May up short. 'How could you possibly know that?'

'Because Bryant gave it to you for your birthday,' the unit chief explained. 'He had his landlady sew your name on it.'

32

IN & OUT

Longbright followed the devastated May back to his office and sat on the corner of his desk. 'How did she end up wearing it, John?' she asked. 'Surely you must remember.'

May tried to recall the details of the meeting. 'She was cold. I put it around her neck.'

'And you didn't take it back when you left her?'

'I probably meant to and forgot.' He ran his fingers through his silver mane, exasperated. 'I can't believe she's gone. It must have been my fault in some way. What the hell am I going to do? They're going to find my DNA all over her.'

'You mean you touched her.'

May looked guilty. 'I kissed her.'

'Oh John, you *didn't*.'

'Yes, but you know, like an old friends' kiss, except it was a hug and a kiss. She always had this aura of toughness and independence, but I could tell she was unhappy.'

'So you hugged her long enough to transfer God-knows-what from your hands and jacket.'

May looked like a smacked dog. 'It never occurred to me, obviously. I suppose when they put that together with the scarf it'll be impossible to disprove.'

'Except that anyone who knows you wouldn't believe it for a second.'

'What about a jury, Janice? How are they going to know me?'

'That's ridiculous – you have no motive.'

'Of course I don't.' He dropped down into his chair. 'What a bloody nightmare. What was I thinking?'

'You weren't to know. The Met lads won't believe—'

'The Met lads? They're not our friends, Janice. This will play out very conveniently for them. Obviously they know it wasn't me, but how perfect that I get caught interfering with the legal process! There'll be an internal inquiry, and you know as well as I do that we wouldn't even pass a health-and-safety inspection, let alone a full investigation. It'll mean the end of the unit.'

'Then we have to find a way of clearing your name before it goes any further.' Longbright knew she sounded unconvincing.

'How? You heard Land. I'm out. If Darren Link discovers I'm still here after today he'll turn us over to the IPCC and shut the place down himself. I can't be party to anything concerning the case. With Arthur's mind gone AWOL and me under suspicion, you're on your own.'

'Then we need a plan,' said Longbright. 'Who else knows you went out with her? What about her daughter?'

'I don't suppose so. You'll have to talk to her and see what she knows. All I can say is that the whole thing was a massive error of judgement on my part.'

'Why didn't you take the scarf back?'

May shrugged. 'She was cold, and when I kissed her I just slipped it around her neck. I was being a gentleman.'

'Maybe you left it with her because you wanted an excuse to see her again.'

'What, and then she strangled herself with it?' May looked aghast. 'Am I that bad at reading people?'

'No,' said Longbright carefully, 'but sometimes you don't think about the position you put other people in.'

May felt betrayed. He had always enjoyed the unswerving support of his staff, but for the first time he saw doubt in Longbright's eyes. 'Didn't Arthur say that Lynsey Dalladay killed herself?' he asked. 'It certainly didn't look like suicide. What if Marion managed something similar and made it look like murder when it wasn't? She knew they were about to come under scrutiny in the course of the investigation. If she had a link with Dalladay, maybe she took the same way out.'

Janice had always felt closer to John than anyone, and hated seeing him like this. She relied on him to be the centre of any storm, the voice of calm reason. Now he was shaken up and unfocused. 'Think about it, John; wouldn't you have sensed something when you saw her? Wouldn't she have given some indication of what she was about to do?'

'I can't see anything clearly,' he said, as if he hadn't heard her. 'I don't know where this guy Gilyov fits in with North and Dalladay. They inhabit different worlds. They have no connection.'

'Then we need to find one,' said Longbright, catching his panicked gaze and trying to hold it. 'I've always been here for the pair of you, you know that, but we can't solve this with you both out of action. We'll clear your name somehow, but you have to help us find a way forward.'

'Then you've got to get Arthur back,' said May. 'I don't know how. You have to give the case over to him.'

Darren Link walked into Raymond Land's office as if he owned it. He had no sense of containment. He was a man-spreader; his arms fell wide, his chest swelled, he blundered and sprawled in a proprietorial manner designed to invade and threaten and cause offence. He liked to remind people of where they ranked in his estimation. The split shards of his damaged eye seemed to fix upon things of which he disapproved, as if he could destroy them just by staring hard.

Right now he was not at all happy to be in Land's office, with its racing car paperweights and photo frames without pictures in them. He regarded Land as an underling and an idiot.

'How the hell did this happen?' he demanded. 'One of your own men? What was he thinking, arranging to meet this woman? Why didn't you stop him?'

'I didn't know he knew her,' said Land helplessly. 'They met years ago, then didn't see each other again from that time to this.'

'Did he stay in touch with her or did she just suddenly call him up out of the blue?'

Land sighed, knowing that it would all have to come out. 'She'd been interviewed in connection with the Dalladay case. That's why she called John.'

'And he had a secret meeting with her.' Link thumped his brisket-fists on Land's desk. 'Do you realize how that looks?'

'He agreed to see her purely as an old friend, to offer her some advice.' Land cleared his throat nervously, hoping that it would prove to be the case.

'Why did she end up with an item of his clothing? Did she take it from him on purpose?'

'They met in the open air, the night was cold, he put it on her and doesn't remember taking it back,' said Land, realizing how lame the story sounded. 'He's not guilty, obviously.'

'How do you know that?' asked Link with slow menace. 'Your unit has a long, embarrassing history of getting too close to its suspects.'

Land knew that Bryant had always encouraged this culture, blurring the lines between officers and the accused, dragging in outlawed academics and fringe practitioners to offer advice and sometimes becoming directly involved.

Link thought for a moment. 'You say Marion North made the jump to calling May because she was interviewed. Who interviewed her?'

'Mr Bryant,' Land admitted, heavy-hearted.

'That's not possible, though, is it,' said Link with heavy irony, 'because Bryant was suspended from operations after his doctor's report. Unless you let him continue working on the case.'

'*I* didn't, no,' said Land. 'He was confined to his office, then sent home on leave. I can't control what he chooses to do when he's not here.'

Link released a bull-snort of frustration. He had the tenacity of an Exocet when the occasion arose but his attitude was mitigated by a sense of fair play. 'Let's try and be clear about this. North died just after your top man met her in the vicinity. It's circumstantial; let's not worry about that. But he'll have left behind a murder victim smothered in his DNA, and that's the real problem. Has Kershaw seen the body yet?'

'He's had a quick look,' said Land.

Link paced heavily about the room. 'I'm guessing the river may have removed some evidence, and we can argue that there's been contamination caused by multiple first responders, but there could be other matches. They won't be able to claim that there's an actual crime scene as the body was found in the water, which may help matters. It moved downstream.'

'Yes, Mr Bryant has a theory—'

'I'm sure he has, and it probably involves sunspots and pyramids so let's not go there. Depending on the amounts we may not be able to claim transference. They'll go for epithelial evidence.'

Land knew that this was a big problem. The scarf around North's neck had been pulled so tight that it had abraded the skin. Forensic serology was about identifying traces containing antigens and polymorphic enzymes from blood. Touch DNA – epithelial evidence – lay in the skin cells, as few as five or six, that could be transferred from a body to an object. If North's coat buttons had any cells dislodged from

May's hands that had survived immersion, there would be just cause for conviction.

'He made a mistake, he should never have met up with her,' said Land. 'He knows that. So what can we do?'

'Pray he's not a shedder,' said Link. Some people lost more skin cells than others. The number of cells lost dramatically increased with applied pressure, so if May was telling the truth and had touched the victim lightly he might have only resettled material that had since washed off. 'I can't give you advice on this, not without being accused of exerting influence on the investigation,' Link warned. 'John can't have any further contact with his partner.'

'But they talk every day – they always have.'

'You *do* understand that it's possible your senior investigating officer could be charged with murder? Read my lips; he must have no more contact with Bryant.'

Land's voice went up half an octave. 'What about the rest of us? Bryant's at home but he still has lucid periods, and he's using them.'

'So he's still working on the case? God, what does it take to stop him?'

'It comes as naturally to him as breathing.'

Link jabbed his index finger in Land's direction. 'I can't prevent you from speaking to him but you *cannot* pass on anything he tells you that pertains to the case. You need to keep the rest of the staff away from him too, so that you're the only point of contact. I'll provide an internal investigations officer with immediate effect, and John is on gardening leave until the investigation gets handed over to another body.'

'Could we get someone in from outside and sort of make it look like we're impartially co-operating?'

'Absolutely not,' said Link. 'No outsiders. This case can't take any more clowns.'

Land waited until the Serious Crimes superintendent had left, then grabbed his coat. 'I have to go out for a while, Janice,' he told her. 'I'm putting you in charge.'

'What are you going to do?' asked Longbright.

'I'm taking Darren Link's advice: "Don't bring in an outsider." There's only one person who can save us now,' said Land. 'Link says he can't prevent me from speaking to him, so that's exactly what I'm going to do.'

33

SPOONS & SPADES

'Don't let him in,' called a wavering voice from the living room. 'Tell him I'm having another one of my attacks. He's up to something. There'll only be trouble.' The doorbell rang for the third time. 'Tell him I think I'm at the battle of Waterloo or something. There's trickery afoot or my name isn't . . .' There was an unfeasibly long pause.

'Don't be silly,' said Alma, dragging a trolley full of religious pamphlets along the hall. 'I have to go out. He can at least sit with you for a while.'

'I'm not five years old!' The doorbell rang a fourth time. 'Where are my jelly babies?'

'They're in your head.'

'I'm not imagining things!'

'I mean in that horrible Tibetan head, where they always are. I'm going to let him in.'

'If you do I'll never eat any more of your cabinet pudding again.'

'Then I'll take it to my parishioners.'

'Why would you be so cruel? You could sell that stuff to Holloway Prison and no one would ever have the energy to try and escape. Please don't open the—'

It was too late. Alma had undone the London bolt and flicked up the latch. 'I need to talk to you, Arthur,' said Raymond Land, handing Bryant's landlady his wet umbrella like a curate entering a country house. 'I know you're there, I saw your wrinkly little head poking out of the window just now. This is no time for messing about. Are you all there?'

Bryant appeared at the living-room door in an indigo quilted dressing gown and matching slippers, a Turkish potentate exiled to Bloomsbury. 'If you're referring to my mental state it's a mixed bag,' he admitted. 'As you're already in you might as well come in.'

'He had a blackout in the bathroom last night,' Alma mouthed.

'It was not a blackout, you silly woman,' said Bryant. 'I nodded off and woke up thinking I was in Spain because I'd been staring at your stupid matador poster.'

'Alma, could you leave us for a few minutes?' asked Land. 'Arthur, I wouldn't turn to you unless the situation was desperate, you know that.'

'Thank you for your confidence.' Bryant wandered into the kitchen and began rummaging in the fridge.

'You know what I mean. You have to listen to me very carefully. If you don't, you're going to lose your partner, the unit and everything you've ever held dear, do you understand?'

'You have my undivided attention,' said Bryant, pulling out a strange-coloured piece of cheese and tentatively sniffing at it. 'I think this is Stinking Bishop,' he said. 'Welsh rarebit?'

Land sat at the table putting Worcester sauce on his toasted cheese and explained the situation in as much detail as he could muster, but Bryant's first question still caught him by surprise. 'Why is Giles so sure she was strangled?'

'There are ligature marks on her neck,' said Land.

'No water in her lungs then?'

'I don't know. Clearly Giles doesn't think so. I only had a

short conversation with him. We're firefighting here, Arthur. I've not caught up with all the reports.'

'How is John handling it?'

'Not well. He's as shocked as any of us.'

Bryant sat silent for a minute, then rose and left without a word.

What have I done? Land wondered. *What if I've pushed him over the edge?* He turned in an agony of faltering indecision. *How did we ever get in this mess? John framed for murder, and the only person who can help him has lost his wits.*

Bryant reappeared in the doorway. 'I have decided,' he announced. 'I accept your challenge.'

'I haven't given you a challenge yet,' said Land.

'You were about to ask me to take charge once more.'

'Are you sure you're up to it?'

'No, not in my present state, but I have a spade up my sleeve.'

'You mean an ace.'

'No, one of these.' Bryant produced a small trowel in his right fist. 'I can't help John unless I first help myself.'

'Mr Bryant, you're not making any sense,' said Alma, appearing in the kitchen doorway with her coat on.

'And I'm not about to start now,' said Bryant. 'Go about your business, both of you. I have to get started. There's no time to waste.' He shooed them towards the front door. 'Raymondo, give my lovely landlady a hand with her biblical tracts, would you? She's off to thrust them into the hands of poor dupes outside King's Cross Station. Don't read any of them yourself; they'll make your brain fall out. I know a thing or two on that subject, trust me.'

'But what are you going to do?' asked Land. 'Where do you even start?'

'Spoons!' said Bryant, slamming the door on them and bolting it.

The head of the PCU and the chief steward of the United

Church of the Holy Saviour found themselves locked out on the third-floor landing of number 17, Albion House, Harrison Street, Bloomsbury while its tenant got to work.

Bryant ran to the window in his bedroom and opened it. He thrust his trowel into the wooden plant box outside and began digging, showering earth on someone below.

'Oi!' shouted a familiar voice. 'What the bleedin' 'ell do you think you're doing?'

'Who is that?' Bryant squinted over the window ledge. 'I don't have my trifocals on.'

'Brad Pitt,' the unhappy man in the XXXL Arsenal T-shirt covered in earth called back. 'You just chucked dirt all over me.'

'Ah, Mr Pitt, I remember you. You've put on weight. I thought it turned out that your name was Joe; I wish you'd make up your mind. It wasn't dirt, it was compost mixed with aluminium sulphate and iron filings designed to increase the soil acidity.'

'I'll come up there and increase your acidity in a minute,' warned his next-door neighbour, who had been taking out the rubbish when he was hit with debris.

'Yes, you must pop up sometime and regale us with some more of your colourful working-class exploits,' Bryant called back, shovelling more earth out. 'Not now, though, I'm busy.'

Something else fell out of the window box. Joe was hit on the head with a spoon.

'I say, could I have that back?' Bryant called. 'I have some more but that one's part of the control experiment.'

It's fair to say that Mr Bryant's next-door neighbour was steaming by the time he reached the front door. 'This is a block of flats, not a bleedin' science laboratory,' said Joe, holding the spoon in one meaty fist. 'We have to live here.'

'Yes, I know – ghastly, isn't it? I never thought I'd end up in a council flat, but it's been instructive. I've learned a lot about hip-hop, swearing and vehicle maintenance. I'd invite you in for a sherry but I don't want you sweating on our furniture. Thank you kindly for this. Give my regards to Mrs Pitt.' Bryant took the spoon and closed the door.

Back in his bedroom he laid the spoons out side by side and noted the difference between them.

Oddly enough, it was the long-dead Brighton entertainer Dudley Salterton who had planted the thought with his remarks about cockles and people who had a natural ability to control others. What he needed now was the book. Unfortunately he couldn't remember what it was called, what it was about or where he had left it. He began calling around. On his fifth phone call he found himself talking to Dr Gillespie.

'Ah, Mr Bryant, how are you feeling?' Dr Gillespie enquired unenthusiastically. 'Mr Land tells me you've been suffering from waking nightmares. Why didn't you come in to see me?'

'Visiting you is one of them,' said Bryant. 'How's your neck?'

'It's rather worse than I—'

'I'm not actually interested, just being polite. They're not nightmares, more like lucid dreams, and they're proving rather enlightening. I'm calling to see if I left a book with you.'

'Yes, you did,' said Gillespie.

'You don't happen to remember what it was called, do you?'

'I have it here. *Diseases and Treatments of Congolese Tribal Elders 1870–1914*.'

'Did you have a chance to read it?'

'I had a flick through the photographs,' Gillespie admitted. 'The chapter on body scarification was positively revolting. I'm not sure what point you were trying to make.'

'I was hoping you'd take more than a cursory glance at the text,' snapped Bryant. 'Physician, forget healing thyself, I wanted you to heal *me*. What an utter poltroon you are. No matter, I'll work from my notes.' He rang off and returned to the study of his spoons. The coatings on the various pieces of cutlery had eroded to markedly different degrees.

At least Dr Gillespie had served his purpose by jogging Bryant's memory. In the book, all of the elders in the M'boochi tribe had started suffering from depression, forgetfulness and blackouts, and had later experienced powerful lucid hallucinations culminating in loss of sanity, attempted suicide and, ultimately, death. No common factor could be discovered between them until a Victorian anthropologist named Bertram Siddeley investigated their ceremonial drinking cups.

He discovered that the cause of the disease was not genetic, as had first been assumed, but could be traced to the traditional silver alloy goblet from which each elder daily drank. The author had proposed various theories including a reaction between the acidic liquids they consumed and the alloy, and another caused by the home-made fillings in their teeth reacting with the cup itself, but the mystery had never been fully unravelled.

As Bryant studied the damaged spoons, he realized he had the answer lying before him. In most cases the plating had burned off to reveal a brownish compound metal underneath. Clambering on to the corner of the ottoman, he grabbed a filthy leather-bound volume from the top of the bookcase and threw it open. It didn't take him too long to find the section he needed. He read:

Some metals become toxic when they form poisonous soluble compounds in certain forms. Particles of lithium, aluminium, iron and beryllium can build up in the body to form highly toxic bioaccumulation. The toxicity of metals depends on their ligands. Organometallic forms such as tetraethyl lead and methylmercury may prove fatal. Toxic metals are elements and therefore cannot be destroyed. They can, however, be quickly treated by dilution or chelation, which introduces agents that can remove the accumulated particles. Chelation therapy is a relatively simple but very specific medical procedure with a high risk factor that can leave lasting health problems if incorrectly administered. Its effects are immediately felt.

It was a risk he was willing to take, particularly as he had no other options left. Casting the book aside, he headed for his bedside table and lifted the offending item in his hands.

The Tibetan skull. It had sat there beside him grimacing for so many years that he never even considered it. When they had moved to Harrison Street it had been transferred from his office to this apartment. The skull had been plated in silver panels with chased swirls and curlicues running over its frontal and temporal bones and around its mandible, its teeth capped with matching silver crowns, its eye sockets filled with false opals and metal ruffles. The brain pan opened to reveal a tray lined with another heavily patterned alloy on its lid and base, but as Bryant ran his fingers over it now he saw that the chased sections had exposed dark metals beneath the thin silver plating just like the spoons – and it was into this that he had insisted on Alma placing his uncovered sandwiches, sweets and cakes for the past months. All that time, the particles were being transferred to his food and ingested to form a residue in his system.

He considered lobbing the skull from his bedroom window but realized that it would prove useful in testing for specific toxic elements. This time, though, he would not go to his hopeless GP. It was a rush job for an old friend.

Jamel Letheeto had been working at University College Hospital, specializing in toxicity therapies, until he was thrown out for stealing medical instruments. The hospital board was not mollified by his explanation – that he had been stockpiling them for the coming nuclear winter – and had demanded that he undergo psychiatric evaluation, which had found he was suffering from Apocalypse Syndrome.

Letheeto was still a good doctor, even after the nervous collapse that had been brought on by his long hours and over-dedication to work, and with any luck he could still lay his hands on chemicals. Bryant set about finding his phone.

'If we can get the process started straight away you'll still be able to work, if that's what you're asking me,' said Letheeto. 'I can run chromatographic tests on the metal and tailor a specific drug cocktail to remove its particles. We'll need to get rid of the most serious symptoms before they cause permanent brain and liver damage, but I'm afraid there's a strong chance that you'll still experience disturbing side effects for the remainder of your life.'

'The remainder of my life could be the length of time it takes to get through a box set of *Breaking Bad*, so let's do it and be damned,' Bryant pointed out. 'Can you get me into a surgery?'

'No need,' said Jamel. And Bryant could almost hear him grinning down the line. 'I have everything I need in my underground bunker.'

'Jamel, do you think there's a chance you can cure me?'

'Mr Bryant, if I can't do this without killing you, I'll be very disappointed in myself.'

'So will I,' said Bryant. 'Let's do or die.'

PART TWO

COMING BACK

'What strange tides bring a man to London, where o'ervaulting ambition swiftly washes him back to earth!'

ALEXANDER BENDO (1676)

34

ROOT & BRANCH

Imagine we are in a plane above the United Kingdom, the third most populous island in the world. Great Britain is surrounded by over one thousand smaller islands with names like Arran, Jura, Benbecula, Ulva, and Bardsey, which has just four inhabitants. Looking down through clouds of charcoal, slate and pearl to its rain-grey capital, we see the jigsaw pieces of a medium-sized transverse city built around a switchback river: London in the second decade of the third millennium. Thanks to the fact that it set the world's time zones it is very rich, as Venice and Constantinople had been in earlier centuries. For London's bankers the working day is seventeen hours long, so that more money can be made. It is a very fast city that can only become faster.

Those who built London thought about their home in the long term. Westminster Hall dates from 1393 and has the largest timber roof in northern Europe. When it needed restoring in 1913 a lot of the roof had to be replaced. The original timbers came from Wadhurst in Sussex. The estate's owners must have realized that new wood would be needed in roughly five hundred years because they had planted a stand of oaks for that specific purpose. By 1913 the wood was ready to be cut and the hall was repaired. By comparison, many of the City of London's new skyscrapers are reckoned to have a shelf life of about fifteen years.

Despite its accelerating pace, the metropolis is ultimately changeless. Its people remain the same because London is a state of mind. They do not make London. London makes them.

It had certainly made Ali. He thought like a Londoner, was as selfish and curious and impatient as a Londoner, but did not behave like one. It was the secret of his success; beneath a patina of English civility was an alien grace that marked him as exotic and unpredictable.

That was how it had seemed to Cassie North until her mother had been pulled out of the Thames with dark bruises around her blanched neck. Now she began to think of him as something else entirely. What did she really know about him?

Although the company was solidly founded on Ali's charisma and Cassie's business sense, it wasn't enough. As time moved on word spread about the deaths of three women connected with the centre, and clients started to melt away. Like coconut oil, YOLO, fixed gear bikes and goji berries, booking a sampler course at Life Options threatened to become another fad that would evaporate overnight. Ali could not control the damage. Their backer sensed the storm before it hit and warned them that if the problem worsened he would be pulling out his money. Life Options attempted to carry on as normal but overnight it ceased to be a centre of calm and became fraught with tension. As nervous creditors began to reduce their payment windows, Cassie fought with Ali. It seemed that their overnight success story would quickly turn into a horror show.

With May under house arrest and Bryant confined to quarters, it was down to Janice Longbright to finally secure an official interview with the elusive Cassie North. This time she attended in uniform. The effect was deliberate and had a galvanizing effect on the staff, who hastily swept her off to a quiet meeting room overlooking the river.

'I'm burying my mother on Monday,' said Cassie, standing behind her chair, unable to settle. 'So you'll forgive me if I'm not in the best of moods. We've had the press sniffing around, it's been dreadful.'

'I understand and I'm sorry for your loss,' said Longbright, 'but you're central to this investigation now, and I will do whatever it takes to resolve this matter.'

'Fine.' Cassie pressed her hands together. 'I'm not sure what more I can tell you. What do you need to know?'

'Did Lynsey Dalladay have many friends here? Lovers, enemies?'

'I counted myself as a friend.'

'A confidante?'

'No. She seemed to have a complicated private life.' Cassie's eyes stayed on Longbright's. 'I wouldn't know about lovers, and I'm not aware she had enemies. I think people found her difficult. She was very outspoken.'

'She left Mr Cooper's house two weeks before she died. Do you have any idea where she was staying?'

'None whatsoever,' Cassie replied emphatically. 'She turned up on time for the courses so we mostly talked about those.'

Longbright switched tack. 'How did you get on with your mother?'

'Well enough to offer her a job here. We had our differences of opinion.'

'Was Marion seeing anyone? Having problems? Did you talk about stuff like that?'

'We had lunch,' said Cassie truthfully. 'We talked. She wasn't seeing anyone and she wasn't planning on killing herself.'

'What do you mean?' Longbright asked.

'There's a rumour that you think the women who come here are indoctrinated into some kind of suicide cult.'

'Where did you hear that?' Longbright asked, intrigued.

'Some muckraker from *Hard News* has been adding to our problems. She's been getting information from someone at your unit. We're not Scientologists, we're not locking inmates in punishment blocks. Lynsey was here to improve herself.'

'Perhaps she thought the only way to do that was by starting again,' Longbright countered, but now she wondered who had been leaking information to the press.

It didn't take long to find out.

In his survival bunker, a disused caretaker's basement in a council block behind the Francis Crick biomedical research institute, Jamel Letheeto tested the metal alloy that had appeared underneath the silver plating in the Tibetan skull, only to discover that it contained fourteen separate poisonous substances. Some, like iron and zinc, were easily dealt with. Others, like cadmium, proved trickier because while the patient showed negligible amounts in his system, his symptoms were consistent with the presence of such a metal. There were further substances that proved impossible to identify. Jamel wondered if they were plant extracts that had been rubbed into the bone to season it.

The doctor's chelation therapies involved an alarming series of washes and flushes not sanctioned by the British Medical Association. This was because of the skill required to perform the procedures and the risks they involved, but Bryant knew there was no time to waste. Convinced about the cause of his symptoms, he put his faith in Jamel's skills. A fibre-optic bronchoscope was used to remove the only visible particles from his chest and left him with an incredibly sore throat, but no invasive surgery was required.

The testing and flushing ran continuously. At first they left Bryant feeling feeble-brained and weak-bodied, but as the toxins left his system his strength returned with surprising speed.

'How are you feeling, Mr Bryant?' asked Jamel, tidying away his equipment, pleased with his work.

'Like someone's been dragging fish-hooks through my pipes,' said Bryant.

'That's pretty much what I've been doing. You're a man of immense fortitude,' Jamel replied. 'You know, there are thirteen thousand different ways that the human body can fail and you had to pick one of the most obscure. It's a good job you thought of calling me.'

'I like to be different.' Bryant buttoned his shirt and accepted a hand down from the makeshift treatment couch. 'Do you still think I'll make a full recovery?'

'Honestly? No.' Jamel shrugged. 'It's been more complicated than I thought. There could be some permanent brain damage.'

'Oh, that's all right. What's a little brain damage at my age?'

'You probably won't suffer any more aphasic episodes, but you may never fully get rid of the lucid dreams.'

'I knew I must have come into contact with something harmful,' Bryant said. 'I've always been selectively forgetful but the blackouts started suddenly, as if I'd reached a point of toxic overload. Then I remembered reading about the Congolese tribal elders and began to wonder about poisonous metals. I wish I'd thought of that damned skull earlier. You may wish to keep it as a souvenir. What can I do for you, Jamel?'

'You can't help me with the one thing I really want,' said the doctor sadly. 'I want my old job back. They're not going to give it to someone with an apocalypse complex.'

'Is it really that debilitating?'

Jamel indicated his laptop screen. 'Some people use the BBC as their home page. I use the Centre for Disease Control. I can't help stockpiling for the Big One. I know it's irrational, but all compulsions are. It wasn't affecting my work.'

'Survivalists need medics,' said Bryant. 'I think I could put you in touch with someone who would hire you on a freelance basis. The Safety in Numbers Society has branches in

Texas and Virginia. You could probably handle a couple of
Evangelist Rapture groups as well.'

A deal was struck over a handshake. One week after his
treatment began, Bryant went home. The detective decided
not to tell anyone about his return to health until he was
quite sure that the treatment had worked.

In the meantime John May was confined to his apartment
in Shad Thames, and although the remaining members of
the PCU's staff continued to add information to the case, a
resolution eluded them. May had suffered mild bouts of
despondency in the past, but now a terrible new darkness fell
upon him.

Raymond Land refused to allow Bryant anywhere near the
PCU building, but loyally called him every night to see how
he was faring. Janice Longbright co-ordinated searches and
interviews, Dan Banbury stockpiled such evidence as there
was, and Giles Kershaw delayed the filing of autopsy reports
on the victims while Fraternity, Meera and Colin talked to
potential witnesses. But somehow every one of them missed
making the most obvious inquiry of all.

The infrastructure of the PCU had fractured. Without
Bryant and May to head it up, the unit simply failed to hold
together. Raymond Land had always relied on his detectives
to tell him what to do. Without them he was utterly bereft.
Unable to make even the simplest decisions, he wandered
about looking like a funfair proprietor who couldn't
remember if he'd tightened all the nuts on his Ferris wheel.

To make matters worse, Darren Link's internal investigations officer arrived. Barbara Biddle was a ruthlessly practical
woman attempting to plot a fair course through a tough job,
but with over fifty Metropolitan Police officers and nearly
thirty staff members suspended for corruption in the past
two years, facing allegations of drug dealing, bribery, theft,
fraud, dishonesty, sexual misconduct and unauthorized
information disclosure, she could not afford to make any

mistakes. She had a wide body and a narrow spectrum of interests, and told everyone that she would remain apart from the staff in order to preserve her impartiality, although the real reason was that she had nothing to say to them that did not involve some form of castigation. Her visits soon became feared.

'I think we have to reach an agreement, you and I,' she said, closing Raymond Land's office door behind her and sitting down opposite him so quickly that he clutched his pencils. She was as sturdy as a skip, with hard eyes, hard hair and eyebrows painted in great arcs that gave her a look of permanent surprise. 'It's obvious you have a major problem here.'

'What sort of problem?' Land squeaked.

'Imagine for a moment that you're running a fried-chicken shop and I'm a health inspector. I come in to check on your hygiene and find you blithely battering rats.'

'I'm not good with analogies,' said Land.

'Let me be blunt, then.' Biddle slapped her hands flat on his desk. 'There's hardly a rule I can find unbroken in this building, from contaminated evidence to unbacked-up computers. These are failures in basic procedure. I don't really know where to begin. Do you want to start with the lack of security? Are you aware that you've compromised this investigation?'

'What do you mean?'

'You talked to a reporter yesterday.'

'I most certainly did not.' Land was adamant. 'I didn't speak to anyone outside of the unit yesterday apart from my barber at lunchtime.'

'Did it occur to you that he might not have been a barber?' asked Biddle. 'Have you seen your hair? You look like a dog after an operation.'

'I was only passing the time of day,' said Land, crestfallen.

'All right, what about the cow's head?'

Land looked startled. 'What cow's head?'

'The one with four bullet holes between its eyes in the common-room fridge.' She sat back, awaiting an explanation.

'That's probably Mr Bryant's. He does . . . experiments.'

'I assume he's also responsible for the marijuana plant, the live rounds of ammunition behind his desk, the stuffed animals and the collection of Victorian arsenic bottles, some of which seem to be full and in one case leaking?'

'Yes, that would be him.'

'There seems to have been a disastrous collapse in the command chain,' said Biddle. 'There's no point in singling out a particular fault. It would be like treating an infected fingernail when the entire body is riddled with leprosy. You see my point?'

'I'm beginning to,' said Land warily. He should have known she would be trouble. You couldn't trust a woman with a name like someone blowing through a hose into a bucket of water.

'So here's my problem. If I start with just what I see walking around this place, the unit would have to be immediately closed with a cease-and-desist order, and that would mean I'd be unable to investigate what I'm actually here for, which is to try and find out why one of your most senior officers has ended up being a suspect in his own investigation. You see the dilemma.'

'Ah, erm, yes.'

'Obviously I want to be able to perform the duty with which I am tasked, and I cannot do that if the unit is closed.' Biddle found it hard to be officious with a man who looked as if he might shout at himself in bathroom mirrors. 'So let's cut a deal. I will continue to investigate the circumstances which have led to Mr May being placed in this invidious position by turning a blind eye to your current working practices. I'll present my case by keeping within the restrictions of its guidelines and ignoring everything else, for now at least.

But I'll have to make a secondary report to Superintendent Link upon submitting my conclusions.'

'Couldn't you just – not?'

'How will that help the dead and the living for whom you must bear witness?' Biddle asked. 'Your job – in case I have to remind you – is to convict the guilty, protect the innocent and uncover the truth, aims that might be compromised by the revelation that some of the investigating officers are holding bingo sessions in the evidence room.'

'Are they? I'll have to put a stop to that.'

'There's also some kind of Victorian coffin in the basement.'

'Well, strictly speaking that's not ours. We sort of inherited it.'

'You don't know much about what goes on around here, do you?'

Land thought for a moment, then shook his head. 'They don't always keep me in the picture, no.'

'I think I've identified the weak spot in the chain of command,' said Biddle.

'Oh good,' said Land. 'Perhaps you can help me to get rid of it.'

'Root and branch,' said Biddle, smiling for the first time.

35

CHAOS & ORDER

Cassie North buried her mother's ashes in a short ceremony at West Norwood cemetery on a Monday morning wreathed in discreet veils of drizzle. Her grandfather attended along with her aunt Molly and a few children who barely knew Marion and ran around the flowerbeds in beatific ignorance of death's wingspan.

Freddie Cooper came alone and stood off to one side, trying not to look as if he was ambulance-chasing. Cassie couldn't work out if he was genuinely sorry for her loss or if he was just there to support his investment. Either way, she had to remain on her guard. Two of Marion's most loyal clients turned up, and just as the service was finishing Ali arrived in his new jeep, dressed in a black designer suit that was too fashionable to be respectful. Cassie left her aunt and tried to head him off.

'What are you doing here?' she demanded.

Ali removed his mirrored glasses. The day had barely grown light. 'She was working for me, Cassie. I came to say goodbye, that's all.'

'You didn't know her.' She looked around herself, unable to stop her anger from flooding out. 'You think you know us?

You don't have the first idea. You look as if you're going to a party. This isn't just another social gathering you can charm your way into.'

Ali couldn't understand why Cassie was angry. She and her mother had never seen eye-to-eye, but he figured that loss could resolve differences just as it created regrets. 'You think I just want to be accepted?' he asked. 'That it's about your class system? I don't care about any of you, I want to be rich, that's all. You act like making money is a sin. You've never had to live in a place so screwed up that you'd risk your life to get out of it.'

'We're all the product of our formative years,' said Cassie coldly.

'You can't stop acting spoilt, can you? Look at Lynsey, the way she behaved.'

She turned on him. 'And what was your role in that, Ali? What exactly did you do?'

Conscious that the mourners were staring at them in disapproval, he lowered his voice. 'You'd better start getting the accounts back in order or Cooper will pull out and we will lose everything.'

'Is that why you came to my mother's funeral, to discuss our finances?' Cassie snapped back.

'No, you're right, this is disrespectful,' Ali replied. 'I should not have come here. There is no sight more depressing than seeing the British close their doors. It makes you all look so small.'

As he walked away, Janice Longbright shut her notebook and headed back to the PCU.

If the wellbeing centre was experiencing problems, the Peculiar Crimes Unit was by now in a state of abject chaos. On that Monday morning the operations room looked as if medical students had held a party in it, and Janice now kept it locked for fear of providing Barbara Biddle with further ammunition. Elsewhere, photographic evidence, statements and half-finished reports had been shoved into folders to fool the internal investigations officer into thinking that order prevailed, but she wasn't that easily tricked.

'There's banana ketchup all over my timesheets,' said Meera, giving up. She pushed back from the overflowing desk she shared with Colin. 'I can't work like this, I'm going to get a coffee.'

Colin trotted along behind her. 'There must be something we can do,' he said. 'Someone has to take control.'

'I don't see how any of us can, not when that sodding woman's creeping about taking notes all the time.'

'She's just trying to do her job,' Colin reasoned.

'God, Colin, stop being so bloody *reasonable*.' As usual, Meera took his support as some kind of personal slight and vented her anger on the coffee machine until a bit of it fell off.

In Raymond Land's office there was a new problem. 'I know this is a bad time,' said Fraternity, placing a folded page on Land's desk. 'I'm really sorry.'

Land eyed the piece of paper as if it was a hand grenade. 'What's that?' he asked.

'My resignation from the unit,' Fraternity explained. 'You know my background. My brother wanted to get into forensic technology, specifically into the field of virtopsies.'

'*Virtopsies?*' Land's face wrinkled. 'Is that a made-up word?'

'It's a forensic tool,' said Fraternity. 'Virtual autopsies remove the need for physically damaging the body. The development team is looking for officers with tech experience, and I've been given an opportunity to finish what my brother started.'

'You quisling,' said Land. 'Another rat deserts the sinking ship. At this rate I'll be drafting in the two Daves as DCs. You can't just walk out on us.'

'They've accepted me and want me to start as soon as possible. I'll still be around to work with the unit.'

'But I can't spare you from here. Apart from that you're black *and* gay, which is great for our diversity quota.'

'I'll pretend you didn't just say that,' said Fraternity, eyeing him coldly.

'And to be honest I've actually started to wonder if John did it.'

Fraternity couldn't believe what he was hearing. 'If you don't support your own team, who will?' he asked hotly. 'We could get him off the hook if Giles returned a verdict of Death by Misadventure on North.'

'What are you talking about? She was strangled with his scarf!'

'You know what John said. He gave it to her and forgot to take it back.' Fraternity shrugged. 'It's the sort of thing any of us could have done, a simple act of forgetfulness.'

'No. No. No.' Land had heard enough. 'I can't have two detectives losing their memories.'

'All right, but let's assume there was a reason for her having the scarf. What if she wanted to blame him for jilting her? She might have hooked it on something in the riverbed when she tried to drown herself.'

'There's only one problem with the theory,' said Land. 'It doesn't make any bloody sense.'

'All right, it's a bit far-fetched, but someone has to think out of the box. Why did you give in so easily, Raymond? You're not too old a dog to learn some new tricks.'

'You need to show some respect, lad,' said Land half-heartedly.

'I've tried that,' said Fraternity, 'and with all due respect, sir, you need to grow some gonads.'

After the detective constable had left his office, Land buried his face in his hands and fought the urge to yell. Fraternity's departure would leave the PCU roster with a measly five members of staff. He was tempted to include the cat just to make up numbers. Thinking back, it had all started to go wrong when Leanne had dumped him for her Welsh flamenco instructor. Back when his marriage was still on solid ground he used to go home and tell her all about his day. Now he talked to the TV. Fraternity was right; he'd lost his mojo. He needed some air.

He went to the window and shoved it open. It was raining, of course, a fine cold mist that drifted in and soaked his shirt front. Down below, a lorry driver ran a cyclist on to the pavement and swore at him. Opposite, a man threw a box of curried chicken and rice at a litter bin and missed. *It's not just me, this whole city is operating beyond its competence level,* he thought. *The river's being used like a waste-disposal unit and I'm powerless to do anything about it. It's like those Russian dumping grounds where they don't find bodies until the snow melts.*

He looked around his miserable cupboard of an office. Nobody respected him. There was half a pepperoni pizza on the bookcase and someone had left their damp gym kit on the radiator. He had no idea how to get back on track. It seemed that each new day brought a dozen fresh directives that had to be followed, and each one further detracted from the task of policing. As he looked up, an embittered-looking one-legged pigeon voided its bowels on to the window ledge. Luckily the broken drainpipe on the roof chose that moment to overflow and dissolve the chalky splodge.

I hate London, he thought, *commuters rushing to reach their offices five seconds ahead of each other, that chicken shop on the corner leaving the pavement slick with grease, the artisanal bakery over there charging five quid for a manky-looking rustic loaf, Arsenal supporters treating the street like a public toilet, shrieking hen parties tottering between bars on ridiculous heels and that smug, stumpy, virus-riddled flying rat thinking he can have a turf-out on my ledge without retribution.*

Firing his hand out of the window he made a grab for the pigeon but it simply warbled and strutted out of his way, staring him down with an orange eye. Getting this angry interfered with his blood pressure. He blinked hard and sat down.

Biddle and Link had tied his hands and the only thing that

stopped the case from slipping away completely was Giles's determination to reach the most accurate verdict. Fraternity was right; in the unit's time of deepest crisis he had failed to take the lead. He was just wondering what to do about it when his office door opened and then fell off its hinges.

'I thought the two Daves were supposed to have fixed that,' said Arthur Bryant, examining the splintered lintel. He was dressed in a deafening three-piece suit covered in huge mauve checks, his unravelling olive scarf knotted at his throat, a red carnation in his buttonhole, his hair (what little there was of it) combed and a cleanish chequered handkerchief folded in his top pocket. He looked like a cross between a Bavarian bandleader and a badly colourized bookie from an old Ealing comedy.

'What on earth are you wearing?' was all Land could think to say.

'I thought I should make a statement.'

'Why, who have you killed?'

Bryant sauntered in and waved a finger at Land. 'I can tell you're down in the dumps, Raymondo. I don't like to see you depressed. I prefer to see you in a miserable state of poorly suppressed panic. I rose to your challenge and I'm here to help. Once more I am strong in mind and body – and *mind* – full of pep, zip, whizz, beans, vim, vigour, inner cleanliness, get-up-and-go, and this time nothing will interrupt my train of – hang on, I'm going to sneeze.' He sniffed the air and foghorned into his checked handkerchief. 'Mothballs. I haven't worn this whistle in a while.'

'You can't be here,' Land stammered, suddenly realizing that his depression had turned to alarm. He should never have involved his most unpredictable detective. 'We're under investigation. If they find you in the building—'

'—they won't be able to do anything,' Bryant said cheerily. 'Why is that, I hear you ask?' He cupped a hand around his right ear, listening.

'Why?'

Bryant threw his arms wide. 'Because, *mon petit crapaud*, I'm cured. Fixed. Repaired. Ameliorated. I'm Arthur two point zero.'

'What are you talking about? You can't be cured, you have Alzheimer's.'

'No, I don't. You thought I did but I didn't. I'd been poisoned.'

'Poisoned? By who?'

'*Whom*. I poisoned myself.'

'What on earth for?'

'I didn't do it deliberately, you invertebrate.'

'How did you reverse the effects?'

'I had a wash.'

Land started to feel the old familiar sensation of going slowly mad around Bryant, but for once it wasn't unwelcome. 'I'm not even going to ask about that. Are you really cured?'

'Insofar as we all start dying past the age of eighteen, yes. There may be the odd side effect, but nothing I can't handle.'

'But this is incredible. Do you need to rest? Can we get you signed off and back to work?'

'Already taken care of, old sock. I'm supposed to take it easy for a while but sod that for a game of soldiers. Letters have gone out to all the right people.' He slapped his hands together. 'When you have a convenient moment, call everyone together in the common room. Let's see if we can't get my partner off the hook and back in action. What we need around here is a little order.'

'Are you sure about this?'

'Absolutely. I feel like a million drachmas, as fresh as morning dew and ready for anything. But first I need a wee, two chocolate biscuits and a cup of tea so strong it could send Peter Pan through puberty. Can I leave you in charge of that?' He beamed a terrifying grin at Land and headed off in the direction of the toilet.

'I never thought I'd say this, but welcome back, Arthur, I think,' Land told the empty room.

36

READY & ABLE

'Why are we here?' Colin asked Meera. 'What's going on?'

'Your guess is as good as mine,' said Meera, glancing around at the common room with distaste. 'Look at the state of this place. I only just cleared it up this morning. Who comes in here, eats an entire box of Krispy Kremes and leaves the box on the desk?'

Colin coughed and looked away.

'I wanted one of those cronut things,' said a familiar voice. 'I never got to eat one before the craze was over.'

They looked round to find Arthur Bryant sitting behind them, counting out on his fingers. 'Pea-shooters, ant farms, spud guns, mood rings, hula hoops, Sea-Monkeys, mullets, "Gangnam Style", Google Glass, planking and twerking. All the things that didn't last. I'm still here, though.'

'Mr Bryant?' For a minute Meera thought she was hallucinating. 'Is that really you?'

'It seems to be,' said Bryant, poking himself with a sausage-finger. 'Actually I cheated on that list. I'm still not sure what twerking is. There was a lot of waiting around between treatments. Colin emailed me with pub quizzes and memory tests.'

Colin grinned sheepishly.

'I don't understand,' said Meera.

'No, none of us do,' Bryant agreed. 'That's what makes life so interesting. But I'm here now, refreshed and restored, so perhaps I can help.'

The room quickly filled. Dan Banbury arrived with Giles Kershaw. Fraternity DuCaine and Janice Longbright lugged in a trolley filled with case files. Raymond Land entered, expecting to sit at the front desk but found himself without a chair. Only John May was missing. Usually the briefing-room meetings were marked by a level of chatter that reminded Land of a classroom when it starts to snow, but today there was total silence. Everyone was clearly amazed to see Bryant calmly standing before them, just as if he had never left. London's most senior detective now walked to the front of the room, lowering himself on to the edge of the desk. There was something different about him, Meera thought, more focused and controlled.

They anxiously waited for him to speak.

'It only takes forty-eight hours for a trail to evaporate,' said Bryant. 'What happened? You've all seen how John and I work, yet somehow the investigation stalled.' He paced across the front of the room, studying each of them in turn. Colin noticed that he wasn't using his walking stick.

'Let's recap.' He stabbed at a photograph on the white-board. 'Lynsey Dalladay, seven weeks pregnant, chained to a chunk of concrete on the Thames foreshore at Tower Beach. We assumed from the contusion on the back of her skull that she'd been beaten unconscious, locked in place with her boy-friend's neck-chain and left to drown. Freddie Cooper's a shifty little bugger who showed no remorse upon hearing about his girlfriend's death. It could have been straight-forward but complications arose: Cooper hadn't seen her for two weeks, turned out not to be the father and it wasn't his neck-chain. Whose was it? Did any of you try to find out?

'Dalladay had a history of dysfunction and depression. She stayed on the move, joined self-help organizations, rarely contacted friends or family, stopped taking her medication. She was lost and on a downward trajectory. She walked out on Cooper. Where did she go? Hold that thought in your head while you consider this. There have been four other deaths.'

The atmosphere in the room tensed. People shifted in their seats. 'The engineer Dimitri Gilyov, a second engineer named Bill Crooms, a former CEO and river suicide called Angela Curtis and New Age guru Marion North, making five people drowned, three of them with the same spear-like contusions. Curtis had one in her lower back. Her coroner had made a note of it, but nobody ever followed it up. Why kill them in the river? Because it's not covered by cameras, and it was convenient. Even so, there should have been witnesses.'

'We looked,' said Colin. 'We talked to everyone and didn't get anything.'

'Perhaps you talked to the wrong people,' said Bryant. 'I can believe there was no one on the embankments but on the Thames itself? There are houseboats, barges, canal boats all on short moorings, which means they move on and you need to track them down. Did you liaise with the River Police?'

'We talked to them but they had nothing to add,' said Banbury.

'Maybe they're being territorial. They have a problematic history with the CoL police. Gilyov had a dodgy background and his severed left hand was found near Dalladay's body. He'd been tortured and then killed for some transgression. A few of his pals are known to us, but you don't seem to have pursued this line of inquiry with any rigour because you weren't linking the cases together. Why not?'

'The only evidence we have is circumstantial,' said Land. 'Come on, you thought they'd all committed suicide.'

'It was a line of inquiry, and I was not thinking as clearly as I am now. I'll return to that in a minute.' He faced the whiteboard, tapping another name. 'Crooms died after checking on Gilyov. Why did he go back to the body?'

'We assumed he murdered him,' said Banbury.

'Do you have any evidence?'

'No,' Banbury admitted.

'Then let's move on to Angela Curtis and Marion North, both linked to Dalladay by Life Options courses. Curtis signed up for them, North taught them and North's daughter is the co-owner of the company running them. All of this would seem to be sending you in one direction, but only Janice checked out the St Alphege Centre. At this point the next logical step would have been to apply for a search warrant.'

'We didn't do that because we found nothing out of the ordinary,' said Longbright defensively.

'Of course not,' Bryant replied. 'Why would you? You weren't looking for tax infringements, you were trying to find evidence of multiple murder! The CID would have been all over this like a rash. And perhaps they're not murders as we usually see them.'

'What do you mean?' asked Kershaw.

'Let's deal with these matters seriatim. You assumed that because of the locked chain and the contusion that Dalladay had been dragged there by her killer. But I kept coming back to the idea of the Thames as a sacred source of rebirth. Dalladay had reached the end of her tether. She was tired of making mistakes in her life and wanted to be "reborn". She was attending classes designed to teach her how to do exactly that. But it isn't what Marion North taught – she specialized in astrology and aromatherapy, and sold bits of coloured rock to dunderheads. Marion North was there to do some social climbing and make money. Her daughter got her the job. You see my point.'

'No,' said Raymond Land, slightly too emphatically.

Bryant ploughed on. 'Angela Curtis was a woman in need of help, but her need was a physical one. She suffered from depression and hormonal imbalance. I went through her doctors' reports. Ten days before she killed herself she suddenly stopped taking all her medication and handed her prescription pills to her daughter for safekeeping. Why? Because she couldn't trust herself not to start taking tricyclic antidepressants again. The daughter didn't want her to stop taking them but Angela blamed them for her sudden weight gain. She'd stopped them once before and had become suicidal.' He looked around the silent room. 'I trust the connection's clear.'

'Not remotely,' said Land.

'Well, let's move on. Giles made a more detailed examination of the damaged tattoo on Gilyov's hand. It's been subjected to hydrolytic tissue collapse, so this is the best he could get.' He pinned the design on the board behind him. 'It's still not clear, but what I took to be a lighthouse and beams of light could be snakes around a head: a Greek symbol for the Medusa. The name of Freddie Cooper's company. An odd coincidence.'

The general sense of puzzlement increased.

'If we could just pop our Dan Brown novels down for a moment,' said Land impatiently, 'can I point out that there's nothing here that we don't already know?' He waved his hand at the design. 'Er, apart from the Gorgon thing.'

'There's nothing new except this,' said Bryant, holding up a folded yellow sheet of A4 paper. 'Giles?'

Kershaw rose and addressed the group. 'Gilyov had a scar on his left thigh, a messy exit wound, the result of a bullet being fired into him some ten years earlier. It had damaged his muscle tissue and had never healed properly.'

'He also had a girlfriend who left him because she thought he was mentally disturbed,' said Bryant. 'She says he was obsessed with the idea of conquering pain because his leg hurt so badly. When he stopped seeing her he vanished and never called her again, and all she could find in his belongings was this.' He unfolded the page and pinned it on the board.

The paper read: 'Mind Over Matter – An Evening of Magic, Mystery & Mentalism'.

'Take a look at this magician, the Great Hidini, and his assistant,' said Bryant, pointing to two small monochrome photographs. 'Unless I'm much mistaken, they're the couple who took over the St Alphege Wellbeing Centre and turned it into Life Options. You had a single source connecting the deaths. Why didn't you continue testing for paternity down there, starting with Cassie North's business partner?'

'There's no indication that he and Dalladay—' began Land.

'Don't worry, I did some further checking and got Dan here to take a cell sample. We're awaiting results on that.' He unfolded a flyer for Pastor Michaels, and another for the sacred Thames course. 'Thornberry's real name is Ali Bensaud. He has no criminal record but he did accidentally sign his real name once, and that's all it took to track his ID. On the surface of it he has only the most tangential of connections to any of the victims, which I presume is why you didn't interview him.'

'He hasn't really been on our radar,' said Longbright.

'Why not?' Bryant demanded. 'He's hungry, ambitious. According to you, his persona is largely based on his sexual charisma. That means women must at some level think he's available. Isn't that why movie stars keep their partners invisible? A pregnant girl could ruin him. It shows he's fallible.'

'But the company's his. He's got more to lose than anyone.'

'The earliest phone and tax tabs I found for Bensaud start when he began appearing as an evangelist. You can see his career path quite clearly. A showman, a charlatan, and now an unqualified therapist with vulnerable women attending his classes. I want a warrant to take his Life Options clinic apart. And I want to know more about Marion North. John hadn't seen her for years so why would she suddenly call out of the blue?'

'You don't know it wasn't the other way around,' Land said. 'John might have made one of those – what do they call them? Bounty calls.'

'My partner is a gentleman, not a serial Lothario,' said

Bryant. 'Why didn't you pull a transcript of the call?'

'Look here,' said Land. 'She was an astrologer, wasn't she? Why didn't she know what was going to happen?'

Bryant threw him a look of exasperation. 'She wasn't a fortune teller, you echinoderm. There are dozens of New Age therapies, some fallacious, others based on irrefutable medical research. Life Options was newly minted out of a bankrupt business by people with no previous expertise in the field, and employed snake-oil sellers like Marion North.' He slapped the board. 'At the centre of it all, hiding in plain sight, is Ali Bensaud. Clever and highly motivated. I want him broken open. And find someone who saw my partner with North. They were standing on an exposed section of the Thames Embankment, for heaven's sake! Somebody out there noticed them. I've drawn up task lists for all of you.' He fixed each member of the team with a gimlet eye. 'If we can't close this case in the next forty-eight hours I'll shut the unit down myself.'

'What's an echinoderm?' whispered Dan.

'A species that includes the sea cucumber,' said Colin. 'When it gets frightened it expels its innards out of its anus.'

'I think I preferred him when he was talking rubbish,' Dan replied.

37

AFLOAT & ON BOARD

Colin and Meera found him first.

The retired lighterman lived on a barge called the *Penny Black*, its deck covered in spider plants and oil drums filled with grasses and shrubs. It was moored near the landscaped riverside park known as Bernie Spain Gardens, beside the Oxo Tower. Sammy Maisner had inherited the vessel from his father and had a long lease on the mooring rights, but was now under pressure to move because the developers behind the South Bank's latest rash of luxury hutches wanted their residents to have unimpaired views.

'Those bankers in Notting Hill are starting to move out,' said Colin as he and Meera approached. 'They say the area's become really boring since all the bankers moved in. No sense of irony.' He waved his hand at the barge in front of them. 'Next they'll get this bloke out and start moaning about the lack of atmosphere on the river.'

'You've been spending too much time with Mr Bryant,' said Meera. 'Look at it, Colin, it's a floating rubbish dump.'

'Are you coming aboard or are you just going to stand there slagging me off?' Maisner called out. He looked to be in his early seventies, but the outdoor life had kept him fit and fresh. His sailor's cap didn't look very official; more like the sort of hat worn by someone in charge of a funfair boating pond, but he sported the requisite white beard and a navy blue cable-knit sweater. Colin pushed Meera in front, on to the gangplank.

'People don't realize how clearly you can hear everything on water. It can look a bit of a mess, but then there's this.' Ahead of them, sitting low on the deck and shielded by the greenery, was a glasshouse filled with herbs and flowers of every hue. 'I sell them to the restaurants,' Maisner explained. 'I grow everything from scratch and water it from the river. Nothing is wasted. And I hear everything. So what is it you want?'

Meera realized now why no one had interviewed the old bargee. Although the *Penny Black* had an uninterrupted view of Victoria Embankment and Temple Gardens diagonally opposite it couldn't be clearly seen from the far side.

'Before you ask,' he said, patting the side of the barge, 'it's called the *Penny Black* because when my old man was declared bankrupt he sold the stamp albums he'd kept as a child, and the one rare stamp he owned financed the boat. Why don't you come below deck and I'll make some tea?'

Meera couldn't be bothered with social niceties and ran through times and dates. 'We need to know if you saw or heard anything unusual.'

Maisner's amiability faded. 'You're talking about the couple on the bank. I heard them fighting, if that's what you mean.'

'If you knew, why didn't you report it?'

'The river's a noisy place to live,' said Maisner. 'Police launches, party boats, tourists and restaurants; you hear every clank of a knife and fork from up here. It's when the hen parties kick off that I really think about upping anchor. Then the sun comes out and everything's all right again.' He scratched at his beard. 'They won't get me out.'

'The couple who were fighting,' Colin prompted.

'You only hear people on the opposite embankment when the wind's in the right direction. I reckon the wind changed just then.' Maisner pointed to the far shore. 'I'd seen them a minute or two earlier, a man and a woman, middle-aged maybe, I don't know. My eyesight's not what it was. Then I went below deck. My window was open. I heard her shout then suddenly stop, like her vocal cords had been cut. You hear a lot of drunken yelling but it doesn't normally sound so desperate, it's more your co-ordinated mooing-into-the-sky sort of thing. That's why I came back up and looked over again. It looked like she was trying to get away from him. I'd had a couple of whiskies, you know, so I can't really be sure. I glanced back over again and she was gone, and he was standing at the balustrade leaning out, looking down into the water. It was a very high tide, well over seven metres. For a second I thought—'

'What did you think?'

'That she'd gone in. But he kept looking for a minute then walked away, sort of relaxed, strolling like, not a care in the world, so I figured she must have got in a taxi and left him behind.'

'Can you fix a time on it?'

'It had to be closer to midnight than eleven. The Oxo Tower restaurant looked like it was shutting. Most of the tourists had gone off to catch their trains.'

'Did you see which direction this man went?'

'Towards Blackfriars, I think. It's a long bare stretch – there's nothing much along there but the station.'

'If he left by public transport that means he used the District and Circle on the tube, or Thameslink to St Pancras and Bedford or down to Gatwick and Brighton,' said Colin. It was the worst possible outcome; between them the lines ran in every direction. 'You didn't get a good enough look at him to be able to say what he was wearing? What colour his hair was?'

'Maybe he had a brown or grey coat?' Maisner thought for a minute. 'Wait, though, there was something, only—' He looked around at the flowers, crimsons, yellows and purples. 'Red. The first time I saw them he was wearing a red scarf. But when I looked back it was on her.'

Meera shot Colin a knowing look. The scarf had just become a noose around John May's neck.

'I should have called out maybe, just to make sure there was no funny business going on.' The old man looked tenderly at a trough of alpine daisies, his fingertips brushing their leaves. 'I used to live in a council flat in Wapping. You never saw anyone from one week to the next. I could have died in there and nobody would have noticed. Here, everybody on the embankment says hello. When they finally manage to kick me out, it'll be the end of me.'

Prowling past the windows in his Shad Thames flat, lost in thought, John May jumped when the phone rang. Nobody ever rang his landline.

MAY: Raymond, are you sure you've got this right? Arthur's recovering? How is that possible?

LAND: How do I know? Nothing that happens around here makes any sense to me. He says he poisoned himself and now he's washed it out, but he may still see things that aren't there. You'll probably have better luck getting sense out of him.

MAY: Why do you know before me?

LAND: I wasn't expecting him to just turn up, was I? And I couldn't say anything until I was sure he was OK. I didn't want that old cow Biddle reporting me. Your partner has been having some kind of illegal chemical treatment. He's already back at the unit.

MAY: Won't he need permission to return?

LAND: Yes, from his superior officer, which as far as I'm concerned is me.

MAY: My God. Raymond, you've finally done something good.

LAND: Er, thank you.

MAY: So what happens now?

LAND: We're all working to get you off the hook.

MAY: Has Giles had the DNA report back from North's body?

LAND: I was getting to that. She's covered in your cells. The good news is that they're all on the surface of her coat and the exposed parts of her skin. There don't seem to be any on her neck or the palms of her hands. She would have raised her hands to stop you. Giles says that's suggestive, but not enough by itself.

MAY: What about my clothes? Any transference?

LAND: No, but they'll argue that you knew how to clean them.

MAY: What, I cleaned them but left my scarf around her neck? Do you know how ridiculous that sounds?

LAND: It's no dafter than you not remembering to take the scarf back from her. Bryant originally thought the women all committed suicide, although he's changed his mind about that now. He's zeroing in on a suspect but it seems a bit left-field if you ask me. If this Ali bloke's that smart he'll have got rid of any evidence long ago.

MAY: Can't you get me back into the unit?

LAND: Not a chance while I've got the old bag under my feet. You stay there until you're cleared or committed. But at least we can be in contact again. I'll try and ditch Ballbreaker Biddle. (*Raymond had not noticed that Barbara Biddle was in his office doorway listening in.*)

MAY: I have to go. Someone's at the door.

Arthur Bryant stood there in his bookie's suit, a dry-cleaning ticket stapled to his lapel, a bag of wintergreen cough drops in his left hand, a metal catapult sticking out of his pocket, egg down his waistcoat and pipe ash in his turn-ups. He pulled off his hat, raising his tonsure of fine white hair. 'Good morning,' he said, as if it was the most natural thing in the world.

May was speechless.

'You might at least invite me in,' said Bryant, 'I'm spitting feathers. My word, it's poshed up a bit since I was last down this street. It's all very well if you want hand-crafted macaroons and an armchair made from reclaimed railway sleepers but not much cop if you're after a mug of builder's. Don't worry if you haven't got biscuits, I brought my own.' He removed a packet of Jammie Dodgers from his top pocket and tried to bite them open. 'Go mad, take two. And put the kettle on, we've got work to do.'

When May returned from the kitchen with mugs of tea strong enough to strip the enamel from their teeth, he found Bryant standing on his balcony with the steel catapult pulled far back.

'What are you doing?' he cried, trying not to spill the tea.

'I got some pebbles off the foreshore,' Bryant said, in that way he had of providing an explanation without answering the question. There was a twang of elastic and a bang as the stone hit metal somewhere below. He reloaded, closed one eye, stuck out the tip of his tongue and tried again. This time there was a shattering of glass and some shouting. May pulled him off the balcony.

'I think that settles one argument,' Bryant said, pocketing the catapult. 'You can't span the Thames with a stone.'

'Why would you want to?'

'To leave a contusion on the back of someone's head. Curtis and North both had them as well, all on the backs of their bodies. I had this idea that someone might have fired something from the other side of the river. It's much narrower than it used to be. You know Rudyard Kipling's "The River's Tale", which is narrated by the Thames itself?' He cleared his throat.

'And life was gay and the world was new,
And I was a mile across at Kew!
But the Roman came with a heavy hand,
And bridged and roaded and ruled the land,
And the Romans left and the Danes blew in –
And that's where your history-books begin!'

'Good for Kipling,' said May without enthusiasm. 'So you think she was murdered after all?'

'I'd come up with another theory: managed suicides. A charismatic, persuasive man convinces vulnerable females that they'd be better off leaving this world. Dalladay is told she can have a fresh start. Curtis is talked into stopping her meds. North – well, I have to say she seems stronger than the other two but perhaps she also had some weakness that could be exploited. People choose to end their lives for reasons other than money. Out of love, for example. Ali Bensaud teaches them—'

'This is the guy who runs the health courses?'

'Yes, yes, do keep up – he teaches them about the sacred river and its power to heal their souls. He plays to their fears and doubts about themselves. We need to get to him before we go anywhere else. I wanted us to tackle it together, but I'll have to go it alone. You see, there's something I know that you don't.'

'You'd better tell me, Arthur.'

'I'll tell you everything after I've interviewed him.' Bryant glanced at his stopped watch. 'He's still down at the centre, and there's no time like the present. Can I borrow your car?'

'No, you certainly can't,' said May. 'The last time I lent it to you I found the glove box full of maggots.'

'Ah yes, the lid came off my Brachyceran Diptera. Fear not, I can get the tube.'

'The unit got into a terrible state without you,' said May as his partner set about taking his leave. 'Do you really think you're cured?'

Bryant tucked his biscuits into his coat. 'My head is clear. My brain is sharp. My Tibetan skull is at the bottom of the Thames. I feel like a man at his physical peak so long as I don't look in a mirror.'

May was trying to catch up. 'Your skull – I'm sorry?'

'Don't be, I'll fill you in later. I say, you didn't strangle her, did you?'

'I can't believe you'd ask that. No, of course I bloody didn't.' May looked horrified. 'This interview. I hope you're going to play it by the book, use some restraint and subtlety.'

'Certainly not. I'm going to make a total fool of myself. It's the best way to get information.' Bryant thumped his hat, attempting to give it some shape. 'Right, stay where you are, I'm heading out into dark waters.'

38

Q & A

The centre was already facing the loss of its clients as the taint of unsolved crime lapped at its doors. Now Bryant was prepared to stir things up further, especially when the receptionist explained that Mr Thornberry was taking an induction class and wouldn't be able to see him. 'Don't worry,' said Bryant, flashing his PCU card, 'I'll sit in on his talk. I have a lot of questions for him. I'm sure you won't mind.'

The receptionist did mind, very much. The man standing there emptying out his pockets in the search for a notebook reminded her of an over-loved Victorian teddy bear. The ladies on the Life Options client list ran book clubs and charities and lunched in garden nurseries along the Thames Valley. The presence of this benign shambles reeking of peppermints and rolling tobacco would surely add to their growing suspicions. 'Perhaps he could see you at—' she said before looking up from her screen and finding nobody there.

Bryant found a space at the back of the induction room, sat down, blew his nose loudly and opened a box of Liquorice Allsorts. The woman next to him moved her chair away an inch.

Ali Bensaud bounced into the room and began his

welcoming address. He perfectly matched the description Janice had provided, moving back and forth before the women with a loping grace that reminded Bryant of a benign leopard. His accent had now been refined in a language school and defied accurate location. Until 1940 most English families had only travelled a short distance, so their intonation could be pinpointed to within a few streets. Bryant knew that dialects broke down into nine broad types, with Received Pronunciation representing the language's gold standard. Non-native English speakers tended to carry over the phonemic inventory of their mother tongue. *North African Arabic,* he decided. *I'll have to tread carefully. If he wriggles off the hook I'll never get him back.*

It was clear that Ali had constructed his persona with precision and would be wary of traps. He stopped before each of his new clients, first reserved, then light-hearted, then earnest. At the end of the induction the good ladies of the lower Thames Valley dutifully filed out to sign up for classes, and the detective rose to meet his key suspect.

'A few minutes of your time, if I may?' Bryant wiped his hand on his coat and held it out.

'We can go in here.' Bensaud shook his hand and led the way to Cassie North's office. 'My partner is busy dealing with problems arising from the death of her mother, as I'm sure you can appreciate.' He had an easy, affable charm and held the eye with authority.

'So you know who I am?' Bryant seated himself facing Ali in one of his elegant consultation chairs.

'Certainly. I would rather have an open, honest discussion with you than have any more officers prowling around the place undercover.'

'I was very impressed, watching you in there. You use some form of neurolinguistic programming? You think all behaviour has structure that you can learn?'

'No,' said Ali, unruffled by the question. 'I just try to put clients at their ease by adopting their natural speech patterns.

We use a variety of different therapies to help them with various problems.'

'What kind of problems?'

'At the moment we're offering advice on a variety of lifestyle issues, but we'll soon be able to deal with depression, phobias, habit disorders, allergies, learning issues, psychosomatic conditions and so on.'

'But you're not doctors.'

'We specialize in the areas that GPs won't cover.'

'Forgive me, but this is largely pseudoscience, isn't it?' said Bryant. 'The mind-over-matter thing has been discredited again and again.'

'Control trials aren't the best way of discovering whether a technique works, Mr Bryant. Our clients would not return if they didn't feel a change in themselves. We receive many unsolicited commendations—'

Bryant knew a clever mimic when he heard one. Ali was spouting jargon like a paid expert fielded by a TV network, but it didn't sound as if he entirely understood what he was saying. 'Where do your therapies cross over into mysticism?' he asked. 'Marion North was selling "energy rocks" from here, wasn't she?'

'Our clients choose from a wide spectrum of therapies, from those with a scientifically quantifiable health basis, like yoga, meditation and stress control, to more psychic energy-based disciplines.'

'Do you diagnose?'

'We offer advice.'

'What was your advice for her?' Bryant pulled Angela Curtis's pill-pot from his pocket and rattled it. 'I understand she was taking them for depression.'

Ali took the pot and read its label. 'They were prescribed by her doctor, not by me. She was seeing Marion North.'

'What happens if you don't think someone has a problem? Do you send them away?'

'We deal with their perception issues.'

More recited jargon, thought Bryant. 'So it's a win-win for you, isn't it?' he said. 'If they arrive complaining that they're overweight but have a normal BMI, you say let's deal with how you perceive yourself, and – forgive me for mentioning anything so vulgar as monetary gain here – you cream off the ackers.'

Ali was smart enough to realize that he had been caught out. 'I don't know what that means.'

'Ah, yes, English as a second language, I forgot. You still get your mitts on the moolah, the dosh, the deep-sea divers, the loot.'

'I'm not very familiar with this language,' Ali replied, 'but I assume you're suggesting we're in it purely to make money.' His reply was tinged with just the right amount of snobbery and irritation to pass for gentrified English.

Bryant took out one of the glittery drawings Longbright had filched from the centre. 'Surely you admit that when it comes to selling "magic" children's daubs and hand-painted lucky rocks the line has been crossed?'

'People throw coins into wishing wells but it doesn't mean they believe their dreams will come true. If it makes them feel better it's a working therapy.' Ali's brow furrowed. 'Forgive me but you are not here to get tips on running a business, surely.'

'Three women have drowned, Mr Bensaud. That is your birth-name, isn't it? It's quite hard keeping up with your identity changes. Two of the dead were your clients and one was your therapist. And here you are running courses in sacred rivers, informing vulnerable clients about the cycle of death and rebirth.'

Bensaud shook his head. 'You're very much mistaken if you think they're vulnerable, Mr Bryant. They're customers, not patients, and they're buying what they want to hear. I'm not your enemy, I'd like to help you as much as possible.'

'I'm glad to hear that. Your paternity test for Lynsey Dalladay's child came back positive, in case you were wondering, which is why we're having this conversation.'

'Yes, I thought it had.' Bensaud sat back with his palms on his thighs and studied his opponent coolly.

'Don't you think your relationship with her was unprofessional?'

'There was nothing wrong with her.'

'But given her background—'

'She was not helpless or at risk in any way, if that's what you mean. She was healthy and entirely responsible for her actions.'

'She was pregnant, and you are the father.'

'You think I deliberately abused any authority I had? She told me she used contraception.'

'She told you she was pregnant.'

Bensaud looked pained and sat silent for a moment. 'Yes. But she did not suggest I was the father.'

'It was lucky she died before she could talk to anyone else,' said Bryant. 'I mean, from a business perspective. I imagine it would be difficult to get other women to, if you forgive the phrase, open up to you. For example, Angela Curtis—'

'Mr Bryant, I did not have relations with that woman. She attended one of Mrs North's courses. I had no dealings with her socially.'

'She's still dead.'

Bensaud held his gaze. 'You're telling me I'm a suspect.'

'It sounds as if you're telling me. We'll be interviewing your colleagues and clients and searching the premises, as well as examining all of your online data.'

'You have a warrant for this?'

'It will be here first thing tomorrow, so I must ask you to leave everything untouched.'

Ali rose. 'I'll expect you then. In the meantime I'd like to get on with my work.' He waited for the detective to join him, then left the room first.

As he departed the centre, Bryant rang his partner in Shad Thames.

'About Bensaud's positive paternity test,' he said, 'would

you like to hear a theory? Marion North was just starting out at the centre. She got a little over-enthusiastic and failed to follow the centre's carefully plotted boundary lines about its holistic-homeopathic advice. She told Angela Curtis to throw away her medication and start buying their manuka honey or whatever. As soon as Curtis did so, her depression went untreated and returned.'

'Curtis's death occurred earlier than the others,' May pointed out. 'Could you stand still? You're fading in and out.'

'I'm trying to get across a road without being knocked down. Listen to me. Perhaps Bensaud failed to follow his own rules. His new power corrupted him; he wouldn't be the first. As for Gilyov, maybe the engineer had something on him.'

'So Bensaud seduced Dalladay, and when she became a danger to his career he turned to murder. It doesn't sound—'

Bryant would not be moved. 'As for the contusions, they're either deliberate or accidental. Giles thinks Marion North went over head first and hit the stone wall of the embankment on the way down. Sorry, I'm not exactly sparing your grief.'

'You're saying that whichever way we go, Bensaud is our man. How do we prove that?'

'He's not able to acknowledge that he's capable of killing. At the moment we don't have anything on him other than the paternity result.'

'That's enough to bring him in for formal questioning, Arthur.'

'And how do you propose we extract a confession, by breaking out the rubber truncheons? He's smart enough to have set you up for murder, John. You didn't see it coming and we won't see it when he vanishes again. There has to be another way of proving his culpability.'

'So how can you get me off the hook?' asked May,

'I have a date with Daisy,' said Bryant. He rang off and headed for the tube.

*

Fraternity DuCaine and Janice Longbright were running out of desk space. Raymond Land's 'paperless office' initiative had spectacularly failed, and half-eaten trays of dhal, aloo ghobi, chicken korma and beef randang teetered on stacks of overstuffed cardboard folders.

'Let's call it a night,' said Janice, clearing up the meal. 'When I look away from the screen all I can see is dots. I can't believe you're leaving us for the geek squad. Why did you order minced turnips in dried ginger?' She sniffed the tray and dropped it in the bin.

'I'll only be up the road in Holloway. And I'm a vegetarian, remember?'

'Then just order chicken. If I had any sense I'd get out too.' Longbright sighed. 'I haven't had a holiday in seven years. I thought you liked working here.'

DuCaine sighed. 'The forensic tech is a game-changer. I can't advance here. Look what happens when the old boys aren't around; the unit falls apart because nobody except you knows how they work. The only reason Darren Link hasn't taken the case away is because it must suit his purpose not to. He was on vice in Dalston, wasn't he?'

'For a while, yeah. His mates are still there.'

'What if he knew they were on the take and figured we wouldn't go there? We could have another look at the club.'

'If there was anything on the premises it'd be long gone by now. I'm not pulling up their carpets with these nails.'

'You're such a girl,' Fraternity said, grinning. 'You've still got the contact list, yeah? Everyone who knew Dalladay at the club?'

'Sure.' She pulled a single page from one of the files, cascading brown rice on to the paperwork. For the next hour DuCaine worked in silence. At the end of it, he turned his screen around.

'You wanted some answers,' he said. 'You were just searching in the wrong place.'

'I tried to track all the addresses, phones and credit cards of members who were known to hang out with Dalladay but came up short,' Longbright admitted.

'Because the names you were given by the club were phonetically anglicized from the Cyrillic alphabet. The ones you couldn't find are Macedonian, Russian and Ukrainian – I haven't started checking Chinese names yet. I think these three all have criminal records in their native countries, although I can't get access to the Russian files. I figured if they were specifically requesting Dalladay's company they were doing it for a reason, and they had to have paid her.'

'I tried that,' said Longbright. 'There was nothing in her account.'

'No, but there were several international bank transfers made to her via a private bank in Switzerland that according to these dates bypassed the money-laundering checks that are supposed to be in place for overseas transfers.'

'Surely there's no way you can directly access their statements from here.'

'Not directly, but I can get hold of the currency-exchange transactions this end because I've got her payments received. You missed them because they went into a separate account.'

'So how much did they pay her?'

'In total? I've got six amounts so far totalling one point eight million euros. There could be more.'

'What was she, the most expensive call girl in the country?' Longbright whistled. 'Where did it all go?'

'That's the best part,' said DuCaine. 'They briefly entered the second account and went straight back out into a business account owned by Bensaud. It looks like she was helping to finance the expansion of his Life Options franchise.'

'You're saying that Bensaud had both Cooper and Dalladay giving him money?'

'It seems that way. But looking suspicious isn't a crime, Janice. Sorry, I'm speaking out of turn—'

'No, go on.'

'Separate the facts from the speculation and all you've got

is some circumstantial stuff that's not enough for a conviction. I mean, is Cassandra North implicated in the death of
her own mother? Where does the responsibility lie? There are
too many interpretations of what might have happened. If
you try to prosecute now, the case is dead.'

'It's the only break we've had,' said Longbright. 'There's
nothing more we can do tonight. Let's close this up and go
home. Tomorrow's going to be a big day.'

39

PIGS & SHEEP

Arthur Bryant knocked his pipe out against the embankment balustrade and pocketed it. He looked around. The early morning mist softened the river and its bridges, as if a fine layer of tracing paper had been laid over the scene. The traffic was light, and there were few pedestrians on this stretch of the embankment in front of Lincoln's Inn Fields. After a few minutes a taxi hove into view and pulled up in front of him.

'You Mr Bryant?' asked the driver, reaching back to open the rear door.

'Yes, how did you recognize me?' asked Bryant.

'You're joking, right? Here you go, mate, some bloke at Smithfields asked me to drop this off. It weighs a bloody ton.'

'Ten stone seven, to be exact,' said Bryant. 'Can you get Daisy out for me?'

The driver came around and dragged the huge red nylon holdall from the rear seat of the cab. 'You sure you ain't got a body in here?' he asked jovially, looking for a way to balance it on the pavement.

'A body, ha ha, very good. Thank you. Clear off.' Bryant tipped the driver and waved him away, then waited for the coast to clear.

Unzipping the holdall, he peered inside. A big pink face smiled back. He removed Daisy and attempted to stand her upright. The eponymous flower was stuck behind the pig's left ear, a joke from the butcher. Her head flopped to one side but she still managed to fix him with a beady black eye.

Bryant thought he had planned everything carefully, but hit a snag. He couldn't hoist Daisy up the wall. After five minutes of useless effort he was panting with the exertion and Daisy was diagonal.

Shortly a group of Spanish students passed, and Bryant was able to enlist their help after convincing them that he was a police officer and not an escaped lunatic. As they hauled the creature upright he wondered if he should have dressed Daisy, but decided that the pull of clothing in water would make little difference to her overall speed. The students took selfies of themselves with the animal. Daisy was now sprawled across the balustrade. After one more push they managed to get all of her to the top, so that her front trotters dangled above the water.

Setting his mobile's camera to video (following instructions from Dan Banbury that had only taken three years to master) Bryant pummelled the carcass and gave it a shove into the river below. Peering over the balustrade, he was surprised to find that Daisy did not touch the embankment wall as he'd expected but fell clear, hitting the water cleanly and immediately submerging. A few moments later she surfaced head first.

The students cheered and went on their way. Bryant rolled up the bag and began walking beside the pig's drifting body, attempting to keep pace with the outgoing tide, but she was now moving too fast.

By the time he reached Blackfriars Bridge and waited for the traffic lights to change so that he could cross, he knew that he had lost her. He decided to call his partner.

'John, how are you getting on?'

'I'm going stir-crazy here, Arthur. I can't clean my apartment again. Are you any closer to getting me out?'

'I'm afraid this might be a bit of a last-minute rescue,' Bryant replied. 'I'll try not to leave it until your neck's in the noose.'

'You sound out of breath.'

'I'm racing a pig.'

'What's all that noise?'

'A cyclist just swore at me.'

'What are you doing? You shouldn't be exerting yourself.'

'Don't worry, the students helped me push her over the wall.'

'You're not making any sense.'

'Listen, you know we talked about the river providing an easy way of getting rid of a body?'

'Did you say a *pig*?'

'It's not. An easy way, I mean. Daisy weighed exactly the same as Marion North and I couldn't get her over the parapet by myself. I think we can rule out her daughter.'

'Her daughter was a suspect? You just threw a pig into the river?'

'Is there some particular reason why you feel the need to repeat everything I say?' Bryant asked. 'She was a dead weight; it took several of us to get her over the wall and she didn't hit anything on the way down, so there's no explanation there for Marion's contusion. I'm hoping she'll wash in at Tower Beach but the river's flowing much faster than I can walk. You see, I was thinking . . .'

'Oh no.'

'. . . it's not such an easy way to kill someone after all, lifting a dead weight over a wall. But if the victim *wanted* to drown, you could assist them.'

'If they wanted to drown in order to be reborn. You've already been there and discarded the idea. Are you sure you're better?'

'I haven't felt this good since Meera ran over the Mayor's

foot on her motorbike. I have a theory of sorts but the odd one out is Dimitri Gilyov, obviously. He doesn't seem like someone who would have been susceptible to the power of suggestion, so he had to be killed in a more straightforward manner, one that involved a higher level of risk. He was drowned and hidden under the bridge.'

'Wait, why did Crooms come for him? Did Crooms kill him?'

'I think he knew where to stash the body until he could get around to disposing of it. Of course I don't have proof of anything yet. Goodness!'

'What's happened?'

'I think my pig just hit the bridge. Excellent, that would explain it! I have to go. If I can get the carcass up on to the foreshore I fancy there'll be chops for supper.'

Bryant's belief that Ali had persuaded the women to kill themselves was now partially restored. But his nemesis seemed impregnable, and so much time had been lost that he feared it might not be possible to regain the lead. He was at least determined to keep the element of surprise. By 9.30 a.m. that morning, the entire PCU team was down at the centre sequestering its documents. Cassie North turned up and furiously demanded to know what was going on.

'Your partner is an unofficial suspect in the murder of Lynsey Dalladay,' Longbright explained.

'What do you mean, unofficial?' Cassie asked angrily, checking that none of her clients were within earshot. 'Either he's a suspect and you have to take him into custody for questioning with a lawyer present, or he's not.'

'There's an outfit called the Metropolitan Police, you might wish to try them if you'd prefer a milder service,' said Longbright as Colin squeezed past her with a stack of clear plastic boxes. 'We're more your Take It Away and Smash It to Bits to See if Anything Incriminating Falls Out Brigade.'

Two smartly dressed middle-aged women stopped on their

way back from a treatment room and stared at the fracas in the foyer. 'But you're required to stay within the limits of their laws,' Cassie hissed.

'That depends on who wrote our laws, which in this case was our Mr Bryant. The wording he settled on isn't very precise. In fact it doesn't even make sense.'

Cassie looked around wildly. Doors were opening everywhere. 'You are going to drive a stake through the heart of this business.'

'It's better than somebody killing off your clientele,' said Longbright. 'I don't understand you. Don't you want your mother's murderer found?'

'Well, of course I do but—'

'That's the problem right there,' said Longbright. 'There can't be any conditions to murder. Now let us do our job.'

In one of the unused treatment rooms that had been commandeered for evidence, Dan Banbury was standing in for John May, sorting through the online records they had printed out from Cassie North's computer.

'Nothing out of the ordinary so far,' he warned. 'The bookkeeping's almost too clean; there aren't even any admin errors or spelling mistakes.'

'I've got an admin error,' said Meera, holding up a pair of pages. 'The weekly schedule of events repeats itself after one month, yes? These are the courses actually taken by the clients.' She pointed to the second document. 'I've matched them against the hours billed but the numbers don't tally.'

Banbury read over her shoulder. 'Why not?'

'We're a course short. Look, seven classes paid for by Neema Pradesh, six marked on the schedule, eight classes paid for by Amanda Kirkland, seven marked on the schedule. I checked the list of courses offered in the online brochure and the one that's not listed is something called "Sacred Nature: Death & Rebirth",' Meera said. 'Why isn't that down here?'

'Maybe it's not held at the centre,' said Banbury. 'They also run site-specific classes. According to the spreadsheets—'

'For God's sake, go out there and ask someone,' said Longbright. 'You're like kids walking down the street staring at phones instead of looking up. You—' She stuck her head out of the door and grabbed a passing staff member. 'The sacred nature class, where is it held?'

'I think it takes place outside,' said the startled manicurist. 'In another building.'

'Where is it?'

'By the river in Chiswick.'

'Meera, were any of the victims booked on it?'

Meera Mangeshkar ran a bitten nail down the list. 'It looks like Dalladay was.'

Meera ran out to find Bryant. Of the other women who had taken the course Neema Pradesh was not at the centre, but Amanda Kirkland had just finished a relaxation class. Bryant thanked Meera and took shelter under the eaves of the centre's internal courtyard.

A few minutes later Mrs Kirkland came hopping across the wet grass in a white bath-robe to tap him angrily on the shoulder. 'Excuse me, but you can't come in here smoking that thing.'

Bryant removed his pipe from his mouth and looked about. 'Come *in*, madam?' he said. 'I haven't come in. That thing above us is the sky. I'm not "in" anywhere. It only becomes an enclosed space if you're looking at it from beyond the earth's atmosphere, and even then that's metaphysically debatable.'

'The grounds are private and the secondary smoke drifts back,' Mrs Kirkland complained.

'Tell me, do you drive a car, use a phone, get on a plane?'

'Yes, but—'

'Then you might as well smoke.'

'I voted Green,' said Mrs Kirkland, wilting.

'I once voted for Tony Blair. We all suffer disappointments

in life. Go on, have a fag, don't be a coward. I can see the
bulge of the carton in your pocket. If you light up they'll all
want one. We could start a revolution.'

With a sigh of relief, Mrs Kirkland stuck a pastel-coloured
cigarette between her lips.

'That's not a proper oily rag, have one of these, you can
feel them biting your lungs.' Bryant dug in his coat and
dragged out a battered packet.

'Woodbines?' said Mrs Kirkland, reading the carton. 'How
old are these?'

'I bought them in 1982. I keep them in a humidor to preserve their flavour.'

He held out his lighter. She inhaled and coughed violently.
She glanced sideways at him. 'You're a very strange man.'

'Tell me,' Bryant said, 'what do you think of him?'

Mrs Kirkland looked at him in surprise. 'Who, our dashing
guru? You mean apart from the fact that Thornberry is obviously not his real name? He's very charismatic. Rather
sharper than your average counsellor.'

'What do you mean?'

'He has an answer for everything.'

'Give me an example.'

'Well, if you tell him that you're unable to visualize spiritual energy, he'll always explain how you can change – and
how much it will cost.'

'He's running a business.'

'Yes, but he lets you see that he is and then negotiates,
which I find rather refreshing. I mean we all *know*, but he lets
you know he knows. If you see what I mean.'

Bryant studied his smoking companion. 'Why are you
here?'

'The truth?' Mrs Kirkland jetted blue smoke over a potted
clump of love-lies-bleeding. 'My husband runs the third
largest insurance company in Toronto. Do you have any idea
how ghastly that is?'

'The money isn't boring,' Bryant observed.

'Why must these things always be mutually exclusive? If you have an interesting job you get paid peanuts. If it's deadly dull you command a high salary.'

'The therapies that take place off-campus, know anything about those?'

'I think one is ceramics, at a potter's workshop in Putney. The other is just past Barnes, at the Death House.'

Bryant's interest was piqued. 'The Death House?'

'That's what they call it. Something to do with cholera victims in the nineteenth century. Bodies washing into the river or some such nonsense. I went there once but didn't take to it.'

'Why not?'

Mrs Kirkland waved away smoke, recalling the day she went. 'There was a most peculiar atmosphere. I was the oldest pupil in the class. There was something about the way the younger girls all hung on his every word. It felt like—' She stopped.

'Like what?' asked Bryant.

'Like a bit of a cult. Some women can be such dreadful sheep.'

'You think he exerts a strong influence over them?'

'Oh, definitely.'

'And there are improprieties?'

'I wouldn't be at all surprised. But then that's what we oldies always think about the pretty ones, isn't it?' The watery sun vanished again behind black clouds. Mrs Kirkland shivered and pulled her robe more tightly over her bosom. The Woodbine had burned halfway down and was putting its knee into the back of her lungs, so she ground it out. 'I'm going in,' she announced. 'Thank you for the cigarette; I'll probably have a sore throat for a fortnight. It was interesting to meet you, Mr—'

Bryant had vanished.

40

DECEPTION & SUGGESTION

'He's a very *attractive* charlatan,' said Maggie Armitage as they walked from the station, 'there's no question about that. But why would he kill? That's what you want to know, isn't it? Does he deliberately set out to harm?'

'In a nutshell,' said Bryant, looking around at the dank, shadowy railway arches that lay ahead of them. It was lunchtime, and the rain was back with a vengeance. 'Do I really have to see this woman?'

'She might be able to help. You sent Mr Land to see her last time. The poor man must have had the fright of his life.'

'He did. How we laughed. You were saying.'

'It was about two years ago, at the Finsbury Park Rainbow just over the road. They called themselves the Ministry of Compassion. He had a choir with him, but the show was careful to avoid any mention of religion. There was a lot of vague nonsense about spiritual energy, life waves and the mental path to healing. His name back then was Pastor Michaels. I rather liked him. There was intelligence in his eyes. But I couldn't sit there and let him deceive people, so I cut him off.'

'What do you mean?'

'I severed his earpiece cord. He had an assistant who was

feeding him information. They'd probably downloaded it from Facebook or something. You could argue that he was providing comfort to those in need but I think such people do a lot of damage, whether they realize it or not.'

'None of his staff have professional qualifications,' said Bryant, helping Maggie over a pond that had been formed by broken paving stones. 'Marion North was persuading clients to give up their medication with a load of old bobbins about natural energies replacing toxic pharmaceuticals. As a result one of them became suicidal and drowned herself. That doesn't make Bensaud a murderer because it was surely not his intention to kill off his clients, but it could make him a joint principal. Did he independently contribute to causing the *actus reus*, the "guilty act", rather than just giving advice which she was free to take or discard?'

'From what you've told me so far, it sounds as if your man knows his legal position,' said Maggie as they crossed the road, slipping between shushing vehicles. 'That'll make him hard to trap. I could mix you a potion that would force him to tell the truth, although I'd have to swing by the Co-op for a sliced white loaf, and I don't know how you'd get it on him.'

Bryant was puzzled. 'Why?'

'It's a bread poultice. Esmeralda should be somewhere over here.' The waste ground was all but invisible from the road, but she knew exactly where to go. She held open a torn section of chicken-wire fence for Bryant to climb through. Ducking down, she peered through the passenger window of an upturned blue Nissan. 'Esmeralda? Are you here, dear?'

'I have a feeling she's over there,' said Bryant, raising his index finger in the direction of a particularly unappetizing railway arch festooned with dirt-encrusted power cables. A strange burbling noise, something between a pregnant pigeon and a tyre being tested for punctures underwater, emerged from the shadows.

'That sounds like her,' Maggie said, peering ahead. 'I bring her food and medical supplies whenever I'm passing. She doesn't trust doctors. She thinks they want to steal her organs. Why don't you like coming to see her alone?'

'Oh, she thinks she's married to me,' Bryant explained, pulling his scarf higher as if preparing to hide. 'It's hard to believe that she once had a fine academic mind. The establishment punished her for teaching sedition.'

'Why does she think you and she are—?'

'Don't worry about it; she also thinks she's married to Robert Redford and Batman.'

The pair advanced through low light and falling rain to find a strange scene reminiscent of a bad touring production of *The Mousetrap*. A living-room set had been laid out under the protection of the archway: sofa, armchairs and a Primus stove stood on a mouldering carpet beside a table with only three legs and a moth-eaten, yellow-tasselled standard lamp. Bundled in the armchair was an object like a poorly rewound ball of grey wool.

'Esmeralda,' said Maggie softly, venturing nearer. 'May we come in?'

The crooning stopped and a filthy head appeared out of the bundle. 'Who is at my door?'

'It's me, Maggie. I brought you something to eat.'

'If it's curried goat from the Ethiopian takeaway, you can stick it up your arse. The last one I had was old enough to vote.'

Maggie stepped on to the mildewed carpet and opened her shopping bag. 'Here you are, everything you need to make a nice mutton stew.'

Esmeralda snatched the bag and peered inside. She removed a large onion and bit into it. 'Lovely,' she said, spraying pieces, 'I'll have the rest later. Who's that with you?'

'Hello, Esmeralda,' said Bryant, reluctantly moving into the tramp's odour zone.

'My husband! Where have you been? With that other woman, I suppose. I knew you'd be bigeramous.'

'What other woman?' Maggie asked.

'Princess Margaret,' said Esmeralda. 'I suppose you're here to see your son. This apple's off.' She chucked the onion into the shadows and hauled herself to her feet, leading them over to a broken crib stuffed with filthy blankets.

'My God, she hasn't kidnapped a baby, has she?' whispered Bryant in horror. Esmeralda rose with something coddled in her arms. Whatever it was, it seemed to be thrashing about and crying.

'This is little Arbuthnot. Say hello to your daddy.' Esmeralda crept up to Bryant and presented him with the infant. It was brown and woolly and had big red eyes the size of ping-pong balls.

'That's a sock puppet,' said Bryant wearily.

'I'm not,' said Arbuthnot in a ridiculous high-pitched voice, its little mouth squirming as Esmeralda moved her fist. 'I'm born of the loving union between Esmeralda Sparrow and Arthur Bryant in this year of Our Lord, 1978.'

'Oh God,' Bryant whispered to Maggie, 'that was the year I met her, when she'd just been sectioned after trying to set fire to Trinity College.'

'Esmeralda, we need your advice,' said Maggie firmly. 'Do you remember those lectures you used to give about hypnosis and the power of suggestion?'

'I still give them,' said the tramp, gently placing the sock puppet back in its filthy bed. 'I can cure anything, heating disorders, anemorexia, fear of yoghurt, you name it.'

'Do you think a person can be made to do something against their will?' asked Bryant.

Esmeralda's manner changed as she gave the matter her professional attention. 'Not against both the conscious and subconscious will, no. That's a mythicism. But you can get someone to change their behavioural patterns. And it can produce secondary harm.'

'What do you mean?'

The little tramp flopped into an armchair and forced her

wandering wits to a level of deeper concentration. 'First you need a suscepterible subject,' she explained. 'Suppose you hypnotize them into believing that they're about to experience an electric shock – one of the oldest hypnotic tricks – a hormone called prolactin is released from the pituitary gland that can actually kill the subject. In very rare cases hypnosis can cause schizophrenia or exaggerate existing conditions.' She raised a filthy digit. 'But, but! There's no such thing as a properly qualified hypnotherapist, not in medical terms. Coaching suggestions can be used to weaken negative messages which are already in the subconscious. And they can help in healing processes. They can reduce pain and symptoms of dementia, stop cravings, enhance the memory. Are you staying for tea? There's trifle. I didn't make it, I found it.'

'No thank you,' said Bryant politely. 'Who's most likely to prove susceptible?'

'Children, readers, artists, open-minded and emotional people, seekers of enlightenment, people who like trying alternative therapies. And hippies, of course.'

'Why hippies?'

'Because of the terrible times we live in – Vietnam, Kent State, Watergate.'

'She taught American politics in the late 1970s,' whispered Bryant.

'People get into transcendental mediteration because they already feel lost and are looking for peas. Peas and quiet.'

'Do you have to be put into a trance?'

'No, but there are many ideas about what trances are. Hitler appeared to put his followers into a trance with cleverly placed verbal signifiers. There's such a thing as hypnotic language, which plants structured commands in the mind. It can be learned, but some people are born naturals.'

'Could you encourage someone who was suicidally inclined to kill themselves?'

'You can only draw out what's already there. I can offer you bark tea.'

'That would be lovely,' said Maggie. Bryant glared at her.

'I may have a packet of Garibaldis saved. After all, we have something to celebrate, now that Arthur's come to take me home.'

'Esmeralda, I didn't come here to take you home,' said Bryant gently.

'But I want to go to the shore,' she said plaintively, digging out the biscuits. 'Won't you take me to the shore? I can't stay here with my rheumaterism. London Transport's taking away my arch. They're going to build luxury.' She pointed to the sign that had been pinioned to the brickwork above their heads: 'Number One Finsbury – Luxury Loft Living. One Bedroom Apartments starting at 1.2m'. The words 'Loft Living' had partially fallen off. 'They want a million. They don't say a million what, but I haven't got a million anything. Or even a hundred anything. I haven't got anything except my memories and I haven't even got those any more because I've lost the key.'

'I know your memories,' said Maggie gently. 'I'll stay with you a while and we'll write them down.'

'Thank you,' said Esmeralda, her eyes filled with gratitude. 'Have a Garibaldi.'

Maggie accepted the biscuit and surreptitiously held it out for Bryant to inspect. 'Those aren't currants,' she whispered, 'they're dead flies.'

They sat beneath the railway arch as yellow-windowed trains clattered overhead and the rain tumbled into brown iron gutters, rattling down drainpipes and flooding the last remaining liminal spaces around Finsbury Park Station. The elderly detective, the white witch and the tramp discussed abstruse matters that seemed of no possible concern to anyone in the bright new London of glazed towers and steel cathedrals, yet the outcome of their talk had the power to affect the lives of many. From such discarded remnants of the city could great ideas be woven.

41

LIFE & DEATH

'I'm not at all happy about this,' said Dan Banbury, checking the boot of his car. 'Do we have to black up?'

'No, of course not.' Colin zipped his jacket shut and checked his pockets. 'We're not on army manoeuvres. You don't need to stick dirt all over your face and poke twigs into a bobble hat. The main thing to worry about is whether the place is alarmed.'

'Thank God for that.' Banbury closed the boot and bipped the car. 'Couldn't we wait and do this legally, preferably in daylight?'

'John says the warrant only covers the centre's main building. We're running out of time. Have you got everything?'

'I've got a crowbar, a pocket knife, a torch and a whistle for attracting attention.'

'What are you, a flight attendant? Come on.'

They made their way across the soft wet grass towards the Death House. It was almost midnight. This far from the main road it was hard to discern the outlines of the riverbank. 'No wonder Angela Curtis went arse over tit,' said Banbury. 'I can't see where I'm putting my feet.'

'I can,' said Colin, scraping his boot against an elm. 'Bloody dogs.'

'What are we looking for, anyway?'

'Anything that will help us convict Bensaud. According to the old man nobody can agree on what his off-site courses are actually about. There's no documentation at the centre and the suspect's not talking, so that leaves you, me and a crowbar.'

The building was a stilted brick box with green wooden window-frames and a mossy stepped roof. It was attached to the river's overhanging stony edge like a G-clamp, so that one side of it almost reached down into the water. Banbury shone his torch across the door. 'It's not barred, it's got a Dorland lock,' he said. 'They don't make them any more. I can't get that open.'

'Window.' Colin padded around to the side, pushing his way past low-hanging branches. The windows were fitted with steel grilles.

'If you force those off he'll know someone's been in,' said Banbury, always conscious of other people's property.

'Yeah, well, I'll try and put it back after,' said Colin without much conviction. He wedged the crowbar under the grille and put all his weight on top of it until something cracked. The window itself was not locked and slid open easily, but as he pushed it up the entire frame fell out.

'Nice one,' said Banbury. 'Why didn't you just back your car into the front wall?' He climbed through the torn hole with some difficulty and ran his torch beam over the floor.

The Death House had been decorated more luxuriantly than the treatment rooms at the centre. Thick maroon rugs and Persian tapestries were matched by half a dozen brightly coloured beanbags. In the room beyond was a workspace designed to hold laptops. The only terminal actually connected, a silver MacBook, was on standby and password-protected.

'In here,' called Banbury. Colin found him beyond the kitchen and bathroom in the only other open area.

A double bed was covered in silver scatter cushions and artificial roses. 'It doesn't look like a treatment room to me,' said Banbury, sucking his teeth. 'View over the river, a client list of bored attractive women, it's almost worth getting struck off for.'

'You have to have a medical degree to get struck off,' said Colin. 'This bloke's Mr Showbiz.'

They checked cupboards and drawers but found nothing out of place or untoward. 'There must be something. He can't take everything every time he closes up after a class,' said Dan, whose terrier instinct had now been awoken.

'No cameras. There's a router over there,' said Colin. 'Maybe he's stashed another laptop somewhere?'

Banbury stamped on the floorboards, testing them. 'What's underneath holding this place up? What would they put down there?'

'Bins,' said Bimsley. In his last year at the PCU they had virtually become his specialist subject. He and Banbury lifted the window-frame back and wedged it in place as best they could. They attempted to replace the grille for a while, then gave up.

At the side of the house they found an access panel leading to a crawlspace. Bimsley pushed open the wooden trapdoor and climbed inside. 'Thank God for recycling,' he called back, shoving out a green plastic crate filled with paper. They set down their torches and began going through the printouts.

'I've got a feedback questionnaire from the sacred nature course,' said Banbury. 'Sounds like a bunch of old toss to me.'

'Show me.' Colin felt at home sitting in the pile of sodden rubbish that had become caught around his boots. '"From the alignment of sacred barrows on its shores to the mysteries of the moon-driven tides that lap its banks, the Thames represents the healing power of Isis, a path of hope, a living fluctuation of life and death." So that's "a bunch of old toss", is it?'

'Totally,' said Banbury. 'The sort of thing my wife likes, along with pedicures, *Fifty Shades of Grey*, scented candles, coconut oil, book clubs and the box set of *Downton Abbey*.'

'That's a bit harsh.'

'She's not soft, though. She started reading all this stuff about warrior women and empowerment, then replaced our bathroom stopcock. If she can figure out how to update her phone software I'll become surplus to requirements.'

'It says here the nymphs of the river guide lost souls to healing lands on the Other Side. Doesn't say the Other Side of what. "The fair nymphs of Thamesis, keeping time with the billow of her crystal waves, carry us to the Ocean with her ebb." "Crystal waves" is pushing it. I saw a dog with its guts out in there last week, right by Dead Man's Stairs. You think he gets them to believe in all this?'

'It's not enough,' said Banbury. 'There's a difference between sounding like Barry White and persuading someone to padlock themselves in the river. There's got to be something solid.'

'Like what?' Colin asked. When no reply was forthcoming, he looked up at Dan and found him reading pages in the torchlight.

'Like this,' he said, turned the page around. '"Death & Rebirth: Removing Anxiety from the Last Taboo".'

'What's the picture at the top?' asked Colin. 'I recognize it.'

'It's a painting.' Banbury read out the caption. '"Théodore Géricault. *The Raft of the Medusa*. The work depicts survivors from a ship wrecked off the coast of Senegal in 1815 who survived by eating their dead companions. Of 147 crew members set adrift on the unstable raft, only fifteen survived." That's a bit grim.'

'Grim?' said Colin. 'It's a masterpiece of French romantic chiaroscuro, you nonce. The painting's an analogy of France's corrupt government. The commander ran the ship into sandbanks, then took the longboat for himself and the high-born, leaving the rabble to the raft, which was so loosely tied together that men got their legs trapped between the logs. The abandoned crew rioted. They were forced to eat their leather ammunition pouches, then they ate each other.'

'How come you know so much about it?'

'Mr Bryant showed me the picture in one of his books.'

'Confronting death, eh?' said Banbury. 'I can't imagine too many people signed up for that one.'

Colin took the pages from his colleague and carefully folded them away. 'Maybe there were three women who did,' he said. 'We need to check everyone who took the course.'

'This is the big revelation, is it?' asked Land, his patience rapidly fraying. 'You're telling me this fellow Bensaud holds separate private meetings at his "Death House" or whatever you call it in order to make sacrifices to the river?'

It was Wednesday morning, and Bryant had brought his tea into Raymond Land's office while he explained the previous day's events.

'I'm just telling you what Colin and Dan found, *mon petit cafard*.' Bryant fished a teabag from his mug with a tuning fork, the only item he could lay his hands on which approximated a spoon. 'They think he's bedding his clients and preying on their fragile states of mind to offload them when things get messy.' He flicked the teabag nonchalantly in the direction of the wastepaper basket and missed.

'I've never heard of anything so ridiculous. Are you trying to tell me we're dealing with a modern-day Bluebeard?' Land picked up the teabag, which had landed on his foot, and dropped it into the bin with distaste.

'I've been doing some checking on the way he runs his businesses. He's been a very busy lad in the last couple of years. "All human evil comes from a single cause, man's inability to sit still in a room" – Blaise Pascal.'

'Spare me the cod psychology, Bryant. If you really think this bloke's knocking off women, why are you so against bringing him in and sitting on him?'

'Because we'll lose him that way.' Bryant passed Land a mug of tea and gave him a small electric shock. 'Sorry, I keep doing that. Something to do with my treatments. I think Bensaud is teaching them how to live, then taking away that gift when they no longer deserve it. "Men live as if they were never going to die, and die as if they had never lived" – the Dalai Lama. "If we don't know what life is, how can we know what death is?" – Confucius.'

'That's enough!' Land raised his voice in a forlorn attempt to sound authoritative. 'You've searched the premises and turned up nothing. You've questioned him, his staff and his clients. If you're not prepared to drag him off the streets and subject him to some decent psychological torture, you're going to have to admit defeat and let someone else take over.'

'No,' said Bryant. 'I need something that will irrefutably incriminate him. Talking won't work. He's mastered mental manipulation magnificently. Try saying that with my teeth.'

'So he turns up out of nowhere as a mind-reader, a healer and what-have-you – but what does he actually want?'

'I imagine he wants what people like him always want,' said Bryant. 'A foot on the throne. The attention of those in power. Rasputin had the ear of the Tsar of Russia.'

'Cherie Blair had an astrologer,' added Land.

'We need to find the anomaly that will undo him. Before we bring him in here, the case has to be absolutely watertight.'

'How are we going to get that?' asked Land. 'We're out of time. Link is pressing to go ahead with charging your partner tomorrow.'

Bryant needed to be alone for a few minutes.

The events of the past few weeks had been tumultuous. He had solved the riddle of his own decline; he had glimpsed oblivion and had been spared. Taking a Northern line tube south, he now stood at the centre of Waterloo Bridge looking down into the fast-flowing waters, hoping to find further answers, but the shape of his life still eluded him.

He thought of Nathalie, small and dark, laughing, the touch of her hand as she balanced above him. It had been the evening of her twenty-first birthday. She'd climbed up on to the balustrade and was tripping lightly along it, right where he was now standing. He reached out and ran his hand over the stonework, wondering if it held the imprint of her dancing feet.

Young and broke, they had been invited out to drink and celebrate and were both a little tipsy. He had just asked her to marry him.

It was a spontaneous request foolishly spoken aloud, and yet the moment he heard the words he knew his intention was true. He would never love another.

She had suddenly stopped laughing and looked down at him. Her features had blurred with the passing of time but he could never forget her smile.

She was about to give him her answer when a bus horn sounded behind them, and the noise made her start.

She lost her balance, and when he turned around to grab her she had gone. Arthur threw himself into the water and tried to find her, but the tide was against him and the current was too strong. Nathalie had never learned to swim. In his heavy overcoat and hobnailed boots he was nearly pulled under, and for a moment he wanted to be drawn down with her.

The search teams dragged the river for days, but they never found her body. Across the years, whenever he looked into the Thames he saw her. Even now, she was still there. When the waters turned and began to rise, he imagined her drifting back into the city to find him. He had never loved again, not truly. How could he when she was still here, borne into the city on lunar tides?

Focus on closing the case, he told himself, digging into his coat pocket and producing a smooth pebble. He threw it into the scudding waters, a symbolic act designed to make him banish thoughts of Nathalie, and turned his attention back to work, and the problem of Ali Bensaud.

He enjoys controlling others. He preys on the lonely, the bored, the vulnerable, the directionless. But is he a Jim Jones, a Colonel Kurtz? Someone who would inflict the madness of control upon others? Is he merely callous and ambitious or does he genuinely believe he's doing good? It would be a matter for a court to decide, and it will mean the difference between capture and release. Someone this Machiavellian might well be able to influence a jury and avoid a conviction.

You shouldn't be worrying about that, he thought. *Someone else can deal with the problem. Your job is to find a way of reeling him in and to get John off the hook before it's too late.*

He had one slender lead left. Mrs Kirkland, the client at the St Alphege Centre to whom he had given an ancient cigarette, had given him the name of another woman who had taken the 'Sacred Nature: Death & Rebirth' course. Rose Nash, a retired NHS psychotherapist, had agreed to meet Bryant and talk about her experience at the Death House.

From Waterloo he caught a direct train to Shepperton, the picturesque Thameside village mentioned in the Domesday Book that paradoxically became the home of dissident writers and movie executives.

There was certainly something defiantly odd about the place, he thought, alighting from the train and heading for the winding High Street. The locks, weirs and riverbanks seemed to belong to the forgotten summer days of the Edwardian age, and yet it was strongly associated with science fiction. *Star Wars* and *Captain America* had been filmed here.

'Sometimes I go into my local pub and find a Hollywood legend sitting at the bar,' Rose Nash told him. 'It's like living in a place that has become unmoored in time and space. I suppose that's why I like it.'

Rose might have been a figurine, Wedgwood or Waterford perhaps, designed to fit a doll's house representing a typical half-timbered English cottage. Her cosy living room looked like a film set designed for Hobbits, and was crowded with horse-brasses, paintings, brass pitchers and thick earthenware pots. Bryant looked perfectly at home amongst the bric-a-brac, sunk into a floral sofa in his great tweed overcoat.

'I didn't finish the Life Options course,' she explained, serving tea. 'It all felt so ridiculously bogus, and he was constantly upselling us. I don't like to be coerced. They're peddling inner calm but everyone seemed very tense.'

'What do you think they were coercing you towards, exactly?' asked Bryant.

'That's rather the question, isn't it? I'm not sure he knows himself. I didn't think he was talking literally about death and rebirth, not if you mean he wanted anyone to kill themselves and be reborn. Let me show you something.' She went to the sideboard and returned with a pack of tarot cards, sorting through them.

'This is the Death card,' she said, turning over the familiar figure of a cloaked skeleton riding a white stallion against a sinking sun. In his bony right fist he clutched a black and white flag. 'His bones live on. His armour makes him unconquerable. His horse is the colour of purity, because Death is the ultimate absolution. Everything that's reborn is fresh and untainted. The rising sun behind him is a symbol of immortality because it dies and lives. But see what else is in the picture – a river. You'll find it on all the Death tarot cards, symbolizing the cycle of death and rebirth. Sometimes there's a boat too, the ferry that transports the souls across the River Styx. Death is associated with the number thirteen, a female number.'

'I didn't know numbers had sexes,' said Bryant.

'It's sacred to the lunar goddess as there are thirteen moons in a year. So everything is tied together, death, rebirth, life, all controlled by the moon, which in turn controls the tides, making the river the access path to a new state of purity.'

'And you believe this to be true?'

'No, Mr Bryant, I think it's an evocative and rather charming mythology, and I quit the course. I was older than most of the women there, more cynical and still happily married after thirty-five years. We don't listen when we're being told straightforward facts; we would much rather accept what some charismatic character tells us. I got the distinct impression that some of them would do anything their teacher wanted.'

'So you think he's just in it for the money?'

'I don't know. He doesn't seem to have any actual qualifications. But there's certainly an air of mystery around him. He talks about reinvention and rebirth a lot. Perhaps he went through something similar himself.'

'You mean an intimation of mortality? We all have those.' Bryant was thinking of his own recent brush with fate.

'Yes,' said Rose. 'Maybe he's encouraging others to cope with the same thing.'

Bryant called his partner on the way back. 'We could search for some kind of by-law infringement and get the centre temporarily shut down, but it's not going to solve the bigger problem. We simply don't have the evidence to make it stick.'

'If he's impervious, you need to find a weak link in someone close to him,' May replied. 'What about Cassie North? If we could prove he killed her mother—'

'John, I think she believes you did it, although even she can't come up with a motive.'

'There's something that's been bothering me,' said May. 'Bensaud wasn't born in the UK. All this "sacred Thames" stuff means nothing to him, so why would he run courses in uncovering its origins?'

'It doesn't have to be about the Thames. He could have a problem with the sea, anything with a lunar tide.'

'No.' May called a stop to Bryant's thought process.

'Arthur, you have to stop theorizing and find physical evidence. You've passed your own deadline. Raymond says the internal investigations officer is going to be submitting her report first thing tomorrow. They're going ahead with the charge of murder. She's also going to blame him. At the very least, my career is over. There must be *something* you can do.'

'It's not just about you, John. I have to protect vulnerable people from this man. Guess where Daisy ended up.'

'Your pig? I dread to think.'

'At the exact spot where you found Dalladay's body and Dimitri Gilyov's severed hand. As I suspected, it's a quirk of the tide.'

'If you tell me the river's sending you messages, I'm going to hang up.'

'Actually, I'm beginning to think the Thames tricked me. I've listened to everyone telling me what the river means and I'm none the wiser at the end of it. If a girl is attacked in a park it doesn't mean her attacker is obsessed with trees. What if this isn't about the Thames at all? It could simply be the connection between a number of events.'

'I was trying to tell you that—'

'Dudley Salterton said the trick was to make yourself invisible or become the most visible person in the room.'

'Are you telling me something or just thinking random thoughts aloud?' May asked. 'Do you have anything at all that can get me out of here before tomorrow? I've paced a hole in the rug. Can't you do what you used to do, look up something in one of your weird books or study a painting for clues?'

'I have one last idea to try,' said Bryant. 'I've been seeking out academic experts on the sacred Thames, but now I can see they were the wrong people to talk to. I should have been interviewing people with more practical knowledge.'

May sounded nonplussed. 'I really don't see how it's going to help—'

'Maybe it's why the river was used, not for some sacred purpose but simply because it's familiar territory. The Thames provides the easiest and most obvious solution for the disposal of bodies.'

'No, you've lost me,' said May. Sometimes his partner was like a poorly tuned radio, fading in and out of comprehension. 'We decided it was impossible to get a girl on to that beach and leave her there to drown.'

'Yes, impossible, exactly,' Bryant agreed, which wasn't a useful response.

'I just hope you know what you're doing, Arthur. My life is at stake here.'

At least Bryant's abnormal thought processes showed he was thinking normally again. But it was now a matter of time; if he didn't come up with the goods, they were sunk.

42

FAST & STRANGE

The Lighterman looked like the sort of pub that turned up in old horror films. From its doors drunken doxies were expected to fall and fights erupt. Once it had sported a pleasing amount of stained and mullioned glass, but too many lads had been put through the windows. Even gentrification had failed to stop revellers from staggering out and being sick in the river. At the rear a small beer garden stood on a platform of warped wooden pilings, and the menus now featured the pub's new faux-handcrafted logo above the dish of the day (crayfish focaccia), but no matter how often the design changed, most of the clientele remained anchored to the river beneath.

Bryant sat with 'Bad Oyster' Stan Kipps and his old skipper 'Blotto' Otto Farmingham, who had been born and raised on the Thames at Woolwich. They preferred to sit outside even though it was bitterly cold.

Stan had his own pewter tankard, Bryant noticed, and wiped foam from his walrus moustache as he set it down. 'We transferred to the ferry when the Pool shut for good,' he explained. 'It was a bit of a comedown after the tankers. Funny thing was, we got more seasick on the ferry than we ever did in the Atlantic. There's a right old churn to the tide in the dead centre of the channel, and the constant docking means you're reversing engines all the time. It messes up your guts.'

'I remember Tower Beach,' said Otto. 'The P&O liner *Rawalpindi* was shelled off Iceland at the start of the war and went down with most of her crew, but its ladders was saved and they was installed to get down to the beach. Big steel grilles with hooks and chains they was.'

'You didn't get no more fogs on the river after the Pool went,' said Stan. 'Hay's Wharf had all these panels along the front, pictures of barrels and crates and drums – "The Chain of Distribution" it was called – is that still there?'

'It's all flats for them oligarchs now,' Otto told him. 'Shad Thames had hundreds of walkways for moving goods. They got tore down in 1983. My old man used to be down there shovelling tea, spuds, tapioca, you name it.'

'Did both of your families work only on the river?' Bryant asked.

'Of course.' Stan sounded surprised by the question. 'My grandma worked at Tilbury Dock passenger terminal 'cause most people travelled by boat back then. But we was mostly lightermen. Your watermen carried passengers but we shifted goods. You can still see some of the old lighters, the flat-bottomed barges, down towards Southend, but they was replaced by tugs. Right up and down the Thames, they was, tanners at Bermondsey, candle-makers at Battersea, soap-makers at Isleworth, lots of breweries.'

'Does it surprise you that body parts were found by Tower Beach?' Bryant asked.

'Not really. We used to see all sorts washed up on the starlings.'

'Starlings?'

'Yeah, the stone palings that protect bridge arches. They've got curved iron spikes around them.'

Bryant's eyes narrowed. 'What kind of spikes?'

'Sort of Victoriany ones with four sides.'

Now it made sense – the contusions on Dalladay's skull, Curtis's back and Mrs North's shoulder had been caused by the spikes around the starlings. The river had hurled their bodies at them. Even Daisy had picked up a scar on her journey when she had slammed into the bridge.

'It flows fast and strange around there,' said Stan. 'Rather than risk going under London Bridge, passengers used to get off at Old Swan Pier and walk around the bridge to get back on board at Billingsgate. So many watermen drowned. My old man had six brothers and we lost two to the river.'

'Did all the families know each other?' Bryant asked.

'Of course. We were all members of the Guild, so our kids went to school together,' said Otto.

'And you still see each other?'

'Yeah, at special occasions and that, down the Waterman's Hall. We knew everyone, didn't we, Stan?'

'Did you ever come across either of these?' Bryant unfolded a photocopy showing mugshots of Gilyov and Crooms.

'Blimey, that's Bill Crooms,' said Stan. 'I don't know the other one.'

'Me neither,' said Otto, 'but that's definitely Bill. He got himself into a lot of dodgy stuff.'

'What sort of stuff?'

'You have to remember, Mr Bryant, when the lightermen went out of business they still had to make a living. We weren't fishermen, saving the wages from three-week trips out of Grimsby.'

'I had a cousin at Grimsby,' Stan added. 'They were a superstitious lot; no women on board, nobody could wear green, you couldn't draw a pig or a rabbit on a boat. We were all Londoners so we needed London jobs. Some went to the boatyards; Bill started repairing engines for the MPU.'

'The Marine Policing Unit?' Bryant was surprised. 'I thought you said he was dodgy. The MPU have a reputation for being above corruption.'

'The officers themselves, yeah. But Bill and some of the others ran rackets on the side. Import-exports.'

'So he was smuggling?'

'Machine parts mostly, and we heard' – he checked his mate's face for approval – 'that him and his mates was selling recon goods to a boatyard in the East End.'

'Do you have any idea how they hooked up with buyers?'

'We don't want to get no one into trouble, Mr Bryant,' said Otto. 'It's hard making a living on the river now.'

'There have been five unnecessary deaths,' said Bryant. 'There could be more. I'll keep your names out of it but I need to check out every lead.'

The pair discussed the matter between themselves for a minute. 'All right,' said Stan finally. 'There's this club in Dalston. I can give you some names.'

Meera and Fraternity descended on the Cossack Club and found Joe Easter in his usual place at the bar, reading Virginia Woolf's *Orlando*. They left with one name circled from the club's guest list, and headed towards an address in the City Road. Here, a new corridor of luxury apartment buildings had been built along the north side, creating an intimidating palisade of angled steel.

Mick Draycott's apartment was on the twenty-third floor. A bored-looking concierge sat in a bare Plexiglas cabin, blue-skinned in the light of the monitors that guarded the secure compound. He might have been protecting a prison. His filtered voice reached them through a window microphone. Draycott was home, and he wouldn't let them use the swipecard-protected elevator because they didn't look like police officers.

Fraternity slapped his PCU card against the glass but the concierge stood his ground. 'You've got no rights here,' he said. 'We have our own private security unit based on the site.'

'You're all still under city police jurisdiction,' Fraternity replied. 'Open the door before I come in there and taser your ears off.'

The concierge hit two buttons, one to unlock the lift, the other to buzz Draycott's apartment and warn him that they were coming up.

'Can you believe he just did that?' said Meera. 'I'm taking you in, mate.'

They barged into the security cabin and saw a figure on the concierge's monitor.

'He's already in the hall,' said Fraternity. 'He can get straight down to the car park from his flat.' He pulled Meera back towards her Kawasaki. 'I've been in this building before. The underground levels are a maze. Let's wait for him to come out.'

Back on Meera's bike, they headed around to the car park exit just as the shutters rolled up. 'He's in a Ferrari,' she said, 'now what?'

Fraternity shrugged. 'Maybe he'll pull over?'

The guttural roar of the customised yellow 488 GTB suggested that its owner might not be amenable to a stop and search. The Ferrari came out at such speed it nearly ended up in the front garden opposite. Fraternity glimpsed a cannonball-headed man behind the wheel and called in the licence plate just as the vehicle took off in the direction of City Road.

Meera figured the Kawasaki had an advantage over any high-performance car attempting to negotiate London's afternoon traffic at speed. 'He doesn't know how to drive it,' she called back. 'It's not a car, it's a chromium-plated posing pouch. He's probably never taken it over thirty.'

They were coasting awkwardly towards Old Street round-about when Draycott realized he was losing ground and jumped the lights, clipping a builder's van. Meera winced. Her motorcycle was easily able to nip between the circling vehicles and draw alongside. The traffic on Great Eastern Street was building up towards the rush hour. The Ferrari hung a right into Bishopsgate.

'Smart move,' Fraternity shouted. 'He must know about the closure.'

These days the venerable ward of Bishopsgate looked like a Minecraft scenario. A third of the office buildings along its length were being torn down and replaced with immense glass boxes. Mobile cranes stalked the highway, which was shut to general traffic. The Ferrari was able to manoeuvre at speed around the obstacles but it couldn't second-guess the behaviour of pedestrians, who were likely to recklessly sprint across the asphalt.

Fraternity had expected the Ferrari to pull over somewhere here, but it accelerated. 'He's screwed if he crosses into Gracechurch Street,' he called out. 'It's one way at the end.'

The only exit open to Draycott was via a series of ever-narrowing junctions and clogged dead-ends. Ahead lay the Thames, and unless he could find a way on to London Bridge from these corridors, most of which were blockaded by Department of Works machinery, he would be forced to abandon the vehicle.

He had made a mistake; turning left on to Eastcheap, he would now miss his only route to the bridge. The makeshift layouts would have defeated the presenters of *Top Gear*. Not a single road led to the edge of the Thames unless they were traversed on foot.

The Ferrari roared to a halt and its owner made an ungainly scrabble from the driver's seat. He ran for it, but part of Monument Place, which lay ahead, was filled with steel Portakabins, reconfiguring the cityscape into a labyrinth that befuddled seasoned foot patrols. Meera slammed the Kawasaki up the kerb and across the pedestrianized square, cutting off Draycott's exit. Their suspect decided to cut between the cabins and make a beeline for the bridge. Meera pulled the bike over and they followed on foot.

'I love it when we get a runner,' said Fraternity. 'I could do with the exercise.' He caught the slow-moving Draycott with ease but decided to go for a more aggressive form of obstruction by landing feet-first on top of him.

'You got an urgent appointment somewhere?' he asked amiably, allowing Draycott to draw just enough breath for a reply.

'You're making a bloody huge mistake, pal,' the man beneath him managed to gasp out. 'I've got a lot of pull around here. I'm a senior partner of the Findersbury Bank.'

Fraternity burst out laughing. 'If I'd known, I would have worn my kicking boots.' Then he read Draycott his rights and booked him for dangerous driving. An hour later, after an argument with Draycott's lawyers, they were reluctantly forced to release him.

43

HOUSE & YARD

As he had only been drinking lemon squash at the Lighterman, Bryant was able to take Victor, his ancient rusting Mini Minor, from North Woolwich to Chiswick. As he parked and alighted outside the tree-covered Death House, a gang of kids pushed away from the shaded wall and came over.

'Mind your motor for you, mate?' said one who looked somewhere between eleven and thirty years old.

'Not unless you want me to mind your broken arm for you,' said Bryant cheerily. 'What do you know about this building?'

'A lot of fit birds go in there,' said a lanky lad with terminal acne.

'They come with this man?' asked Bryant, showing them a photograph of Bensaud on his phone.

'That's a picture of a kitten in a shoe,' said Spotty.

'Ah, hang on.' The boys waited patiently while he tried to find the right photograph.

'Yeah, he's the one.' They all agreed on Bensaud's identity. 'There's a lot of singing in there an' that,' said the oldest. 'And I think he's giving 'em some of *that*.'

'Some of what?'

'You know, some of *that*.'

'If you aren't even able to articulate your grubby little fantasies I'm not listening,' said Bryant. 'Anyone else ever come here?'

They talked among themselves. 'Nah,' said the oldest. 'Not since Finston's.'

'The estate agent?' asked Bryant. He'd assumed the building had been rented out to the centre.

'Yeah, them. 'Cause it was like empty for years before that.'

'That's useful to know.' Bryant attempted to make a note on his phone and succeeded in erasing one of the specialist apps that Banbury had painstakingly installed. Since his cleansing treatment electrical objects were behaving more erratically than ever around him.

'Useful enough to pay us?' asked Spotty.

'You'll have to settle for the knowledge that you've earned the heartfelt thanks of a grateful nation,' Bryant told them.

'You what?'

'Oh, sorry, complex sentence structure, I should have realized. Well, it's been a pleasure to trade monosyllables with you. Anyone want a sherbet lemon?' He dug out a crumpled packet and offered it around.

'Peedy bait?' said one, snapping a shot of Bryant on his phone just in case. 'Cheers but no, ta.'

'Oh, for God's sake, I'm not trying to poison you. Go on.'

Another lad reached out a hand and received an electric shock. 'Ow.' He thrashed out his hand.

'Oh, sorry about that,' said Bryant. 'I've got too much energy.'

Yong-nyeo Kim, the agent at Finston's, was surprisingly helpful. 'It was on our books for quite a while,' she told Bryant, waving him into a giant lime-green oven glove that turned out to be some sort of fashionable sofa. 'Sparkling water or cappuccino?'

'I'm not a punter,' said Bryant, presenting his PCU card, which he had managed to crumple in spite of the fact that it was laminated.

'Oh.' She seated herself beside him and had such a disheartened look on her face that he wondered if she was going to be beaten later for not making a sale. 'What can I do for you then?'

'So it was empty before?' asked Bryant.

'Yes, for many years,' she said. 'It wasn't very helpful that the building was known locally as the Death House.'

'Why did it get that nickname?'

'Hang on, I have some notes on it.' Tapping her tablet, she pulled up the property's file. 'Purchasers love a bit of local colour, even when it's scandalous. It was once a tavern called the White Hart. In the late 1800s some local men who worked on the barges disappeared after drinking there. The landlord and his wife got them drunk and robbed them, then supposedly sent their bodies down a chute into the river. They thought the men would wake up further downstream, but they drowned. The landlord and his wife were hanged and the nickname stuck. We tried changing it back to the White Hart, but that didn't work. It's not a residential property. The new owner was very keen.'

'Mr Ali Bensaud?'

Yong-nyeo Kim consulted her notes. 'No, it was a lady. She paid cash, which was a problem for us because of the revised money-laundering laws.'

'Cassandra North?'

'No, let me see – the money was paid by a Lynsey Dalladay.'

Bryant tried to contain his surprise. 'Did she say where the money came from?'

'I believe it was part of an inheritance, although I wasn't dealing with that side of the sale. We still have the transaction details but I'm not sure if I'm allowed—'

'Oh don't worry about that,' said Bryant reassuringly. 'I'm allowed to stick my hooter in wherever I like.'

Yong-nyeo Kim went off to locate the documentation while Bryant studied the properties on offer in the Finston's brochure and realized that he could not afford to buy a part-share in a collapsed garden shed from them. He was still staring forlornly at page after page of perpendicular palaces when she returned with some photocopies. 'This is all I can give you,' she said apologetically.

Bryant scanned the sheets and his beady eye snagged on the only quirk he could find. In the transfer reference box, where you were supposed to write something that would remind you about the nature of the transaction, was handwritten 'Athena Marine'.

It's possible that no one else would have made the connection, but to Bryant it struck a significant note. As he thanked Yong-nyeo Kim and left, he called Longbright. 'Janice, I need you to find something for me; a boatyard somewhere on the Greenwich Peninsula called Athena Marine. There used to be an Athena Road around there. It was where the lightermen went for their piecework. It's possible either Bill Crooms or Dimitri Gilyov were hired by the company. See what they're up to.'

'Is that it?' said Longbright. 'No explanation, no plan of action, just have a poke around?'

'All right, find out who Crooms and Gilyov were working for and see if he transferred one point eight million euros into Lynsey Dalladay's account before she died, how about that? She used the money to buy the centre's outpost at Chiswick. Whoever gave it to her either knows how Gilyov died or killed him themselves. Is that enough for you?'

'On our way,' said Longbright.

There was only one boatyard listed with that name, and it was on the Isle of Dogs in South-East London, where once the stubs of ancient quays had formed a maze of basins and docks. Now the slums had been torn down and replaced with apartment buildings, lushly photographed on websites and in brochures, but somehow still melancholy and inhospitable in the gathering darkness sweeping in from the river.

The sky had become blemished, but it was hard to tell whether it was nightfall or just the next wave of bad weather rolling in, until Longbright looked up and saw the seagulls tumbling against the wind, driven inland by the approaching storm front.

Developers were still building around the old quays. A few street names were all that remained of the area's dockland past: Tiller Road, Pepper Street, Ferry Street, Crews Street, Spindrift Avenue. Longbright had seen photographs of masted schooners in dock with their bowsprits thrusting out across the pavements, so closely were they moored to the dockers' houses.

Longbright checked the map on her phone. 'This is the place all right.'

Colin Bimsley stepped back into the road to get a better view. 'It looks like it's been closed down. What has this got to do with the Dalladay murder?'

'That, my clumsy young friend, is a question only your boss can answer,' said Longbright, walking up to the black-painted main doors and looking for a bell. 'See any way in?'

'Down here.' At a broad-shouldered six foot one the spatially challenged Bimsley was a hefty lad who could prove surprisingly nimble when he wasn't confronting immovable objects with his head. Longbright had to trot to keep up with him. He shot down the yard's side alley, to a wide steel shed where an Alsatian was barking.

'Police officers, take him inside, sir,' he called as a young black security guard appeared with the dog on a chain.

The guard obediently unlocked the gate and backed away. 'What's in the shed?' Longbright asked.

'It's where they repair the launches,' the boy explained.

'We just need to take a quick look inside.'

'I thought you said Mr Bryant wanted us to check for Gilyov's contact?' said Bimsley.

Longbright shrugged. 'Well, while we're here.'

The guard removed the padlocks from the boatyard door and pushed one side back. 'There are no lights any more,' he said. 'They've been taken out.'

'Don't worry, lad, we've got torches,' said Longbright. 'Make yourself scarce for a few minutes. Go and have a coffee somewhere.'

The tarpaulin-covered boats were raised on trailers and standing in dry-dock supports. Long steel bars hung on chains, homemade block and tackle rigs ready to haul engines into place. As they made their way between the hulls, rain began rattling the roof overhead. It sounded as if someone was emptying gravel on to the corrugated metal.

'What are we looking for?' Bimsley shone his jacket-torch across the starboard deck of a battered cruiser, picking up the flat glare of a rudder, a glint of chromium railing.

'Whoa, back up – what's that?' Longbright stopped beside a black-painted hull and ran her hand over the paintwork. 'This is a chop-job. Look.' She pointed to the crooked seam that ran beneath the hull's paintwork.

'Fraternity told me there's a trade in reconditioned boats, just as there is in road vehicles. There's nothing wrong with that.'

'Who are they selling them to?'

'You'll need the log books.'

'Then let's find out who's running this set-up.' She walked to the bow of the longest vessel and climbed the stepladder that had been placed beside it. 'Someone's here; the paint's still wet.' She tilted her head on one side, thinking. She turned suddenly and sniffed the air. 'What's that?'

An overpowering smell of scorching varnish filled her nostrils. Still balanced on the ladder, Longbright scanned the shed with her torch beam. A low light source flickered in the corner, throwing strange shadows on the roof. She could make out the shape of a human figure, someone inside the boatyard with them. 'Colin, I don't like the—'

It was as far as she got. The explosion was muffled by the presence of so many large structures in the boatyard, but the wave of heat it generated still knocked her from the steps. She landed hard on the concrete floor. When she managed to get back on her feet, wiping her bloodied left palm on her thigh, she saw that the entire end wall of the shed was engulfed in rising flame. 'Colin!' she called. 'You OK?'

'Yeah, think so.' He came around the corner to find her.

'Your back's on fire.'

'Oh, right.' He tried to see over his shoulder. 'I can't get injured again; Meera will kill me.'

'Hang on.' Longbright grabbed the end of a tarpaulin and pulled it free from a tender, throwing it over Colin's head and slapping him hard on the shoulder blades.

'All right, blimey, go easy,' he yelled.

'I've already been set alight once this year, I'm an old hand at this,' said Longbright.

Smoke from the burning varnish was replacing the oxygen with an acrid, unbreathable poison. Crouching low, they ran between the hulls, searching for an exit. The torches had been knocked from their hands and had spun beneath the boats. The door by which they had entered was now locked from the outside.

'Other end.' Colin waved and led the way back.

By now the smoke was so thick they could barely draw breath. Away somewhere to the right of them, a series of canisters overheated and detonated. Janice's lungs were burning. She stumbled on, following Colin. A fresh wave of searing air blasted over them. She slipped and fell on to one knee. It should have been easy to get back up, but instead her other knee gave way and she dropped flat.

A strong hand pulled her back up. Colin's face appeared through the smoke, his nose and mouth masked by a rag. He began dragging her towards the side of the building. She couldn't understand what he was doing – there were no doors or exits of any kind here.

Behind them, a series of fresh discharges detonated in the boats. The whole of the yard was now burning fiercely.

Once she started coughing, she could not stop. Colin was pressing his hands against the wall. Her head hurt so badly that it was impossible to think clearly. What was he doing? As she tried to understand, he grabbed one of the steel bars overhead and pulled himself up, swinging high and forward, hitting the wall with an echoing boom. His boots broke through the panelled side of the shed. At the end of the second swing it fell away and he was able to drag Longbright through the gap into the open air.

They fell down together as further explosions rocked the shed.

'Your leg.' She tried to speak but doubled over, hacking out dark mucus. Colin's left calf was pouring blood from a jagged tear in his jeans. He sat her down against a low brick wall and ran off. She coughed hard again, trying to understand what had happened, then lay back with her head on the brick-work and lost consciousness.

Colin ran. The cold rain-dashed air he drew in cleared his burning lungs. Ahead, the bald, thick-set man he had seen inside the boat-shed was heading towards the end of the road and the dock beyond. For once there was nothing in Colin's path, which was just as well because right now, any collision involving the DC and a moving vehicle would have resulted in the latter coming off worse.

Pounding across the road without stopping to look, he caught up with Mick Draycott just as he made the fatal mistake of turning around. Colin lifted him off the ground with one spectacular uppercut to the jaw, sending him over the low chain-link fence and down into the pungent mud of the dock at low tide.

44

CALL & RESPONSE

John May paced back and forth across his living room, listening to Raymond Land's excuses on the phone.

'I can't do it, John,' Land insisted. 'If I let you back in now you'll be in violation of your house arrest and the case will be automatically prejudiced against you. If you really want to do something, forget about the Dalladay girl and concentrate on your own defence. Think about why someone wanted to get rid of Mrs North.'

The detectives generally used Raymond Land as a kind of reverse barometer, taking his indications to mean that the absolute opposite was true, but once in a while he accidentally hit the nail on the head. When May rang off, angrily throwing his phone on to the sofa, he realized that the unit chief was right; he'd been considering the investigation as a whole only to find that each new fact contradicted the previous ones. Going back to the notepad he had been filling with ideas, he seated himself before his coffee table and went over all the possibilities again. He'd assumed he had been deliberately set up for a fall, but now he concentrated on finding a reason why someone would specifically wish to kill Marion North.

He tried to recall exactly how she had looked, standing before him on Victoria Embankment, a handsome woman, facing him squarely and holding his gaze, her red lips catching the light – red lips, red scarf – and in that moment he regretted not having seen her sooner. His decision not to continue seeing her was linked to his history with married women; he had always found reasons to end relationships before they became too demanding. But he was sure he had left her with his scarf to give her a reason for seeing him again. The whole passive-aggressive thing was absurd in a man of his years.

I've been a bloody fool, he thought, *allowing each of them to escape and pretending to be sorry when they didn't call. I wanted to see her again, but how I enjoyed letting her go in the first place! I told myself I was putting the needs of the unit first, as if I was committing an unselfish act by pushing each of them away.*

For too long he had been content to act as the straight man to Arthur in their little double-act. He only had himself to blame for his present situation. May always took the path of least resistance, and this time he had ended up as a suspect in his own murder investigation. Well, no more. Grabbing his coat, he headed for the door.

Raymond Land was nervous. His detectives were missing and almost everyone else had disappeared. He was left with Crippen, currently spraying gravel about in her litter tray, the two Daves, who sounded as if they were taking the basement apart with road-drills and gongs, and Barbara Biddle, who was locked in the common room with boxes of files, wearily checking her watch while she searched for further infringements. At least she hadn't submitted her report yet.

When Longbright and Bimsley came in through the door looking as if they'd been standing too close to a controlled demolition, he got a definite sense that things were rapidly moving on without him. 'What the hell happened to you two?' he asked, rising in alarm. 'What have you done to your leg?'

Bimsley shrugged. 'It just needed some butterfly stitches.'

'We had a run-in with the guy Fraternity arrested,' said Longbright. 'This time he won't be getting out on bail. Is Mr Bryant back yet?'

'Back from where?' asked Land. 'I can't raise him on his phone. I can't get hold of anyone.'

'Who's looking for me?' Arthur Bryant sauntered in eating a banana. 'I've been hearing about you, Colin. How's the leg? Nice punch, by the way. You broke Draycott's jaw in two places. Couldn't you have just stamped all over him like Fraternity did? He's unlikely to sue, though, what with the attempted murder charge and all.'

'Could somebody please tell me what is going on?' Land demanded.

'It's simple, *mon petit beauf*,' said Bryant, munching. 'The banker met Lynsey Dalladay at the Cossack Club and paid her one point eight million euros through a private Swiss account for services supposedly rendered, which she used to buy real estate for Ali Bensaud's wellbeing centre.'

'What did he get out of it?'

'He was shifting dodgy money into UK property and did a runner when he got wind that we were on to him, but I think there's more to it than that. While he was out on bail, it looks like he attempted to murder two of our staff when they turned up at his place of work.'

Land gave a low whistle. 'Dalladay must have been something special to get paid that much.'

'Draycott couldn't have gone there with the specific intention of killing our staff,' said Bryant, ignoring Land's lascivious thoughts about what a high-priced call girl might get up to. 'He'd just been released from police custody. What was he doing in the boatyard?'

'He was repainting one of the vessels,' said Longbright.

'Ah yes – that makes sense,' said Bryant.

Land looked first at his detective sergeant, then at his most senior detective. 'That *makes sense*? Is there something you know that I don't?'

'You mean apart from everything?' Bryant thought for a moment. 'I know that John had nothing to do with the death of Marion North. And I think I know how to bring this chain of tragedies to an end.'

By the time the fire control officers stationed at Deptford had managed to douse the Athena boatyard, there wasn't much left of the shed or its contents. May arrived just as the engines were packing up. As he slipped under the plastic ties of the cordon, Senior Fire Officer Blaize Carter came out of the security guard's hut carrying boxes and bin bags. She looked even more athletic and magnificent than he'd remembered her, despite her hi-vis yellow jacket and the baseball cap that hid her kinked auburn hair.

'What are you doing here?' asked May. 'This isn't your manor.'

'Nice to see you too, John,' said Carter. 'You didn't just come down to see me, did you?'

'As a matter of fact, I did.'

'Your Mr Bryant is giving me the run-around.' She indicated one of the bin bags. 'Boat registration records. He wants these so you might as well take them to him.'

'How does he know what he needs without coming here? It's like he's watching us all from somewhere above, moving pieces around.'

'You're asking *me* how he operates? What do you think happened?'

May accepted the bag from her. 'Looks like we interrupted an arson attack.'

She nodded back at the smoking shed. 'It wasn't very well planned. Draycott left a nice clear trail of petrol drips all the way from the garage to a stack of combustibles he'd piled up just inside the doors. And if he was looking to burn the contents of that bag he hadn't done his homework. They were stored in the security office safe.'

'Where is he now?'

'The EMT took him to the Docklands Medical Centre suffering from a nice bit of police brutality. Well done, your team. You'll have to wait until his sedation wears off.'

'So you had the combination for the safe in there?' asked May.

'Not exactly.' Carter pointed back to one of her fellow officers, who was dragging the largest sledgehammer he had ever seen. 'Wanton destruction of private property. It's why I joined up.' She headed past him and shoved the rest of the boxes and bags into the fire tender's secure area. 'I hear your partner made some kind of miraculous recovery.'

'Yes, he'd been accidentally poisoning himself.'

'You lot don't do anything by halves, do you?'

May squinted at her through the pattering rain. 'We have a reputation to live down to.'

'If he's better I guess you won't need to look after him so much any more.' She stuck the tip of her tongue between her teeth, teasing him.

'It doesn't look that way, no,' he said. And then: 'So, what I said before . . .'

'. . . about always having to put your work first, you mean?'

'Yes, that part. I may have been mistaken. I've been thinking.'

She stood up and studied him. 'Oh? And what did you decide?' She was waiting for him to say it. He tried to think of an intelligent answer, but the words dried in his mouth.

'Well? Cat got your tongue? I guess finding yourself on a murder charge makes you stop and think. You have a lot to learn.'

'Then teach me,' he said. 'What time do your men disappear?'

'When my shift ends. We can go to that disgusting Italian

restaurant in King's Cross.' Every police officer and fire-fighter in the area knew La Veneziana. It had a resident crooner called Gary Garibaldi who smoked while he sang and fiddled with his flies whenever the waitresses passed by. Bryant had once found a dog-end in his *calzone*.

'Why would you want to go there?' he asked.

She shrugged as she turned to leave. 'It was where you turned me down, Mr May. I'm going to make you eat your words.' She climbed up into the fire tender.

What a woman, he thought, watching her go. Then: *What have I done?*

As he walked back to his BMW he saw someone leaning on the bonnet, hidden beneath an enormous black umbrella. It tilted back, cascading water, to reveal a familiar wrinkled face.

Arthur Bryant gave him an old-fashioned look. 'Did you learn nothing from your incriminating embrace with Marion North?' he asked. 'Do the fairer sex blind you so much that all common sense simply flies out of the window?'

'Everybody has a weak spot,' said May, his cheeks colouring. 'I suppose women are mine.'

'I hate to interrupt your amorous dalliances with anything as sordid as work, but I thought I'd better come here in person. I need those registration documents. There's still one key factor missing. I'll tell you about it if you like.' He raised a finger and pointed at May. 'We *are* a team, after all.'

'What can I do?' asked May. 'I'm not even supposed to be outside my apartment.' He handed over the black plastic bin bag and unlocked the car. 'I guess you're in charge now. Find what you're looking for while I drive.'

Bryant slid on to the back seat and tore open the plastic bag, rapidly sifting through the files. 'I made a fundamental mistake,' he explained. 'I assumed the killer was intelligent. I should have realized earlier what was going on.' He checked the immobile hands of his watch. 'We need to get going. There's a life in danger. We still have time to save him.'

'Who?' asked May.

'Why, Freddie Cooper, obviously.'

'Sometimes I wish I could see the world through your eyes.'

'You wouldn't want to with my vision, trust me. There's no answer from Cooper's mobile or his house phone.'

May put his key in the ignition. 'Where do you want me to go?'

'I think he's going to be drowned, so you'd better head for the river.'

'Would you like me to aim for any particular section?' May asked. 'As you keep reminding me, it *is* a couple of hundred miles long.'

'Just put your foot down,' said Bryant. 'I'll figure something out on the way.'

45

TIME & TIDE

Raymond Land looked at the stack of coffee cups on his desk and realized he'd drunk enough caffeine to power him up the side of Snowdon. There was no answer from John May's apartment and obviously Bryant wasn't picking up. He was sure that they had illegally joined forces once more and were out there putting the entire unit at risk. Even if they managed to close the case, John would at the very least be in violation of his house arrest.

To make matters worse, Barbara Biddle knocked and entered without waiting for a response. 'I don't know where to begin,' she said, pulling off her Alice band and shaking her head at the pages in her fist. 'Everything is wrong here, every single thing, from evidence contamination and witness-statement policies down to health-and-safety infringements. Each of these points, taken individually, would be enough to close you down for the next thousand years. How am I supposed to identify a problem when the entire operating procedure of the unit is contradictory and downright dangerous? Every aspect of the unit's working structure is anomalous.'

Raymond thought hard but couldn't remember what

'anomalous' meant. He suspected it wasn't something good.

Barbara threw the paperwork down in disgust. 'So now I have a problem. In my job it's helpful to uncover one or two specific causes for concern and recommend a way of removing them. So what am I to do when none of it works? I can't simply recommend shutting the entire unit down. That's not within my power, and besides, the PCU still seems to have a few key political allies. But I have to do my job. You see my dilemma?'

'No. Yes. Yes,' said Land nervously. He felt as if his shirt collar was strangling him.

'If you hadn't allowed your detectives to run roughshod over you creating their own climate of chaos, things wouldn't be as they are now. I've identified the source of the problem. It's you.'

Land swallowed. This was the worst of all possible outcomes. If Biddle blamed the unit's catastrophic procedural misdemeanours on him, he would be booted out without a pay-off, and if he simply agreed to fall on his sword he would still get nothing. Dreams of a retirement bungalow on the Isle of Wight suddenly evaporated.

'I feel for you, I really do,' Biddle continued, softening a little. 'I don't want to be seen as a walking hatchet, chopping away at the roots of venerable institutions. I'm human, I have feelings. There's more to me than this uniform.'

Land tried for the image and failed. The thought of there being a woman behind all that make-up had honestly not occurred to him.

Barbara set her pages down on his desk and took a step closer. 'I'm prepared to make allowances. I know you've been under a lot of pressure, what with the divorce. I don't listen to gossip but it's been hard to ignore what the others have been saying.'

What have *they been saying?* Land wondered.

'You can imagine how much harder it is for me. I know what they say about me behind my back. "She's a cold bitch."

"She enjoys destroying people's lives." "She should never have been acquitted." We're supposed to remain impartial but it's impossible not to form opinions. And right now, you could do with an ally.'

'What do I have to do?' Land all but squeaked.

'You'll have to think of something,' said Barbara, flicking the end of his tie. 'Let me know what you come up with.'

'They're heading for the Thames,' said Dan, tracking Bryant's second GPS. 'Why are they going it alone?'

'Mr Bryant's protecting us,' said Colin. 'If he's wrong, he'll take the blame.'

'Then we have to back him up,' said Dan, 'particularly after the way everyone has treated him lately. We should have had more faith in him. Go and get the others.'

Colin collected the rest of the team with the exception of Raymond Land, who he felt would be neither use nor ornament. Leaving instructions with the two Daves to keep an eye on the phones (something they had come to enjoy doing), they took off in pursuit.

'The Thames was considered a place beyond laws, a free zone of water gypsies and smuggling bargemen,' said Bryant as his partner drove. 'Water moves constantly, so it's a symbol of liberty.'

'As usual I'm missing your point,' said May, attempting to squeeze between buses.

'The point is that we checked the riverbanks and fore-shores, the barges and moorings, before thinking of the river itself, and then we went for the few small craft that passed on the Thames that Sunday night,' said Bryant, 'but we didn't go to the most obvious place where a criminal might be hiding, and you know why? Because they use boats which are so ubiquitous that we never even notice them.'

'What are you talking about?' asked May. 'We thought of everything.'

'No we didn't. The Marine Policing Unit is based out of a station on Wapping High Street and has twenty-two vessels at its disposal at any time of the day or night, plus they can call on the services of the RNLI. The building is close to the first murder site, but set back from the shoreline. They're the only small craft allowed to move near areas of sensitivity after dark.'

'I could see their launches moored at one of the reaches near Dalladay's body,' said May, 'but the MPU can't be implicated in this. They've a reputation for being incorruptible.'

'Who says they were in on it? Who else has access to the boats?'

'Oh – got it.'

'Precisely. The engineers and mechanics. MPU Wapping doesn't have them on staff because they use registered shift-workers.'

Much of Wapping High Street had been relined with new apartments, but the oldest part still retained its narrow cobbled road and its converted wharf buildings connected by iron walkways. The light was fading now, and the street lamps turned the rain into gilded needles.

'He must be around here somewhere,' said Bryant, wiping the window with the back of his hand. 'The MPU moorings are directly behind its headquarters.'

'You honestly think he's right on the unit's doorstep?'

'Killers have a habit of remaining in a tight geographical area,' Bryant pointed out, 'and they often return to the same sites.'

May's BMW pulled up beside the blue steel gates of the MPU's vehicle yard. 'How are we going to talk our way through this?' May asked. 'We have no jurisdiction here.'

'We don't need it,' said Bryant. 'Wapping Police Stairs has a causeway leading straight to the moorings. It's part of the MPU site but it's accessible from King Henry's Stairs, the next staircase along. There are twenty-eight staircases along this stretch alone, but quite a few are illegally locked.'

May turned in his seat. 'Arthur, it's dark now and raining, and the steps will be covered in algae. I've only just got you back; I don't want to lose you again. Why don't you wait here?'

'I have to see for myself, John. We're wasting time.'

'All right. On your own head be it.' He held the car door open.

Meera climbed off her bike and leaned through the window of the Renault, scowling at Dan's phone. 'I thought you said the tracker was accurate?'

'On roads, yes, but it's only approximate when it goes off-piste.' Dan and the others climbed out of the car and gathered on the pavement of Wapping High Street. The rain had grown heavier in the last few minutes, and the street ahead was deserted. 'It says they're within a few metres of us. Maybe they're inside the marine unit itself.'

'This thing started on the river. Isn't that where it has to end?' Fraternity crossed the road, looking around for access. 'The tide's out. They have to be on the shore.'

They found the narrow ginnel that sliced between the buildings, but its gate was locked.

Colin needed no GPS to know where he was. The old pubs of London provided a ghost map in his head. 'We're between the Captain Kidd and the Town of Ramsgate,' he pointed out. 'They've both got river steps.' He set off in the direction of the swinging pub sign as the others followed after him.

46

WATER & SMOKE

As May had predicted, the worn stone stairs were virid and slippery with weed. Ahead lay the rocky foreshore, mournfully cloaked in rain. A jetty and the police launch moorings stood beyond, but all of the boats were tarpaulined and locked up.

'There's nothing here, Arthur,' he called back. 'Where else could he be?'

Bryant was concentrating on not tipping headlong down the rain-lashed staircase. 'Crooms knew how to unlock and pilot old MPU cruisers,' he called back. 'Nobody pays any attention to the police launches. They sit so low in the water that they can barely be spotted, and they're all but invisible on the river at night. Can you see anything?'

'There's a boat moving,' called Meera from the top of the staircase. On the far side of the jetty a rusted cream and brown cruiser was slowly chugging away from the boarding platform.

Colin was on to it, closely followed by Fraternity. In seconds they had reached the wooden causeway and were pounding over the rain-slick boards towards the departing vessel. The pair reached the boat's departing stern and without hesitation jumped for it.

Colin slammed on to the starboard deck and landed on a coil of rope, noisily sliding into a stack of tethered yellow plastic crates. Fraternity, slightly behind him, was less lucky and only just managed to reach the side of the vessel. Colin grabbed his arms and pulled him on board.

'They must have heard that. Why hasn't anyone come up?' Fraternity asked as they headed towards the bows of the cruiser.

Colin tried the door leading below deck and tore it open. Inside, an elderly skipper and his wife looked back at him in surprise. The skipper threw his joint out of the open window.

'It's a no-go,' Fraternity radioed back. 'Just some stoned old couple on a private vessel. They thought we'd come to bust them for smoking a doobie. We're heading back.'

'Now what?' said May. 'I hope you have another idea. I wouldn't be surprised if the Met was on the lookout for us by now.'

'Water,' Bryant replied, checking his phone. 'Freddie Cooper was seen being driven away from his office in Nine Elms an hour ago. He has to be drowned.'

'How could you possibly know that?'

Bryant ignored him. 'Where, though? God, we live in one of the wettest countries in the world and what do we do, build canals and ponds and fountains and lidos. He could be anywhere. Meera, call Cooper's company and find out if any of his trucks have moved away from their usual routes.'

She made the call and waited while the controller checked. 'One,' she called back. 'It's heading along Upper Ground.'

'On the South Bank? In which direction?'

'Going east towards Barge House Street.'

'How fast can we get there?'

'Buckle up,' said May.

The gun-metal-grey BMW was followed by an unmarked squad car outridden by Meera's Kawasaki. Traffic was light until they hit a jam on Blackfriars Bridge ten minutes later. London's deepening storm skies had driven many vehicles from the streets.

'Where is it now?' Bryant asked.

Meera's headset crackled. 'He's just turned down towards the South Bank, but the road's a dead end.'

May was puzzled. 'It might be nothing. He could be making a delivery.'

'Meera, contact the nearest local unit and get the truck pulled over,' said Bryant. 'He's got his work cut out if he's planning to kill again. The whole area is smothered with cameras.'

'There's some kind of event going on,' said Meera. 'I can see lots of floodlights, banners and balloons, people milling around. You're not going to like this.'

'What is it?'

'According to the Londonist website the Mayor is here. Does something called the Thames Night Pageant ring a bell?'

'I read about that – it's his new initiative, another public regatta,' said Colin. 'Why do they always hold these things in winter?'

'All the streets surrounding the pedestrian zone are closed off,' said Meera. 'The truck won't be able to get any further.'

The BMW nosed its way through the slow-moving revellers, balloon-sellers and street-food vendors, but was forced to pull up on to the pavement. 'It'll be quicker on foot,' said May, leading the way.

Along the embankment dozens of small craft were bobbing on the incoming tide. Some bore sponsor banners; others were decorated in styles from different periods of history. Red and yellow flags hung limply from the lamp-posts. Beneath them groups of bargees, watermen and sailors were represented in quilted jackets, leather breastplates and striped jerseys, monkey-coats and buckled shoes, flat tarred hats and fur caps. They held burning torches aloft as they pushed the wooden boats out with oars and bargepoles dipping into the murky water.

The lights flickering through the falling rain, the drums and yells, the pungent smell of river mud and burning wood lent the scene a pagan immutability.

'How are you going to find anything in this?' asked Dan. 'You haven't even told us what we're looking for.'

'Janice, you were at the Athena boatyard,' Bryant said. 'You saw the kind of vessels that were stored there.'

'They were mostly light cruisers and small motor launches,' the DS replied. 'Dan's right, we're not going to find anything in this chaos.'

'Look for this,' said Bryant, unfolding a worn piece of paper and handing it to Longbright.

She studied it for a moment. 'Linseed oil, drain unblocker, carrots?'

'The other side.'

Janice found herself looking at a redrawn version of Gilyov's tattoo.

'It'll be on the stern of the boat,' said Bryant. 'We have to spread out.'

The team split into pairs and worked their way to the embankment railings, concentrating on the section between the two piers.

The illuminated crimson pageant banners strung between the embankment lamps reminded Bryant of Holman Hunt's famous painting of London Bridge beset by flags and torches. Wooden beach huts, reconditioned from the South Bank's annual Christmas festival, had been set up along the length of the road to sell hot toddies and roasted pork, so that the riverside gathering resembled a thawed-out frost fair.

Meera found herself crushed against the stone balustrade. Below, the water was streaked with crimson and emerald, lit by the crackling golden lanterns that hung from the backs of the festival vessels. It had started raining hard, but only the tourists seemed bothered. Most Londoners expected two things from any evening of public celebration: torrential rain and an aura of joyless melancholia. The only available shelter was under the bridge arches, and these were quickly filled.

Colin searched the seesawing craft, checking the painted sterns as they twisted and turned. The low smoke from the fair's braziers drifted above the heads of the crowd and was beaten down on to the shoreline, where the tar torches pierced the gloom with lambent shards. A stage erected at the end of the street bled electronic feedback, compounding the cacophony and sending echoes from the buildings across the river.

Even Fraternity wasn't sure how he managed to spot the rowing boat. Around six metres long, it was drifting away from the shore ahead of the other parade vessels. A lone oarsman stood poling his way from the rocky beach. He was the only one ignoring the chaos surrounding him, so intent was he on escaping the interlocking boats.

Fraternity and Colin were still a long way from the stair-case to the shoreline. The crowd was a living creature, unyielding, enclosing, impossible to penetrate. Only someone as small and tough as Meera had any hope of getting through. They caught her eye and signalled to her.

She dropped low and shoved forward, causing revellers to yell and fall back as she hammered her way through. Emerging between the legs of a surprised brewer selling hot porter in commemorative tankards, she caused him to slop the boiling ale on his customers. The ensuing argument caused others to fall back, allowing her to reach the break in the balustrade that led to the beach staircase.

Popping up again, she surveyed the scene on the floodlit water before running for the steps. The boats along the shore-line were all attempting to set off, but were so densely packed that many could not get clear. Following Fraternity's mimed directions, she jumped on board the first vessel, hopping from one deck to the next, using them as stepping stones. At the outer reach of the last launch she threw herself forward as the rowing boat passed, and landed hard on its deck.

As the pilot raised his oar, Colin cried out a warning. Pushing forward, he tried to reach the shoreline but a group of incensed Indian lads shoved him back into place. He and the others could only watch, helpless, as the figure on the boat swung the oar at Meera, sending her over the side.

47

SINK & SWIM

As Meera surfaced she fought to stay clear of the dancing prows and stabbing oars that surrounded her. May spotted one of the supervising MPU cruisers and prayed it would find the spot where she thrashed the bitter water. As its spotlight picked her out and Meera was pulled aboard, May tapped his phasing headset. 'Fraternity, can you follow her path over the boats? Don't let Colin try.'

'Getting hard to hear you, John,' Fraternity shouted back. 'Not enough bandwidth.'

May waved his arms, pointing frantically to the route. Fraternity finally nodded back and set off.

'Here, give these a go,' said Bryant, handing his partner a pair of pocket binoculars. 'They're no use with my eyes even in the night-vision mode.' May was not in the least surprised that his partner should be carrying such an item. Bryant had been known to produce everything from a soldering iron to a portable easel from his inside pocket. He scanned the scene and quickly located the longboat with the Medusa logo.

There was someone lying in the bows, but the figure was stiff and silvered, like the effigy of a venerated elder being committed to the depths on a funeral barge. Crimson smoke drifted across its prow as it inched forward towards clear water.

'I can see Cooper,' said Fraternity into his crackling throat-mic. 'He's either unconscious or dead.'

Freddie Cooper was cocooned in duct-tape, his ankles and wrists bound together, a strip sealing his mouth. Standing astride him was Ali Bensaud. Gone was the look of benign gentility; in its place was a fixed mask of anger.

May refocused the binoculars. Fraternity was bouncing across the decks of the locked-together vessels. A moment later he had landed on the rowing boat, almost capsizing it.

Bensaud regained his balance and raised his oar again, swinging it hard, but he only caught the young officer's shoulder. The others were too far off to help. The MPU cruiser was forcing its way towards them, but its path was blocked by a rat-king of oars and tangled pennants. In the chaos of the mass launching most of the craft had become hopelessly interlocked. On the shore, the Mayor was having an argument with a group of Russian sponsors he was seeking to impress.

When May was next able to focus he saw that Bensaud had turned away and was picking something up from the deck: a long-barrelled shotgun.

Fraternity's rubber-soled boots found purchase on the wet boards. Bensaud swung the rifle, took aim at Cooper and fired both barrels. The noise was lost amid the cacophony of drums and firecrackers.

'What's happening?' asked Bryant. 'I wish I was taller.' The drifting crimson smoke obscured his view. When it cleared, he saw that the rowing boat on which Fraternity had landed was sinking bow-first.

May trained the binoculars on the vessel. Bensaud had fired through the boards beside Cooper's head. He smashed at the planks with the barrel as an arcing spout of muddy water sprayed into the boat and tipped it sharply. Within moments Cooper was submerged. Bensaud leaped away across the boats, into the firework smoke.

Fraternity hauled himself forward but the craft was rising to a steep angle. The bales and coils of rope around Cooper were sliding over him, trapping him.

Fraternity climbed down and pulled at the body, raising his head and tearing at the silver tape across Cooper's mouth. The boat lurched deeper, throwing him off balance and dropping Cooper below the waterline once more.

Fraternity grabbed at his arms, trying to free him, but water flooded in as the boat sank. He was forced to head over the side and into the river.

May tried to see what was going on but the boat had now vanished between the other craft that had crowded around it. Fraternity appeared thrashing and spluttering near the spot where the boat had submerged, and dived again. When he surfaced, he was hauling Cooper beside him. Several of the costumed watermen who had gathered from the maze of marine craft reached down and dragged them out of the icy tide. They returned to the shoreline bearing the officer between them, and in a second cortège, Cooper's bound body.

Of Ali Bensaud there was no sign. There were only silhouettes of mariners and revellers moving through a haze of green and scarlet smoke, like ghosts of the river risen from the depths to wage war with those upon the land.

48

GUILT & INNOCENCE

The gathering at the PCU was unusually sombre. The team had decamped there after the disastrous turn of events at the river pageant. Raymond Land was the only member of staff whose clothes were not steaming and sodden. Fraternity had his arm in a sling. Meera's shoulder was taped up.

'I don't know where to begin,' said Land, pacing past them. 'Do you want the bad news or the *really* bad news? Because of your incompetence we've a murderer on the loose planning God-knows-what. By now he'll no doubt have changed his name and appearance again, so we may never find him. He got into the country; I dare say it'll be just as easy for him to get out. Meanwhile, your latest little escapade has left a banker in St Thomas' having his jaw wired up, and Mr May here is being charged with the murder of Marion North.'

'You didn't do much to stop it happening,' said Meera angrily.

'That's enough out of you, missy,' snapped Land. 'I've had nothing but disrespect and insubordination from you from the start.'

'Don't pick on her,' warned Colin.

'Yeah, leave her alone,' said Fraternity.

'Oh, am I being addressed by the pair who've single-handedly put police brutality back on the agenda? The suspect you duffed up has launched a lawsuit against us. Luckily, by the time it goes through the unit will have ceased to exist. We'll be closed for business.'

'Again?' groaned May. 'This is getting to be a habit.'

'That's it, treat it like a joke.' Land was now nodding like a dashboard mascot. 'Well, this time there's no eleventh-hour rescue. The entire investigation was a monumental cock-up from beginning to end. When textbooks come to be written about the policing failures in Britain you'll have your own section.'

'Is this going to affect our pensions?' asked Dan Banbury, his hand half-raised.

'Bensaud can't get far,' said May. 'He needs to contact Cassandra North because he'll require money to get out of the country, and he won't be able to use his credit cards. She controls the finances. She'll have to get him cash from their company account. When he contacts her we'll find him.'

'Have you spoken to her?' Land asked.

'Of course,' Janice replied. 'She's ready to do whatever we say. Her first priority is to save her business.'

'I would have thought her first priority would be finding her mother's killer, then hiring a lawyer,' said Giles Kershaw, 'before her clients all start suing her for feeding them quack potions and giving them life-threatening advice. Stupidity was never an impediment to a lawsuit. Do you know how much the pseudo-medical industry brings in?'

'No, and I don't care about a bunch of gullible—' Land looked around. 'Where's the hell's Bryant?'

May had assumed one of the others had brought him back. 'Wasn't he with you?' he asked.

Bryant stood before the bringer of life and death.

Beyond the lock gates on the Isle of Dogs the river was high and wide. At this point he was almost entirely surrounded by

chill waters. You could feel it on the skin, taste it in the air.
Here the breaches in the river's sea defences had once formed
an inland lake known as 'the Poplar Gut', London's own ali-
mentary canal.

He stared past the rotting green stanchions, down into the
puddled mud studded with polished stones, pieces of pottery,
car tyres and shredded knots of blue nylon cord, and a distant memory surfaced.

He was seven years old, waiting for the bridges to close so
that he could visit his father's family on the Isle. 'It's like
Venice,' his father had said admiringly, with what was probably the least appropriate simile ever chosen for the Isle of
Dogs. There was no purpose in searching for London's past
now, so completely had it been erased. But the old man
remembered.

'Mr Bryant?' A young Malaysian boy appeared carrying
something the size and shape of a painting wrapped in plastic.
'You're waiting for this?'

'Thank you, yes,' Bryant replied. 'I thought it was quicker
to come and collect it. Just stick it down there.'

'It's really heavy. Have you got a way of—'

'Thank you, I've a taxi booked to take me to St Thomas'
Hospital. You can get along.'

The young man carefully stood the board against a wall
and took his leave. *The final piece of evidence,* thought
Bryant. *Even if Bensaud makes it out of the country, his
dream is over now.*

'We should call it a night,' said Raymond Land, irritably
checking his watch. 'The only lead left is testimony from
Cooper and he's still having his stomach pumped. There's
nothing to be gained by staying here. Go home, the lot of
you.'

'You're kidding. It's so windy out there that the rain's going
sideways,' said Meera. 'Let's at least wait until it eases off
a bit.'

'You're not dossing down here, young lady. This is a police unit, not Airbnb. Not that any of you actually solve crimes here any more, it seems. Maybe after we've been closed down we could go into the hospitality industry, turn the place into a community centre or an artisanal coffee shop, start serving cappuccinos in the evidence room.'

'Not every case ends the way you'd like it to,' said May. 'You should know that by now, Raymond. None of the Met's specialist units would have got any further. We know who to look for. Bensaud will have to surface eventually.'

'What about Lynsey Dalladay?' asked Longbright. 'We didn't manage to do very much for her, did we?'

'What did you expect, vengeance?' asked May.

'We don't even know what really happened,' said Banbury, who hated loose ends.

'It's fairly easy to work out a sequence of events,' May replied.

'Well, could someone else do it?' asked Land. 'After all, you are actually under house arrest and suspended from duty pending a murder charge. Or does nobody think that matters?' An accusatory silence ensued. 'Oh, for God's sake.' Land waved him on.

'Bensaud got her pregnant,' May continued, 'and when she told him she wanted to keep the baby he figured she was going to destroy his career. He killed Marion North because she discovered the truth and threatened to tell Freddie Cooper. The two women were going to destroy everything he'd tried to achieve. He was ambitious and when it all went wrong he was forced to clean up. The engineer and his mate had nothing to do with the case.'

'That's not exactly true,' said a familiar voice from the door. 'I've just had an interesting little chat with poor old Freddie Cooper. He's a bit woozy, but sitting up and taking notice.'

'We were told no one could see him,' said Longbright.

'Oh, I just slipped in when the nurse left her desk. Can

someone give me a hand in with this?' Arthur Bryant un-strangled himself and threw his scarf on to a vacant chair while Bimsley obligingly dragged in the bubble-wrapped object. 'Open it up, would you, Colin?'

Bimsley knelt and tore the plastic away to reveal a ragged piece of black painted wood. Along the top, picked out in gold lettering, was a single word: 'Medusa'.

Bryant rooted about in the vast repository of his overcoat and produced a Swiss army knife. Bending down, he began scraping away at the paintwork. Everyone peered forward to watch him. If ever an example of the PCU's peculiar behaviour was needed, it would have been this sight: a roomful of officers silently watching a strange old man scratching away at a piece of wood. Even Land decided to keep his mouth shut.

'Bill Crooms *was* involved. He had a nice little business going.' Bryant flicked shreds of paint from his knife. 'He was running off fake engine parts on 3D printers and selling them to interested buyers with forged IPR from China.'

'IPR?' asked Land.

'Intellectual property rights mean you can trace anything back to the original manufacturer,' Bryant explained, hunched over and concentrating on his task. 'Unless it comes from China, Russia or, oddly enough, California, where things get murkier. In avionics all components require registered provenance, and although the legislation covers all types of marine equipment it doesn't always work out that way because there are plenty of people who are prepared to turn a blind eye in favour of profit. It was Géricault's *The Raft of the Medusa* that finally confirmed my suspicions.'

He stretched and waved the penknife about, loosely outlining the painting, then returned to scratch at the paintwork. 'I had so many elements in my head but my poor befuddled brain couldn't fit them all together. The unmarked beach. The blurred tattoo. The magic act. The chairs stacked in the nightclub. The neck-chain with the puzzle link. The cauterized stump. The health centre. And at the heart of the case, joining everything together, the river. I wanted a unifying theory but I simply couldn't make sense of it. I felt the way poor old Raymond here must feel all the time.'

Land thought of taking exception but decided against it as no one was watching him.

'Then there was Ali Bensaud, so handsome and clever, so ruthlessly ambitious. Seducing credulous women and dumping them. And as proof of his guilt, there was this.'

Bryant set down his penknife for a moment and pulled out a tattered photograph, which May passed around. It showed Bensaud dressed as a magician, with the silver chain around his neck. The crescent moon glistened at his clavicle. It was, without doubt, the same chain that had attached Dalladay's wrist to the rock in the Thames.

'Finally, physical evidence,' Bryant said. 'But it felt wrong. What *really* confused me was the Thames, meandering, switching back and forth, deceiving. That's the odd thing; in most other major cities built around rivers, the waterway acts as a plumb line that provides you with compass points. But the Thames doesn't do that. Quite the reverse; it deliberately obscures your point of view, because whenever you stand on the north bank you assume you must be facing south, but you're not. The river follows the contours of a jigsaw piece, and it led me away from the truth.'

'Which is what?' asked Land impatiently.

Bryant gave a shrug. 'That despite how it looks, Ali Bensaud is not the killer,' he said.

49

INNOCENCE & GUILT

Fraternity was incredulous. 'But Meera and I both saw him sink the boat and try to drown Freddie Cooper.'

'Yes, I know, and that's exactly what he did. But something still felt wrong. Ali Bensaud is a sharp-witted man. I thought if he planned a murder he'd be too smart to leave evidence – so why would he use his own neck-chain to tie Lynsey Dalladay to the rock?'

'You tried to convince us she committed suicide,' said May.

'True. I thought that Bensaud possessed the perfect murder weapon: his charismatic powers of persuasion. But my theory had to be wrong, because as you pointed out, John, he had no allegiance to the Thames and its meanings. He was simply out to make money. Why would he come up with such a strange idea? Bensaud has assimilated our culture, but the concept of the sacred river eludes most Londoners, let alone those learning English as a second language.'

'My thought exactly,' said May.

'There were other things that bothered me, like the amounts of cash that were suddenly passing through Dalladay's account which couldn't possibly have been made from immoral earnings. It was an easy matter to implicate Bensaud, but there was no single hypothesis that would make logical sense of his actions. Persuade Dalladay to kill herself just because she was pregnant? No matter how confused she was, would she really be that weak? And she was known at the centre; being implicated in any sort of crime was the very worst thing that could happen to him.' Bryant turned to address the others. 'I started thinking of Bensaud as something even he didn't foresee: the victim, not the perpetrator. And that meant looking at everything differently. At the heart of this wasn't revenge at all, but a love story. That was when I came to the realization that we were looking for a killer who wasn't smart, just opportunistic. I knew we needed to know more about Bensaud's past. How had he arrived here?'

'He had no records, no background history,' Longbright pointed out.

'That's not an uncommon thing in London,' said Bryant, 'but I still thought it might hold the key. Bensaud accidentally left his real name in the stage-door log of the Rainbow Theatre, Finsbury Park. Maggie Armitage spotted it. Of course, the silly woman forgot to tell me for ages. I knew we wouldn't get the truth merely by asking him. It was when I was looking at Géricault's painting *The Raft of the Medusa* that I realized he might be a refugee. After all, we had an actual Medusa in the case – Freddie Cooper's company. Medusa transports engines, and that gave me links to the others.'

Bryant picked up his penknife again and began carefully removing black paint from the scorched wooden panel on the table. 'Did you know, in rural Spain and Turkey it's not unheard of for neighbours to gamble away the adjoining rooms in their houses? When they have nothing left to put on the table they use their property rights. The Cossack Club is a proper old-fashioned gambling den where people will gamble anything, despite what its manager told Janice. So those were the pieces; all that remained was to put them in the right order. Anyone?' He peered around the room as if expecting to see raised hands.

'Oh, for God's sake!' Land exploded. 'Just for once can you drop your Miss Marple routine and give us the bottom line?'

Bryant would not be rushed. 'Marion North's daughter Cassie was an enigma. She didn't really get on with her mother but still hired her to work in the company. She had an affair with Bensaud but stayed long after it ended, and didn't walk out when she discovered he'd got Lynsey Dalladay pregnant. She was at the centre of everything but kept such a low profile that we never suspected her for a minute.'

'What, you're saying that Cassie North killed her rival and her own mother?' asked May. 'That doesn't seem right.'

'No, that's what I thought,' Bryant agreed. 'As soon as I stopped thinking of this as the work of a clever manipulator and imagined someone trying to make the best of a series of disastrous accidents, I arrived at the only possible answer.' He paused for dramatic effect. 'Freddie Cooper. It had to be him.'

'But you just saved his life,' said Land.

'I haven't finished.' Bryant silenced him with a hard stare. 'It's a matter of looking at Cooper differently. He's feral and instinctive, a self-preservationist haphazardly covering up consequences. This time, all of the pieces fit except one. He had the most to lose if Life Options went down. But I thought he might kill for the simplest reason of all – in order to survive.'

While Bryant let that sink in, he walked to the front of the room and drew an odd pattern on the whiteboard. 'Medusa delivers engines, trucks and boats. It's also involved in the smuggling of parts and people. Four years ago one of its vessels sank, drowning a hundred and eighty desperate refugees. One of the survivors was Ali Bensaud. I deciphered Gilyov's tattoo as a gorgon because it fitted, but I was wrong. If we draw in the missing sections we get something else – not snakes but tendrils. Not the Gorgon but a jellyfish. Not a Medusa but a *méduse*.'

Having filled in the image, he returned to the section of painted wooden hull and picked a scab of paint from it. Underneath the silver 'A' in 'Medusa' was an 'E'.

'Cooper's French-registered boat, the *Jellyfish – La Méduse* – was taking refugees from the coast of Libya, and its owner cared less about its human cargo than its contraband. It was never traced because he changed the company name. Dimitri Gilyov had the tattoo because he was the captain of *La Méduse*. By this time ship owners were regularly being prosecuted, and when Gilyov tracked the owner down in London he tried to blackmail him. Cooper punished Gilyov by cutting off his hand – the proof he bore on his tattooed skin – and throwing it in the river. The current did the rest. Gilyov harboured the grudge and drunkenly came at Cooper one night in the boatyard. He was knocked out and drowned in the shed's water trough. Cooper put the body in his car and drove it to the bridge.

'By now Cooper was making more money than he could handle and needed someone to help him launder it, so he looked around for a dupe and chose Lynsey Dalladay. He got her a job in a gambling club and had his players pass her their "winnings". She wasn't a call girl, she was a mule. There was a problem, though. Money couldn't stay in Dalladay's account without someone noticing.

'Dalladay introduced Cooper to Ali Bensaud and Cassie North, and Cooper seized the investment opportunity they offered him. London is the dirty-money capital of the West. It arrives from Russian and Chinese sources and gets dumped into property and companies before it can be traced.

'Everything should have gone smoothly – but something unexpected happened. Ali Bensaud fell in love with Lynsey Dalladay. He even gave her his precious neck-chain, to remind her to be strong. Dalladay announced she was pregnant by Bensaud and told Cooper she was donating his laundered cash to Life Options. She loved Ali and she would do any-thing for him.'

Land looked as if he was having trouble keeping up. It had been a while since his most senior detective had made this much sense.

'Cooper insisted on meeting Dalladay at Tower Beach,' Bryant explained. 'She had to climb the gate to get inside, but it was the kind of challenge she liked. He was waiting under the pier in the decommissioned MPU boat he used, and chained her with the neck-chain Ali had given her. Then he headed upriver, leaving her to drown. Hence, one set of foot-prints leading to the tideline.'

'But he still couldn't get his hands on the money,' said May.

'That's right. So he asked Marion North to help him. But by now Marion knew he was the owner of *La Méduse*.'

'How did she find out?'

'One of his invoices read "Méduse" instead of "Medusa". Before Cooper could rectify the mistake she showed it to Bensaud. He must have been devastated. Cooper heard that a man called Bill Crooms was asking around in the Finsbury Park cafés where Libyans and Syrians gathered. Like Bensaud, he'd arrived in the UK under a new name. He heard rumours that Cooper owned refugee boats and had amputated Gilyov's hand. When Gilyov vanished, Crooms searched for evidence.'

'Cooper must have felt that everything was closing in on him,' said May.

'And that made him panic,' Bryant replied. 'Police and press were sniffing around and gabby Marion North was likely to talk. Cooper moved in as soon as you left her, and strangled her with your scarf. Maisner, the skipper of the *Penny Black*, didn't see you, he saw Cooper.'

The truth dawned on May. 'So Cooper directed blame on to Bensaud—'

'—by encouraging you to investigate the centre. He didn't care about losing his investment. He painted out the evidence by changing the names of the remaining boats which were in for repairs. But he missed the vessel that was being used for the Thames pageant.'

'The contusions,' Longbright reminded him.

'Dan thought the wounds were similar but Dalladay didn't get dragged along in the tide like North. She wasn't hit by a starling. Cooper hit her with an old-fashioned boathook. A curved metal spike almost identical to the bridge starling that the bodies of North and Curtis ran up against.'

'Do we have any proof for all of this?' asked Land.

'We have Cooper's confession,' Bryant replied, 'although his lawyer won't be pleased that I took it while he was still under the effects of medication.'

'And you're telling me you got all of this from a bloody *painting*?' said Land, still unable to fully comprehend the details.

'Actually it was John who gave me the idea,' said Bryant. 'He suggested I should look at paintings.'

'So you were working as a team behind my back.' Land thought about showing annoyance but decided to be magnanimous. 'I suppose I should never have tried to stop you.'

'I'm just sorry all this has probably come too late to save the unit,' said Bryant.

Land looked suddenly sheepish. 'Actually, I may have found a way of temporarily protecting us from closure.'

'You?' It was Bryant's turn to be surprised. 'How?'

'Hello, everybody,' said Barbara Biddle, leaning in the doorway and smiling conspiratorially at Land.

'I don't care who you are or where you're from,' said Supervisor Elena Drosio, checking the call board above their heads, 'all I want is results. You were top of your team last week. Now you're three places behind. I thought you wanted to be a winner.'

'You don't have to worry,' he replied. 'I'll make it up before the end of my shift.'

'See that you do,' said Elena. She looked at him and softened. 'Look at the people around you. They're from all over the world and they all want to make something of themselves. But you're smarter than any of your workmates. I'm sure you could get whatever you want if you put your mind to it.'

Bowing his head in deference, he took his place at the desk once more, donned his black plastic headset and checked the dazzling blue screen in front of him. 'Good morning,' he said, picking up his pen, 'am I talking to the lady of the house? My name is Ali Bensaud and I have a special offer for you today that I think you'll be very interested in . . .'

As he reeled his caller in, he shaded the drawing he had made of Lynsey's face, to remind him of who he had loved and lost.

In the great windowless grey hall of the call centre, 197 other employees set out to be kings of the city.

50

BRYANT & MAY

'I don't think I'll be going near the Thames for a while,' said Bryant.

'Nor will any of the others,' May agreed. 'They've all got colds. I thought you deserved a treat after saving me like that, even if you did leave it until the last minute.' The detectives were perched on stools in the atrium bar of the Shard. Bryant was unable to obtain a pint of nice cloudy bitter and, at a loss for what to order, had settled on an Acapulco Sunset. It arrived with a sparkler, a curly straw and a red umbrella, and couldn't have looked more 1980s if it had been wearing legwarmers.

'It's funny to think that the Thames was so essential to Victorians. From up here it seems utterly insignificant.' Bryant traced a forefinger on the angled glass wall. Below him was spread an alien city, a vast plain of winking lights. 'You can hardly make out any landmarks at this height at all. Perhaps that's the appeal of buildings like this.'

'What do you mean?' May asked, turning his glass.

'Anonymity. We could be looking down on Shanghai or Bangkok. Urban sprawl as far as the eye can see, and from up here it's the same as anywhere else. London and New York are roughly the same size, approaching eight and a half million people. Guangzhou is five times as big. But from far above all cities are the same.'

'Then you have to get down into the streets again and start rediscovering what makes the place unique,' said May. 'You can't let London beat you.'

'It beat Ali Bensaud,' said Bryant, extracting the kiwi and raspberry kebab from his drink. 'He came here with an ambitious dream and the city poisoned it. London took his girl and his money and it corrupted him. And the river – it's not sacred or dangerous any more, it's forgotten. I'm finding it harder and harder to stay in love with London, John. It's failing those who come here looking for a better life.'

'Not all of them,' said May, trying to offer his partner some hope. 'We don't know where Ali is now. He's had a taste of success. I don't think he'll give up easily. Hey, come on, no more depressing thoughts. You should be celebrating. You got your mojo back.' May raised his glass.

'Perhaps,' said Bryant, disdainfully removing a baby tomato from his concoction of tequila, pineapple, rum and almond liqueur. 'But I do feel different now. Something inside me has changed. I've seen glimpses of something else. I'm not sure what exactly but there are – images.'

'What of?'

'I don't know. A ghost city, an alternative version of London I imagine and long for rather than the place I live in. I was warned there would be after-effects.'

'Then there's only one thing you can do,' said May. 'Learn to enjoy them. Time is short but it hasn't run out yet. I'm going on a date – yes, at my age, have your laugh. After decades of worrying about everyone else I'm going to finally start enjoying myself.'

'You're right, of course,' said Bryant, setting aside his glass. 'That's exactly what I should start doing. Embrace the changes, and if any more phantoms appear I'll sit down for a pint with them and ask them about the London *they* know.'

'So you remember who you are now,' said May as the waiter dropped a terrifying bill on their table and beetled away. 'The last time we finished a case together you weren't so sure.'

'Yes, I think I'm getting the hang of it again,' said Bryant. 'You have no idea how nice it is to be able to remember where you live.'

'And where do you live?' asked May.

Bryant pointed to the chromatic matrix of lights that lay in every direction beyond the angled glass. 'Out there,' he said.

Janice Longbright closed down her computer, folded up her make-up box, turned off her desk lamp and hunted for her coat. Now that the case had been closed and the unit's demise had been deferred she felt strangely empty inside. It was late. Looking around her eerily tidy office, she wondered what to do next.

'How come you're always the last one to leave?' asked the square-set silhouette in the doorway.

Longbright squinted. 'Jack?'

Sergeant Jack Renfield stepped into the room. She hadn't seen him since he broke up with her on the towpath of the Regent's Canal.

'What are you doing here?' she asked.

'I heard about Fraternity moving on,' he said casually. 'A shame that. He's a decent guy, just like his brother was.'

'We'll still see him. He's going to be working with Giles.'

Renfield looked around the room. 'That means there's a vacancy here.'

'Not for long,' said Longbright. 'John has someone in mind: a German forensics specialist. She's supposed to be very good. Brilliant, in fact.'

'Oh. I guess that ship sailed without me.'

'I thought you hated it here,' she said, folding her arms.

'I didn't say that. I said I couldn't stay here after what had happened between us.'

'You asked me to marry you for the wrong reason, remember? Because you thought you'd lost me.'

'Yeah, I thought about that,' said Renfield. 'I shouldn't have asked you to give up the job. That was selfish. Sometimes I forget it's a vocation.'

'So – why are you here?'

'Oh—' He didn't know what to do with his hands, so he stuck them in his pockets. 'Your internal investigations officer asked me to collect some files and shred them. It sounds like she's not going to present her case against the unit.'

'And?' Longbright was waiting.

'And I've got them stacked in boxes in the hall, all ready to go. I told you, I'm not like Bryant and May, Janice. I'm not like the rest of you. But I do miss it. The Met's boring compared to here. The PCU isn't like a regular unit. It's more like—' He struggled to think of an appropriate simile. 'Like working in a condemned funfair.'

'Well, you gave it up.'

'I gave you up.' He bit his lip. He was never the most articulate of officers, and hated talking about his feelings. 'It made me realize. If someone makes you happier when you're with them than when you're alone, you shouldn't let them go.'

'And what the hell makes you think that person would ever take you back?'

Renfield screwed up one eye. 'Er . . . I was counting on a sudden endorphin rush.'

'Jack, did you just make a joke?'

'I think so, yes.'

She laughed. 'Blimey, there may be hope for you yet.'

He looked up at her sheepishly. 'Then what should I do?'

'Apply for the job.' She smiled. 'We'll see how it goes.'

Fraternity DuCaine sat under a dripping plane tree beside the canal and watched the rain creating sound waves on the water. Beside him, in a plastic bag, were the few personal items he needed to keep from his days at the PCU. He couldn't bring himself to tell Raymond Land the real reason for wanting to leave the unit. It was true that he had a great job lined up, but every day when he entered the office a wave of sickness swept over him.

His brother had been killed while working for the unit. At first Fraternity thought he could handle it, but everyone around him had known and loved his brother, and the awkward pauses that followed every mention of Liberty's name were more than he could bear.

It hurt him to go because he liked them all, even Raymond Land. They tried so hard and often failed but still they stayed, underappreciated and underpaid, like employees in a company manufacturing children's toys that had long since fallen from favour. He couldn't understand what kept them at their posts until he realized that they had no other option. Like many public sector officials they were institutionalized beyond the point where change was possible, and that was what made them happy.

He smiled to himself and rose from the damp grass. *I did it for you, Liberty,* he said to himself. *Now it's time to move on.*

'Is there a bone running through this?' asked Colin, sawing away at the orange brick on his plate.

'There shouldn't be,' said Meera, 'it's chicken Kiev. Normally all it does is spit boiling garlic all over you.'

'Yeah, like that dinosaur in *Jurassic Park.*'

'That wasn't garlic. It was venomous sputum.'

'It was a joke, Meera. Lighten up.'

They were chewing their way through mountains of carbohydrates in La Veneziana while Gary Garibaldi sang 'My Way', pulling at his gusset every time he hit a high note.

'I wish he wouldn't keep doing that,' said Meera through a mouthful of spaghetti. 'Why do Italians always have to play with themselves?'

'It's a matriarchal society,' Colin replied, still sawing.

Meera put down her fork. 'What's that got to do with it?'

'Well, they have to keep checking everything's still there.'

'I suppose that was a joke, too.' She sighed. 'I'll never get used to you.'

'I don't know, you came on a date.'

'We're having dinner.'

'But a dinner is a date.'

'No, dinner is dinner.'

'What about if you have dessert?'

'Trust me, you're not getting dessert.'

There was a controlled explosion of garlic sauce. Colin wiped it off his shirt with a nonchalance that suggested it happened every time he ate, which wasn't far from the truth. 'Don't look now,' he said, still wiping, 'but John's on the other side of the – I said *don't look!*'

Meera turned in her seat. 'Oh, he's with the fire officer. She's quite attractive without her helmet and gumboots.'

'Is *he* on a date?' Colin asked.

'He's having dinner, like we are.'

'Yeah, but whatever you say, we're here because I won the bet.'

Meera gave in. There wasn't any use in arguing any longer. 'OK,' she said, 'we're on a date.'

The idea dawned on Colin. 'We're on a date,' he said, jumping up and grabbing her.

'Colin, what are you doing?' Meera tried to wriggle free but he only held her tighter. He was like Pepé Le Pew hugging a black cat that had accidentally got white paint down its back. He gave her an over-emphatic garlicky kiss before releasing her and plonking back in his chair.

'Sorry,' he said, 'I know you don't like PDAs.' He looked down at his wet shirt. 'I'm a mess.'

Meera gave him an old-fashioned look. 'I've seen you covered in bits of cabbage.'

Colin smiled. 'I've pulled you out of a bin.'

The thought that perhaps they deserved each other after all crossed both their minds as they ordered dessert.

In the unlit basement of 231, Caledonian Road, one of the two Daves called to the other. 'Give me a hand with this, will you?' He pointed his torch at the great box, approximately eight feet long and three feet wide, that they had uncovered in the centre of the river-damp floor. 'The lid weighs a ton.'

The other Dave sidled over with a cage lamp and set it down. He took up his place at the corner of the lid and together they strained to lift it. As it was made from a single slab of Portland stone it proved too heavy to raise, so they were forced to slide it over, and even then it would only move inch by painful inch.

After twenty minutes they had managed to shift it halfway, but then it reached its tipping point and dropped, slamming to the floor, where it split in half. The Daves jumped out of the way to avoid having their toes crushed.

One of them crept forward with the cage light and gingerly lowered it over the edge.

'Is there something inside?' asked Dave One, straining to see.

'Not something,' replied Dave Two. 'Some*one.*'

Before heading off to meet Blaize Carter, May had given his partner a lift home. Pulling up on the corner of Euston Road and Judd Street, he reached over to unlock the passenger door. 'Are you going to be all right from here?'

'Of course I am,' Bryant replied. 'It's only a short walk through to Harrison Street. We won't find Ali Bensaud, you know, and nor should we look for him.'

'He tried to kill someone,' said May.

'Let's say there were extenuating circumstances.' He smiled ruefully. 'I'll see you in the morning, bright and early.'

'You don't need picking up?'

'No, I can manage perfectly well, thanks.'

The sky had cleared and diamond stars augured the first winter frost. Unable to clear his palate of the taste of the raspberry and almond cocktail, Bryant headed down into Cromer Street, to the scruffy little Irish pub on the corner called the Boot. It was always empty at this time of night.

As the wall-mounted television was showing football highlights on Sky Sports with the colour turned up so high that the entire room was emerald green, he bought himself a cleansing pint of Camden Pale Ale and took it outside. Although it was cold, a lone stranger sat at the single wooden bench table with his hands around a pint of stout.

'Do you mind if I join you?' Bryant asked.

'Not at all, sir,' said the gentleman, shifting his book over to make room.

Bryant sneaked a look at his fellow imbiber. He had a peculiar tonsure of dark chestnut hair swept forward and up at the sides, and a straggling, greying beard that seemed determined to fly in all directions at once. His velvet-collared jacket had the widest lapels Bryant had seen since the disco years. He was perhaps in his mid-fifties, although it was hard to tell for his eyes were young and shone brightly.

'What are you reading?' Bryant asked companionably.

'Not reading,' said the gentleman, with a look that suggested he was pleased to be asked. 'Rehearsing, sir.'

Bryant tried to see the cover of the book and failed. The light from the overhead globes was low. 'Are you an actor?'

'We are all actors in the pantomime of life, are we not?' The reply came with a knowing smile. 'But no, too itinerant a life. I am merely a reader. At least, I shall be reading aloud, from this.' He raised the cover of the book and Bryant saw that it was *Our Mutual Friend*. 'I cannot countenance the idea of making another assault on Tiny Tim this Christmas, so I thought I would give them something of a rather more demanding nature.'

Bryant took another look at his companion, and his blue eyes widened.

He recalled that between 1868 and 1869 Charles Dickens gave a series of so-called 'farewell readings' across Great Britain. He was contracted to deliver one hundred in all but the strain proved too much, and after he collapsed the tour was cancelled.

'Your most far-sighted and sophisticated work, I've always thought,' said Bryant, filled with awe. 'A beautiful combination of psychological insight, satire and social analysis, woefully underappreciated.'

Dickens barked out a laugh. 'It is about money, sir, money and nothing but, the getting and giving of it, the raising up and falling down of it. Which is to say it is about London. I thought it would be more popular. The public prefer the sentiment of Little Nell and the death of Nancy, and who can blame them?' He looked hard into his beer, as if staring into the depths of the river. 'Money,' he repeated, 'the spread and taint and stink of it. I thought the city would change in my lifetime. I thought that the poor would rise, that injustice would be levelled like a dust-pile. I was sorely disappointed to find that the tides would continue to lift and fall on the dispossessed and those who feed from them. I tried to be kinder as I aged. Why could not my city do the same?'

Bryant knew that there was no one in England more qualified to rail against the injustices of London. Dickens had spent his life seeking social reform, only to become bitterly disillusioned by its end. He had even sought to make amends for his writing, softening the character of Mr Riah in *Our Mutual Friend* to apologize to critics who had misread Fagin as representative of all Jews, and what had happened? Those same critics had turned and accused him of being too kind. There was no pleasing them. The great man was too much everywhere at once, and needed to be torn down.

'You're still here, though,' said Bryant, seeking to encourage.

'Ah yes – well. Every traveller has a home of his own, and learns to appreciate it the more from his wanderings. I used to live down the road, you know, in Doughty Street. I was much younger then, and green.'

'It's a museum now,' said Bryant. 'You were born over two hundred years ago.'

Dickens released another alarming yelp of laughter and suddenly seemed very young indeed. 'Then I am thankful for my longevity. And this little pub is still here! I mentioned it in *Barnaby Rudge*, you know.' He cleared his throat. '"The Boot was a lone house of public entertainment, situated in the fields at the back of the Foundling Hospital; a very solitary spot and quite deserted after dark." Something like that, my memory is not what it was. I only put it in because I passed it on most days.' He pointed at Bryant. 'But you, sir, if you are the Ghost of Christmas Yet to Come, tell me – does London find a way to shed its venomous skin and start afresh with a kindlier heart?'

Bryant later had time to think long and hard about the answer he gave that night.

'I would like to say that its people have more compassion now, because they know how others have to live. I fear that for every stride forward there is always someone who would have us take another step back.'

'But the people of London know what is wrought in their name?' asked his companion. 'We did not, you see. It was easier to turn away from our fellow men.'

'They know,' said Bryant, 'because London is no longer a city. It is a world. We share the stories of our lives with each other.'

'Then it must be harder for us to hide our failings from one another, and that is surely a good thing,' said Dickens, draining his pot and rising. 'Forgive me, but I still have many pages to learn tonight. I must be on my way. We can never afford to stop learning, any of us.' He turned and shook Bryant's hand. 'An honour, sir, and my gratitude to you for indulging an old man's foolishness.'

'The pleasure was entirely mine,' said Bryant. He knew

that the author would succumb to a stroke after a day spent hard at work on his unfinished novel, the world's first whodunit, *The Mystery of Edwin Drood.*

No, he thought, his heart soaring at the thought, *we must never stop learning. I've always felt that, but now I've heard it from the master.*

Bryant rose to his feet and looked around but Cromer Street was deserted once more, the tops of the great dark oak trees rustling in the rising night breeze, a copy of the *Metro* fluttering along the pavement.

The trouble with you, Charlie boy, he thought as he twirled his walking stick and set off for the warmth of home, *was that you had so much righteous anger boiling away inside you and no one to truly share it with. You were only ever the great Charles Dickens. Us, we're Bryant & May.*

ACKNOWLEDGEMENTS

In the interests of playing fair, I had woven the solution to Mr Bryant's malady into the last three books. The novels are complete in themselves and are designed to be read out of sequence without any discernible loss.

The idea for this particular novel came from talking to neighbours whom I simply regarded as Londoners without ever considering their backgrounds, and discovering that they came from countries like Iran and Bulgaria. 'To Londonize' should be a verb, because it's what happens to many people who arrive here – London is a city in which newcomers are quickly adopted and can quickly adapt, to the point where their speech patterns perfectly match those of born Londoners. So this book is for them and their new lives.

As always, I must thank Simon Taylor at Transworld for his perspicacious notes, Kate Samano, and Richenda Todd for her excellent edit. Thanks also to PR Sophie Christopher, agents James Wills and Mandy Little, and to the bloggers, librarians and booksellers whose passion keeps us working through the night.

Bryant & May will return in *Wild Chamber*.

For advice, comment and constructive argument about writing, London, movies, books and just about everything else, talk with me at www.christopherfowler.co.uk or on Twitter @peculiar.